BALLOON DAYS

Kristi Strong

Published by Pen It Publications in the U.S.A.

812-371-4128

www.penitpublications.com

ISBN: 978-1-63984-268-1

Edited by Dina Husseini

Book Design by Ralph Peter

ACKNOWLEDGEMENTS

Over the span of ten years, the seed of an idea grew into a heavily revised novel. A novel of my own to place on my bookshelf, a novel with the fingerprints of all those who helped shape it. Who knew that sitting in a cubicle at twenty-three years old, passing silly notes back and forth with my dear and talented friend, Lexi, would spark the concept of Balloon Days.

A monotonous life was not for us. I wrote, "I wish we could take a hot air balloon and escape to wherever, with whomever, for as long as we wanted—whether a real-life place, or an imaginative one." She responded with a drawing depicting just that. The idea evolved from there. We eventually left that desk job.

Thank you, Lexi for being a part of the inception. Your brain is brilliant, and our conversations spark and expand my creativity.

Four editors are forever to be praised for elevating this book into a much more readable version than the meandering, embarrassing mess it once was: Kristen Tate, Lynne Griffin, Eric Wyman, and my present editor, mentor, and newfound friend at Pen It Publications, Dina Husseini.

Kristen Tate, at The Blue Garrett, I thank you for your willingness to step into the first draft of my book. You were the fairy godmother of my story, waving your wand to repair the damage. I am grateful for your dedication, expertise, and your delicate way of pointing out where paragraphs were ill-fit, unnecessary, and clogging the story's flow. Your encouragement, ongoing support, and endless book recommendations on learning how to write a fulfilling story—not just spitting out a book—have been invaluable.

To Lynne Griffin, I used your beneficial coaching advice to cut or merge unnecessary plotlines. Because of you and your expertise on what readers want, my characters run into obstacles, not situations.

Thank goodness for finding editor Eric Wyman—the push you gave me to "show," not "tell," turned sentences into paragraphs. Your honest feedback not only transformed my book but made me laugh and have more fun with the writing process. I cannot thank you enough for your wisdom, your reassurance, and your responses to my random panic-induced messages seeking feedback over something as simple as a word choice. Yet, no matter how trivial, you answered. My favorite feedback of yours is that I write miserable characters very well.

Dina Husseini! What a gem you are. I'm so appreciative of you, because meeting you has changed everything. You're my gal. My book's champion. I am forever indebted to you for your belief in my book, your genuine love for it, and for connecting me to Debi Stanton at Pen It Publications. You are the defibrillator my book needed. Your ability to ignite scenes and increase the tension is exceptional. You are my hype woman, always pushing me to take it to the next level. I love brainstorming with you. Your imagination is boundless.

Thank you to Debi Stanton and Kenney Myers for believing in me, for giving my story a voice, and for all those at Pen It Publications for making this book a living, breathing entity.

Thank you to my beta readers—your feedback revealed unresolved issues and gave me the fun insight into how readers could interpret my character arcs, scenes, and plotlines. I was satisfied to learn my book's mission was clear while maintaining surprises along the way.

My family, in-laws, and friends—I am beyond appreciative for your outpouring of love, interest, and support, for the excitement over every milestone in my book's journey.

Shout out to my amazing mother, Eileen, for being my cheerleader and supporting my passions. It means the world to me when you compliment my writing. Thank you for always letting me make my own mistakes while guiding me along the way. Many of those experiences inspired the events in my book. I couldn't have gotten through any of it without you.

To my beautiful sister, Kerri, for being another voice to lift me up and provide me with wisdom—and for raising my amazing little nephew, Owen, who I hope one day will read my book and be proud of his aunt.

Thank you to my father, Ralph, and my stepfather, Charley, both who beam with pride at my endeavors. I am lucky to have you both by my side.

To my creative, talented brother, Ralphie, you not only helped with and voted on word choices at odd hours of the day, but you dedicated your time to create my ideal book cover. It brought my vision to life and let me see my book as a fully realized novel. You gave me a special gift.

To my cousin, Katie, who is my best friend, the "Julie" to my "Elliott," I thank you for your willingness to read and provide smart advice for my various versions of Chapter One, no matter how often I changed it (quite often). Your reassurance when I'd want to give up helped me more than you know.

To my stunning, quirky, energetic Rat Terrier Sophia. Thank you for sitting on my waist when I'd open my laptop on the couch. Thank you for staring up at me with those big, round eyes and a wagging tail when I wrote at my desk. Thank you for coming on my weekend-long writing retreats to do nothing but write, eat, sleep, and take you outside for walks. Best dog ever.

Thank you to my loving husband, Ryan. Thank you for always calling me an author when I felt like a fraud. Thank you for the seemingly little things, like having a favorite character—Orson—and having bookmarks made with each character's name on it. Those little things made it feel more real, something to be taken seriously, not to be seen as just a hobby. You endlessly inspire me with your myriad musical talents, your daily encouragement, and your advice on how to phrase a sentence, or "if a comma makes sense there" (but, like, does it?), and what the scene evokes. Meeting you jumpstarted the confidence to lift my book to a serious level to invest time, money, and emotion in. You allow me the space to pour my soul into my writing and help me achieve my goals. You keep me laughing and hopeful. That is a partner's dream. Thank you for choosing me and being my number one fan, as I am yours. I love you, always.

And to the readers: Thank you, thank you, thank you. I hope you find yourself in a character. I hope you feel inspired for change. I hope you remember you are not alone.

DEDICATION

To those we have lost. Imagine how we will meet again.

*The mind, without senses, without frantic noise or external guidance,
will naturally cling to any thought. When all thoughts fail,
the brain will create its own senses,
its own world, and, therefore,
its own reality.*

CONTENTS

CHAPTER 1
ELLIOTT

Elliott Bailey stood uncertain of what would happen next after she hit the button and the brainwave-altering chemicals diffused into the room. Piano music hung in the air like a dream, and the dimly lit Day Room smelled of cedarwood and lavender—yet her heart rate climbed as if she were being chased.

She lowered herself onto the plush, white sofa and hit the activation button on the remote control. She wrapped her arms around her legs as the lights switched off, the music fell silent, and her two minutes of preparation time came to an end.

No colors. No tastes. No scents—all remnants of life vanished.

Elliott had prescribed this very psychological treatment dozens, if not hundreds, of times, during her first year of working at the Center of Balloon Days, but it wasn't until now she found herself on the receiving end. Elliott would closely watch her patients on camera, to ensure their own safety as they engaged in the procedure, of course, but those observations didn't offer her much comfort now. After the chemicals took their effect, some of her patients would pace while others would rest on the fleece hammock or loveseat. She would watch them smile and laugh or weep and yell. The patient's brainwave activity reports summarized the rates at which their brainwaves fired throughout the process—mostly rapid, but sometimes slow and steady.

As far as their inner experiences, the information that actually mattered, she had to rely on their subjective descriptions. While she could hook up a patient to every modern sensor neuro-technology offered, there was nothing she could use to analyze the data in someone's mind.

In truth, the unknown alarmed the hell out of her.

Elliott's gaze roamed around the room as she prayed to see the white feathers along the walls. The carpet white as snow. The sky-blue pillows resting upon the sofa—to see anything, anything at all, but her world remained black as shadow.

A sudden blanket of warmth soothed her stomach, her head, her throat. Her jumbled nerves, which flickered incessantly, quieted and like a lake untouched, her mind calmed, freeing it of polluted thoughts. Still, there was nothing yet to see.

What am I doing wrong?

Elliott recalled Dr. Heller's advice for a Balloon Day session: Let your perception be your guide.

It was the Center's motto she knew all too well. After all, she had parroted that same advice to all her patients—as all staff members were required to do. It was Elliott's turn to follow the seemingly simple direction, and she had zero clue how to open the map.

Sure, our perceptions are our way of understanding the world, and sure, the reality our brains create for us is not derived solely from our senses but from our interpretations and experiences as well; even emotions play a role in how we perceive the world.

Anything that threw her off—like when her boyfriend canceled their plans at the last minute—proved tolerable if she was in a pleasant mood. If she was irritable and sensitive, forget it. She'd ask a hundred and one questions, view his behavior as distrustful, then fall under the haze of guilt hours later. Reality is often filtered through one's blueprint embedded within. The brain repressed painful memories in order to move onward, in order to survive.

Elliott knew these things, but she still couldn't find a way to relinquish control and let her unconscious mind do all the work. The whole point of Balloon Days was to disturb the unconscious junk, let it float to the mind's surface, and then do something about it already.

As if switching on a light, a new world began to form as she finally let her unconscious mind take over. Within seconds, soft carpet bloomed beneath her, and four walls of royal purple rumbled through the floor as they encased her in a room fit for a queen. A four-poster bed with sheer lilac curtains popped into place like magic. Elliott craned her neck to see a stuffed Big Bird and Elmo resting beside the pillows.

This is wild.

She stood on the floor of an enlarged version of her bedroom, except it was arranged as it had been when she was a child. The bed was quadruple its normal size, the purple comforter neatly tucked into the mattress, just as Dad demanded it be every single morning, or else she'd endure his rant of how a neat bed starts every day off with an accomplishment to feel good about.

A made bed seemed foolish as its unmade existence didn't harm anyone. She absolutely never considered it because it was a snore chore. Done further to alleviate him than it was to fulfill her own understanding of fulfillment. Sometimes Elliott left it messy on purpose. As she recalled these memories, a splitting sound from the bed, as if someone ripped the teeth of a zipper, broke the silence.

The mattress expanded and contracted, slowly and continually. Audible inhales and exhales with each swell and collapse. The bed was alive. Too anxious to step forward, yet, too curious to escape through the bedroom door, Elliott remained where she stood.

An indistinguishable voice from the bed whispered, "Help."

Elliott stepped forward, concern overriding her nerves. "Hello? Is anyone up there?"

Her father's head sprouted from the middle of the mattress. Out came his torso and arms to reveal a bulky figure in a black button-down shirt, with a maroon tie around his collar. He turned and glared at Elliott with stormy eyes, his face contorted in rage. He yelled and raved, yet no sound came from his mouth.

The figure's movements were sudden, almost twitch-like, the way he wriggled out from the mattress and darted toward Elliott. His limbs twisted in unnatural angles, like a spider with crippled legs, as he scampered across the floor, rapidly closing the distance between them. Elliott hugged her knees and made herself as small as possible. Inches from her feet, he multiplied into hundreds of miniature spider-like creatures. The implacable army crawled down the walls, up the furniture, enshrouding her in a black sea.

She shut her eyes as they crawled against her skin, the ends of their legs sharp like daggers, pricking her body with their every step. Specks of blood replaced the freckles along her arms. She squealed as she stood and shook, trying to get the spiders off her. They clung to her skin.

Go away.

Go away.

Go away.

"Get out of my head," she yelled.

She opened her eyes and heaved a deep sigh of relief. The horrible spiders were gone; the blood disappeared. It worked. The room shrunk back to its normal size. Still, the bed remained only a foot below her. Swiveling around to find her framed mirror on the back of the bedroom door, she pressed her hand against the glass.

Standing in the reflection before Elliott wasn't her at her present age. The figure was short, tiny-limbed, with faint freckles and straight brown hair, not Elliott's typically dyed auburn hair, that reached her elbows. She wore a black skirt made of tulle, and a black sequined t-shirt. This was Elliott's favorite outfit when she was six years old.

A sudden shudder at the bedroom door seized Elliott's heart and clutched her throat; the mirror confirmed the blood had drained from her already pale face. She rushed to lock the door, pressing her body weight against it; she was so small, so little, so helpless. Her weight wasn't nearly enough to blockade the door. All Elliott could do was listen to the chatter of the people on the other side and hope they didn't try to enter her room.

She pressed her ear against the wall. "You did what?" It was Mom, dejected, pleading. Her speech was strained from her sobs. "Please tell me it's not true."

A wetness touched Elliott's bare feet, as if the ocean licked her toes and swam beneath the arches of each foot. Except this wasn't seawater; it was a torrent of her mother's tears.

"Frankly, I don't know why you're all that shocked," Dad said. "You had to have seen this was happening."

Dad's next words would be forever etched in Elliott's memories, as clear as when she had first heard them in real life so long ago. Above and around her, each one of his words pushed through the margins of the door into Elliott's bedroom. Each taking up space, stealing the air. The words were enormous and flaming and glistening, welding themselves in a chain above Elliott.

Now I'm seeing words? Am I losing my frigging mind?

"I've been searching for a way out for years," he continued. Elliott listened closely as more words flowed into the room. Each one perfectly legible and taking up further space, emanating heat, as scorching as the sun. "You've pushed me away at every turn. You let your ridiculous worries ruin your life. You're poisonous, goddamn poison, Charlotte. I can't let you wreck my life any longer."

The words worries and poison took up more space than the other words. Elliott soon found it difficult to breathe. She yearned to escape through the window on the other side of the room, but she couldn't move the heavy words blocking her way. She tried shoving the word ruin, but it wouldn't budge. It remained earthen and still, like a mountain. As more words flooded the room, she found herself trapped and drowning and dripping with sweat. If Elliott didn't do something soon, she'd be buried here.

"You're the controlling one," Mom said. "Just because I ask you to do more things than you ask of me—because God forbid you help around here—does not mean you aren't constantly criticizing in other ways. You are just like your mother."

There was a pause before Dad spoke his next words. "The divorce will be good for both of us."

"Warren... you're really going to give up?"

The sound of Mom's defeat landed in Elliott's heart and sank like a stone.

"There you go again, always trying to guilt me," Dad said. "I spent enough of my time catering to your misery. I have zero sympathy left. Zero. It's high time I start breathing free air again. Hell, if it weren't for Elliott, I'd have left sooner." His voice boomed. The door shook as more words forced their way into the bedroom. "I wouldn't have made Holly wait so goddamn long."

Holly was the word that took up the most space, but unlike the other words, this one grew and grew and grew like a balloon that wouldn't pop. Taking up what little space there was left in the room. Elliott gasped for air. None would enter her lungs. The words squeezed her body against the door—she couldn't move. The heat burned her skin.

She barred her eyes and proceeded to struggle for breath, wishing it would all pass, expecting these infernal words to surrender their grip. She knew how this finished. There would be no happy ending here.

This was a Balloon Day. Balloon Days weren't real. They would conclude. She hoped her unconscious mind made whatever message it dropped through smoother, easier to understand, so she could stop this self-inflicted torment.

Let your perception be your guide.

She drew a breath and gradually opened one eye to see if any floating words lingered. There they were. Words of red. Words of green. Words of blue. Words of yellow—each hanging in the air like blinding Christmas lights.

They were Mom's words. "I'D-BURN-THIS-WHOLE-GODDAMN-HOUSE-DOWN-WITH-YOU-IN-IT-IF-IT-WEREN'T-FOR-OUR-DAUGHTER-IN-THE-NEXT-ROOM."

Elliott dashed toward them, the verbal evidence her parents would never love again—if they had ever loved at all. She flailed her arms to knock the words away, and they each fell to the floor, shattering like glass.

"What the hell was that?" Dad shouted.

Shit.

His voice roared from below her bedroom.

Before she could react, the center of her bedroom floor dissolved into a red muddy substance and began to swirl like quicksand. The gravity of the blood-colored sinkhole devoured the edges of the remaining rug with a deafening gulping and gurgling sound, and sucked Elliott along with it.

She scrambled to grip whatever she could, but her body was too small to hold onto anything as more and more of the floor morphed into the slippery form. Her feet pushed away, but the mud quickly engulfed them. Her ankles. Her shins. Her knees. Wiggling proved impossible as the thick sludge locked her in its grip.

"Help. Please. Someone, help me." Elliott cried, startled by her own voice—it was that of her little girl self, matching her current stature.

She cried out again. But no one answered.

She could achieve nothing but weep as she watched her waist go under. Then her arms and her chest. As the mud neared her neck, she surrendered. She closed her eyes, bracing for death.

Death never came—nor the expected suffocation.

This was still a Balloon Day, she remembered. You don't die in Balloon Days.

The hole widened and released Elliott to fall from the other side. She landed on a cold leather couch and found herself in the family room below her bedroom. The sofas perfectly positioned around a dark blue rug.

Portraits of Elliott and her parents hung on the wall, with the crackling fireplace bathing every inch of the room in a sinister reddish ambiance. In front of her were four gargantuan legs. As her gaze trailed upward, both Mom and Dad loomed above her like redwood trees.

"Elliott," Mom called out. "It's okay, baby. I'm here."

"Why did you guys have to fight, so much?" Elliott said, straining her voice in hopes they could hear. "You never stopped to think about me. You fought in front of my friends; you ruined holidays, my birthdays, my school plays. Nothing stopped you from arguing," she said. "No matter how hard I tried."

Elliott cowered as large droplets of cold, bright blue tears poured out of Mom's eyes, bursting open and spilling onto the rug, the sofa, and Elliott, like water balloons. As more tears flowed from her mother's eyes, she shrank, soon stopping at a foot above Elliott.

"I'm sorry you had to suffer, honey. I never wanted this for you."

"Stop babying our daughter, Char," Dad howled from above. "You're making her as weak and dramatic as you are. She needs to toughen up. It's a shit world out there. Coddling her all the time will make her useless. Or, perhaps you want our daughter to become some welfare queen who can't rub two sticks together to make a fire. I won't allow it." He lifted his leg, and the sole of his monstrous shoe came crashing down on Mom so rapidly the flame of her scream was snuffed out almost before it began.

"No," Elliott shrieked. "We are not weak. You're a huge, heartless asshole who—"

He lifted his leg again, about to do the same to Elliott. She shielded herself and he let out a grating laugh.

Please. No more. I want this to be over.

The bottom of her father's shoe reached her, and Elliott's forearms pressed against her skull. As the weight of his foot became too great, the pressure lifted.

As Elliott lowered her arms to see what had happened, she noticed her limbs were no longer small and frail or scarred with burns, but the body of her twenty-eight-year-old present self. The giant had vanished and instead replaced by serene, white-feathered walls, the soothing scent of lavender, the spell of lulling melodies. Elliott had returned safely to her Day Room, having escaped the mayhem of her mind in one piece.

CHAPTER 2
HOWARD

It was time to construct the perfect life—even if it would exist wholly in Howard's head. Jillian Mark didn't love him. Nor was he rich. Not even close. In real life, he didn't have much, aside from loneliness. A loneliness so consuming it rotted him from the inside out.

He could have it all at the Center of Balloon Days. At least, that's what he'd heard. On a Balloon Day you could do anything, anywhere, with anyone. Hold on to the string and let it take you away.

Howard stared at the pearl-white surface of the waiting room floor, the sweet scent of fresh flowers overwhelmimg him. A bouquet of plum-colored roses rested in a vase on the remarkably clear glass table next to him. If it wasn't for the golden legs of the table, he'd have thought the vase floated in midair.

The clock on the wall showed it was 11:58am, two minutes away from Howard's appointment time. He retrieved his journal, more like a diary—but Howard felt childish calling it that—out of the plastic bag he carried it in. The rustling sound of the bag disrupted the ambience of the strings and chimes of the music streaming from the speakers.

I don't belong here.

He opened the tired, creased notebook, flipped to a fresh page to dump his brain chatter, or else the doubt would continue to knock around in his head. He wished he sat in his local library absorbing book after book, back where he belonged. Howard wasn't fancy enough for this place. Virtually everything had a silk-like sheen, except for the glowing color-themed elevators, and the lavish art lining the walls. Any staff member he crossed paths with wore white—but not lab-coat white.

9

This attire consisted of ruffled blouses, button-downs, and slim pants or skirts. Their hair styles were as meticulous, arranged in ways he'd only seen people use for weddings. It was the type of place his brother John would go to, or anyone else who made over $200k a year.

"Howard Nor?" a woman called out. A waft of lavender hit his nose, an earthy scent he immediately recognized. It had been Mom's favorite.

Howard shut his journal and lifted his head. She stood in the wide threshold of the open office doors. Sunshine from the grand window illuminated her satin outfit, weaving light through her hair, like she was an ethereal angel sent from the heavens to save him from his small, pitiable life—one could only hope.

"Hello," she said. "I'm Dr. Heller."

Howard removed his navy-blue beanie. It seemed the appropriate thing to do. As he stood, his journal and pen had been forgotten and dropped to the floor. The doctor remained smiling as Howard scrambled to pick both up, his cheeks warming as he stumbled like a bumbling high school freshman.

She shot a look at his plastic bag as he placed the journal in it. She could see how pathetic he was. He should bolt and call the whole thing off. His hard-earned cash would be better spent on whiskey.

I'm here to get better. Get up and go to her, already.

Putting his humiliation to the side, Howard followed Dr. Heller into her office, the sliding doors shutting out the world behind him.

Regal and serene, Dr. Heller had wavy, honey-brown hair tied loosely behind her head. Not one strand out of place, matching the hue of her wide-set, almond eyes. The corners of her mouth curled slightly upward. Everything she wore was white except for a symbol, the size of a quarter, of a black balloon stitched into her blouse, placed on the area underneath her right collarbone.

The balloon's string looked like a stretched-out capital S. He visualized the balloon gliding toward the sky, nearing the clouds, then disappearing out of sight. "Welcome to the Center of Balloon Days. I am the neuropsychologist and clinical director here."

One leg crossed over the other, she rested in her chair. Dr. Heller didn't appear too much older than Howard, maybe by a decade or so at most, unless she had some type of powerful skin regimen. Yet there he sat in the smooth leather chair, at twenty-six years old, with a prematurely balding head that was freshly buzzed to beat the process.

"Nice to meet you," Howard muttered, offering his best smile in return—strained and awkward.

She remained poised behind the glass desk between them; the desk, positioned in the center of the room—more like a table—had four slender legs of gold. The rest of the room was bare, except for a white sofa and chair in the far-left corner and a bookshelf. The shelves occupied by dense textbooks, each a perfect glossy white, too far away for Howard to read the titles. Were they filled with words, or simply for décor?

"Here at Balloon Days, we offer you an exceptional treatment you won't find anywhere else," Dr. Heller said. "Imagine your wildest dreams come true. All your fears? Worries? Doubts? Everything holding you back, magically disappeared." She snapped her fingers. "Like that. Think of it as an induced lucid dream."

Howard's heart felt like the balloon on her blouse, her words the helium inflating him with hope.

"Your chart says that you would like two credits. Two credits are not that much, but enough. A lot can still happen in thirty minutes." She handed him a tablet. It was cool against his hands, and the screen was covered by a wall of text. "I need you to sign the contract and waiver. It includes today's intake payment, each of the credits you purchased, and your key card for your assigned Day Room. But don't worry, we'll keep your credit card on file so you won't need to do this again."

Howard pictured the brown bag filled with his savings underneath his bed and his heart quickly deflated. Each credit cost him fifty dollars. Working as his brother's personal assistant didn't pay much—enough to get by. Picking up extra hours became essential.

To experience the way his life could have gone—to have been successful, to have lived a life he could be proud of, and to be with Jillian, a woman who was easygoing, creative, and had a smile that softened the most hardened of hearts—meant the world to him. Maybe he could be someone's role model one day.

He scrolled to the bottom and signed.

The doors behind him opened. A staff member appeared wheeling in a white cart. As she neared, she picked up a glass teapot. Steeping tea leaves and petals of various colors rested at the top, creating pink-tinted water and a sweet floral scent.

"Would you like some of our exceptional tea?" Dr. Heller waved her arm, palm up, as if selling a product. She put her hand back in her lap. "We have plain black tea as well."

"It is my favorite tea today," the young girl said. "Rose petals accented with orange blossoms. Good for the heart and the soul. And all organic."

"Black is fine," Howard muttered.

"This is Romalda," Dr. Heller said. "After you and I finish our meeting, she will escort you to your first Balloon Day."

Romalda bowed her head. "I look forward to helping you."

Petite and pretty with slightly wavy ivory-blonde hair, Romalda wore a white sleeveless blouse and matching white dress pants, complete with white heels and elegant, white-rimmed glasses. The brightness of it all hurt his eyes, like a sunny morning when Howard had downed two too many shots of Evan Williams the night before.

Romalda poured tea into one of the glass mugs, a black balloon etched into the side of it. A drop of tea missed and spilled on the white surface.

Romalda's face dropped. She briefly closed her eyes. "I'm so sorry, Dr. Heller."

"Hmm," Dr. Heller hummed. She stared raptly at Romalda with the hint of a grin. But the area around her eyes possessed zero wrinkles. The expression was a peculiar mix of caring and annoyance. It reminded Howard of Miss Rory's face, his apathetic third-grade teacher, whenever he misspelled something on the chalkboard.

Romalda eyed Dr. Heller, flashing a nervous smile. She frantically grabbed a napkin to absorb the liquid. She tossed the used napkin in a small waste basket on the bottom tray of the cart. Within seconds, it was as if Romalda's worried face never existed.

Howard shifted in his seat. It seemed like the sort of thing one shouldn't be witnessing. As if he was watching a Broadway show and one of the actors tripped up in a dance.

"Okay. All is wonderful. Here you go," Romalda said, placing their tea-filled mugs on coasters before she left. He took a sip: perfect temperature, not too sweet.

"Now tell me," Dr. Heller said. "How would you like to see your life changed by Balloon Days?" She leaned forward and placed her smooth, manicured fingers on her laptop keyboard.

Her words spun and sank in Howard's mind. He said nothing aside from a murmured "um." The heat returned to his cheeks.

What is wrong with me?

No one else seemed to have this much difficulty expressing themselves. With a shaky hand, he touched his wiry beard, which he kept in an in-between state: not messy, but not trimmed either. He surveyed the room some more and noticed to his right were floor-to-ceiling windows tinted light blue. They must make a bleak rainy day in Manhattan appear bright and cheery.

Dr. Heller momentarily took her hands off the keyboard. "For example, common goals are processing a trauma, working on phobias, or playing out different challenging or high-risk situations to avoid real-life consequences," she said.

"I don't want to be sad anymore," Howard said.

The words hung pathetically in the air. He sounded like a child whining about his math homework.

"Well, you are not alone—many patients desire the same," she said plainly. It was a cold, rehearsed line. One that said she didn't give a damn if he was about to step off the Brooklyn Bridge. "What would that look like for you?"

Howard assumed this intake would be simpler, but he was wrong. Like he'd been wrong about most things in his life. "A real career. A home. A life worth living." Getting his thoughts out was like pulling sticks out of mud. "With the woman I love." *Who is preferably not a backstabbing, reckless, cold-hearted woman who sleeps with anyone who gives her a wink and a smile, like his ex-girlfriend, Kimmy.* "Her name is Jillian."

"Those are great goals—I can already envision your Balloon Day," Dr. Heller said with a dutiful wink as she typed away. She probably didn't hear a word he said. "Tell me the last time you had experienced anything close to that."

That answer wasn't simple either. Visions of piano notes along with his parents filled the air. "When I was fifteen."

Howard could tell Dr. Heller about his music, he remembered it well—the weight of the piano keys pushing back on his hands, the coolness of them against his fingertips. The awe he felt when not only one note sang, but several burst at once into a melodic haze or a visceral warning.

He wasn't ready to tell her why he'd stopped playing; why the keys collected dust.

"And why is today the day, Howard?" Dr. Heller said, her eyes subtly squinting. "Why is now the time to start your therapeutic journey?"

He stared at her open-mouthed, unsure how to answer. Too many reasons had piled up for quite some time now. It was hard to know where to begin.

"Don't think too much on it. You've shared a lot with me already, which is strong of you. This is a question I ask all of our patients to ensure they are ready to commit to healing."

"I am ready," Howard said. "I needed time to save money."

Howard was too mortified to admit he allowed coked-up Kimmy back into his life, yet again. Only to be dumped like trash, yet again, two days ago. At this point, he lost track of the amount she came and went during these last few years. He was a book she continually picked up, then put down again, without any intention of ever reaching the end.

But Jillian.

Jillian gave him hope—with her encouraging nature, with her hazel eyes swallowing him whole, with her kind words relieving his Kimmy-induced heartache. He'd rather get help for her instead of for Kimmy any day.

"I'm looking forward to a Balloon Day. Is that a picture of one?" Howard pointed to the strange artwork in the middle of the left wall hoping to distract Dr. Heller from pressing for more answers. The painting sat between two other pieces—both portrayed white brainwaves on a sky-blue background, like outlines of narrow hills and valleys. Up and down, up and down, his eyes traced along them.

"That's another painting of mine. It's not a Balloon Day per se, it's the mere representation of one. You see, the man is walking down a staircase—clouds for steps, of course—holding a black balloon to represent the freedom of the imagination as he explores the inner depths of his mind.

One of my favorite pieces." She gazed pridefully at it. This was the most enthusiastic Howard had seen her for this entire meeting.

Howard questioned her fondness for it. There was something eerie about a man with a wide smile staring straight at him, walking down a spiral staircase, despite it being made of clouds. Maybe that was simply because the depths of Howard's brain were more like a dungeon, nothing anyone would beam for.

"It's great. He looks happy," Howard lied.

"Of course he does, because he is. You will be too." She blinked and smiled like the man in her painting.

Before Howard could quench any more of his curiosities, she carried on. "Romalda will escort you back to the elevator to take you to your Day Room, S44. The S is for the silver elevator. The first 4 is for the fourth floor, second 4 is for the Day Room. This is your Day Room every time you visit, so it is imperative you keep this key card and not lose it. We can issue a replacement, but with a fee."

Another fee?

No one discussed this in any of the reviews he read, but perhaps those reviews had been "carefully curated." He was right to think this was a place only for the rich. Howard took the key card from her hand: all white, with the same black balloon as on Dr. Heller's blouse printed on it. S44 was written underneath it in silver. He slowly rose, sliding his beanie on his head as he listened, trying to remember it all, grabbing onto her words and storing them neatly in his memory.

"You will have two minutes to settle in once you're in the room. There, you'll find a remote control on the wall. Once you press the activation button on the control, your brainwave activity will be rerouted by our proprietary blend of therapeutic oils released into the air. These oils gently alter the frequencies in your brain to initiate a controlled dream-like state, immersing you into your Balloon Day—the first one can be unsettling for some, due to the newness of it, but it still comes with plenty of insight." Dr. Heller paused as he met her gaze, her eyes miniature pots of golden honey.

"Unsettling?" Howard said.

"Be mindful of your time," she continued. Howard's question swept under the rug. He didn't blame her; he lacked assertiveness. Story of his life.

"You can hit the switch and enter your Balloon Day before the two minutes of prep time is up. However, if you don't press the button after your preparation time—you will be using your credits regardless. But I can tell you are a smart man and will use your credits wisely. With all of that said, any other questions before you sign the consent form?" Dr. Heller handed him the tablet again.

The print was small and the form lengthy, a black balloon at the top. "Are there any risks?" Perhaps this question would get Howard a clearer answer.

"Such a curious mind." Dr. Heller paused, her smile in place yet the disagreeing eyes reappeared; warm and frigid. "Your well-being is paramount to us, so I have ensured the technology is safe. There are no side effects of the oils. Emotions arise, of course. If anything is triggering, we will work with you to explore how it matters and help you understand the emotions you equate with a negative experience. But they're only feelings, and feelings are manageable. What kind of therapeutic place would this be if we didn't let you feel in order to heal?"

That wasn't exactly a no, but it was good enough for him. Maybe he should have researched more.

"No need to worry—we are here for you. You can always end your Balloon Day whenever you want. As we say: let your perception be your guide." Dr. Heller motioned her arm toward the door, signaling for Howard to proceed, Romalda smiling while waiting as promised.

Well-rehearsed and right on cue, both women ushered him toward the silver elevator. Yet his head was still filled with questions.

Did it work?

What did it feel like?

Was it easy?

The intake was so finely tuned that Howard was the one who had forgotten his lines, even if he hadn't been given the script in the first place.

"Romalda, please lead Howard to his Day Room, S44." Dr. Heller turned to Howard. "Have a great Balloon Day," she said, then returned to her office.

Could Howard make Jillian love him on his Balloon Day? Maybe he could have everything he wanted, like Dr. Heller said.

Or maybe this would only bring him more misery.

CHAPTER 3
ORSON

The opened windows poured the summer sun into Orson Thatch's living room, where his wife lay in a hospice bed. The breast cancer had spread to her lymph nodes.

Orson did not want his wife to die. She was only thirty-eight years old, with countless plans for the future. Every night, on his knees, he prayed for one more day.

One more day to be with her.

He wanted Madison's strawberry blonde hair back, not the wig that poorly imitated its true color. He wanted the conversations to return without her having to fight to remain awake. He wanted the weekend movie nights after their seven-year-old son Ryder fell asleep. He wanted everything back to normal.

Losing her meant losing half of himself.

How could he be all he could be for his son if half of him was missing?

If there was ever such a way to get it all back, he would risk whatever it took to obtain it. A friend mentioned that his late mother spoke to him through a medium, with details no one else would know, but it was something to be chary about.

Orson had witnessed the silly ways people tried to hold on to a person who had to let go of life, grief-stricken love making fools out of them. Would he ever be that fool?

He placed the newly delivered lilies from Madison's parents on the round table in the middle of the foyer, in between the vase of fresh roses from his own parents and an exquisite ceramic bowl from their last trip to Spain.

Returning to the living room, the Long Island news channel quietly prattled on the mounted television, explaining where the top local wineries could be found. Orson shut it off. He gazed at the bed in the corner to the right of the fireplace, the nook previously occupied by his favorite sand-colored recliner. Madison had drifted into sleep once again.

The moments when she was lucid had thinned out. But she came around, especially with Ryder; he read her one of their favorite books earlier, the one about that wizard boy, Harry Potter. The memory alone cracked Orson's heart, the image both sweet and stinging.

Pale sunshine carried into the kitchen as Orson grabbed a bottled water, the spilled rays brightening the grays of the hardwood floor. As the cold water traveled to his stomach, Orson pondered the proposition his boss had presented him weeks ago—to become a senior partner.

The offer remained in the back of his mind. And the front. The medical bills were ever-increasing, and more money meant more security. Possibly greater healthcare for Madison. But Orson's career as a lawyer for wealthy physicians had already stolen away most of his time, time he now needed to spend with his wife.

As Orson returned to the living room, his younger sister's laugh carried through from the playroom; Rose kept Ryder occupied. Ever since his neighbor Elliott had to step back from babysitting as frequently, Rose happily took over.

Rose had always been wiser than her years. In grade school, she hardly had to study to obtain honors. Orson, on the opposite end, buried himself in books just so he could get his tests hung on the refrigerator alongside his sister's.

His efforts eventually paid off—he was now a successful lawyer, and Rose was a blogger with an online business selling her artwork.

Ryder's bare feet stomped on the hardwood floor of the foyer, then slowed down as he entered the living room. Rose swiftly followed. Her coral lipstick on yet again, a recent trend she said that complimented her summer tan and one of her self-made bracelets.

"Hey, bud. Where'd your socks go? I thought we were matching again today." Orson revealed his dinosaur patterned socks underneath his navy-blue dress pants.

Ryder shrugged. "Felt like taking them off. Besides, you forgot to wear the car ones yesterday." Lately, Ryder developed a talent for talking back, acting as fiery as the strawberry-blonde hair atop his head.

"Ryder, be nice to your father," Rose said. "He's trying."

The urge to tug at his collar nagged him but Orson put his hands in his pockets instead, clearing his throat. As he contemplated how to respond, Madison stirred.

"Mom," Ryder rushed over to the bed and half-hugged her body. "Guess what? My magical rocket is almost done."

"Easy, buddy," Orson said.

"It's okay." Madison struggled as she reached for Ryder. He moved closer and kissed the top of her head, although the expression on his face was filled with hesitance. "Really. Sweetie, it's okay."

Orson gently took Madison's hand—the hand where her wedding band used to be. With her fragile state and an alarming amount of weight loss, they had believed it best to keep her ring in the safe.

Orson ran his finger over his own wedding band. Envisioning the word "always" engraved on the inside, and in her handwriting, stabbed him with unutterable pain, penetrating deep into his chest.

"I love you guys," Madison said, her voice cracking and thin. "No matter what."

"Always?" Ryder said.

"Always."

The knife twisted further inside Orson's heart.

Over the next several days, family members came in and out of their home. So many people came through that Orson had considered keeping the door unlocked at all times. Part of him wanted to selfishly pretend they weren't actually home. Another part of him wanted them all to fuck off so he could get as much time with his wife as he could, to make up for every single minute he had taken for granted.

Finally, alone, Orson sat in the recliner at Madison's side as the morning sun cocooned them in a tangerine haze. He wished he could have a pain-free conversation with her, wished he could ask her all of the things he never had a chance to: How to take care of Ryder better? How to soothe him? How to parent without her? How to feel alive without her?

Instead, he watched her while she slept. The delicate rise and fall of her chest, the faint reddish-brown freckles on her forehead and cheeks. The twitch of her mouth, the sound of her breathing. He took it all in, as much as he could. He knew he wouldn't be able to soon.

The peace was short-lived as his phone buzzed on the end table. Orson's boss flashed on the screen. He lightly kissed Madison's cheek in hopes to not wake her, then walked upstairs and closed his bedroom door half-way.

"Hey, Jack. How are you?" Near the window, he caught sight of their garden, a blend of rose bushes, hydrangea, and inkberry hollies beginning to wilt.

"Sorry to bother you, Orson, but Darnell is adamant you remain his attorney, regardless of whoever else I offer. Wants you to be the one to handle the jury selection. Won't adjourn either. The problem of being too good, am I right?"

Orson rubbed between his eyes. Darnell was a big-shot millionaire and an orthopedic surgeon being sued for operating on the patient's right knee instead of her left knee, yet blamed everyone but himself for it, his exact words being "Well, the surgical team didn't double-check the chart."

Incompetent fool who couldn't find his own asshole if it wasn't on a chart.

"Would he be willing to postpone another two weeks?" Orson said.

"Another two weeks? He'll call you unreliable. Do you want to keep your job, or not?"

If Orson didn't oblige to protect Darnell's practice, and Darnell smeared his reputation, he could lose myriad clients.

"Alright then." Orson's collar tightened again, but this time he pulled at it and undid the top button. "I'll be there bright and early."

"I know times are beyond bleak, but if it helps, you're on the right track to becoming a senior partner sooner than later, Orson. Keep up the good work."

Giving up the case would be in Orson's best interest. But to sit home all day, every day, in misery without any distractions at all was unappealing.

He then realized that Jack didn't ask about his wife once.

Orson pocketed his phone.

"I assume I'm watching Ryder tomorrow?"

Rose stood in the doorway, her hands on her hips. He should have closed the door completely.

"Oh, hey, Rose. Yes, actually." He attempted to win her over with a humble smile, but his sister's sour expression remained. Charisma, he continued to learn, could only go so far with family. "I'm sorry, sis. I know you already have a lot on your plate."

For roughly two years, Rose and her husband have attempted to conceive, and Orson did feel sympathy for them, truly. The accumulated bills for infertility treatments were staggering and Orson offered to help pay for them, but when Madison's cancer took a turn for the worse, he had to pull away the offer. Rose had displayed underlying bitterness that popped up here and there ever since.

"I'll stay over. Again. You're lucky Ryder is a sweet little angel, and that my husband is so patient." She crossed her arms, and as she spoke Orson could make out her slightly crooked front tooth. It wasn't quite a snaggle tooth, but it surely was a relative of one. "Plus, I haven't been able to blog in over a week. I might lose followers."

"I appreciate it. Let Jeff and your other dozen followers know that I certainly appreciate them too." She let out a small laugh that seemed to take her by surprise. Taking that as a good sign, Orson took a step toward her. "Madison also does. You are always a tremendous help. And right now, there's immense pressure at the job on top of all of this. Surely you understand."

Her sneer returned, and Orson could swear her sapphire eyes possessed a reddish tint. "You said that two months ago, Orson. Last year. And the year before that. Your wife is dying but you gotta go get some asshole surgeon out of trouble? You know I'm always here for you and you don't have to be there for me, but you do need to be there for your kid, and for your wife."

"You think I don't want to be here? I don't want to be anywhere else, but how are we supposed to pay for these treatments?" he said. "I don't know if you know this, but I can't blog my way through life and still have the money needed for treating my wife."

23

Rose turned on her heel, disturbing her dark hair, almost black like Orson's, flowing down her spine. She ventured down the hall, back to Ryder's room. His son's sweet, high-pitched voice bounced into the hallway before she slammed the door.

Orson sat on his bed. The soft fabric of the silky gray sheets against his hands reminded him he hadn't made the bed this morning. Duties like that were tended to by Madison. She had a way of fluffing up their pillows to make them feel brand new. She chose the coziest linens to match their modern white-black-gray color scheme, broken up with crimson accents, maintaining a romantic flair.

He sighed. Surely, Orson was not chasing the wrong things. She's envious, her bitterness showing again. Orson did work a lot, but he provided his family with a gorgeous home, food in the fridge, vacations, access to the top physicians. It was a hell of a lot more than he had growing up.

Orson traipsed down the hallway and knocked on Ryder's bedroom door, opening it a crack.

"Who is it?" Ryder said.

"Hey, bud." Orson's hand hovered over the knob.

"Password?"

Ryder changed it weekly. Orson gave his best attempt. "Boogers."

"No-o-o," Ryder yipped. "That was the old one."

"Okay. And the new one?"

"Guess."

"Snot."

"Guess again."

"Just tell me, Ryder."

"You're no fun." Ryder sounded like he was joking, but the words still hurt. Orson knew there was truth to them. "It's wizard now."

Orson cupped his hand by his mouth. "Wizard."

Ryder giggled. "Come in," he said.

Ryder sat in the middle of the bedroom floor, legs crisscrossed next to Rose, building a Lego tower with a sly grin on his face.

"What's going on with that smirk? What are you not saying?"

Ryder cracked up and stood. "Look." He lifted reddish strands of hair off his forehead, revealing a lightning bolt sticker. "I... Am... Harry... Potter," he said with a puffed chess, deepening his voice.

"Oh, my goodness. Look at that. You are." Orson bent down to take a closer look.

"Can you show me your mark again?" Ryder said.

Ever since learning Harry Potter had a lightning bolt scar, Ryder had taken a sudden interest in foreheads, learning that Orson had an ink mark on his; where the tip of Rose's pen landed after she flung it at him when they were children, all because Orson finally beat her in Monopoly Jr. Orson lifted his hair.

"Cool." Ryder grinned.

"Thanks, son." Orson couldn't help but chuckle at what Ryder's idea of cool was.

"Now, Dad, watch out." Ryder waved an imaginary wand and Rose moved out of the way. "Stupiferous."

Orson pulled a pen out of his shirt pocket. "Shmoop dadoop."

"What?" Ryder rolled his head back, howling with laughter.

"Good one, Orson." Rose said. Orson shrugged and they both laughed along with Ryder.

Collecting himself, Ryder said, "You need to read the books." He pointed to his bookshelf, the set complete and calling. "You promised you would." Another thing Orson didn't have time for.

"Dad will soon, Ryder," Rose said. "Hey, why don't you shoot another spell at him?"

To Orson's relief, Ryder grabbed a crayon from his small blue desk and snapped around, the crayon's end directed at Orson. "Blast, blast, blast. Dad, pretend my spell hit you, and big green sparks flew out of my wand and then fall on the floor."

"On it, son." Orson gripped his chest, dramatically lowering himself to the floor, delighted to redeem himself any way he could. "Oweee." The laughter echoed down the stairway into the living room where Madison lay.

Orson's wife, and Ryder's mother, breathed her final farewell.

CHAPTER 4
HOWARD

"Silver is nice, right?" Romalda chirped as Howard followed her into the illuminated glass elevator. "I like the turquoise one myself, but silver is wonderful too." She pressed button #4.

"So, your first Balloon Day. Are you excited? Because it is exciting. I love Balloon Days. You can go anywhere and do anything—with anyone. I've flown on a dragon and battled a girl on another dragon. It's amazing how Dr. Heller managed to give this opportunity to the world. Dr. Elliott Bailey is wonderful too—I saw on your chart she's your assigned psychologist."

As Howard nodded, the door slid open to a miniature version of Dr. Heller's waiting area. It was sophisticated, with white walls and floor, a comfortable plush sofa, bundles of lavender on the end tables.

"Welcome to your pre-room," Romalda said.

The door straight ahead to his Day Room shined like ice: frameless and tinted light blue, like the windows in Dr. Heller's office but he could not see through it, although the glass still had a translucent appearance. S44 was etched in black writing at the center, with the signature balloon above.

"What's that door for?" Howard gestured to a white door with a large black knob.

"That's the pre-room bathroom."

He poked his head in. Pristine as expected, unlike his decaying bathroom at home.

"No mirror," he said.

"Oh no, mirrors don't belong here." Romalda waved her hand to brush away his words like a foul stench.

Howard stared at the blank wall again above the sink. As if he didn't already feel invisible enough.

Then again, it was nice to not be reminded of his sad existence anyway.

Romalda pressed the elevator button and the silver-lit glass glowed. Within seconds, the elevator doors opened. "Have a great Balloon Day. Let your perception be your guide."

As the elevator doors closed, worries dripped in his mind like hot tar. What if Jillian stopped talking to him again, even here? What if he messed up his fantasy life too?

Howard turned to face the door. A screen on the wall to its left lit up and released a pleasant chime signaling his Day Room was ready. Howard slid his key card in the slot. A touch screen underneath displayed his initials as well as his credit balance. He selected to use both, figuring he might as well go all out for Jillian where he could.

He stepped into Day Room S44 and the door slid closed behind him. The air smelled of lavender and gentle piano music played as if from a distance. Long white feathers gently swayed, covering the walls of the room, which was a perfect square. Above him, the ceiling resembled a blue-black sky. Stars were scattered like twinkling gnats. Translucent, light gray clouds floated by, and the white carpeting cushioned his feet through his worn sneakers.

Against the wall to his left, was the loveseat as promised, with pillows of the same dark blue as the realistic sky above. The sofa looked like the kind of couch he could get a restful nap on, which was tempting as he already felt drained. Near the right wall hung the floating fleece hammock. He grazed his fingers across the material.

It was certainly the most elegant room he had ever been in.

Howard grabbed the shiny control from its holder. It had a smooth round button in the center with the words "Have a Great Balloon Day" curling around it in black letters, in some type of swirly cursive font. The button lit up to signal that his two minutes of preparation time were over.

Falling back into the hammock, Howard pushed the switch as to not waste any time. Immediately a strange, airy sensation warmed his body. The music fell silent, the lavender scent disappeared, and the lights of the room vanished. He was in complete darkness. His mind quieted as he closed his eyes.

Moments later, Howard sensed the weight of someone on his chest. A sheet lay over their bodies, the comfort of a bed underneath.

Hesitating, he let one eye squint open, the other slowly following. His vision was hazy, but he could make out a pair of hazel eyes looking up at him.

Those eyes.

Jillian's eyes. A meld of autumn leaves on the forest floor, their brightness the reflection of the sun on a quiet lake. The few freckles sprinkled across her nose and cheeks laid a path in between and below them.

Eyes that turned Howard into a modern-day Lord Byron.

"You're awake." A cheerful grin stretched across her face.

Her peach scent filled his lungs.

Howard was awestruck—he ran his hands through her soft hair, they roamed around to her arms, then her back; all was solid, and warm as can be, as if she were a real human. Alive and true.

Jillian rolled onto her back, her raven hair spreading out like a deck of cards beneath her head. He lifted the covers to make sure all was as it should be, kicking his legs against the mattress, then pinched his cheeks.

"Are you okay?" Jillian said.

"I'm more than okay."

"Let's make coffee," she said, swinging her legs over the bed, her bare feet grazing the carpet. "And then watch The Apartment. I want to enjoy the day before we have to fly back to the city and your big tech company steals you away again." Jillian pranced off into the next room.

Howard slowly nodded, still in a daze. This was his brain's creation. He had to go with it, had to enjoy it, believe what the doctor said. He looked around at their cottage. As he did, it became clearer and more defined, all of it immediately assembled by his mind.

Flames crackled in the living room fireplace opposite the plushy sofa. A dark red blanket rested upon it, rumpled from recent use. Their bedroom at the back of the house had walls painted buttercup yellow. The entrance was a lovely wide-open archway, allowing them to see out to the rest of the home. Two pairs of shoes were on the floormat by the front door. Peacoats hung on the nearby coat tree.

He lifted himself off the bed, startled to see a photograph of Kimmy, with her teal hair and ratty plaid button-down, on the floor, a line of cocaine on the table in front of her, her hands dripping with blood.

What the hell?

He blinked, and the photo was gone. Was he imagining things? Was that possible in an already imaginary world? He shook it off and wandered into the kitchen, unsure of where Jillian went.

The kitchen was small and charming, the walls a light wood, cabinets and countertops frosty gray, with a table and chairs of the same color in the corner. The sultry fragrance of chocolate chip cookies wafted upward. As he neared the sink, used spoons and bowls covered with leftover cookie dough came into focus.

The window above the sink was slightly open. The snow-white curtains billowed with the magic of a soft breeze that carried into the room, touching his cheek. He drew the curtain out of the way to view the Irish countryside, a patchwork of vibrant shades of green—grass on hills as light as kiwis and limes, with valleys the color of evergreens and emeralds—as he had seen in the travel books.

"Come here, my love."

Sitting on the sofa, Jillian wore an orange sundress, twirling strands of dark hair around her finger. Her hair, thick and gleaming, flowed past her shoulders, skimming her porcelain skin.

He settled himself on the spot next to her.

She ran a hand through Howard's hair, hair that suddenly appeared as he recalled how it had been. Golden brown, soft, its length short but long enough to still see its slight wave.

Howard cupped her chin and delicately fixed his lips against hers, pillowy and warm as they parted. It was unlike any kind of dream he had ever experienced. Seamless and clearer than his waking state—no booze-filled blurriness or robotic motions, no more thoughts of having to push through one more day only to start all over the next.

Gently pulling away, Jillian looked at his face, tears welling up in her eyes. "I love you," she whispered. The sweetest words, a precious gift.

"I love you too," Howard whispered.

Jillian didn't know that, not in the real world. Would he ever tell her? Would she say it back?

Should he ever tell her?

No. Nothing good will come of it.

Her hands clutched his and tugged. "Let's get dressed and go." She tugged again. Her voice was suddenly distant, fuzzy and faded. "Howard, why are you so behind all the time?" Jillian turned airy, her eyes a fusion of yellow-green and brown, brimming with disappointment.

Howard wobbled as if drunk, though he hadn't a drop of whiskey all day. But he knew he was slipping. Heavy-headed, blurry-eyed, and woozy. Something went wrong, and it was growing worse by the second.

There was no such thing, no such goddamn thing as lasting joy. How could he forget that?

As Howard tried to figure out what was happening in his Balloon Day, Jillian began fading along with her voice. "You need to change everything, then I will love you..."

Before Howard could react, a black shadow crept in, framing the scene, the image of her shrinking exponentially. Howard's eyes darted everywhere, begging to understand, his legs wobbly with alcohol.

He closed his eyes and opened them. The darkness still spread.

What was going on?

The darkness vanished with Jillian, and the drunk wore off with it. The fog that dizzied his brain dissipated. Still, his legs were unsteady, as if he were standing on marshmallows.

He looked down. It wasn't marshmallows, it was clouds—a staircase of clouds in the middle of the sky that appeared out of nowhere, confusing him further. He followed the trail downward, gaining his footing on the cushions beneath his feet.

Four cloud steps away, he froze.

At the bottom was a grand piano resting on sand. Mom sat next to it, with her feet in the ocean lapping at the shore. She leaned back, her russet brown hair skimming the sand, and fixed her gaze on him.

"Howard, I love you." Her voice carried like a chill breeze, haunting but soft. "You need to not lose yourself. Don't forget how important you are."

In the distance, the shadow of a man walked along the shore and Howard could make out the distinct shape of a knife in his hand. Howard's heart pumped faster than his racing thoughts.

Hastily rushing down the clouds, Howard yelled out for her to run. The man neared Mom, and as Howard reached the last step, a new cloud formed.

Then, another.

And, another.

Then, another.

Every step he took, a new cloud appeared.

He was close and yet impossibly far away. Too far to save her. Just like when he was fifteen.

He was useless.

A blanket of darkness crept in, stripping the color and shapes away from everything until all that remained was Mom's fearful eyes.

And—there was nothing. Nothing at all.

Howard blinked gently. He stared at a dimly lit Day Room. The music returned and rose in its volume. Lavender filled the air, the activating control unlit and lifeless. The exit door slid open.

A female voice addressed the room. "Breathe in deeply and exhale gently. Proceed to the exit elevator. Your next Balloon Day awaits. Come back soon." Howard could tell it was a recording.

He trudged into the post-room. Why did his Balloon Day have to end there? He should have saved more money. Thirty minutes felt like five. He needed more time for Jillian. Now for mom. He could've saved her; it was his fault that she died. Howard had to pull more from his savings, he had to work harder for John. He had to come back.

As he entered the elevator, his phone vibrated in his pocket. It was his brother. He could be a tough boss, but to John's credit it was unlike him to call on Howard's day off.

The service was weak in the elevator, but Howard answered his phone anyway.

"Howard … sorry … a drag. I … hoping … be able to stop in an hour." John's words were choppy, but knowing him well, he was assigning a task to Howard. "I … you to wait … a package for me. Gotta … away, man. Me and … the airport. Itching for a change of scenery."

The elevator doors opened to the lobby.

"I decided last minute to take Jillian to Paris for the next few days. Is that cool? Can you do that?"

"Oh. Sure. No problem."

If only Howard could have been the one to whisk Jillian away.

CHAPTER 5

ELLIOTT

Elliott laid on her bed as the moonlight draped her room in a white glow, still racking her brain as to what had happened during her Balloon Day. The red haze throughout it all stumped her. She knew the color to be symbolic of myriad things: passion, power, aggression, anger. And blood and warfare—clearly there were hostilities.

Passion had admittedly been nonexistent for most of her life, aside from her career. Power? More like powerless, unless Elliott counted when she had escaped moments of absolute terror. But had there been strength in sheer panic and desperation?

The Dad-headed spiders had frightened the crap out of her. Although Freud believed spiders in dreams symbolized issues with one's mother, Elliott disagreed. Her mom and she had a wonderful relationship. Yes, Mom could get emotional at times and overshare—she mentioned Dad had stopped initiating intimacy, and how he had used gifts to manipulate her into fashioning excuses for why he'd miss Elliott's dance recitals and Science Fairs. But Mom endlessly supported Elliott. She was a great mother. Freud was the one to have mother issues. Elliott was more of a Carl Jung type of gal anyway.

According to Jung, spiders swarming you in your dreams meant you had trouble facing the despised, darkest parts of yourself, hidden in the "shadow." What the hell would that mean for Elliott? She supposed she did resent her anxiety. Anxiety weakened her mentally. Physically, it wore her out.

As for Dad's critical approach, well, that was nothing new, but it was still exhausting. Did the giant-sized version of him mean she still had much to overcome? One thing was certain—she had to have another

Balloon Day session to let her brain unravel and make further sense of it all.

Elliott's phone rang and her stomach flipped. She hadn't heard from Asher since their fight earlier this morning, about those flirty girls at his job. He said he "needed time alone to think."

"I'm so glad you called," Elliott began. "I've been—"

"This isn't going to work."

Elliott sat up in her bed. "What do you mean 'not going to work'?"

"I'm sick of constantly fighting with you. Plus, we have Dave's big Halloween party this year, and I don't want this bullshit drama to ruin all our plans."

"Is that what you care most about, the stupid Halloween—"

"I thought of a good idea." He crunched what sounded like an apple. "Let's give it until the day after the party. A couple months for you to step up and make things better, Ellie. That makes sense, right?"

Elliott rolled off of her bed. She stared out the window toward a sky full of darkness as she began to pull at her eyebrow. "Are you giving our relationship a deadline?" The stars hid themselves amongst the thin cloud cover as the crickets chirped their nightly lullaby, preparing most of Long Island for sleep. Except for her. She wanted to scream. "And over the phone? Are you twelve?"

Her boyfriend paused. "I guess so."

"You guess that you're—you know what? Forget it. Get it over with then." Elliott paced back and forth, then sat on her bed. The opened blinds dropped lines of moonlight across her pale legs down to the floor.

"You're not listening," Asher snapped. "It's annoy—no, Mom, I am not talking to you, promise—but yeah, enough fighting already. You've been so goddamn insecure lately. You call me twelve when you're the one acting like a child. I need you to be more mature. More optimistic. Like how it was in the beginning. Or, unfortunately, our relationship will have to end."

She picked at the hole in her white cotton sheets, its circumference growing like the hole Asher was digging in her heart.

"Fine," she said.

Was he being absurd? Or had she deserved his scolding? Deep down, Elliott believed the argument valid, asking her twenty-eight-year-old boyfriend to stop letting girls behind the smoothie counter sit on his lap or throw stupid straws at his toned rear-end while he worked. All harrowing events which Elliott witnessed a few too many times.

Elliott didn't actually want to ruin her first long-term relationship. She was pissed off and resentful, but she wasn't willing to let Asher go. Not for this.

With Nate, her ex-boyfriend in college, dumping him was a no-brainer. After three years of dating, he had confessed he'd been cheating on Elliott with his family doctor.

Asher James came along—a year and a half ago. Elliott met him at the Superflex Gym he managed. It was also one of the gyms her father owned. Dad loved Asher. To his eyes, Asher was perfect—looks, manners, money.

Each time Elliott went to work out, Asher had aimed to impress her more and more. Free smoothies, otherwise, Dad gave her a measly 40% discount, a reserved treadmill, weekly private training sessions with him. Asher was handsome, persistent, and charming. Dad kept pushing Elliott to go out with him and it didn't take long before she relented and said yes to a first date at Rothmann's Steakhouse, and to the next date at Eleven Madison Park, and to the next...

Mom wasn't as convinced; she had said he lacks "depth." Which wasn't always true. He created effective gym routines and found off-the-beaten-path cities to take Elliott to, like Bremen—a small but stunning destination, straight out of a fairytale.

As for herself, Elliott had the perfect job: Clinical psychologist at the Center of Balloon Days, with freedom to use Balloon Days as she pleased. Now all she needed was the perfect relationship. Apparently, that was too much to ask for.

"I care about you. About us," she said, digging her toes into the rug.

"I care too. Have more positive energy, alright?" Asher said. "Can you go to a psychiatrist? Try a medication for stress, maybe."

"No." Elliott pulled at a thread in her sheets, another hole in the making. "Dr. Heller is insisting I continue to use Balloon Day sessions. I would rather do that."

Dr. Heller encouraged Elliott to further gain insight from the patient's perspective, in order to better help them understand what they're truly processing—and it would also help Elliott better explain what Balloon Days are to potential patients. Elliott got the feeling it was mandatory, regardless of Dr. Heller suggesting otherwise.

"Why, what good will that do?" he said. "You said it sucked."

"I did not say 'it sucked.' I said it was jarring but informative."

"I don't remember you saying that."

"Well, maybe if you listened to me, you'd remember. I am working on releasing my anxiety in them. It will help with—us." Elliott flopped backward on the bed, her foam pillow momentarily comforting. "Can you please reconsider telling those girls to stop?"

"Oh my god, this again. This is a part of the job. Girls will be there. I can't tell your dad to stop hiring women. Plus, I don't have feelings for them. They do that with all of the guys there. You're making up stories in your head." There was a long pause before he spoke again. "Fine. I'll see what I can do about getting them to tone it down."

His curtness killed her. What was he thinking? Did he still not see that what he had done was wrong? If only he would talk it out more, she could make it right.

"Thanks," Elliott said, feeling little relief. "Can we get breakfast in the morning?"

"No. I am meeting with Clara before work for acai bowls."

Elliott's throat tightened. Clara was one of the gym's smoothie girls who playfully touched and complimented him the most.

"Why?" she said. "Why wouldn't you want to eat breakfast with me instead?"

"Because I want to see my friend," Asher said plainly.

"Clara's a coworker... not a friend."

"Coworkers can be friends. Don't act stupid," he said. "You're jealous again, aren't you?"

"No, it's just that it's not normal for a guy to want to have breakfast with another girl instead of his girlfriend." Elliott wished her bedroom floor were red quicksand, as it had been in her Balloon Day. She'd throw Clara into it.

"She's a friend. Get it through your head. It's normal for guys to have friends. You'll never find a guy who doesn't."

In a way, Asher was right. But why did the notion still upset her?

"I'm a good guy, Elliott." His tone softened. "It hurts when you accuse me. I know your experience with guys hasn't been great, but you need to understand that not every single one cheats."

"You're right," she said. He made a good point. "I'm sorry. Can we talk more about the deadline thing? I think—"

"I don't want to talk about that right now," Asher said. He yawned. "I'm tired. I'll call you tomorrow."

Asher hung up before she could say another word.

Elliott kicked her legs against the mattress. The conversation played over and over and over again in her head, like gunk she couldn't wash out. She attempted one call to see if he'd answer and apologize for the terse goodbye.

Alright, maybe three times. Elliott's helplessness was akin to being suffocated by the words in her Balloon Day, except they were her own because Asher wouldn't listen. If only he would understand her reasoning, like her cognitive-psych professor finally had when he bumped her grade to the A she deserved, Asher's stupid deadline could've been avoided.

Maybe she shouldn't have said anything about the flirty girls in the first place. Grades were different. God, Clara and those basic bitches were so horrible and dumb and desperate.

How couldn't he see that from the start? It was one of those topics they sometimes made fun of together. How childish the girls could be at work; how they appear unprofessional. When it came to flirting with him, apparently their childlike choices were acceptable. It made her sick.

She hopped out of her bed and flicked the lamp on. She prepared her outfit for tomorrow. All white. Her closet was mostly white now, ever since working at the Center. Dr. Heller said the color symbolizes positivity, illumination, and rebirth. Honestly, Elliott thought it was blinding and bland.

With all the white and her red-dyed hair, now a fiery copper hue, sometimes she wondered if she looked like a blood-tipped tampon. She chose different textures to break up the menstruating visual; a sleeved eyelet dress with flats. Elliott respected Dr. Heller greatly, and she respected her rules.

Elliott slipped back into bed. She tried falling asleep but another restless night lie ahead, her thoughts spinning away like spiders building webs inside her skull.

Challenges with anxiety were nothing new. Pulling out her eyelashes at the age of seven one by one and counting each in the palm of her hand wasn't normal. She knew that. But it scratched an itch she could never permanently relieve. Her childhood therapist, Dr. Jenni, told her she developed maladaptive ways to control what she could not.

Elliott was a firm believer that with enough effort and willpower, she could control it all.

The following morning, Elliott headed to her friend's apartment for solace, and a helpful distraction. There'd been no word from Asher since their last conversation and she had no clue whether he met up with Clara.

Driving through the first cafe she could find, she prayed caffeine would help her function enough for her Balloon Day session later that day, although the fragile, uncomfortable state of wired and tired was one she'd never liked but knew all too well.

Julie's place was bright and calming, homey and inviting; just what Elliott needed right now. The sun beamed through the row of windows lined with small pots of pretty succulents and reflected off the cream walls. The scent of jasmine emanated from a lit candle on the coffee table, its three flames flickering above a pool of melted wax. Elliott nestled into the sofa.

"A deadline for a relationship is not normal." Julie turned on the air conditioner awkwardly positioned high on the wall, but with her height, a few inches taller than Elliott, she barely had to stretch to reach the switch. Returning to the sofa, she scooped her chestnut hair into a ponytail at the crown of her head.

She stared at Elliott, waiting. "I can fix it," Elliott said. "It'll go away." She swiped her thumb over a chipped nail, feeling the groove where the cherry polish, Ash's favorite, had cracked. "I'm sure he was acting out of frustration. He'll come around."

"That's not true." Julie shook her head. "Not everything can be fixed, Elliott. Especially relationships." Julie's pale blue eyes were lasers when she was upset, which was unnerving; it also meant she cared. "Look at our moms. They tried and tried. Look where it got them. Back in the dating pool, anyway. Sure, your mom finally found someone worthy of meeting you. But think of how much time she wasted investing in a dead-end relationship." Elliott recalled the image of Mom being squashed by the giant version of Dad stomping her to death. "Hey. You're tugging on your eyebrow again."

Elliott dropped her hand to her side, restraining the urge. All she could think about was her eyebrow. It wasn't exactly like an itch, no, but a need, to alleviate a sense of wrongness. Like a hair was moving or the muscle was loosening, and she needed to squeeze it or else the strange sensation wouldn't stop and something bad would happen.

She started tracing the lines of her palm instead, like Dr. Jenni had suggested. "You don't have to be mean about it. At least I'm not pulling any eyelashes out."

"What? I'm not being mean." Julie wrapped a throw around her shoulders.

"I'm sorry," Elliott said. "I'm on edge."

"I'm trying to help. Please start seeing the difference." It was hard for Elliott to see the difference. She started doubting her emotions a long time ago. "Listen, you know how much I care about you. I wonder if you'd be this anxious if you weren't with him. It says a lot that you're, like, freakishly good at work. But outside, not so much."

It was true. Elliott was masterful at her job. More like a divine calling to help others rather than a career. Just because she was good at it didn't mean that Asher was the sole source of her anxiety.

"Asher does make me happy. The other night he surprised me with dinner and a bottle of my favorite perfume," Elliott said.

"All I'm saying is that I think you deserve better," Julie said. "Anyone can buy you Chanel and make you dinner. I'm worried, is all. It's like you're trying to wrap a dead mouse in a beautiful gift box—inside is still a rotting, dead mouse."

"Ew."

"You know what I mean."

"Obviously I understand your analogy. It's a good one, actually. I might use it in a session someday." Elliott said. "But you don't know Asher like I do. It doesn't fit here."

Julie's fingernail met the plastic cup—tap, tap, tap—she then set the coffee on the table. "I cannot pretend to like him. Sorry. The dude is a complete douche."

"Every guy can be annoying at times."

"Annoying is different," Julie said. "Annoying is not manipulative."

"He's not manipulative."

"Maybe I don't know every single thing about Asher. All I'm saying is you would do so much better with someone more like, well, more like you." She squinted in thought. "Speaking of, my cousin Evan should be on his way over soon. He's another nerd."

Elliott jokingly gasped. "How dare you. I'm not a nerd."

"You watched a documentary on 'competitive endurance tickling' last night."

"I simply needed to know why one would want to compete in something like that," Elliott said. "There was an intense twist by the end, you should watch it."

Julie stared at her with a pinched mouth and Elliott could see she restrained herself from laughing.

"Alright." Elliott laughed. "It's not the most common documentary to watch."

"You also collect sugar packets from restaurants you visit."

Elliott released a quick laugh. "Yeah, but that's only when it's meaningful."

"I know, I know." Julie playfully rolled her eyes. "Evan does the same, but with receipts."

Elliott couldn't help grinning. To share a secretive collection of sentimental souvenirs was strange to have in common.

Was Julie right? Was there a more suitable paramour out there for her?

"Enough about me," Elliott squirmed. "Did you decide if you want to keep the new job?"

Julie rolled her eyes again, but this time in aggravation. "No. I can't tell if Maria is in way over her head. She's so kind, don't get me wrong, but she seems to have zero clue on how to run a business."

"That sucks. I'm sorry." Elliott didn't know what else to say—she couldn't relate. Dr. Heller ran her business successfully.

Julie blew out the candle on the table. She watched the smoke rise like a snake above the wick. "I hope she keeps it afloat."

"Me too. I know you love the patients there." Elliott glimpsed the clock on Julie's bookshelf. "Shoot—I'm so sorry. I have to get going to meet with Dr. Heller." She took the last sip of her iced coffee, thick and goopy from the caramel syrup that had settled on the bottom before chucking it in the trash can.

After a quick goodbye, Elliott dashed out into the tidy courtyard of the apartment complex. The smell of freshly cut grass carried in the air, the clouds few and shapeless against the baby-blue sky.

Elliott dropped her phone on the pavement.

"Let me get that for you." It was Julie's cousin Evan. Yankees cap on, in jeans and a mossy green t-shirt, wiry white headphones hanging off his neck.

Elliott pulled her sunglasses off and rested them on her head. "Thank you." She quickly tucked her phone back in her bag.

"No problem. Very cool case by the way. I'm a Lord of the Rings fan myself."

"I'm actually a huge fan of the books more than the movies," she said. "But it's totally fine if you hadn't read the books though."

Evan rubbed his chin. "Hmm. I've only read them a dozen times or so, so I'm a bit overdue for another read-through. I think they're better too."

She laughed, realizing she hadn't laughed much in the last couple of days. "I have this theory that people who prefer books over their on-screen adaptations have bigger imaginations than those who don't. They prefer the world they create in their heads." Except she hoped her mind would create a friendlier world within her next Balloon Day.

"I suppose it's kind of arrogant too," he said, flashing a warm smile. As his mouth fell natural again, the top lip appeared almost oval-shaped.

"Really? How so?"

"Well, if you prefer your own creation over another's, couldn't that be considered self-centered in a way?" he said. "Even if unintentionally? Also, it's fairly limiting to rely only on your perspective."

Elliott bit her lip. She was impressed. Aside from Julie, no one challenged her theories, or pondered how the mind works with her. It must run in their family.

"Or maybe it's fun to imagine a world outside of reality," she said. "Reality can often be disappointing."

Right now, it was not.

"True." He stroked the stubble around his mouth. "But I think expectations create disappointments. I've learned how to be more flexible. Living life rigidly has only caused me to break. I have to remind myself to go with the flow. There's control and then there's laziness, and there's something in between."

She looked at the grass clippings strewn across the freshly mowed lawn and nodded—although that gray area existed far out of reach. She looked back at him. Evan's eyes were bewitching, something she never noticed at those parties or in Julie's family pictures. Around each black pupil was a ring of pineapple yellow, electric blue. Like sunflowers against an azure sky.

"You're Elliott, right?" He remembered her too. It was nice to be remembered, even if she had not spoken to him much. Whoever was near him at parties always seemed to be smiling or laughing. He was easy to spot, a floating head above the others. Probably a hair over six feet, he was almost an entire foot above her now that she was up close.

"That's me." Her cheeks warmed and the heat pressed against her skin more than it had before.

"I'm Evan." He reached out and shook her hand. His hand was soft.

"We were just talking about you, actually."

"All good things, I hope?"

"Maybe," Elliott said.

That sounded flirty.
Does he think I'm flirting?
That's not good.
That's inappropriate.

He laughed, but it was a sweet laugh, quelling her nerves. "Are you heading back inside?"

Shit. The time. "I wish, but I can't. I'm running pretty behind. I have to head back home to catch the next train to the city." Elliott squished her bottom lip between her fingers, then quickly dropped it, hearing Julie's voice in her head.

"That's a bummer." He tugged at his backpack straps. "But I'm sure we will get some good hangs in soon."

Is he flirting with her now?

"Oh, yeah, for sure—Julie would like that."

"Sure," he said. "Julie would like that."

Strolling to her car, the sun seemed to be shining brighter than before. She couldn't shake those sunflower eyes out of her head.

CHAPTER 6
ORSON

The sounds of death followed Orson, haunting him like a curse. When all was quiet at nighttime and Orson laid himself to restless sleep in the half-empty bed, Madison's strained voice whispered. Her rattled breathing crowded his head as he dealt with his clients. The words "Madison" and "wife" rang louder than before. Sat heavy in his chest.

Any time he entered the living room, the whimpers of Madison's parents standing next to their daughter's lifeless body, questioning how her life could end before their own, echoed off the walls. Ryder's fervent and frequent sobbing tightened his heart.

Even Orson's cries felt distant, outside of himself.

If only he hadn't left the living room that day—if only he had stayed at her side. If only he could have saved her.

Orson sat uncomfortably on his son's bedroom floor trying to figure out how to tell Ryder that his mother was gone and that Orson's fictitious claim she had returned to the hospital for a few days was, indeed, untrue. He fidgeted with his wedding band. Next to Orson on the blue and red area rug that matched his bedsheets was Ryder playing with his Lego blocks.

What should he tell him? That his mother, the one who did everything for all of them, the one who loved him so much that it poured from every cell of her body into every choice she made, the one who took care of them so tenderly, so carefully, was now gone? How there was nothing Orson could do to prevent it? How, as a father and as a husband, he had failed. Where does one start?

Ryder was so young. He didn't yet know about the horrors of life. He wasn't supposed to. Children were supposed to play and imagine and feel safe, blithely sheltered under their parents' love.

Accidentally dropping a Lego piece, Orson returned to the present. Ryder groaned at the fallen block but Orson ignored this. There were more important matters at hand. He checked the time on the wall clock, its numbers along a cartoon racetrack, the cars of each hand telling him it was only getting later.

"I'll be right back, son. Stay here. Keep, uh, building—you're an architect." Orson left the bedroom and made his way down the hallway to call Rose.

"Rose," Orson said, his arms suddenly feeling useless and light. They ached for Madison. "I haven't told Ryder yet. Honestly, I don't know what to say. I tried, but nothing came out. I don't know what to do." He was doing this all wrong. Was there some kind of Dummies guide for how to grieve your wife while also parenting your child?

"Do you want me to?" Rose said. He could hear her sniffling. "Actually, don't answer that. Listen. Don't try so hard. Think about what Madison would say."

What frightened Orson more were the inevitable questions a bright, analytical boy like Ryder would ask, questions with nebulous answers that would never suffice.

"You're right," Orson said, scratching the stubble on his chin. He was long overdue for a shave. Maybe he should do that first.

"Just don't wait any longer." It was as if Rose could read his mind.

Orson rubbed his left shoulder, the knots building up day after day. The grandfather clock chimed. Seven o'clock had arrived, and Orson's stomach churned. Lately, the top of the hour was one of his least favorite things and he had been meaning to disable the clock's announcement of it. He hated the constant reminder of time's ever-forward, unrelenting advance. No matter how much you want it to pause, no matter who and what you have to leave behind, time raced by.

Full of dread, Orson headed back down the long hallway, clutching onto the smooth brown railing, his feet heavier with each step. He passed the two guest bedrooms, remembering long ago plans of having more children. A distant dream now that will never be fulfilled.

A few steps into Ryder's room, Orson froze.

Ryder was still so little. His little hands, his wrinkle-less fingers. His little smile. His teeth not fully there yet. His little brain, his growing brain, should be stretched to the brim with dinosaurs and dragons, magical stories, books about space. He should be full of wonder, full of curious questions like how do planes fly and how do pill bugs roll into their famous potato-like shape?

With one conversation, the innocence will disappear, and it will be Orson's doing.

Madison once told Orson it would not be until around nine years old, the start of puberty, that Ryder would truly start to understand what death meant. When was the official mark for shedding innocence? The line we all must eventually cross, where naivety and unadulterated wonderment begin to fade. Whatever age it was, Orson knew it wasn't seven. But the news Orson had to share, well, that would jumpstart Ryder's fading childhood.

And so, Orson let Ryder continue to build his creation one small block at a time, so he could stay a kid for a little longer.

"Dad, check this out." Ryder looked up, eager and wide-eyed.

Orson stepped closer and crouched. "That looks great, truly."

Ryder beamed with pride. "So, listen, son. There's something I need to tell you." Orson fidgeted with a Lego block. His insides were squirming around, and he wished he were one of those pill bugs, curling up, and rolling away.

Ryder kept building, then connected one last yellow piece on top. Snap.

"Okay." He looked up, his expression innocent with a patient smile stretching across his rosy cheeks. His big green eyes locked onto Orson's.

"You know how Mom has been sick with cancer, right?" He wanted to lie to Ryder, tell him his mother was still alive, simply out with a friend. He wanted to pretend the same to himself. "Well, she—"

"I am building her this rocket so I can take her to outer space." Ryder fumbled with more pieces to connect on top.

Snap. Snap.

"To a secret hospital. And she will be all better again." He said arrogantly as if he'd solved world hunger in a single stroke.

"Oh, my dear sweet Ryder. You're right. But..." Orson did the best he could to swallow the tears clogging his throat. "Can I have your attention for a minute, bud?"

"Oh. Yes." Ryder nodded—snap—connecting one last yellow piece. "Okay. Done." He scanned Orson's face for a reaction.

"Wow. What a wonderful, magical rocket," Orson said, his weight shifting as he lowered himself completely onto the rug, his position what Ryder called pretzel style. "So, what I was starting to say was, Mom got too sick for Earth. Remember when she taught you about Heaven? When your fish Pinocchio died?"

"Aw, I miss Pinocchio," he said, his head bowing down.

"Me too. But, do you remember? About Heaven?" Orson put his hand on the top of Ryder's head, and smoothed his light reddish hair back, the hair that forever reminded Orson of his wife's strawberry blonde locks. He was trying his best to be as gentle as possible, but he had a feeling he was doing a terrible job.

"Duh," Ryder said with confidence. "Mom said it is where all the spirits go when they finish their time here. That we all have time here and then we go to other places—and Heaven is the best place." He extended his arms to the sky. "Where God lives." Ryder looked back up at Orson, pausing to see if he was right.

"Correct. You are so smart, kiddo, wow. The memory on you. The scientists in Heaven saw what you were cleverly creating with the Lego pieces." The back of Orson's neck, and his forehead, burned up like a sudden fever. "They are very special. They took Mom up there for you. We can see her once more soon, but she will be sleeping, because Mom and her spirit... are in Heaven now. She is so, so happy there."

"Wait," Ryder said, his forehead creasing as his little mind tried to make sense of something Orson couldn't make sense of. Why did people have to die so early, when so much is left to live for, and when so many others needed them to still be around?

It wasn't fair.

Ryder conjured up his next words, slowly working themselves out. "But. W-why would they do that? Did my rocket take too long?" He frowned at his creation, to him, now rendered useless.

"No, son. It's not that."

"Then why would Mom not tell me?" Ryder's voice rose as he stood, his head above Orson's. "Why would she not take us with her?"

"I don't think she wanted to leave us here. But we..."

Ryder glared at him, waiting. Waiting for answers one could never give. Orson spent his life arguing case law in front of judges and using the power of crystal-clear syntax to get what he wanted. His words were his sword, his power, a weapon he wielded to slay his enemies in the court room, and he was good at it—exceptional in fact.

Why couldn't he tell his son that his mother was dead? Why was he at a loss for words when he needed them most? Perhaps there was no logic as to why this had happened to Madison, why it had happened to them. Perhaps grief wasn't something that could be reasoned away.

"She didn't want to leave us, son," Orson settled with.

"Why would they take her from us then?" Ryder's small voice grew louder. "I want to see her. Bring her back."

"I-I don't know. I can't do that, but I certainly wish that I could," Orson faltered.

Ryder slowly looked around his sizeable room—the room Madison and Ryder had decorated differently each year. The current theme was from the Pixar movie Cars. The plans to morph it into Harry Potter were now halted.

Ryder looked down at his Lego rocket creation. He swung his leg back, and to Orson's surprise, kicked his rocket—along with all the hard work that went into it—with such force most of its pieces scattered all over the room, yellows and blues and reds flung away, some under his bed, some ricocheting off the hardwood floor into the bathroom.

"Son—" Orson quickly kneeled with his arms outstretched toward Ryder.

Ryder turned back and looked at Orson, his eyes shining, his voice cracking. "Tell her to come back. Tell Mommy to come back." Ryder fell to his knees and began to cry. "Please, Daddy, please."

"Come here. It'll be alright." Orson knew that wasn't true, just as he knew that he wasn't convincing. It was all a lie, a lie, a lie—and Ryder's mouth opened wide, letting out a wail that pierced Orson's already shattered heart.

Orson pulled Ryder close and held him tightly. "I'm so sorry, son. I wish she could come back too. I wish I could fix it. If there is ever a way, I will. I promise."

"You're lying." Ryder squirmed and pushed away. "Mom fixed everything, and now she's gone." He fled into his walk-in closet and slammed the door, shutting Orson out. Shutting reality out.

Orson buried his head in his hands, tears streaming down his face.

Ryder's reaction proved he did everything wrong.

Later that evening, after Ryder eventually returned from the closet, he cried himself to sleep in his bed with his thumb in his mouth. He started the habit back up after Madison became more ill. Orson didn't know how long he should allow his son to rely on this coping mechanism, but it clearly seemed to work.

Ryder had denied Orson's invite to lay with him. Feeling crushed, Orson headed outside and rested on the porch swing, staring up at the stars. It was quite possible that Heaven did exist for the good ones like Madison, and that she could see him right now.

Was her spirit surrounding them? He wanted so badly to believe. He was starting to consider the whole psychic medium-thing. Anything, anything out there, that could bring her back to him—he now understood why people tried the things they did to try and bring back their loved ones.

There had to be something. There he was—wifeless and alone.

What if he had been around more? Maybe Orson could have helped her, saved her somehow. At the very least, he could have tucked away more moments, more memories with her and his son. Money was the only thing his career gave him. That and the power-trip in the court room as he swept the floor with his opponent's attorney.

None of that amounts to anything significant. If only he could feel Madison's hand interlaced in his once more, hear her laugh once more, run his hands through her soft hair again, before the cancer stole her bit by bit.

With death, there were no second chances, no matter how persuasive he was.

CHAPTER 7
HOWARD

Sitting at the computer in his brother's apartment, Howard stared at John's MacBook as he sipped a hot coffee from Dunkin Donuts—his treat for the day. Howard was sorting through John's work emails, while John romanced Jillian in Paris. The only thing that took the sting away from Howard envying his brother's life was to daydream about the Balloon Day version of Jillian as well as the possibilities of what to do with her in his next one, as phony as that might be.

Others steered their lives in better directions while Howard had crash-landed his. Dropping out of high school should have forewarned him. At the time, it seemed like the best idea. Fifteen-year-old Howard had fallen behind in everything as the homework accumulated while he flattened. He became trapped underneath it all. His mother was dead. Piano was dead. His father had become the living dead before he, too, gave up and passed away. Howard had no longer cared about planning his future.

When Howard met his ex-girlfriend Kimmy years ago at a local dive one night, it had seemed like a turning point. She had walked right up to him, looked him up and down, smirked and stood on her tippy toes to kiss him on the cheek. Just like that.

Kimmy was pretty in a raw, wild way. When she laughed, she laughed with her entire body. She'd throw her head back, sometimes clap and infectiously cackle, or she'd stomp her feet. Howard loved making her laugh.

He quickly fell in love with all of Kimmy—her vibrant teal hair with dark roots, and how it always appeared slightly unbrushed, like she recently woke up no matter the time of day. He loved her passionate gazes as she planned fun escapes for them, sometimes as simple as laying in the park at 3am to look up at the stars.

But nothing ever felt simple with Kimmy. She said things like "Dance with my body," when she wanted to have sex after she'd light up a joint. The first time she told him she loved him, was through painted words in her own blood on an otherwise blank canvas.

Months later, she snapped the blood-adorned canvas in half after a heated argument. It started when Howard asked her to stop disappearing for days on end. She had scolded him, stating she didn't want to be bothered when using cocaine. Howard soon learned why—who would want to be pestered by their boyfriend when fucking strangers? Stupid Howard.

When the love was good again, it was as intense as the fights. On and off their relationship went for years, sucking him in and spitting him out, withering him away more and more each time.

It sounds dumb, but Kimmy had made him feel special. She brought life back, like the human version of a defibrillator. It was poetry and romance and sexually mesmerizing. He had lived inside himself for too long, the depression having nearly swallowed him whole.

She'd vanished again, and this time it felt final. If it weren't for Jillian and her grace as she helped him through the withdrawal of the break-up, he'd let the depression swallow him completely this time.

If it weren't for Jillian being John's girlfriend, maybe Howard would've had the slimmest chance of dating her instead.

Howard churned out the last of the work emails and then he did what he always does when alone in John's apartment. He opened the computer folder labeled, "J & J." Instantly, hundreds of thumbnails of Jillian stared back at him from the screen as he scrolled through. Some with John—

A selfie of the two together, holding waffle cones filled with gelato in Florence.
Side by side with glasses of red wine at Raphael Vineyards in Long Island.
But many without—
Jillian jumping in front of Big Ben in London, her raven hair caught in the wind.
Jillian laughing on the Brooklyn Bridge, stuck behind a group of confused tourists.
A close-up of Jillian's profile, her cupid's bow sloping into her delicate, yet full, upper lip.

Howard double-clicked his favorite one to enlarge: Jillian enjoying chocolate cake, but she had dropped a piece, swiftly catching it in her hand. Her smile was open and wide. Her eyes were closed.

There was something comforting about her glee despite dropping her dessert. It was a perfectly imperfect moment captured in time, despite who was on the other end of the camera.

There was a jingle at the door and Howard turned. John wasn't supposed to return until tomorrow. The lock continued to be undone, and not only John's voice, but Jillian's, too, carried through the wall. Of course. He whipped back to the laptop and immediately shut it closed in a panic.

"Oh, hey," John said as he dropped his duffle bag on the floor.

Howard nodded. Jillian waved, then looked down at the floor.

"Yeah, we came back early because one of my clients—you know, douchebag Jake—he's having a financial crisis apparently," John said as if Howard had asked. "I'd have told you to take care of it, but it's too important." John laughed. He glanced at Jillian and she gave a quick laugh in return. It sounded like a pity laugh. Howard wished he could telepathically let her know that he thought it wasn't funny either.

"That sucks," Howard said, trying to sound convincing. "Sorry your trip was ruined."

"I was sad to leave the City of Love," Jillian said. She was doing that thing again with her eyes. Like there was a hidden message inside of them, more words behind the words.

"We can always go again," John said, shrugging. "Can you help Jill unpack my things?" It was more of a statement than a question. Jillian looked down at the floor again.

Almost two years ago, when Howard turned twenty-four, and John twenty-eight, John had moved out, and bought his fancy apartment, so Jillian could come over more and John wouldn't have to worry about "being overheard" at night. He had also told Howard it was time to stand on his own two feet.

Howard wobbled.

"Hello? Earth to Howard," John said. "I need the laptop. Go help her."

The laptop. Jillian's picture would be the first thing that John would see upon opening it. How the hell could Howard excuse that? A lump lodged in his throat. He didn't know what to say. The discomfort inside him was expanding by the second, like an overfilled balloon about to burst.

"I still have some stuff left to do," Howard settled with.

"Fine. You don't have to help her, just get out of my seat," John said, walking toward the desk.

Howard could lie and say John had the picture of Jillian on the screen already opened, so Howard had kept it there. Why would it be on the main screen now and not minimized?

Not good enough. He could say he was working on an anniversary gift for John and Jillian.

But their anniversary was nowhere near close to coming up.

John nudged Howard to get out of the desk chair. "Wait," Howard said.

"What the hell? Give me my laptop, idiot."

"I ran a virus scan. Let me make sure it ran its course. It's a new software, you won't know how to use it."

Howard realized Jillian was staring at him now with furrowed brows. Like she knew Howard was anxious.

"John, let Howard finish. I need your help with something."

"What is it?"

"Um. It's private. Can we talk in the bedroom?"

Howard looked at John, praying he would take the bait.

"Alright, whatever," John said. "I gotta take a shit first."

As John walked away and closed the bathroom door, Jillian grinned at Howard; his body tingled as all of his capillaries filled with blood at once, a heat so fierce that if he walked around naked in Antarctica, he could melt the snow with each step. Maybe people in love were the ones responsible for climate change.

John was aware Howard and Jillian texted or spoke here and there when she needed gift ideas for John, or groceries. Within months, Howard and Jillian had secretly branched into other topics and discovered many common interests—bands and films and books and dreams of traveling.

Months ago, in late spring, Jillian confided more and more in Howard—especially after harsh fights with John. Howard would listen and support her as best he could; he yearned to do more, to hold her, comfort her, rescue her. She began to do the same for him after intense fallouts with Kimmy. He had unthinkingly, and unmistakably, fallen in love with his brother's girlfriend.

One month ago—which now felt like eons ago—Howard had hinted to Jillian about these growing feelings to see if his hopes were fruitless. That's when their layered and lengthy conversations had suddenly switched to casual and infrequent, and as of two weeks ago he hadn't heard from her at all, outside of sporadically seeing her in the apartment.

He was imprudent to think Jillian would ever, could ever, return his feelings in kind. He wanted to be swallowed up by a drain, like one of the despicable, relentless apartment-dwelling cockroaches he finds scurrying about his home every now and then.

Like them, Howard didn't know when to quit apparently.

She rescued him from John's persistence. There had to be something there.

Jillian inched toward the desk—her peach scent entering the air between them. "There must be something you're hiding. What is it?"

"It's some shoddy poem I wrote." He hated lying to her, but what else should he say? The truth humiliated him. "If John saw it, he'd never let me hear the end of it."

She frowned. "Please tell me it's not for Kimmy."

"It's not."

"Promise?"

She still cared. Howard couldn't help but smile. "Promise."

"Let me see it. Maybe it's not as bad as you think." She reached to open the laptop, but he placed his hand over it.

Her hand landed on top of his.

Life paused.

Nothing existed but the warmth and softness of her skin. They looked at each other. She glanced at the bathroom door. Still shut, with no sign of John emerging any time soon.

Before Howard could stop her, Jillian snatched the laptop off the desk.

Howard's blood kicked throughout his body, as she sat on the couch with the evidence proving he was a creep. He was mortified. Howard froze behind the sofa as she slowly opened it, as if she were relishing in his torture.

There it was. Her gorgeous face, closed-eyed and smiling, filling the screen reflecting back at her.

"Oh," Jillian whispered.

That was it. One simple "oh."

That was it.

The toilet flushed. The bathroom sink ran. Howard was sweating now. Jillian continued to stare at the photograph of herself, but he couldn't see her facial expression. This had to be the most humiliating moment of his life. Worse than the time he soiled his underwear in first grade and the two-faced Clarence Thomas announced it to the class, granting Howard the nickname "Craptain Howard" for a solid four years.

As John opened the bathroom door, Jillian closed the photograph, then the folder, just in time.

CHAPTER 8
ELLIOTT

Elliott blasted her car's AC to battle the thick, stinging heat as she pulled away from Julie's apartment complex. Fair skin was no match for August humidity, and her Irish roots made her wilt in the sun.

The familiar drive through her town was lined with outdoor restaurants, banks, and her favorite clothing boutique, Mi Amor. She turned right onto Weaver Street, then left soon after, entering the cul-de-sac and parking in the wide driveway of 65 Summer Avenue.

Elliott's house was indeed beautiful; the front yard impeccably gardened, surrounded by crisp, clover-green grass, but it came with a caveat: she was renting it from Dad. After Elliott's parents had divorced, Mom moved to a two-bedroom apartment in the same town as to not disrupt Elliott's schooling. Nothing had confused and frustrated Elliott more than shuttling back and forth between the two homes. She missed having one bedroom, one place for friends to come to, one place to call home. At times, she missed Mom and Dad fighting. At least that meant they were all under one roof together, and still a complete family.

Years ago, Elliott returned from graduate school, and Dad moved to a town further out on the island with his new wife, the fake-titted, "I-hate-kids-I'm-glad-I-never-had-them" Holly. She's almost fifty now, so Elliott wasn't sure why she needed to remind anyone of that. Dad had decided to keep the family house for Elliott. He had been motivated by guilt, even though he steadfastly denied it.

Elliott parked her gifted-by-Dad black Mercedes-Benz SUV—only ten minutes until the next train into Manhattan came, and she lived about an eight-minute walk away from the station. It was worth rushing. She hated driving into the city. Finding parking was a bitch and paying for it was bitchier.

She grabbed her work bag from the passenger seat and scrambled past her neighbor Orson's house. Usually, family members and friends came and went, but since his wife's devastating death, their home went quiet, as if the house itself was in mourning.

The rest of the block was a blur of landscapers' buzzing blades and dogs rattling away as she ran by. The blaring horn of the train and obnoxious tinkling of the bells as the flashing red gates lowered on the crossing sparked a rush of adrenaline.

Elliott's heart pounded as she slid in before the train doors shut. She found an empty row and sat down. Her picturesque town—on the North Shore of Long Island—disappeared as the train sped onward. Outside the window, the scenery changed as the train zoomed by. Going from a peaceful suburbia with its plethora of trees and bushes and flowerbeds, she now found herself riding through run-down apartment buildings, with clothing lines strung between windows and garbage decorating the streets. The landscape then shifted into a post-industrial wasteland with the looming city skyline as its backdrop.

A tunnel soon swallowed the train, disrupting Elliott's gaze and phone signal, reminding her she still hadn't heard from Asher. Slowing down, the train finally approached the last stop.

Elliott was practiced in dodging Penn Station's bustling tourists, commuters, and locals. Still, someone managed to bump into her, his suitcase banging hard into her leg. She then made way for a woman in a yellow dress sprinting to make a train, feeling generous after having recently won her own battle with the restraints of manmade time.

After twenty minutes of stop-and-go traffic, and shifting scents of roasted peanuts, perfumes, and cigarette smoke, the taxi dropped Elliott off at the Center. It was an impressive building on the Upper East Side, near Lexington Avenue, on E 76th.

Tall and alluring with twelve floors in total, the Center of Balloon Days took up a decent portion of the block. Inside, nearly everything was pearl white, pristine, and sterile, yet still sophisticated, much like a palace.

At the front of the lobby, a row of ten glass elevators gleamed—they led to the patient Day Rooms and to the luxurious psychologist's suites located on the top two floors. Each elevator had its own color: red, yellow, pink, silver, violet, green, blue, turquoise, orange, and brown. The order of glowing lights elegantly arranged. It was mesmerizing.

In the center of the lobby, an impressive glass wall, tinted light blue, separated the entrance and the back area of the building. A duplicate row of illuminated elevators positioned on the other side of the wall were the exit elevators that lead out to E 75th.

Dr. Heller constructed the building in such a way so that each client would barely interact with one another, as to not influence each other. A patient would enter the lobby. Then enter their designated elevator and be lifted to their Day Room. Once finished, the patient would exit through the post-room and exit elevator.

Entrance—Balloon Day—Exit. Brilliant.

Footsteps echoing throughout the main lobby, Elliott took in the beautiful ceiling high above. It was a bright blue sky full of billowing clouds. The illuminated glass elevators seemed to disappear through those clouds as they ascended. When Elliott arrived on her first day, she had soon found out the science behind the magic. It was a condensation effect to create clouds for the elevators to pass through.

It was essentially a state-of-the-art fog machine that cost more than her salary. Dr. Heller spared no expense.

Elliott strode toward the glowing violet elevator, smack in the middle of the row, and pressed the up arrow. She watched as it worked its way down, while the green one to its right carried someone to a higher floor. Once in the elevator, no one could see in or out. Everything was so well thought out, so intricate; Dr. Heller was simply a genius.

A bell chimed as the elevator opened. Her phone rang.

It was Asher.

She had completely forgotten to worry about him since leaving Julie's apartment. She tugged at her brow, checking the time. She was cutting it close to her meeting with Dr. Heller. But she let the elevator go, as it would disrupt her signal, and answered anyway.

"Hi, Asher. I miss you." The urge to ask if he had seen Clara for acai bowls poked at her, but she didn't want to know the answer.

"What are you up to?" he said, but not in a curious way; it was in the way people asked as if they were already disappointed in what the other's answer will be.

"I'm at work."

"Oh." As predicted, he replied with judgment. "I figured you'd be seeing a psychiatrist today."

"I told you I was continuing—"

"I thought we talked about how to move forward. Don't you want to go to Dave's party?"

"Yes." She fidgeted with the hem of her white dress. "Please trust me to fix this."

"Clara said she went to his party last year, and that it was awesome. That he goes all out," Asher said with excitement in his voice.

Elliott bit her tongue hard. "Sounds good."

"Only a select few from the gym get invited."

She stared at the artificial clouds above with tears in her eyes. Her relationship with Asher seemed as fake as those clouds. How could he go from rolling on grass with Elliott, tucking a daisy behind her ear, and declaring his love on one day to being cold, critical, and dismissive the next? He cared more about this stupid party and his reputation than he cared about her. It was an emotional seesaw. Funny how people change as they grow a sense of safety with someone.

"Anyway, I do trust you, Elliott. I don't always say everything the right way. And I'm sorry for that. It sounds good in my head. But then you get upset so..."

"It's okay," Elliott said, surprised by his admission. "I'm sorry, too. I overreacted. You know I don't want to lose you." She hit the elevator button.

Come on, open again.

"I know," he said. "I love you for that."

The chime sounded again as the elevator opened.

Elliott's mouth twitched as she said goodbye to Asher, trying not to feel upset. She rushed into the elevator as it was about to close, then quickly texted him, asking if he could come over later.

Deadline. Balloon Days. Medication. So much to change. The perfect life was worth it. Right?

The elevator opened on floor twelve, revealing a spacious area flooded with natural light; the double sliding doors straight ahead were to Dr. Heller's executive suite. Elliott's office was on the floor below, along with the other psychologists' suites lining the perimeter of the building, giving each their own window.

"Hi, Elliott," Romalda said, spraying a cleaner on part of the office door, then wiping the area in a circular motion. "So much to clean." Everything looked spotless. "I believe Dr. Heller is awaiting your arrival. Better hurry on in. I'll get out of your way."

"Right, thank you," Elliott muttered. The doors mesmerized Elliott every time she approached them—blue-tinted glass, adorned with white translucent clouds. She hit the button on the left of Dr. Heller's office door, then waved at the tiny white camera above. The door immediately slid open, the clouds temporarily disappearing into the pockets of the wall.

Dr. Heller checked her watch, then looked up with a quick raise of her eyebrows. If Elliott wasn't already sweating, she sure was now.

Sitting behind her glass desk, positioned in the center of the room, Dr. Heller wore a silk blouse and dress pants. Elliott admired each of Dr. Heller's outfits, how immaculately assembled she appeared—always white, serene, fashionable, and tasteful, each with a tiny black balloon threaded on the right side near her collarbone.

Elliott envied Dr. Audrey Heller immensely; she was the Center's founder, a neuropsychologist and Elliott's clinical supervisor. Dr. Heller had it all. She married a handsome anesthesiologist who believed in her vision for psychological health, and together they had invested in her dream and bought the building that now housed the Center. Maybe Asher would one day do the same for Elliott.

Elliott took the seat across from Dr. Heller. Like the rest of the Center, her office was beautiful in its modern simplicity. The glass desk had an open laptop next to neatly stacked folders and a tablet. In the far-left corner of the room was a plush sofa with powder-blue pillows. Directly across from it was a leather chair. A round, light-blue ottoman was positioned in between the two.

Dr. Heller had explained how certain patients chose to remain at the desk, and when Elliott asked why that was, Dr. Heller told her they preferred a clinical feel because they feared intimacy. After that, Elliott wondered if Dr. Heller parsed her own decisions, so she sat at the desk during some visits while asking to sit on the sofa for others.

"I apologize for being a few minutes behind," Elliott said. "It won't happen again."

Dr. Heller crossed her legs. "Let's not waste any more time then. How are your patients?"

Elliott was definitely sweating now. She did her best to shift into professional mode and detach from her nerves. "They're progressing positively in their Balloon Days. Each patient is satisfied with their treatment." Hopefully, she could soon say the same for herself.

"That's great news, Elliott." Dr. Heller clasped her hands together on her desk. "Any interesting insights?"

"Yes." Elliott sifted through her work bag, struggling to swiftly retrieve her work tablet with all her patient files.

"You know, they have tote bags with compartments," Dr. Heller commented. "Makes it easier to find things."

"I'll have to look into that. Thank you." Doing her best to hide her embarrassment with a nod and a smile, Elliott pulled out the tablet.

She quickly accessed one of her patient's files, and explained how one of the newer patients, Mack, said he tested out what it would be like to have an affair with his coworker Nancy, who was flirty with him.

He played out the likely aftermath—of seeing his wife leave with the children—and it broke his heart. He said he'd stopped flirting back—as he already should have known to do—and the temptress moved on to another colleague.

"Wonderful. See? More proof of how Balloon Days has helped your patients. I love the various ways our patients use them. The treatments are endless."

Dr. Heller's caramel eyes seemed to twinkle, and herself.

"I agree," Elliott said. "I do wonder if there was a point for some patients where we could focus on talk therapy and then they could have Balloon Days as needed?"

"Hmm," Dr. Heller hummed. "That's a good idea, Elliott, but no," she said, smiling. Barely blinked. "I'm sure you understand that Balloon Days is the primary focus here. Why do you ask?"

"My neighbor recently passed away from breast cancer, and her husband and son aren't doing so well. I was thinking they could use a gentler approach first."

"Balloon Days can be calm—it's all under the patient's control. You will see that. It's why I wanted to make sure you begin your own. As for his son, there are plenty of child therapists I can recommend. Remember, no minors are allowed. Their brains are too vulnerable, not fully developed yet."

Elliott rubbed her lips together.

"I can see you are hesitant," Dr. Heller said in a soft tone. "When you have more Balloon Days, then you will be recommending it to everyone you know because you love helping people, and this helps." She leaned forward. "There is something special about you, Elliott. I can tell you take your position seriously, and maybe one day you'll receive a promotion."

"Thank you. I did learn a lot from my first Balloon Day. I will continue to recommend it, absolutely." Elliott couldn't admit the disaster her first Balloon Day had been and risk looking like an amateur. Dr. Heller's admiration meant the world to her.

"Perfect," Dr. Heller said, smiling. "Balloon Days offer a wealth of information to process, as you know. Don't feel bad if your first session was more intense than you expected. It's easy to forget you're the director, the one in control." It's as if she could read Elliott's mind. Was her body language that telling?

As Elliott said goodbye and reached the office doors, Dr. Heller stopped her. "One more thing, Elliott. Have fun with it. You are in control. Let your perception be your guide."

Inside Day Room P93, Elliott laid on the sofa with the control in her hand, repeating her new mantra—I am in control. I am in control.

Nothing could be worse than her first one. If she could survive that, she could tackle anything else her mind hid within its walls. With one more minute of preparation time left, Elliott took a deep breath and pressed the activating switch.

To her surprise, she slipped into her Balloon Day more smoothly than the last time. The darkness vanished as Elliott willed her imagination to take over, forming vibrant green pastures all around her.

Tall, gorgeous, globe-shaped flowers sprouted from the ground, in colors of fuchsia, teal, and bright orange. The breeze in the air was soft, carrying a sweet and fruity scent that lingered. She finally understood how to create, how to be conscious while her unconscious mind let loose.

Elliott wore a long-sleeve black shirt falling above her slim waist; a hint of skin peeked above a maroon swinging skirt. Her feet cozy in black shoes.

She was perfect.

She thought of a hot air balloon—instantly, she was in the basket of one. The hot air balloon carried her upward, the burner roared above her head. Clouds—puffy, pearly, bouncy whites—rested against a light blue sky, and the silhouette of a castle tower appeared ahead, wrapped with vines of yellow roses. Gliding to the top of it, she hopped out, admiring the landscape, a mosaic of colors, and soaked up the sights, scents and sensations.

A table with paint brushes and trays of watercolors appeared at her side. She picked up a brush, dunked it in water, swirled it around different shades of green, unapologetically mixing the colors. Peering out from the tower again, she began to paint using the landscape as her canvas. Hill tops and valleys emerged in the distance. Grass blanketed the ground, a shamrock-colored sea.

Paint on the tip of her brush again, black bristles dripping wet with color, Elliott swiveled her wrist, spreading flowers around the hills. Pink and peach zinnias, royal purple alliums, white lilies, and yellow roses sprang from the fields below, a forest of flowers, swaying a slow and elegant dance.

The flowers filled the air with a fragrance awakening every splendid memory she held. Like smelling pine and instantly thinking of winter or smelling seaweed and remembering the ocean waves crashing along the shore.

But the scent-tied memories hit her all at once—Mom ringing bells at Christmas time to signal Santa's gifts had arrived. Dad carving the turkey at Thanksgiving. The cologne of her eighth-grade crush who stopped the world when he planted her first kiss.

Elliott painted a waterfall flowing gently into the river near the tower. A guitar melody played as the water traveled onward, music notes ascending and twirling up toward the clouds.

Where the waterfall met the river, bubbles rose out of the mist. Revolving slowly, floating upward, they neared the top of the tower—nearing her. As they moved closer, she realized each bubble was filled with a running memory, unfrozen in time, playing the way a film would. Except here the images were not flat. Miniature versions of herself and the ones she loved were preserved inside the floating orbs, the treasured scenes of her life alive once again.

There in the bubbles was Dad holding her up on his shoulders at five years old, walking her around an amusement park, the air fragrant with salty popcorn and sickly-sweet cotton candy while kids screeched on the nearby rollercoaster. A teensy Elliott soon waited in line for a fun house with fear on her face, excitement in her restless legs. She clutched onto Mom and Dad as they walked through the labyrinth of silly illusions and moving obstacles.

Another bubble passed by of Nana swinging Elliott around in her pool tube at four years old, singing her silly made-up songs. The cool water glided like a silk blanket over her skin. Nana's caring touch guided her throughout the pool.

More floated on by, picking out her first pet, a cat named Cutie, who had a thick coat of peanut butter fur. Mom was smoothing her hair back after her first break up. It abruptly changed to drinking red wine by the Eiffel Tower with Julie and her friends. The recent run-in with Evan in Julie's courtyard...

She smiled in silent wonderment.

In the distance, red-tinted bubbles crept forward, their clarity increasing as they swam by, the red color alone alarming her. A bubble nearby held Dad punishing her because she wouldn't finish her supper, telling her she was ungrateful and spoiled. Asher calling her stupid for being paranoid when he had lunch with his coworker Clara; the text messages from her ex-boyfriend, Nate, to his doctor, admitting he didn't feel bad for cheating on Elliott; one of her professors, Mrs. Scott, telling her she was too rigid to ever be an effective psychologist as Elliott presented a mock client case in front of the entire class.

Lastly, one of her most humiliating moments: her second grade crush, Liam, letting her friends know he'd never like her back because her eyelashes were ugly and that she was a freak for pulling them out.

She promptly popped each of them with tears in her eyes, leaving only the pleasant ones behind. Why did the others even show up? Was she doing her Balloon Day wrong again in some way? Was it possible to be bad at a Balloon Day?

Determined to regain control, she wiped her eyes and focused her attention back on the sweet memories. With each deep breath, the crystallized memories inched closer. She held out her hand and one of the bubbles kissed her palm like a butterfly's landing, popping and melting into her skin. More bubbles landed, splashed, and enmeshed, diffusing through the layers of her body, lighting up a warmth from within.

Everything was perfect again.

The glowing sun waned, and a mellow breeze swept across her skin. She wanted to stay with these memories forever. The ones that softened her anxiety reminded her of all the good in life and all she had accomplished.

Within seconds the colors muted and dimmed, until they, along with everything else, disappeared only to have her surroundings be replaced by her Day Room.

The door to her post-room opened. Overall, her anxiety lessened. Maybe her two Balloon Days ignited her transformation already. She held her shoulders high and marched into the exit elevator.

As she sauntered back to Penn Station, thoughts of what she had processed abound, the smell of pretzels and hot dogs teasingly wafted into her nostrils. According to a nearby street clock, the next train home was less than ten minutes away, so she snagged an overly priced hot dog and devoured it, a glob of cold ketchup landing on her finger.

Only good things could come from this treatment, she was certain, as long as she figured out how to use them properly. There were several points during the Balloon Day where Elliott's anxiety proved manageable. Maybe her relationship could be remedied after all. She would prove to anyone who was doubting it that it would be okay. She would prove she had not failed, that she was inarguably capable of a healthy relationship. She could beat anxiety once and for all.

After squeezing into a seat on the train, Elliott eagerly opened her phone to see if she got a message from Asher.

It read: can't come. sry. busy.

CHAPTER 9
ORSON

The days had been a blur since Madison's death, and soon the memorial service for his wife was upon them.

Orson had requested the grand bouquets of lilac-colored roses, white calla lilies, and deep purple larkspur cascades to be displayed near the urn that held his wife's ashes. As beautiful as the urn was—deep blues and purples, etched butterflies, cloisonné style—it was unnatural, surreal to know his wife had been reduced to dust. He respected Madison's wishes though, despite how dreadful the entire process had been, and he would soon sprinkle some of her ashes in the flower garden with family by his side.

The funeral parlor, Viola & Blooms, was tasteful and modern, a palette of soft whites, grays, and blues. The room had rows of cushioned white chairs, enough to hold one hundred guests. Portraits of Madison, with her family and friends, were hung along the heather-gray walls. Every time he looked at one of them, he was hurled back into a reality that ripped him into pieces, like a soldier stepping on a landmine in the dark.

"You did a wonderful job arranging all of this. Madison would have loved it, Orson," Rose said in between greeting guests.

"She deserves nothing but the best." Orson shook the hand of Madison's colleague, a nurse named Frankie with dangly purple earrings, and thanked her for coming.

More colleagues, friends, cousins, aunts, and uncles arrived, as well as Ryder's friends. Neighbors soon arrived, including Elliott. She brought a lovely peace lily and placed it on the table near the urn.

Each handshake, hug, and extension of gratitude for every loved one's sympathy drained Orson. It was both paining and comforting to be near those who shared the same grief.

He stepped forward to the front of the room, preparing for his speech. Ryder sat in the first row, repositioning his bottom on the chair, in between Orson's mother and Rose.

The rows of chairs behind them were filled by more loved ones—he could spot Aunt Josie, his cousins Don and Bridget. Others walked around, still perusing the carefully laid out photographs. Orson was slightly surprised that Jack, his boss, was nowhere in sight. Doug, Nancy, and other colleagues were there, and they nodded from the back row when he spotted them.

Orson cleared his throat. When everyone quieted, he began. "Hello, everyone. First and foremost, I would like to kindly thank all of those who have come here today to honor Madison's life, the woman I was lucky enough to call my wife for over fifteen years now. Our time was cut short, but no amount would ever have been enough. Although I am beyond blessed to have had one minute."

Orson paused, hearing many begin to weep again, and he mustered all his strength not to mirror them. He was not ready to say "did" or "had" or "was" yet. Although speaking in present tense saddened him, too.

"As made apparent by today, Madison had lived a life full of love and one filled with genuine, supportive people by her side. She made the world a brighter place, the people she neared lifting in positivity.

"Madison was the most caring, patient, loving, and devoted mother and wife. She always made sure Ryder and I were content and loved—she did this through her exceptional cooking, her displays of affection, the songs she would play on the violin, all she had taught not only to Ryder but myself about art and music and compassion, and about what matters in life—your connections with others, and your connection with yourself. Two things we often forget."

Orson paused, wincing inside at how often he forgot this fact.

"She was dependable, empathetic, loyal, graceful, breathtaking. I think we can all agree that Madison was a wonderful and rare gem. She was, and will always be, the love of my life, my sweetheart, my everything.

I am happy she is no longer suffering, yet, selfish and wish she was still here."

He looked at the urn.

"Grieving often seems like an insurmountable feat, but Madison once told me the harder we love, the harder we grieve—that loving someone is a direct correlation to missing them when they are gone. Therefore, let us not push away our grief, but honor it—and let ourselves miss Madison because we love her so."

Soon after, most of the guests had left aside from close family and friends. Orson returned from the bathroom when he bumped into Elliott in the hallway.

"Your speech was beautiful."

"Thank you, Elliott."

"She was one of the sweetest people I knew."

Was. "Indeed," he said.

Elliott smiled—the smile he saw all day long, one full of mournful compassion full of sympathy.

He was starting to get sick of those smiles. They reminded him he was someone to feel badly for. They reminded him he was a widower.

"How is Ryder doing?" she said.

"Not good."

"Is there anything I can do to help?"

"Babysitting here and there should cheer him up—he always enjoys your company. Rose will continue to help when you're unable to," Orson said.

"I can always come over and be with him, even if you're there, so you can get work done around the house." Elliott offered.

"I appreciate that, Elliott. Thank you." Orson looked down at the light-blue carpet of the hallway and back up again. "This is all unbelievable."

Elliott pulled at her lip. "You know how I'm working at that new therapy clinic, the Center of Balloon Days?"

Orson was sure where this was going—he didn't need to talk to a shrink about his problems. He never had to before and it's not like talking will bring back his dead wife. "Uh-huh, of course. Hope that is going well."

"The reason I bring it up is because it is a completely different type of therapy from talking to a therapist the entire time."

Orson checked his watch as he crossed his arms. "How so?"

"You get assigned a room—a Day Room. There are Elite Day Rooms as well—and the technology in the room is set up to alter our brainwaves to prompt a lucid-dream-like state."

Orson's arms dropped back to his sides. He slipped his hands into his pockets. "Go on."

"The clinical director, Dr. Heller, is the head neuropsychologist there and could explain it better than I can, but to put it simply, you can create whatever you want to process, clearer and better than you would in a lucid dream, which is something many of us never experience otherwise."

"I don't think I need that kind of help." Orson had dealt with death before. Although not as impactful as losing Madison.

"Well, what I'm saying is that maybe there's a way to process grief. Maybe even have your wife be there. I have the business card somewhere in here." She reached into her handbag.

"Listen. I know what you do is important, truly, but as for myself, I'm not convinced it could help, and I am certainly not convinced I could see my wife again—which is cruel to suggest otherwise. I can do this on my own."

"I'm so sorry, Orson. You're right. That was presumptuous of me to assume what you'd want to process, if you did give it a chance." She handed him a small white card with black writing. "In case you change your mind. I promise you, from having tested it out myself, it's worth every cent."

He took the glossy card, a black balloon on one side, the address and number on the other against a smooth white canvas.

Ryder sprinted toward them.

"Elliott." He wrapped his arms around her, his nose, and eyes red from tears. "Can you come over soon? And play video games with me?"

"Definitely. I'm sorry I haven't been able to come by as much lately. Silly work, right? Who needs it? I wish I could play with you every day instead," Elliott said, hugging him back.

Ryder hung his head low. "Me too. Mom used to play a lot."

Elliott took a brief glance at Orson.

"I'm so sorry about your mom," she said to Ryder. "I can see how sad you are. I'm so sad too."

Ryder's eyes lit up as he looked at her, as if her admission released something within him. It was odd. Adults, especially dads, shouldn't show their emotions around children. Whenever Orson's own father had, it scared him. It meant something must be extremely horrific. Orson had to be Ryder's hero.

"Do you think she will ever come back?" Ryder said.

Orson thought his talk with Ryder was sufficient enough for him to understand that Madison could not return to them. Ever.

At seven years old, perhaps it was not the most understandable concept. Or maybe it was Orson's parenting tactics that were severely impaired?

Madison was often the one to handle most of Ryder's misunderstandings, tantrums, and stressors. Maybe it was time to have Ryder see a therapist. The way Elliott was with Ryder seemed to display positive effects. That seems like something a proficient parent would do, despite Orson having zero insight into the process.

Elliott kneeled down to Ryder's level. "That would be amazing if we could see her again, but remember, she's still here, all around us, always with you. She's just invisible now, like how some superheroes can be. Remember when Harry Potter goes invisible?"

Ryder's eyes widened. "Like the cloak?"

"Exactly. That's the only difference now."

Down the hall, Orson's mother waved and called for Ryder. He hugged Elliott once more, dashed away, happily yelling "Grandma." There was no hug for Orson.

As Elliott turned back to Orson, her perfume wafted toward him, a delicate fruit smell, Madison's favorite scent. He somehow hadn't noticed until now. He'd been doing that a lot lately—being there, but not feeling grounded to anything. Like a ghost.

"So," he said. "About what you were saying. Do they offer therapy for children? Ryder certainly seems to need it, right?"

"That would be beneficial for him, yes. But in regard to the Center, I'm sorry, they don't take children. Traditional play and art therapy is highly effective though. I can give you some referrals."

"I'd appreciate that." The tension in his body eased.

73

"But for you, Balloon Days could be worth it. You truly could see your wife again, similar to how you do in your dreams, if you wanted to. It could help with your healing. And, Dr. Heller would be more than happy to have you as her new patient. Take your time to think about it. Shoot me a text if you need anything else." Elliott hugged him goodbye.

Seeing his wife again—the premise sounded unrealistic. Phony, even. A way to leech money off of grief-stricken suckers. It sounded like a lawsuit in the making.

But oh, how he ached for his wife. He ached so badly. Orson stared at his wedding band, wondering how it all came to this. Madison was gone. He was at her memorial. She was dead. Madison—was dead.

The air suddenly became thin and hot and his vision was hazy. He leaned against the wall. He could barely breathe. He was suffocating. He was alone. Alone in this hallway, alone in this life. He slid to the floor and buried his face in his hands. His cheeks were wet, and he realized he had already been crying.

Rose called for Orson from down the hallway. It must be time to go. His legs locked, his body unresponsive.

What the hell was happening to him? He had to get it together. Orson wiped his eyes with his handkerchief. He took a deep breath and the fruit-filled air hit his nose again. Shutting his eyes, he envisioned the scent coming from Madison instead of Elliott's lingering perfume. He inhaled deeply. The memory of his wife, buried in his imagination, was better than nothing.

Could a Balloon Day be better than that?

He looked at the business card again, the glossy letters beckoning him to call. Maybe he should. The idea alone slowed his heart down. It certainly seemed upscale enough. It was also based in hard science, as Elliott had previously explained.

What could be the harm?

CHAPTER 10

HOWARD

Howard placed his umbrella back in his plastic bag. Each tattered sneaker soaked through to his feet as he returned from the library and entered his dingy apartment. Old and worn, the fronts of each shoe flapped open exposing his wet socks—one of last year's hand-me-downs from John.

Misery penetrated his gut the way a rainy day torments a previously broken bone, or so he imagined, having never broken any. That's what Pop had said, so it must be true. He stepped into the bathroom. The faded yellow wallpaper next to the sink was tearing. He pressed it down, but it curled back in defiance, determined to remain worn and torn.

Howard had to shave his stubbly head and trim his beard. As he grew older, time had whittled him down, making him look less and less like his brother. John was slightly taller than Howard, athletically built, with butter-blonde hair that didn't sit quite right but in the messy way that women seemed to like.

Howard was fortunate enough to have landed Pop's symmetrical nose and strong, pointed chin along with Mom's olive complexion, straight teeth, and lips that were not too full, not too thin. The tradeoff, however, was his love for alcohol and premature hair loss.

Dirty and cold from the rain, Howard splashed water on his face and dried it with a washcloth. A cockroach crawled near the sink drain. Howard sighed as he flushed it down the drain. Peace.

He was not going to get it, not now at least. He left his apartment again, checking the date on his phone. The last day of August. Two more days until he was paid again. Two more days until he had enough credits for a thirty-minute Balloon Day.

Once outside of the apartment building, Howard opened his black umbrella, one of the wires needing assistance to straighten out, and ventured forward. The beads of rain slapped down and rolled off the sides, creating a waterfall around him.

He footed the familiar walk to John's place. Usually, he would stop at the local convenience store for alcohol, but he hadn't the time nor extra money to spend until John paid him again. He needed that money for Balloon Days. So far, it seemed worth it. He wasn't missing whiskey that much, come to think of it.

Passing down blocks shadowed by apartment buildings, they soon became increasingly elaborate with brownstones and townhomes, as Howard entered the wealthier side of Queens. Kids played and laughed and yelped in neighborhood schoolyards and fenced-in playgrounds, but they were mostly empty now due to the rain.

The few kids splashed in the puddles as car horns honked and blasted music, the occasional sirens howling in the distance. He hoped, yet again, this walk might be the one he finally received an apology text, or any type of text, from Jillian. Especially after her laptop rescue having given him hope. It never came.

Howard reached John's apartment. The apartment was striking with vaulted ceilings and high-end appliances, but John's messes ruined it. He was a fancy investment banker at the office, but a careless man-child at home. Clothes flung in a corner of the living room. The smell of take-out from the night before reeked from the overflowing garbage bin. Money tucked into a crumpled envelope—Howard's "weekly salary."

John was always messy and Howard was used to cleaning up after him. At least, now it was part of his job, and he was paid for it. Maybe when people made plenty of money, it was okay to mistreat their things.

Howard walked into the bedroom to get the laundry detergent from the closet, sidestepping a used condom on the floor. John must have cheated again; it was the only time he used them—a repugnant fact Howard was unfortunate enough to know.

"Damn it, John," he said to himself. Before he could berate John in his head further, his phone came to life in his pocket. "What do you want now?" He opened the text message.

It wasn't from John. It was from Jillian.

His heart beat faster. He hit open and her words appeared on the screen.

I heard you started therapy. I'm happy to hear that. Hope you are well.

He stared at the message. He rubbed the back of his neck. How did she know? Did John tell her? Why? How would that come up?

He swatted the thoughts and wrote: Thanks. Hope you're well too.

He added: Where have you been?

Howard gathered the dirty clothes and trudged to the laundry room at the back of the apartment. He threw the clothes in the washer and dropped in a soap pod. He checked his message box. Still empty. He checked again.

Turned the wash on. Put the empty basket on top of the machine. Checked to see if she read it. Nothing. Seven minutes had gone by. He went back to the kitchen and began arranging the silver canisters full of ground coffee beans of various flavors—his least favorite being the sweeter one, nuanced with chocolate and spices—on the counter to ensure each had the same amount of space in between.

He checked his phone again, but still nothing. On his way out, he pulled the trash up and tied the bag, brought it outside, and threw it in the dumpster.

Howard returned inside. His phone flashed. One new message. It was short and simple but powerful and stole the breath right out of him.

Take a train to me this weekend.

A rush of warmth flooded his heart, followed by a numbing chill. To see her again. Would it matter? How could he see her alone, and outside of John's apartment? The last time he saw her was a week ago, and briefly—a simple greeting and goodbye as she was leaving to go with John to a local bar, in a snug-fitting electric blue dress, her thick hair effortlessly tossed to one side. It had been the highlight of his night.

Howard reminded himself of what he was: an alcoholic who didn't have a job. A high school drop-out who hadn't bothered to get his GED. Maybe it was his fault, but no one told him to do otherwise.

Jillian might not want to ever leave John; they had their age in common, and John had figured this whole "life" thing out better than Howard ever could. How could he look worthy next to a high-level investment banker with hair?

Yet, she asked him to see her.
This was risky. This was trouble.
But Howard was tired of being lonely. He was in love.

CHAPTER 11
ELLIOTT

Sunglasses on, Elliott sat on a picnic blanket in the park and gathered her hair in a high ponytail, a fountain of auburn. A few bottom strands immediately swung out, flicking the back of her warm neck.

The start of September came with fickle New York weather—heat one day and an autumn chill the next. Today was a mix of the two. The sky a soft, friendly blue with full-bodied clouds; the sunshine made bearable by a cool breeze. A perfect day for flying kites and having a picnic at the arboretum.

Visiting the arboretum was Elliott's optimal go-to thinking spot. Freshly watered grass, a vibrant, jovial green, was the canvas for flower-lined paths, sprightly fountains, and immaculate gardens.

It was color and wonder, a place to get lost in, a place to feel free and alive. It was a shame that the flowers had periods of bloom and beauty, to then drift away, fall asleep, or forever disappear altogether.

At the edge of the picnic blanket was a plate holding sliced pepperoni and prosciutto, meticulously arranged next to slices of aged cheddar and fresh mozzarella. A bottle of pinot grigio sat unopened, alongside two wine glasses and a corkscrew.

Asher wasn't interested in the wine, or the meats or cheeses—he said none were too healthy, which was bizarre, as he'd never mentioned caring about, when it came to cheese boards, until today. Hopefully he would change his mind with the wine at least, because when he did, he loosened up.

"Elliott, what are you doing?" Asher said with a look of amusement on his face.

Elliott had taken out the dollar store kite and was attempting to assemble it.

"I want to fly a kite," she said. "Help me. Please?" Elliott pouted and cocked her hip, giving her best please-do-this-for-me body language, hoping he could pick up on the nonverbals.

"Alright, alright. Let me see it." He stood and walked over.

Success.

"But a kiss first." He leaned forward and she met his lips with hers.

With a satisfied smirk, he connected the plastic sticks to the body of the kite, a zigzag patterned diamond with its tail already flickering in the wind. It was yellow and white, matching her dress.

"You never told me what happened in your last Balloon Day," he said, handing it back to Elliott.

That's because I didn't want to.

She stared at the yellow tail of the kite. "It was much better than the first one. I definitely get the hang of it now," she said. "It was exhilarating to let your brain create anything it wanted."

How much should she tell him? That she was happy, letting go, feeling anxiety-free, until memories, including some with him, stormed in to steal that happiness away? That Evan, someone she hadn't mentioned to him at all, was part of the pleasant ones?

"I felt great during it," Elliott admitted. "Amazing, actually, even though—"

"So, is your anxiety gone now?" He lowered himself on the picnic blanket, finally taking a slice of cheese, but after one bite, he put it back on the plate and covered it with a napkin.

"Anxiety doesn't disappear overnight, Asher," Elliott said. "It's teaching me how to let go and enjoy the freedom. How not to care about my mistakes."

"You not caring about mistakes. That's funny."

Elliott lowered herself on the blanket, next to him. "Why is that funny?"

"Because you want to be perfect. But I love that about you. It's what makes us so good together," he said, matter-of-factly. "You keep me motivated. Lots of competition at the gym—and in the corporate world. Gotta make sure your dad doesn't fire me, you know?"

80

Elliott nodded. She did that when she didn't know how to respond to him, because too many options flooded her brain at once—to hear Asher say they were good together eased her annoyance, until he merged his appreciation of Elliott with his desire to maintain Dad's approval. Something Asher easily obtained. Whereas Elliott chased Dad's approval her entire life.

"Hello? Earth to Elliott."

"Sorry," she said. "What did you say?"

"What else were you saying about your brain before?"

"You mean before you interrupted me?"

"Do you want to tell me or not?" Asher said.

"I was saying, it was weird to have full control over something like that—over an entire imaginary world. But there was one point where the Balloon Day did feel out of my control again. Bubbles of random memories floated along—some unconscious stuff poking through like the first Balloon Day, I think." She paused. "Or maybe I was doing it wrong again."

"Maybe there is no right way, or wrong way, of doing something like that." Asher shrugged. "It isn't real life. Enjoy the freedom of not caring, Ellie, like you said."

She nodded, but this time, in agreeance. "You're right—I'm overthinking it."

He leaned in for another kiss. "Someday, you'll stop overthinking in real life, too."

"Yeah, yeah." She playfully nudged his shoulder with hers. "Okay, it's time to fly this dollar store kite."

Elliott picked up the kite and stood. She began to run across the field. Clusters of friends and families ate, sat under weeping willows, or wandered throughout the grass sea. Some of the children blew bubbles while others tossed frisbees, but she was the only one with a kite, and kids watched with awe. It flew decently high, higher than one would expect for being so cheap. But there it was, soaring gracefully above as she laughed and meandered.

Making her way back to Asher, she yelled to him it was his turn. He shook his head.

"C'mon, really? Why not?" Elliott whined.

"Because. I don't feel like it." His gaze scanned the others who were scattered around the open field. "It's stupid."

"That's not true." She sighted a group of children playing tag nearby. "Please. Have fun with it. Enjoy the freedom, remember?"

Asher opened his mouth, and she hoped for a yes, but no words followed. He looked at the kite, then back at her.

"Alright," he muttered.

"Yay, here you go. Try to keep it flowing against the wind."

"I know how to use a kite." Asher started to jog, and the kite lazily lifted then made its way slowly back down to earth, like a car that had run out of gas. His head low, dragging the kite behind him, he made his way back to Elliott. A few of the kids laughed out loud, others hid their giggles behind tiny hands, and some looked disappointed, returning to their games.

"Aw, no more?" Elliott said.

"We should head out soon—I'm meeting a friend for dinner," he added nonchalantly.

"Wait, what dinner? I thought we were having dinner together." Elliott's hands twisted the kite tail, like her stomach had begun twisting in knots.

"Oh, sorry, but I never said that." He put his hands up in the air like he was pushing a wall, but it was her who felt pushed away.

He had absolutely said they were having dinner together. She wanted to pull out the text messages to prove it.

"Who are you going with? When did you know about this?" she said, the words rushing out of her mouth. He was ruining her perfectly planned evening. "Is it Clara?"

"That doesn't matter. I let you know I'm going out. That should be enough." He placed the neglected meats and cheeses in Tupperware containers and tossed them back into Elliott's tote bag.

He started to fold up the blanket, folding all the money she spent, all the heart energy, the countless thoughts on how to make today's picnic perfect. What cheeses went with what meats; what wine would pair well to impress him.

"What do you mean 'it doesn't matter'? It matters to me." She said.

Asher guffawed as he handed the tote bag to Elliott. "Chill out."

"Chill out?" Elliott said. "I thought we would spend the day together, like we agreed on, but clearly that was stupid of me."

"All of my time can't go to you, Elliott. Relax. You're acting like a child. Let's just go. Please."

"Fine." She choked back tears and started to bend the kite in frustration, not caring if she broke it. The deadline loomed in her mind, so she bit her tongue.

I am in control.

"Oh, stop, babe." He lifted her chin up with his hand. "I'll cook you up a good dinner tomorrow night after we go running. And I'll watch a documentary with you. I found a good one about Phil Heath and his amazing bodybuilding journey. I promise you have nothing to worry about."

She looked at him and smiled, even if that bodybuilder documentary was the last type she'd want to see. "That sounds nice." Elliott felt like she was on one of those mouse-trap rollercoasters, the kind that hurry in one direction only to whip around and go back in the opposite one, giving her mental whiplash.

Asher picked up the picnic basket and headed toward his car, rushing past the exquisite flowers, not once looking back to see if she was behind him.

On the car ride home, they were mostly silent, aside from Asher humming along to the music, until Elliott turned down the radio.

"So, can you please tell me who you are going to dinner with?"

Asher's jaw tightened. "Stop. Don't start this again. What is your deal?"

Whip.

"Can't I be interested in who my boyfriend spends his time with?" She lifted her sunglasses up and pressed her finger against the barely visible bump on the bridge of her nose, trying to resist pulling at anything.

"It's a friend, Elliott. Maybe it is Clara, maybe it isn't. It shouldn't matter either way. You are so insecure sometimes. If you can't trust me, then you shouldn't be with me." Asher's words dangled in the air like bait. Elliott tried to make sense of them, scanning her brain to find an answer that would hopefully please him. It was more of a legitimate reason to end a relationship, but she didn't mean that she didn't trust him.

"Forget it," she said.

Asher briefly turned to look at her with a smug expression on his face. "Things are so amazing otherwise. Look at the great day we had. I flew a kite for you."

Sometimes Elliott truly felt bad for Asher. His mom was more of a dictator than a parent. Part of the reason why Elliott could look past the bad, unlike Julie. Within two months of dating, Asher had confided to her that when he was little, his mom punished him with crackers for dinner. Other times, she would make Asher seek permission to enter and exit each room in the house or take away playdates with friends for a month. Hearing it broke Elliott's heart. And with Asher's dad having left before he was born, there was no way to tell of his influence.

He needed more growing up to do. A lot more.

CHAPTER 12
ORSON

"Orson?"

"That would be me." He motioned to the unoccupied, but exceptionally comfortable, white-cushioned (Everything here is white, he thought) chairs around him.

After sufficient reflection, Orson concluded he should try at least one Balloon Day. It was only right to work on himself if he was considering to place Ryder in therapy, even if it was a different type.

More importantly, Orson wanted to remove his ineptness at being a father. Perhaps Ryder wouldn't need therapy for too long—the thought of anyone seeing Orson bring Ryder to a therapist admittedly embarrassed him. He might as well wear a bright red hat saying, "My dad is a failure."

Ryder's teacher had already informed Orson that Ryder was lacking interest in most games and fell asleep at his desk throughout the day. The way she said it suggested Orson lacked awareness and adequacy. He assured her he would take care of it.

So, therapy for Orson it was too.

"It's great to meet you. My name is Romalda. Dr. Heller will be with you shortly, she's running a bit behind today, our apologies. Busy day." Romalda sprayed and wiped one of the glass surfaces of the end tables; it had already appeared spotless, with a beautiful sheen. She went to another. Again, seemingly spotless.

"You're very diligent," Orson said. "This place is sparkling. My wife is that way with our home. I mean, was."

"Oh. I'm sorry for your loss. Can I get you anything while you're waiting? Coffee? Tea? Water? Anything at all. How about I show you our beautiful paintings?" She led him toward the other end of the waiting area, the sizable paintings hung every few feet in such a way that looked as if they were floating, breaking up the white. Orson welcomed the distraction.

Each was different: vivid sunrises and sunsets in extraordinary colors; fantasy-like landscapes, one with cotton candy for clouds, another with gargantuan flowers; couples sitting in their homes or running along open fields of grass.

All of them had a black balloon in the sky.

"Captivating, right?" she said.

"Quite exquisite, truly." Orson particularly loved the one of a couple flying above a city full of lights.

"And extra special," Romalda said. "Dr. Heller paints them herself, inspired by visions and Balloon Days our patients have experienced. Some are based on what they have told her they would like to see, while others are based on what they have reportedly seen in the visions they created."

"Created?" Orson said. He recalled Elliott mentioning something similar.

"Yes."

"I see. Do they say Dr. Heller has captured the visions accurately in her paintings?"

"Yes. Quite well." Romalda's eyes wandered from painting to painting. "Dr. Heller is special. It's as if she can see what you see. She is that empathetic."

Orson's curiosity grew. All of it seemed quite strange yet promising to him—something he had not felt in a while. As they reached the end of the expansive waiting area, he squinted in the sunlight from the window. Orson peered out and was taken aback.

"That is a fantastic view," he said, peering out at the city, the Empire State Building shooting up toward the sky. "Dr. Heller had certainly chosen a spectacular building for the Center."

"I agree. We can always feel the energy of the passersby just by looking out this window. The buzz of the busy bodies down below." She let out a gentle humming sound. "One by one, they come to the doctor's Center of Balloon Days. Dr. Heller likes giving people the opportunity to slow down. To simulate whatever and be wherever with whomever, away from their worries and stress. Or quite the opposite—to face them. Amazing, isn't it?"

Orson approved with a nod. Except he wanted to escape his pain permanently so that he could become a better father.

A chime sounded.

"Right this way, Orson. The doctor will see you now." Romalda motioned to the majestically crafted frameless double doors made of blue glass adorned with translucent white shapes resembling clouds.

"No one came out," he said.

"Dr. Heller was on a telephone meeting. For in-person appointments though, we make sure there is ample time between each, no matter what, this way no one runs into each other. We do this to protect the identities of all our patients."

This seemed like the type of place that had every corner strategically laid out. As a man of reason and privacy, he appreciated that.

The door slid open again as they approached. A slender woman of great beauty and sophistication rose from behind her desk to greet Orson, and the quiet mechanics of the sliding door let him know it closed behind him. The earthy-sweet scent blooming from the vase of roses on Dr. Heller's desk circulated through the air, their crimson color striking against all the white.

"Welcome. We are happy to have you here." She shook his hand and led the way to a homelike sitting area in the corner of the room. All that was missing was a fireplace. "I trust Romalda treated you well?"

"She was exceptional. Thank you."

"Excellent. Thank you for filling out the preliminary intake information online. We have everything we need uploaded into your file now," she explained, gesturing toward her desk in the middle of the office. Calling it an office, however, diminished the grandeur of the room. Every element of the décor was elegant and scrupulous in its simplicity. Orson had a knack for words but he couldn't find one that conveyed the true feeling this room produced. "Please make yourself comfortable. There is freshly made tea for you." She motioned to the glass mug full of delightfully steaming pink liquid. "Raspberry ginger. Great for the immune system."

He sat down on the sofa across from her. She looked effortlessly dignified in her silky, flowing dress that had a black balloon embroidered near her collarbone.

The loveseat was a buttery leather without emitting the usual creaking sounds as he positioned himself. The floor was covered with a lavish carpet. He had a strong urge to take his leather shoes off and feel the carpet's plush texture between his toes, but he resisted. Instead, he trailed his fingers up and down the sleek arm of the couch—Elliott had been accurate; this was unlike anything he assumed about therapy.

Orson picked the mug up off the tray on the ottoman; although the steam remained, the mug wasn't hot at all. He took a sip. "Wow. That is delicious."

"Truly. Now tell me, Orson. What is it you would like to experience during your time here?"

He placed the mug back down, then smoothed his silver-blue tie against his white button-down. "My wife passed away in our living room about a month ago. She had been diagnosed with terminal breast cancer and suffered for years as it continued to spread, despite endless rounds of radiation and chemo—by the top doctors, no less. We still had hope that she would..."

His voice began to crack. He cleared his throat. He had to get it together. What if something reminded him of Madison during a trial? Who would pay a lawyer who couldn't keep it together? And if he cried in front of Ryder—Orson would surely upset Ryder further than he already was. He had to remain composed for him. Hopefully, this Balloon Day treatment, whatever the hell it was, would help.

"I am so deeply sorry for your loss, Orson. Losing a partner is painfully challenging." She placed her hands upon her lap, leaning closer toward him. "The Balloon Days will be a helpful experience and a wonderful way to assist your grieving. Envision it now—Madison at your side again. You can tell her anything you'd like. Do anything you would like that you hadn't yet been able to. Like old times. The grieving could, undoubtedly, lift—within moments, even."

"I see," he said, noticing the tiniest of pulled threads on his sharkskin gray suit pants. "What are the risks?"

She tilted her head, and the diamond stud in her ear twinkled. "Balloon Days come with the risks you assign them. They work with your comfort level. What do you think would be risky for you to see your beautiful wife alive and well again?"

Orson stared at the portrait on the wall of the smiling man walking down what looked like a staircase made of clouds. "Perhaps getting lost in them. If what you say is true, and I do see her again... what if it's hard to leave her when the Balloon Day is—over?"

"Oh, there is no getting lost, I can assure you of that. I can't promise it will be easy to say goodbye to her, but remember, you can see her again—even within the same week. We have our limits, of course, which is all made clear in the consent form. But you're intelligent. As I'm sure you know, we do not just allow anyone here. We screen potential patients to ensure they are mentally fit and capable of understanding the procedure. We ensure that all our patients who undergo Balloon Day therapy are ready. And you are ready. Your grief is fresh, your emotion is raw. It is the perfect time to work on your healing."

She passed the tablet, consent form open, over to Orson. The limit was three Balloon Day sessions per week, ninety minutes maximum per experience. An in-person check-in session at least once a month was required or else the Center would suspend any further appointments. Scrolling down, he noted at the bottom, as Dr. Heller mentioned, the risks stopped when the patient wanted them to stop.

"I'm in full control then."

Dr. Heller slowly nodded, smiling. "Precisely."

Images of Madison overwhelmed him. It felt right, as if she was telling him to sign on the dotted line and go with it.

He thought of life without her. He thought of Ryder.

He signed.

Dr. Heller nodded, taking the tablet back. "Your Elite Day Room, B107, is on floor ten. You will take the blue elevator. This will be yours to return to as you please for your scheduled Balloon Day sessions. In addition to the delightful perk of Elite Day Rooms being grander in size, we stagger the appointments, so you will not have to wait for anyone, but there is still a pre-room with the bathroom for you if need be."

"Thank you."

"Let your perception be your guide." Dr. Heller smiled and shook Orson's hand.

Orson's waiting room, or the "pre-room" rather, was gleaming white and cozy. As he stepped into the restroom, he noticed an immaculate toilet and sink, complete with a beautiful brass waterfall faucet.

No mirror? Strange.

Although there wasn't necessarily any reason why he would need to see himself at this moment, not having a mirror there gave him a feeling of invisibility; nothing to reflect his existence, no feedback for his mind. Maybe that was the point. Soon, as he was told, all sensory input would be stripped from him, allowing his brainwaves to shift into a blank canvas. Whatever the hell that meant.

He stepped back out. Slipped his Day Room card into the slot, selecting to use four out of his ten credits. Dr. Heller had suggested buying credits in bulk; Orson figured he would stick with the ten to see how things panned out.

The stunning blue, ice-like door slid open. Orson's gaze fell to the floor first—the same thick white carpet as in Dr. Heller's office. He took off his shoes and sunk his feet into the plush, delicate material. The softness against his silver socks, peppered with race cars for Ryder, put him at ease. The air smelled of mulled cider. Soothing sounds of a crackling fire filled the room. White angelic feathers covered all four walls. To his surprise, he suddenly wanted to create art, romantic, dreamy art, the art Madison had inspired. His Day Room was divine.

Scanning the sizable but quaint square room, everything was white save for the cobalt blue of the sky-like ceiling matching the pillows atop the velvety-looking sofa lining the back wall. The ethereal hammock in the middle of the room, hanging diagonally, the thin, clear wires of it barely noticeable, giving it a look of invisible suspension, was pure luxury.

Next, he discovered the control in a small white pocket hanging on the wall to the right of the door. He clutched it in his hand as the lights dimmed further, the white of the room now snow, in the dark.

The button glowed. His promise of refuge. He closed his eyes and envisioned his beautiful wife's face, as he had remembered her long before she had become bedridden, mostly skin and bones. He pushed it. Instantly, he was as weightless as one of the feathers on the wall.

Opening his eyes, astounded and sitting on the edge of his bed inside his old college dorm, he recognized where he was immediately. The room Orson had during his second year—the year he met Madison. He hopped off the bed.

Everything was as it had been. His desk a mess of pens and papers from studying, political science textbooks opened to random chapters on the floor. A mirror hanging on his closet door showing his reflection, which startled him. Orson was his young and handsome nineteen-year-old self.

Hair darker and thicker, body less muscular in his green t-shirt and jeans—he had been scrawny in his youth. Minor wrinkles around his umber-brown eyes smoothed over. All in all, he was impressed at how little he had changed over the years.

Orson left his room and ambled down a path between the fellow residence halls. He didn't feel quite in control of his actions. Not quite out of control either. Drawn to the courtyard as if a string was stitched into his waist, his belly button perhaps, and someone pulling him forward from the other end, he willingly obeyed, having an idea as to what might await him as he reached the courtyard.

There she was.

Madison sat on one of the patio benches. Every cell inside him was buzzing. He was going home. He was going to his girl. He remembered this moment, feeling exactly how he did now. Giddy at the idea of approaching her. Horrified she might reject him, yet confident she wouldn't.

Could she reject him here? Or was this living in the memory?

They said he could create whatever he wanted, yet this unknown force tugged him toward each of his movements, the movements reenacting one of the most joyful, life-changing events in his life. How could he have forgotten how indelibly magical this moment was? Strolling over, Orson cleared his throat. "Excuse me, would you mind if I sat here and admired you? I mean, admired the courtyard trees and flowers with you. Although, neither are as pretty."

Nearly a veritable version of Madison, complete with his favorite beauty mark on the left side of her neck, laughed. "Um, sure. Nice pick-up line. Clever."

"Did it work?" He sat down next to her.

"Got me to laugh."

"Got me to sit."

She looked Orson up and down. "I guess it did. I'm Madison."

"I'm Orson. Did you know, Madison, that I am going to marry you?"

She laughed again as she marveled. "Oh? Is that so?"

"Very much so." Orson stood up and picked a nearby rose blooming before his eyes as he thought of it. He could create—now he understood. As Orson turned to bring Madison the rose, his surroundings suddenly blurred, the colors mixing together. He went to steady himself as he gasped in confusion.

As quickly as whatever had obscured the scene, another became clear in his view again. He was somewhere else. He and Madison were holding hands as they roller-bladed along a bike trail. Orson knew this memory well too. They had many pictures of it, one in a frame on their fireplace back at home.

The familiar magnetic pull washed over him.

Madison almost fell over and yanked on his hand. He held her up, looking in her opulent, bright blue eyes. There she was—alive, alive, alive.

Complete and breathtaking. She wore his university sweatshirt, the large size of it adorable on her. He could hold her, kiss her, see her, breathe her scent in, be comforted by her voice again. Memory or not, he was with his wife again.

They rollerbladed down a path alongside a brook. Butterflies fluttered. Flowers bloomed.

The sunshine beamed through the leaves of trees, their dark, impressive silhouettes against the cloudless sky. They turned onto a path with more trees on either side of it, the branches twisting upward and out, bending toward each other, forming arches.

"Take a picture of me with the trees," Madison insisted. "They're so beautiful. So strong—like you, my love."

She skated and stopped in the middle of the path, waiting, waving, and smiling. It reminded him of another time, later in their relationship, when they had gone hiking, and he had snapped photo after photo of them exploring the forest. As he recalled that moment, the same twisting of the scenery began to blur his vision, his body feeling squeezed as if being squished by a tube.

The memory of hiking was replacing the current one, enveloping them.

Orson trotted behind Madison on their favorite trail, an open cliff area at the top. "Orson, look. A deer. Deer—come here, deer." Orson felt like he was on some sort of fantasy ride he would have loved as a child. He wanted to ask Madison how to help Ryder with his grief, but he was enjoying the moment too much.

In this memory, they were twenty-two now. Giddy and goofy, frivolous and free.

Orson held the camera lens to his eye, ready to go. "Stand still. I'll get a photo of you and the deer in the background. It'll be fantastic."

"But all I am are photographs now. You have to accept that."

Orson lowered the camera. "What did you say?"

"I said take a picture, sweetheart."

Madison jumped. Orson quickly lifted his camera again, clicked, eager to capture the momentum. As soon as he had, she yelped and froze mid-way. Suspended in the air. The camera turned her into a still, lifeless photograph. Suddenly her words broke through the surface of his brain: all she was were photographs now.

Orson looked back at the camera, and when he looked up again, Ryder stood below her fixed body, looking distraught.

"Dad, what did you do?" Although this person looked like Ryder, he did not sound like him. He sounded cold and distant. "Why did you make her life stop? You ruined everything. You always do. You're the worst. You should have been the one to go, not Mom."

As Orson attempted to answer, tears stinging the back of his eyes, he had returned to his dimly lit room back at the center. Utterly confused and upset, he pressed the intercom on the wall in the post-room.

"Romalda," he cried out. Within seconds, she replied.

Minutes later, the exit elevator doors opened. "Is everything alright, Orson?" She walked forward holding a glass of water. "Here, drink, it's electrolyte-infused water. I also added a touch of lavender."

"Oh—thank you." He received the glass and sipped. "Well, I'm not too sure if everything is alright. My head is simply reeling. The way the doctor explained it to me, I thought I would be creating whatever I wanted to see."

"Yes, of course," Romalda confidently responded.

"So, why did mine do the opposite? I had precious little control over what happened. I was being swept through memories, until the last one, where I took a photograph of her, of my wife, and she became lifeless. And my son, he was caustic, hateful..."

Romalda put a finger to her lip; it was unusual to see her without a friendly smile plastered on her face. "Oh dear." She cast a brief look at the exit elevator and then back at him. "Let me book you an appointment with the doctor. Unless you feel it is more urgent than that. It is possible I can bring you up to Dr. Heller now. I know she prefers I handle things first, unless absolutely necessary. Would you say it is urgent?"

"No, no. It's not urgent." He handed her back the empty glass. "Well. Would you say it sounds urgent based on your experience here?"

"Dr. Heller would say this is normal for the first time." Her smile returned, wider than before. She continued. "You will get used to controlling how far you let anything that feels 'risky' go. You can exit any time, don't forget."

If he made it seem urgent, they might suspend him. They couldn't suspend him. Not now. He would stop on his terms.

CHAPTER 13
ELLIOTT

Standing in a treehouse, Elliott was high in the sky on her Balloon Day. She looked down, seeing nothing but clouds and buildings the size of ants. Her legs shook. She wasn't necessarily afraid of heights, but she was afraid of falling unexpectedly. What would happen if she tested either of these fears? Surely nothing bad, right? The millisecond the idea of landing crossed her mind, she would stop.

So, she closed her eyes and jumped.

Elliott's bravery, and shriek, lasted three seconds, before marshmallow softness caught her fall, her nostrils filling with its sweet, delicate scent. She pulled a piece off and savored the soft saccharine taste, enjoying the childlike wonder.

Considering it another success in both her studies of Balloon Days for phobias and her own anxiety, the marshmallow underneath her converted into the soft white hammock in her Day Room. Next time she would fall for five seconds.

She went back into her office. Smaller than Dr. Heller's, it still had an ornate feel and a sizable window. Everything was shiny white, save for the touches of blues and violets within the abstract paintings hung on the walls, along with different arrangements of colorful flowers on her desk greeting her every Monday morning; this week's bouquet was of honeysuckles and orange blossoms, reminding her of spring, the ground awakening, the playgrounds alive with giggles and excitable screams.

Elliott reached for the office phone to call her newly assigned patient. She quickly accessed his chart on the electronic medical records system.

Name: Howard Nor. Age: 26.

Scanning Dr. Heller's therapy notes, Elliott paused at the bottom, in which Dr. Heller concluded he was developing an insecure attachment style with a woman named Jillian, had a deep envy of his older brother, and suffered from moderate recurrent depression and social anxiety.

Apparently, these issues were most likely related to untreated adolescent trauma. Dr. Heller had bolded the words "learned behaviors of not taking risks. Possible alcohol dependency to assess over time. Suicidal ideation not reported, no history of prior attempts or hospitalization."

Howard answered the phone on the second ring.

"Hi, Howard, I'm Dr. Elliott Bailey. I see Romalda was able to schedule your first appointment with me early next week. We can process your first Balloon Day and set some long-term goals. Does that sound good?"

Howard agreed, and Elliott went on to inform him about herself and her approach: that she preferred collaborative skill-building to strengthen a proactive stance rather than reactive stance toward life's challenges. She is a firm believer in the cultivation of self-compassion to aid treatment success.

Elliott enjoyed adding new patients to her caseload—although, she was always nervous before their first meeting, hoping the new patient would be a good fit, hoping he or she would find her helpful.

"Howard, is there anything else I can help you with today?"

There was a pause before he answered. "I was wondering if there was any discount option for the Balloon Days. I can only afford another fifteen minutes, thirty at most."

"Hmm, okay, I understand." Fiddling with a purple paperclip, Elliott pondered. "It might take more time to see progress, which I'm sure is what you're worried about?"

"Yes. It was difficult to leave, as the end became a bit... puzzling. But I understand if that isn't possible." Elliott wondered what he meant by "puzzling." Did he experience anything like she had? She made a note for herself to ask him about this during their session. "I'm sorry," he continued. "It's likely a ridiculous request."

"No, don't be sorry. This is what I'm here for. I will speak with Dr. Heller about some possible solutions. I know she offers package deals from time to time, which offers a small discount. I can call you back as soon as I find out." She jotted "discount?" on a nearby notepad.

"That's nice of you, thank you. And thank you again for your time."

"You're very welcome."

She could see why Dr. Heller tagged him as moderately depressed. He sounded like the human version of Eeyore. Kind and gentle, yet joyless. She wanted to tell him to come in, she wanted to cradle him and tell him it would all be okay, to give him as many Balloon Days as he needed.

After she hung up, she reviewed his file more thoroughly. It appeared he had talked copiously about the woman named Jillian, how he wanted a relationship with her, and how he had admiration for his brother's many successes. Maybe this was the risk-taking Dr. Heller had identified?

That mixed with social anxiety would prevent him from pursuing something more with Jillian in real life. How had Howard met her in the first place? Nothing was written in the notes—Dr. Heller must not have asked for a reason. She was intentional in her decisions, never letting anything slide without reason. Maybe Elliott shouldn't ask either. Not right away, at least.

Elliott headed to Dr. Heller's office; the midday sun shone brightly through the windows of the hallway, dimming every few seconds as the abundant and active clouds played peek-a-boo in the sky. Dr. Heller was sitting in the corner area of her office. Elliott joined her and asked about the sliding scale. Dr. Heller quickly disapproved.

"People tend to undervalue the treatment when they pay less. And we want him to value it, right? He isn't using an Elite Day Room, as it is. I think I've made the prices fair enough for the standard experience," she said, smiling.

Elliott was not aware of the Balloon Day prices, as Dr. Heller said it was not necessary for the psychologists to know. Only she and the billers had to be aware, which made sense. Elliott's stomach pinched at the idea of sharing the news with Howard, but she wanted Howard to value his sessions and get the most out of them.

"Don't worry, Elliott. He can always use fifteen minutes per Balloon Day if need be. It will still be effective." Dr. Heller raised her eyebrows, one higher than the other, and smirked. The last time she wore that expression was when Elliott asked if there were annual raises. She had felt stupid, and she felt stupid now. "If we start lowering one person's prices, then—well, you know the saying, 'if you give a mouse a cookie...' We are not a practice that enables helplessness. He'll find a way to make it work."

Elliott returned to her office in slight confusion as Dr. Heller's words buzzed in her head. Did Elliott agree? Not with everything. Especially when Dr. Heller compared Howard to a mouse. He deserved the same respect as those who could easily afford Balloon Day credits.

Elliott called Howard back, as promised. His understanding provided respite from her anxiety, though he had sounded disappointed, saying he'd have to ask his brother for a raise. Hopefully his brother obliged.

Later that evening, Elliott munched on white cheddar popcorn in her living room. She quickly wiped her fingers of the cheddar powder and pressed pause on a documentary—about the rise and fall of an animatronic character band of animals—when Julie called.

"Are you still watching the creepy Rock-afire movie?" Julie said. "I was terrified of those things. Especially the wolf guy. Those teeth, the cheeks, all of it—disgusting."

"Oh, Rolfe? Yeah, he is bizarre. Honestly, I'm fascinated because they're so creepy." Elliott folded the Smartfood popcorn bag. She sealed it with a snack clip. "I have to finish it."

"You're invested now, you have to. Just stop sending me pictures of Rolfe." She could feel Julie's signature smirk through the phone.

"Fine."

"Tell me how it went at the Center."

Elliott took a sip of water then placed the glass back on the coffee table. "I have my first case of someone going through recurrent depression and I think he might be suffering from alcoholism." Elliott pulled at her lip. "Honestly, I'm nervous. I've only ever treated anxiety-related disorders."

Suddenly, every therapeutic approach was bombarding Elliott. They all seemed to be the best. Or maybe she should try to mimic Dr. Heller. She thought of the bookshelf in her study room filled with psychology textbooks and the latest non-fiction and workbooks about ways to relieve symptoms or understand children or how to dissect and help the trauma-influenced mind.

"I'm certain you will be great at this type of case too," Julie said. "You're capable of basically anything when it comes to helping people. You're one of the most compassionate people I know."

"What if I'm not capable enough?" Scenarios of blanking out and not knowing how to respond during their first session played in her head. Saying the wrong thing and Howard staring at her, frustrated and confused, yelling in her face about how she was not understanding anything he was saying, how she was a horrible psychologist who should be fired, suddenly seemed like the only probable scenario.

"Then you're not, and you'll learn how to be. Anyone who knows you knows that when you want something, you won't stop until you get it. You'll be fine. As long as nothing distracts you." Elliott knew Julie was hinting about Asher. She also knew what the next thing out of Julie's mouth would be.

"How are things with Asher? I'm assuming you guys are still together?" Elliott sighed, put Julie on speaker phone, then picked up a book about depression off the coffee table. She had plans to read the entire thing after the documentary and flipped through the pages.

"Yes, we are still together, Julie. Things are going well actually. He has his good moments. I just complain a lot." Although, the other day he told her she was cutting an onion the wrong way; they bickered so often it was as if a rope lay between them at the ready for tug of war.

"For now," Julie muttered. "Whatever. Sorry. I'm being annoying. But you can do so much better. Oh, speaking of which, before I forget, tomorrow night my friend Laura—you met her once—is celebrating her birthday at a bar called Blue Velvet in Brooklyn, and you must come with me. Oh, and guess who will be there."

"Melinda?"

Melinda was an irritating, flirtatious, shrill girl who would unfortunately show up at random social gatherings, because she was the sister of their friend Nicole. Nicole was the exact opposite of Melinda—a wonderful human being.

Julie laughed. "Oh, god, no, I hope not. But probably. Anyway, I meant my cousin, Evan. He said it was nice running into you."

Elliott placed the book back on the coffee table. She suddenly became lightheaded. Probably her body crashing from the long day. "I see."

"You don't have to talk to him." Julie paused. "Or you could. And like, fall in love and have lots of babies together." Falling in love sounded nice, and so did the "having lots of babies" part, but not yet. She was nowhere near yet.

She remembered Asher.

"I'm already in love."

"Are you?" Julie challenged.

Elliott scanned the framed photographs on the fireplace mantel—her with Julie and friends in front of the Big Ben. Her and Mom hugging during a Christmas brunch; her holding Captain the day she adopted him—then she picked up the one of her with Asher.

It was from earlier in the year, around Valentine's Day, when they had gone to see The Phantom of the Opera on Broadway. She could barely recognize herself, she looked so happy, her smile sweet and genuine. Was it naïve to have been deeply infatuated that early on? In the reflection of the glass, she could see tears pooling in each eye. She put the picture back on the mantel.

"If you can't answer quickly, Elliott, maybe you aren't. Something to think about. Anyway, meet me at my place around seven-thirty tomorrow?"

"Okay," Elliott said. A moth fluttered around inside her stomach, trying to make its way out.

As they said their goodbyes, there was a jangle of keys and the clicking of the front door as it unlocked. Elliott wiped her eyes, the streaks of wet mascara on her index fingers, the tennis bracelet from Asher slightly slipping down her wrist.

"Hello?" a man's voice called out.

It was Dad, the infamous Warren Bailey, big-shot CEO of a Long Island hedge fund; that plus the multiple gyms he owned throughout Long Island and Manhattan. He was the last person she wanted to see.

He came around the foyer, entering the living room. Thankfully, he was not a spider nor a giant. Just his normal jerk self. "What, you don't look at your phone anymore?"

Elliott checked her phone. Two unread text messages from him. "Sorry. I was talking with Julie, I didn't get a chance to open your texts. She asked about my new—"

"Look at this place. It's a mess. I don't let you stay here at such a reasonable price to let the place become a pigsty, Elliott," he said, wiping a finger along her television stand, holding it up to view the dust.

Elliott looked around. Sure, the blankets and pillows on the sofa were disheveled, and a couple had fallen on the floor. Empty mugs were on the coffee table and the edges of the ceiling fan were thickened with gray, furry dust. Hopefully he wouldn't go into the kitchen too. She was pretty sure she left a pot in the sink from making herself poached eggs this morning. Probably crumbs from the toast on the counter. It wasn't dirty, but it was messy. He was right. She had to tend to the house more, but she was hardly home these days.

"I'm sorry... it's been busy at work. I was actually given another new patient today."

Why was it whenever she was around Dad, she regressed to an acne-riddled teenager?

"Alright, but make sure this gets cleaned. Looks like a warzone in here." He shook his head disapprovingly. His inky black hair was thick and barely moved even as he turned his head. "You don't have your glass of ice water on a coaster? The coaster is right next to it, for God's sake."

"It doesn't have condensation yet."

"It will any second. That's no excuse."

"Yes. You're right. Sorry, Dad." Elliott put the glass on the coaster, then picked up the pillows and blankets and rearranged them on the sofa. Dad inched toward the dining room, where many of her books about various therapeutic approaches lay open on the table.

Crap.

"What is this, Elliott?" His voice rumbled. "That's a Benetti you have all your dirty books on."

She winced. "I'm coming," Elliott yelled, hurrying into the dining room. "I'll take care of it. I promise." She gathered a couple, stacking them up to take them back to her bookshelf in the study.

"You know, this place should look spotless. I work tirelessly, Elliott, and my house is pristine—not from the house cleaner either, but from my own attention to detail. That's what you need more of. Get your head out of the clouds." His eyes alone could shame her—each iris a stormy livid sea waiting to engulf her. The eyes of the miniature spiders flashed in her mind, and she winced.

"Anyway, here," he said, softening his tone. Elliott looked up as he pulled an envelope out from the inside pocket of his gray suit, his thin argyle tie momentarily disturbed. He calmly readjusted it, his impeccable look restored. "A little something for you. For doing well at the Center."

She reached out and took it, felt the weight of it, and could tell it was loaded with gift cards, most likely for expensive clothing stores he and Holly approved of. "Thank you," she said. "And I am sorry about the house. It won't happen again."

He swatted the air. "Eh, if not, I'll have my house cleaner stop here too. Anyway, use that money well. You will always need professional clothes. Regardless, you know how important appearances are. We can always look put together. It isn't anyone's business what's happening on the inside," he said, proudly bestowing his miraculous, fatherly wisdom as usual. "You are the psychologist, not them, after all." He chuckled. "I don't say it enough, but I am proud of you. You got my genes when it comes to having the brains for success, despite the inheritance of your mother's propensity to dramatize everything."

The snap was quick—no matter the calming techniques, the self-regulating skills she had learned. Her father's condescending, critical nature made her question everything she had ever done since she was a child.

And there always, always, always was the moment that came when he pushed her too far, clueless that his criticism built the ever-growing barrier between them. She wished she could be the giant and flatten him with her shoe.

"You're so ignorant," she spat. "You clearly know Mom and me so well. Maybe I'm dealing with a lot of stress from school, research, and just anything. You could ask, you know. Mom does."

"Don't you dare start. This is unbecoming of you." He looked at her hair, picking up a strand. "Would it kill you to keep your natural brown locks like your old man's. It's classier." She pulled her head away, smoothing it back in place. He knew very well Mom's hair was naturally auburn.

"Now, be good. See you soon, kiddo."

Just like that, he was gone. Elliott went to the couch and chucked each meticulously placed pillow back on the floor.

CHAPTER 14
ORSON

Orson sat in the waiting area for his follow-up appointment with Dr. Heller. Calming piano music played from seemingly nowhere; he barely noticed it until the doors slid open.

"Good morning, Orson." It was Dr. Heller. "Right this way."

She took a seat behind her glass desk, wearing her lab coat over a white blouse and skirt, appearing more clinical today than last time. Orson lowered himself in the seat across from her, feeling the softness of the cushion underneath his bottom.

"Tell me what happened." She rested her hands in her lap, her gold watch half-exposed and glimmering. "Tell me what troubled you in your Balloon Day session."

"Where do I begin?" Orson cleared his throat. "There were several disturbing moments. Overall, I barely was able to use my imagination—it mostly seemed as though my memories took control, if that makes any sense." He must sound ridiculous, but her expression hadn't changed. She's likely heard crazier happenings. "I felt the same type of physical energy and strength I had in the past, but my emotions and thoughts were from my present self."

Dr. Heller typed away at her computer. "Go on, I'm listening while documenting your experience."

"It was as if I was observing from within as the memories played themselves out, as opposed to being an active participant. I felt myself moving myself, but I knew exactly where to go, as if I was being pulled to it. At the end of the last memory, my wife jumped as I was taking a picture of her. But after I clicked to take it, she remained suspended in the air, frozen and lifeless. That's when my son showed up, with a mature, cold voice and accused me of taking her life away. He also said..." Orson stared at the angelic yellowish-blue glow shining through the windows onto the carpet, similar to the way the sun sparkled through stained glass in a church, before returning his gaze to Dr. Heller. "He said he wished it was me who died instead."

She had stopped typing and put a hand over her heart. "That must have been quite alarming and painful for you at the end, especially after the comfort of those earlier memories, I'm sure."

"I wanted to save her," Orson said. "But it was too late. I hope Ryder knows that, too. God, he was so livid with me, full of hatred, and disgust toward his own father. Is this how your place runs, to make people feel worse? Or is this some kind of fluke?"

Dr. Heller raised her eyebrows and returned her hand to her lap. "Let me first explain the brain's inner processes. This is all perfectly normal." She swiveled her laptop screen around to an image of a brain. It looked like an MRI. Some parts of the brain were blue. Some parts red. "You see, here is the hippocampus, the area where our brains store long-term memories. Memories can also be encoded throughout the brain in the different sensory areas involved.

"For example, if a specific scent is tied to that moment, whenever you smell that particular scent, it will not only light up the area for an olfactory sensation but also the memory—or the many memories—it is linked with. This helps the brain understand and construct the world rapidly, to make sense of it. Think of it as mini reference cards created as you live your life."

She turned the screen back toward her.

"What appears to be happening is that your hippocampus, as well as the associated networks in your brain, are hijacking some of your control throughout the Balloon Days. You are still conscious and aware of your present thoughts and emotions, which indicates a level of control and processing in the now. As you can see, it's nothing alarming. It's simply grief-imposed brain activity. Your unconscious mind believes you could have saved her. Rationally, I believe you know that's not true. It's false guilt."

She clasped her hands together on top of her desk.

"As per policy, though, and out of my utmost concern for your well-being, as that always comes first, let me address the impact your Balloon Day experience had on your symptoms of grieving. Any anxiety, panic attacks, depression, side effects, vivid dreams, nightmares? Anything at all out of the ordinary since then?"

Orson took a moment to gather what had transpired since earlier that week. "No. As horrible as the end was, I did feel happy again to see my wife. She was so... lifelike. The grief has felt lighter. The guilt you mentioned is certainly still there, though." How could he forget about the guilt that ran through him? Whether it was false or not, present issues warranted the feeling. Ryder slammed his door twice on Orson yesterday for getting the bedroom password wrong yet again. He had to remember to log it in his phone.

"It must be indescribable to have the opportunity that we offer here. To see your wife again is nothing short of a miracle, I'd imagine."

"I've been euphoric in a way I haven't felt in years. I feel the infatuation I felt for Madison when we first met. Quite honestly, I am still eager to have another Balloon Day." She was right. How could he be upset with the place that let him see his wife again?

Dr. Heller leaned back in her chair, smiling. "Lovely, I'm pleased to hear. Let's schedule your next session with me a week from today at the same time. That will give you space to see what other changes, benefits, issues, emotions, and so on emerge. Feel free to tell your clients and colleagues about us too. Here are some business cards."

"Sounds like a plan." Orson gave her hand a quick, firm shake after collecting the cards. "I will see you then."

As Orson approached the door, he swung around to face her. "Doctor, one more thing."

"Yes?" She rose behind her desk.

"Do you believe in mediums? Or spirit guides, psychics, anything like that?"

"Hmm." she said. "Interesting question." She walked over to her sitting area, grabbed the vase off the table, checked the water level, and placed it back down. "From a scientific standpoint, our beings wouldn't be able to exist without the electrical firings between neurons, or the blood in our veins. From a spiritual standpoint, it seems some believe our minds, our souls, linger.

"Between you and me, I would consider them a scam. Whereas in your Balloon Days, you will be with the closest, unvarnished replication of your wife. There is no medium in the world who knows her better than you do."

"It truly is remarkable technology. If only it were possible to extract the Balloon Day Madison into the real world." Everything about his life would be complete again.

"Let your imagination roam, Orson. Who knows? Maybe one day that too could become a reality. One could only hope." She winked.

Orson chuckled. "One could only hope, yes."

Orson left, his head buzzing about brains and souls and Madison. Seeing four missed calls from Rose, he rang her back on the way to his car in the parking garage. Sounds of honking cars competed with nearby Park Avenue chatter as he waited for Rose to pick up. After the fourth ring, his sister's voice carried through his ear buds.

"Orson, are you almost here? Your son has been at my house waiting for you. It's nearly dinner time. In case you cared, when I picked him up, his teacher told me he stole a kid's lunch today."

"Hi, Rose. Yes, yes, I'm on my way over now, should be about an hour, hopefully less. I wanted to ask you if you had any of the photographs, we placed around the funeral home for Madi—wait, what did he do?"

Orson climbed in his sleek, gunmetal gray Porsche Cayenne Turbo SUV. After pushing the engine start button, he reached for the leather wheel, relishing its smoothness against his palms, soothing his nerves.

Rose's voice and frustration now transferred throughout his car as he drove out of the parking garage. "One of the other kids saw him going through lunch bags during arts and crafts time. He took one of them. I asked him why, and he said because you hadn't packed him a lunch. What the hell is going on with you?"

"Oh god, Rose. I'm so sorry. I'll speak to him. And I won't forget again."

"But that wasn't all the teacher said. He shoved a kid for not giving him a crayon. You need to do more than talk to him, Orson. He needs his father. He already lost one parent—don't let him lose two."

"I understand. Absolutely. I promise. If you could also get those photographs for me, that—"

The speakers let out a beep-boop noise. Rose had hung up.

Orson slammed the brakes. He was about to turn down a one-way street. He pulled over and knocked his fist at the wheel.

What was happening to him? Rose was correct—Ryder couldn't lose another parent. Was this hunt for Madison worth the anguish? The thought of stopping after only one encounter brought tears to his eyes.

He had to get it together for his son, and surely, this was helping his grieving process. There had to be a better way to maintain Balloon Days while still showing he was an attentive father. Orson was determined to find it.

Upon returning home, after a mostly silent car ride with Ryder—and after many apologies hoping Ryder would forgive Orson's tardiness—Ryder flung his backpack on the hardwood floor of the foyer, an inch away from the hallway closet where it was supposed to go.

Ryder was seven years old with an evolving personality. His attitude and push for independence was beginning to sprout up here and there, now more than ever. Mornings ago, Ryder refused to eat oatmeal and asked Orson to cook him pancakes. Ryder knew it would cause them to arrive late to school.

The next morning, he requested, or demanded rather, to wear his Batman pajamas to school. Orson gave in to both requests.

"Hey, bud. How was it at Aunt Rose's?" Orson said, placing a cast iron pan on the stove. He clicked the gas on, setting the flame on high.

"Fun. And guess what? We played a racing game and I won. Can you believe it? Did you know I could do that?" Ryder sat at the kitchen table, finishing up the last of his homework.

"That's fantastic, Ryder. I did not know that. But I'm not surprised." He high fived his son.

Orson dripped a couple of tablespoons of olive oil into the pan, waiting for the ripple to signal it was ready to sear, and placed two cuts of filet mignon on the pan. The steak sizzled.

Ryder walked over to the countertop next to the stove. "Can I put in the butter?"

"Absolutely, Chef Ryder."

Ryder helped throw in the butter, two cloves of garlic, and a sprig of thyme. Ryder watched as the butter became a pale gold foam, and Orson spooned it over the steak. It had been a while since they cooked together. It had been a while since Orson cooked at all.

"That smells so good." Ryder sat back down at the table as Orson pulled the roasted potatoes out of the oven. "I can't wait to eat. I miss Mom—it's weird seeing only two plates."

Orson plated the steaks and the roasted potatoes and brought them to the table. It was more than weird. It was paining.

"At least you don't make me eat broccoli," Ryder said.

Crap, the vegetables.

"I miss her very much too, kiddo. Now let's eat. This was one of your mother's favorite meals, you know. Next time though, unfortunately, we will need the broccoli."

After dinner, Orson washed the dishes while Ryder watched television in the den. As he scrubbed the dishes clean, the goofy voices of the cartoons cracked his son up.

"Alright, bud. It's getting late," Orson said as he walked into the den. "Tech time is done for the night." Orson turned the television off and was immediately met with a groan. "Before you head upstairs, I need to talk to you about what happened at school today, like with the crayon," Orson said, trying to approach the subject as lightly as possible.

"No," Ryder roared.

Orson was taken aback. Ryder was certainly expected to be upset, but not this upset. He threw a pillow at Orson, then climbed up onto the polished blue-and-white-tiled coffee table. Thousands of dollars underneath his weight.

"Ryder, get off that right—"

"I don't want to. I wanted to play with you before bedtime. You're always working. Mom played with me," he said, crossing his arms. If Ryder would just get down first, Orson could breathe again.

"Please. Get off the table first."

"No." He kicked the remote control off the table, but thankfully it didn't break when it hit the gray rug.

Orson wished he'd paid more attention when his wife would soothe Ryder's distress or outbursts. Most of him wished things would simply go back to normal. Orson was adept at working and coming home to a well-managed home. Ryder was right. He barely played with his only son.

Orson scanned the living room as if his wife would appear. But he was alone. On his own, uncertain of how to handle this situation aside from giving in. He missed every way Madison made his and Ryder's lives better, easier. Should he punish Ryder for yelling and speaking this way and potentially breaking a household item? Should he acknowledge Ryder was right and play with him while groveling for forgiveness?

What would Madison do?

"I see you have a lot of anger, buddy. You're right, though. Mom was wonderful. I know this is hard for you, and that I haven't been there. Do you think you can forgive me? What would you like to play?"

He decided on a mix of both what she would do and what he would do to gain back his son's affection. Ryder was still sulking, although his scowl softened, and he uncrossed his arms.

"Maybe you'd want to quickly go to the toy store and get something new?" Orson said.

Ryder's face lit up—he responded with resounding acceptance to Orson's proposal, jumping down from the coffee table, nearly giving Orson a heart attack, but he was relieved that his son was happy again. Orson quickly checked the surface of the table for any blemishes—still in perfect form, thank goodness—before they headed out.

About an hour later, Ryder hopped out of the car with a bag of new toys in one hand and an ice cream cone in the other. After playing together with his new set of wrestling figures, now strewn about the den room floor, Orson helped Ryder get his pajamas on and made sure he brushed his teeth. He tucked Ryder into bed two hours beyond his usual bedtime.

"I know it's a tough topic, but let the teacher know if someone took your crayon next time. Or tell me, and I'll get you more. It isn't worth getting in trouble for such a silly-goose thing." Orson tickled Ryder with his last words, getting a few choked laughs out of him.

Ryder soon closed his eyes, drifting off to sleep.

Orson returned downstairs to sift through the photographs Rose had reluctantly given him after he reassured her repeatedly it would hasten his healing process. He picked up a special one from their wedding day—the two of them, hand in hand, sitting on a bench near a lake in Central Park.

He spoke out loud in hopes that somewhere, anywhere, Madison could hear him: "Hi, my love. How are you? Can you still feel where you are? Do you remember me? I can still hear you and see you breathing. Laughing even while you were sick. Being with you until the very end. There are so many moments I wish I could forget and yet I'm glad I was with you to ease any ounce of pain I could for you.

"Ryder made a video for you because he thinks it will make you get better and 'come home.' He has your magical mindset. I hate that you felt sorry, felt that it was your fault. I hate that you suffered. I miss you so very much."

The Balloon Day he tried was so peculiar. Seeing Madison young like that felt so foreign, yet, powerful. It had been like watching home videos or looking through photographs of memories, except he had become a moving part of them, witnessing them for a second time, a chance to truly appreciate each intricate detail—a second chance to fully be there with the person he loved most.

He was haunted by remorse—he had become so preoccupied by less important things. How poignant it was, that people, including himself, could take those simple moments for granted.

It was those simple moments with her he missed the most. It's what he craved most for his Balloon Days, and thinking about what his next one would be cradled him to sleep.

CHAPTER 15
HOWARD

Howard boarded the early-morning train from Queens Station and headed to Jillian's new apartment on the outskirts of the city. He usually enjoyed the train, the sense of peacefulness he'd feel when riding them to nowhere.

Today was different. Today he was visiting Jillian and he was visiting Long Island. Two new things.

There weren't many others on the train, which surprised Howard for a Sunday morning. Then again, many people had families to spend time with and homes they wanted to relax in—something he hadn't had for over a decade now, unless he considered his Balloon Days real rather than fictitious.

With each new village the train stopped at along the way, a crumpled ball of paper underneath the seat in front of him gently rustled, stuck within its small radius, barely noticed, no longer needed anymore by anyone.

A message lit up his phone. It was John asking where he was and if Howard could come by later.

The train got closer to Jillian's station and he could feel the back of his neck sweat with worry, his thoughts flickering like a dying light bulb. He didn't know what to tell John. He slid lower in his seat, as if John knew what he was doing. As if John could see him. Maybe this was an awful, childish idea.

Howard settled with the library as his current location, telling John he could come over and clean later tonight. Hopefully, that was enough to quell any suspicion. John replied with a simple, "Okay." A simple response. A little too simple. The period at the end of John's response did nothing to mitigate Howard's anxiety. That period seemed forced, final, like John knew everything.

The train made its last stop. He grabbed the crumpled paper and pocketed it in his jeans before leaving the train.

Jillian was sitting on a bench not too far from where he exited.

Shuffling toward her, he could see and hear the ocean, smell salt in the air. She quickly spotted Howard and waved.

This was indeed a terrible idea. What if he disappointed her? What was she expecting from hanging out alone, anyway?

"Hi," she called out as he got closer. He loved her sweet-sounding voice, her sing-song tone. "It's so great to see you. How was your ride?" She stood and walked toward him.

"It was fine. Your new town looks great." Howard squished the crumpled paper in his pocket, part of him longing both he and it were back in their respective circles, where they belonged.

"Thank you," she said, laughing shyly. "I love it here. Being so close to the ocean is peaceful. Let's walk, I'll show you the beach. It's extra beautiful this time of year. Not so crowded with fall around the corner."

"You look happy," he said.

"Oh, thanks." Jillian stopped walking and turned to look at him. "As happy as that photo of me you left opened on the computer?"

Howard stared straight ahead.

Was this a setup? Did she tell John? If a train passed by, he'd jump in front of it.

"I'm messing with you, Howard. It was unexpected, but flattering. Unless you were making fun of me or something..."

Flattering. So, this wasn't a setup. She didn't think he was a creep, after all.

Surprised and relieved, he continued walking once she had. "No. Not at all."

"Well, thank you." She laughed again, a humble laugh, and made a little dance motion with her arms. Was she nervous too? She led him off the platform and onto the sidewalk toward the ocean. "I'm glad you made it out. You look nice."

Now Howard was the one to laugh, but not humbly. More of a shocked laugh, but he entertained her compliment anyway and thanked her. He adjusted his dark blue beanie. He peered down at his button-down, its many holes in the sleeves and slightly faded jeans. His mangy sneakers made worse after the few days of rain. He would buy new clothes and shoes, but with his saved-up cash now being used for Balloon Days, it wouldn't be anytime soon.

Howard had gone to at least four more Balloon Days since the first. The last two were only fifteen minutes each. Even with fifteen minutes, it was so warming to be with Jillian, albeit she was the fake version—but it seemed as if he was getting through to the real one too. As if the actual Jillian could fall in love with him in the real world.

Overall, his Balloon Day experiences were going well—aside from the random John or his ex-girlfriend, Kimmy pop-ups—in which he would quickly squash them down and regain control. He noticed he had been drinking less too. The Balloon Days often left him in a better haze than alcohol ever had.

Roaming his eyes upward again, passing by Jillian's feet in flats, her long, sun-kissed legs—the tan painfully reminding him he hadn't seen her up close in a while—peeking underneath a knee-length, flowing, brown skirt, and a black tank top tight on her slim figure underneath a dark denim jacket.

Even casually dressed, she was effortlessly and brutally gorgeous. Every time he saw her, she looked crisp, put together, radiant. John was right to want to date her, but why cheat on her?

Maybe he liked the way she appeared on his arm. It must be nice to have a beautiful woman like that on one's arm at a party or social event. Or was John's cheating his way of coping, his flaw, like whiskey had been for Howard?

Regardless, it was wrong.

Jillian shifted toward him and playfully nudged her shoulder against his. He shivered at her touch. "I'm sorry I got weird for a bit," she said. "I had to think about what you said."

A drop of rain hit Howard's nose as he was about to ask her what it was she had thought about. Jillian held out her hand, feeling the rain on her too, as nimbus clouds covered the sun, the bright town now shaded in gray. Her outstretched hand looked so delicate and soft. What would it be like to hold? Would it be as it had in his Balloon Day, or better?

"Shoot," she said. "There's a coffee shop nearby—want to sit in there while we wait for the rain to pass?" She stopped and turned to look at him.

Be in a public place together. That was something they probably could never do in the city, for fear of being seen. Or had she told John? Howard checked his phone to see if John had written again. Nothing. Not yet at least. Was that good or bad?

"I'd like that," he said. He already took a risk to see her, what was one more?

When they entered the plant-filled, well-lit café, the raven-haired barista at the counter looked their way. He assumed anyone who looked at him was judging him. Pretending to take in the detail of the space, all he could think about was his unkempt appearance. He much preferred and felt more at ease in dive bars.

"What can I get you two?" the girl said.

You two.

The words swirled around in his head. He liked the sound of it.

"A medium mocha latte, please. No whipped cream." Jillian turned to Howard. "Want anything?"

"Just a small hot coffee, thanks," Howard said.

"Any flavor?" the barista offered. "Or syrups? We have a new dark bean blend that goes well with the hazelnut syrup."

"Regular black is fine." He was unprepared for such questions.

"One plain coffee, hot. You got it," the barista said. "That'll be $7.23 total."

There was an awkward pause. Jillian reached for her wallet from her purse.

"No, wait." Howard fished through his pockets as his face burned with humiliation. The customer behind them sighed; he forgot his wallet. He could have charged his credit card. "I'm sorry. I must have left my wallet at home."

"No, no, don't worry about it," Jillian said. "You came all this way. Least I can do is get you a cup of coffee. It's on me." She quickly handed her credit card to the barista, who had to be judging now if she had not been already. Howard kept his eyes on the dark wood floor.

He had only brought enough money for the train. He was foolish for not having thought he would need more. Although this wasn't a date, he probably wouldn't know the difference if it was. It had been far too long since Howard had any of that in his life.

"So," he started as they settled into their table. "How's John doing?" He hated uttering the words, but he felt it best to get it done and over with, like a household chore.

Jillian shifted in her seat. "Don't know, to be honest. We've been arguing more lately." She made circles with the wood stirrer, a caffeinated whirlpool in her mug. She stopped and looked up. "Actually, we broke up."

"Really, when?" He was surprised, confused, and a little relieved. But that relief was short-lived as fear moved in.

"Yeah," she said. "A couple of nights ago." That explains her recent texts. "He needs to—sorry, needed to—treat me better, you know what I mean?" She fiddled with the silver bracelet on her wrist. A bracelet Howard was near-certain John had gifted her, which made it odd she had not taken it off. Was she still hopeful of salvaging the relationship? "I hope it wasn't wrong of me to ask to see you one-on-one like this. I hope you don't think it was a dumb idea." She let out a nervous laugh.

His brain froze, his mouth slightly agape. Now it was more real. A faraway infatuation with his older brother's girlfriend was one thing, but now she was single. And telling Howard about it. But that didn't matter. A big stamp on her forehead read "John's" and going anywhere closer to her than he was now would cause him death by electric shock.

He looked at Jillian, her gaze fixed on her drink. Her shoulders slumped, and her mouth subtly twitched. Was she about to cry? That made him feel worse than any electric shock ever could.

"No," he said. "It's not stupid."

"Oh. Good. That's good." Relieved eyes found his, the corners of her mouth curling into a smile. "How are you doing?"

"I'm as well as I can be," he said.

"How's the new therapy? John said you had told him that in Balloon Days your dreams come true. Sounds nice."

"Something like that." Howard said. There wasn't much else to share. He didn't want to discuss his use of Balloon Days, knowing he'd have to lie in embarrassment or risk appearing outlandishly creepy—the laptop was one thing, but playing house with a fantasy version of her was a whole other kind of weird she would unlikely find as flattering.

John telling Jillian annoyed Howard. It wasn't his information to pass along. He had no right to bring up Howard's personal life to Jillian, let alone anyone.

The only reason Howard confided in John in the first place was to make him proud of his attempts to get better; for John to stop criticizing him for his lack of progress. Howard bashed himself enough for being a failure in life—he didn't need John to berate him too. He likely delivered the news to Jillian in a mocking way. Howard could picture John telling her "My brother finally got help, that loser. It's about time."

"Well," she said, "I'm glad you're seeking help. God knows, everyone could use therapy."

"How are your auditions going?" Howard said, desperate to change the subject. The steam of the coffee warmed the top of his lip as he drank.

"Oh, you know. Random things here and there. There's actually an interesting voice-over audition for a new animated show coming out. I've never done anything like that before, you know? But it's been pretty slow, so I've been doing other things." He hated when she was vague. It made him fill in the blanks with awful scenarios. Should he trust that she and John were over?

Maybe she started dating someone else entirely, and that's what she wanted to tell Howard so he would never pester her with his feelings again.

"That's great." He bobbed his head. "I'd love to hear those voices." They both laughed, and Jillian bowed her head, her hand hiding her face as she feigned shame.

"Hopefully, you will hear," she said. "I'd love for you to. It will be the voice of the main protagonist—Sally—of an animated show called Spectacular Sally. It's about a high school student who discovers she has magical powers and uses them to help protect her bullied classmates and eliminate bullying altogether. But there's a female antagonist named Rachel, who also has superpowers."

"Of course, there's always a villain who gets in the way," he said.

"Always." She looked him in the eyes and frowned. "Anyway, it's a bit far-fetched and still being worked out, but that's the gist of it."

"Are you still getting nervous before auditions?" Howard wiped coffee off his upper lip with a napkin.

"Slightly. Nothing like that time for Breaking Ocean though. Remember that?"

"I remember. You were an anxious wreck."

"It had to be one of my worst panic attacks, I barely made it out of John's that morning." She shook her head. "I can't believe he left for work. He didn't help me at all. Thank God you were there."

I can believe it. He left you behind all the time.

"Thank God is right," he said. "If I hadn't grabbed that plastic bag in time, you'd have puked all over the couch."

"To be fair," Jillian said, "I never acted in a thriller before. I kept repeating what you said on the entire cab ride there: 'It's not a crisis; I can handle this.' You always are such a big help."

If only "always" truly meant always—maybe Howard would be happy for the rest of his life.

Jillian reached for her latte at the same time as he reached for his coffee, the backs of their fingers lightly grazing each other, the softness of her skin making him forget the rain hammering down on the pavement ruining their walk to the beach.

Jillian looked down at her phone, blushing, but within seconds her face dropped with frustration.

"Ugh."

"What's wrong?" Howard put his coffee mug down.

"Oh. Um." She shifted in her seat. This was the part, Howard knew, where she'd say it was John and that she'd have to leave and take the call. "It's my sister. She's pissed I haven't called her yet today like I said I would."

Howard's nerves eased. "You two are speaking again?"

"Oh yeah, you can say that. She's going through a breakup. Mindy's still, like, controlling about if I don't respond, you know what I mean? Starts to say I don't love her anymore, especially when she's upset, then she starts talking all kinds of crazy. I'm debating on not responding for longer this time, so she learns I won't put up with that." Jillian tossed her phone in her open purse on the floor. "I'm sorry. I must be the one who sounds crazy."

"Not at all. I'm sorry you still have to go through that. I hate seeing you upset." Howard was sorry, but he did wonder if Jillian felt the same way about him at times, if that's why she'd disappear on him too, leave him all alone. Was he as overwhelming? He had the shriveling-within-his-own-body feeling, the feeling that whispered, "You are a nobody." It made him feel small, quieting him into nothingness.

Jillian sighed, glancing down at her bag again. "I'll deal with it later. Where were we? Aside from you being so sweet. I can't believe you and John are related sometimes. I wish he was as kind as you."

Jillian's praise revived his existence, made it easier to push the belittling voice aside. He had never thought anything like that—that John could, or should, envy something about Howard. It was hard to believe.

After an hour or so of conversing about their reviews of animated shows, to prepare Jillian for her audition (the voices of the characters were indeed important), then the differences in music throughout the decades (both agreed the '90s carried the most diversity), they ran back to the train station, laughing as they surrendered to sodden clothes.

She accompanied him onto the platform—the train already approaching. She looked at him. Jillian was only inches shy of Howard's six-foot stature, standing there with her hair wet, mouth partly opened, hesitant.

"I hope I can see you again soon," she said.

"Me too." Howard filled with anticipation. He could sacrifice another library visit for her. "Next Sunday?"

"I'd love that," she said.

Her eyes met his, lingering there.

Howard panicked. Was this the moment you kissed a girl? Was this the signal? Or Jillian's personal one?

There was no time to consider it. He settled on giving her a hug; she hugged him back, leaning her body into his, warm and drenched, the scoop of her black tank clinging to the delicate lines of her collarbone.

As they separated from each other, it felt natural to take Jillian's hands in his. Balloon Days seemed to be giving him confidence after all—and it was clear Jillian was noticing.

He needed more guidance, more insight. Howard had the choice to pay the electric bill on time or to buy another fifteen minutes at the Center. The answer was obvious: another Balloon Day.

The train that Howard wished would never arrive released the automated beeping sounds that warned the doors were about to close, and he reluctantly released her hands to rush inside.

From the window, Howard watched her stroll away. Even as his phone buzzed from John he was smiling—genuinely—for the first time in years.

CHAPTER 16
ELLIOTT

The awaited evening arrived. Birthday party, pub, Brooklyn. And Evan. As seven o'clock approached, Elliott finally settled on wearing a fitted black dress, a black leather jacket, and black booties.

Perfect weather for it. End-of-summer-soon-to-be-fall kind of weather. Elliott said goodbye to her Havenese, Captain, with a pat and a kiss on his furry head. Off to Julie's she drove, moonroof open, breeze in her hair.

"You look great," Julie said. "I bet Evan will agree."

"Oh, yeah, totally what I was aiming for," Elliott said with sarcasm, although it would be amazing if Evan did notice.

Wait, amazing was too strong of a word—she barely knew him—but it would be "cool." Only because he seemed like a nice guy; he would make a great friend.

Maybe Julie hoped Evan would change Elliott's mind tonight, causing Elliott to immediately dump Asher. A strong catalyst was all it took to set big decisions in motion.

Was that what Elliott was waiting for too? Something out of her control to put her in control and decide officially to stay or go before Asher would decide for them?

The stupid and unnecessary Halloween deadline was pressing in, after all. Why was she jumping through these hoops? There should never have been a deadline in the first place, even if his intentions somehow seemed sincere at the time.

The mind could be so confusing. Matters of the heart more so. It was much easier to help others with their lives than her own.

"What's new with you?" Elliott said. She grew tired of her love life being the topic of discussion.

"Finally got a paycheck after five weeks," Julie said. "Such a joke." She flipped the mirror open and checked her makeup. "I won't stay there for much longer if it stays like this."

"Maybe give it until the end of the year?"

"We'll see. Don't worry. I'll make sure I have a plan lined up before I leave. I didn't take on school loan debt and work my ass off to work for someone who can't pay me on time. My dad said to keep my mouth shut. To suck it up. And for what? To hold myself back? To be trapped in a cocoon of misery like he is. Never."

Elliott envied Julie's willingness to leave a situation that wasn't working well for her. Although she wondered if Julie was too hasty at times, like when she refused a second date with a girl because she talked about why she broke up with her ex-girlfriend. Julie had commented, "Too much, too soon." Elliott believed that kind of information could reveal a lot about someone's character.

When Elliott and Julie arrived at Blue Velvet's, a bar blending the vibes of dive and upscale, they made their way through the crowd to the familiar faces in the back corner near the touchscreen jukebox. Evan perused the songs.

Elliott's heart beat rather quickly. She scanned the crowded room, from the bar's open floor area to the mocha-brown wood booths and tables on the opposite side, her blood nearly jumping out of her veins. What was she so anxious about?

Relax, Elliott. It's your friends. Who cares if Evan is here too?

"Hi there, hey. Did you want to order a drink?" Elliott was startled by the bespectacled nose-pierced waitress, who seemed to come out of nowhere.

"Oh, hey," Elliott said, projecting her voice and hoping to be heard over the music. "I'll have a vodka and Sprite, please." Alcohol would surely calm her nerves.

"You got it."

As Elliott turned back around, there was Evan.

And Nicole, with Melinda by her side wearing a tight shirt squeezing her breasts so high up and so close together that they resembled a rear-end on her chest.

"Hey there, girlies," Melinda shouted, barreling through the crowd. "Excuse me, hello, wake up," she yelled at a guy who was blocking her path. He shot her a look before moving out of the way.

Nicole, with her glossy dirty blonde hair, full, pouty pink lips, and round blue eyes came up to Elliott and Julie. "Ahhh, I'm so happy to see you, Elliott, you look amazing. You too, Julie."

They thanked her, complimented her floral romper, then greeted the rest of their friends.

Evan shimmied close to Elliott. "What's up?" He leaned in and gave her a quick hug hello. His scent lingered. Elliott's nose for smells, a skill she developed since working at the Center, told her it was a blend of vanilla, bergamot, and sandalwood, a refreshing mash-up of romance and masculinity. "Told you we'd get some hangs in soon."

Evan was warm, extremely cute, and his golden-brown hair made the yellow hues of his blue eyes pop. He had straight teeth, his jaw strong and square—a bit like Asher's, except Evan's has a dimple in the middle of his chin—and his cheeks rosy-white.

Oh gosh, he was perfect. Elliott was screwed.

She noticed any woman around him vying for his attention; her sweet friend Nicole transformed into public enemy number one, and she wanted to slap that bitch away. What the hell was going on with her?

The waitress brought her drink, and Evan turned to clink his glass of fizzy brown beer against hers.

"Cheers," he said, holding his drink out toward Elliott.

"Cheers." She tapped her glass against his and drank.

Now, think of a topic, keep him engaged.

It was important to learn more about him after all, and maybe find some type of flaw so that her curiosity could be crushed for good.

"So, what have you been up to?" Elliott said. "Rescue any more fallen phones?"

It wasn't exactly the best or most exciting line, or atmosphere, for delving into someone's lifestyle, but it was better than nothing and him then walking away.

"Just keeping busy with work and volunteering," he yelled over the music. And, no, yours had been my first and last apparently," he said. "It was an honor to be your phone's hero."

Elliott took a sip of her drink, smiling. "Where do you volunteer?"

"I volunteer for a soccer class on the weekends. It's for little kids. I'm one of the coaches. It's a pretty cool gig," he said, his head slightly bouncing up and down with his last few words.

"That's awesome to hear," Elliott said. Some would consider Evan their dream guy, that was for sure. "Definitely not something you hear often." Why was she saying hear so much? She was acting so unbelievably awkward.

"Why do you think that is?" he said.

"What? For why people don't volunteer?"

"Yeah," he said. "You said it's not something you hear often."

"People are too busy working. I mean, that is what we are supposed to do, work—and have to work—in order to get paid and live. We are then typically selfish with our free time."

"Do you volunteer or are you the selfish type?" he said with a smirk, teasing.

Elliott faltered as she searched for the right response. She did volunteer here and there, but it had been some time. Truthfully, it was often to boost her resume. She didn't want to fib, but she was embarrassed.

"A mix of the two," she said. It was true. "You must be selfish sometimes too, though. Don't lie."

He shrugged, smirking. "Depends on how you define selfish. You could say I'm being selfish right now by wanting your attention, right?"

A tingling sensation flowed from her stomach to her head, like bubbles rising in a flute of champagne.

"Where do you work?" she said, changing the subject. She was dating Asher, after all, and she had to ignore the yearning to flirt in return. "Sorry, you don't have to talk about work. I am sure you want to have fun tonight." Droplets of sweat formed on her forehead. She took a longer sip of her drink and quickly wiped the sweat away when he wasn't looking.

"No worries." He raised his glass to her. "I'm in healthcare management. I work for Brain Health and Wellness in the city. It's pretty decent. And they're flexible about hours. What about you?"

"My job is also in the city." What an interesting coincidence. "I'm a clinical psychologist, I work at the Center of Balloon Days. My home is in Long Island though, so there's a lot of back and forth."

"That sounds awesome. I live in Long Island too, and yeah, that commute can be a killer. I've actually heard of the Center I think I work right—"

Melinda popped in between them—her chest barely bouncing suggesting Elliott and Julie were right about the implants—and wrapped her arms around each.

"Birthday shots, y'all?" she said, sounding like she already had a few herself.

Evan pulled away and looked at Elliott. "I'm down. You in, Elliott?"

"Why not?" Elliott said.

"Hey, Nicole, Julie." Evan called out. "Round up Scott and the others, we are going to do some group shot action."

They hustled over, Nicole being the first to arrive. "Hell yeah," she said, smiling at him. He smiled back. Elliott imagined how great it would be if she could erase people.

The rest of the night involved more Evan. They had found a table in a quieter spot, to avoid further shouting at each other. She learned about his hobbies of writing short stories and playing guitar, the new recipes he'd cooked, how he recently took his dad out for dinner to celebrate both of their job promotions.

She also learned that his mom had died in a horrific car accident on the way to the grocery store when he was twenty years old; the image of his younger self, receiving the news from his dad, weighed heavy on Elliott's heart.

"Thankfully, my dad and I helped each other get through it," Evan said.

"I do believe support is the key to healing, not time," Elliott said.

"Time passes regardless of pain," he added. "It's all about who you surround yourself with and what you do with that time that matters most. You learn to move forward with the pain best you can—there's no leaving it behind. That's how it is for me, at least."

Julie was right, darn it. Elliott and Evan did have a lot in common. Questions rooted in Elliott's mind, her confusion growing. Was it possible

Asher and her could actually work on their compatibility? Or had that ship already sunk?

Julie threw several winks at Elliott throughout the night, as she flirted with her own target—a short, dark-and-shiny-haired girl named Lily, a friend of Nicole's. From what Julie spilled to Elliott in the bathroom, Lily was a labor and delivery nurse from the South Shore of Long Island and shared Julie's love of snowboarding.

Eventually, everyone got ready to leave after midnight, Elliott mildly panicking about Captain being okay when she realized the time. Evan gave her a hug goodbye. "Give your dog a pat on the head for me."

Elliott laughed. "I will."

He leaned closer, his breath against her ear. "Let's hang out soon?"

She thought of Asher. Let's give it 'til the day after the party. His words echoed in her head.

Asher hung out with Clara; Elliott could have a new friend, too. "Yeah," she said. "Let's do that."

Elliott tried to hide the stupid cheesy grin pushing its way out.

CHAPTER 17
ORSON

Weekday mornings flustered Orson. The routine of the past dwindled since Madison died. Heart-shaped pancakes for breakfast, Ryder's favorite music playing while he showered and brushed his teeth, then dressing into his chosen outfit (with her help), all were buried fossils lost in time.

The only evidence a morning routine existed, was Ryder's fifteen minutes of television time that turned into forty-five. Ryder refused to budge, regardless of Orson's persistent requests for him to shower and eat breakfast, so they could leave on time for school.

Today, it was extra important for Ryder to shorten his new routine. Orson had scheduled a Balloon Day session for that morning. He did the only thing he knew that worked as the fastest incentive—bribing Ryder with a new toy if he readied himself in a timely fashion.

After arriving at the school with time to spare, Orson asked Ryder's teacher for a quick word about Ryder's recent wrongdoings. He made sure to smooth things over with Miss Taple, by explaining how things were tough right now with Madison gone, effectively tugging at her heartstrings.

Orson headed over to the Center. Realizing he hadn't notified work yet of his absence, he called the firm's receptionist to let her know. Five minutes later, Jack called and filled the car with his booming voice.

"What's going on, pal? Are you really that sick?"

"It seems to be a persistent, relentless little thing."

"This is the third time in two weeks you've called off. You said you were okay to work, but if you're still not, don't pretend." There was a short pause. "We can hand off some of your cases to Veronica, or that new guy."

Orson closed his car windows, glancing apologetically at the car next to him. Thankfully, the light turned green.

"Listen, I'm gonna be real with you, Orson. We need to keep these clients. Your last-minute absences aren't working out for me, or them. I don't want to be a drag, but my wife is bitching how we aren't spending enough time together, need a vacation, blah blah blah.

"You know how invested I am in you, but I am going to have to hand over these cases to another junior lawyer here if you don't think you can handle it right now. I can't keep taking care of your clients for you and making up excuses."

"I understand your concerns. I just need a little extra rest. Nothing to worry about. I'll be good as new after the weekend." A car honked in the other lane at a car that nearly smashed into him. Orson winced.

"Are you driving?"

"No." Orson paused. "Just the television."

"If you say so, bud. Don't disappoint me. See you after the weekend."

Orson could not let his grief get the best of him. Images of downgrading his home, his cars, Ryder's education, played in his mind. He promised himself he would make it to work on Monday to ensure his cases were handled, his future as a firm partner secured. Come hell or high water, he'd make it work.

After suffering through traffic, he made it to the parking garage across the street from the Center.

Orson ascended in the blue elevator, reaching his Elite Day Room quickly. The control hung before him, the button taunting. His stomach let out digestive noises, but they weren't due to hunger—it was the squiggly feeling he got in the lower bowel area after having eaten take-out.

Aside from the recent filet mignon meal, that's what most of his and Ryder's meals were lately, unless Rose came over to cook. It reminded him of his father—but back then fast food was considered a treat.

He pressed the button on the control, as he read aloud the scripted words marked around it to no one: "Have a Great Balloon Day."

The floating sensation swept over him, clearing his body, clearing his mind. By his third blink, the room was replaced with an old apartment. It was the first apartment he and his wife rented together before marriage.

As Orson looked around, everything appeared as they had arranged it then. There was a sense of wrongness to it, a feeling of death and emptiness. There were hardly any noises at all aside from his breathing.

A traditional railroad apartment in Queens, the rooms were all laid out in a straight path, a series of connected rooms. At the start of the apartment was the kitchen, followed by the living room in which the main door was located, a den, and lastly, their bedroom.

The den had been transformed into a shared creative space where Madison practiced violin, and Orson would read or study for mock trials in his squashy, brown corduroy recliner.

He walked along the length of the apartment until he reached their old bedroom. The stale quietness lingered, as if no one had lived there for decades. If his perception were truly leading him, then why could he not hear anyone speaking on the streets below?

Deciding to peer out of the windows to see if he could, at the very least, see any neighbors or passersby, he lifted the sheer white curtain. What he found was unexpected. The street, the lively 49th Street, wasn't there. Instead, there was a sidewalk, blurry and gray.

Was he going blind? He looked back into the room to find his vision was clear. Odd. Once again, he peered through the window, the jumbled gray sidewalk still there.

A chill trickled down his spine. Lowering himself on the creaky, low bed, the comforter still the same pale green as it had been then, he tried to collect himself. It was short lived.

Music abruptly filled the room—a gentle, sweet song his wife used to play. Orson pulled at his collar. He had enough of the mysterious games. He tiptoed back into the den, and to his surprise, there she was, sitting on a stool in the corner of the room, the music growing louder.

Madison was her younger self again, though older than last time, possibly mid-twenties, around the age she had been when they leased the apartment. She placed the violin on the floor and turned around.

"Orson," she yelped, heading toward him.

Orson opened his arms, but as he went to embrace her, he lost his balance, arms swooshing right through. Catching himself, he turned to face her again. She remained where she was, now swaying back and forth, slightly translucent and humming the melody she had been playing a moment ago.

Orson was puzzled. He pushed his hair back in frustration, wanting to pull it out instead. The first Balloon Day was jovial and realistic and he could touch her, hold her, kiss her. Despite its ending, he was hoping to experience that again, no matter how fleeting.

Madison's holographic image disappeared with a popping sound, like a pouncing kernel over the fire. The melody vanished with it.

This was strange and beyond frustrating. He searched through the den in hopes of finding a clue. An old painting lay on the floor of a lake against a sunset. He had painted it himself. Madison encouraged him to keep going, no matter how many times he wanted to give up.

He recalled a song she practiced on the violin the day he finished it, and as soon as its melody entered his memory, the song began to play aloud—the bow of the violin releasing each note as if an invisible player glided it against the strings. The melody was light and beautiful, a melody Madison believed would be a song butterflies hummed if they could.

Commotion near the front of the apartment disrupted the song, the violin now still, and the air silent. He peered down the narrow hallway. Something stirred in the kitchen.

Orson had to walk through the living room first, but as soon as he reached it, a thick and foul smell hit him in the nose and stopped him in his tracks—something rotten, decomposing, like hot trash. It was an acrid, suffocating stench, one of sulfur and skunk and vomit and excrement all at once. He covered his nose with his sleeve, edging closer to the kitchen entrance.

As he took one more step, he fell backward and grasped for the wall, falling onto his rear with a thud. About five feet away, his son Ryder was sitting in a pool of blood, blood that was dripping down from his crying eyes onto his shirt and pants in the middle of the floor. The blood spread like crimson snakes winding along the rivulets of the white tile.

The blood permeated through the floor as if quietly sucked away, the tiles now white again. What the hell was going on? Ryder vanished, but within seconds his small voice returned. Orson spun to face the living room.

"Oh, hey, Dad. Everything is okay now." Ryder sat in a pile of ash-gray dirt. As Orson edged closer to what he thought was a homogenous mound, solid white pebbles came into focus. Ryder sifted through the ashen pile. "Look. I found her jaw. Can I keep it?" He happily held it up, a grin stretching across his face. "If I find more, we can rebuild Mommy."

A tattered yellow dress lay nearby, strands of strawberry red hair lying on top like a wig. Orson clutched his chest at the horrific sight.

Yet, a part of him believed they could rebuild her.

CHAPTER 18
ELLIOTT

October had announced its arrival with shades of orange, golden yellow, soft browns, and crimson reds. Jack-o-lanterns sat alongside speckled green and yellow gourds on porches, and nutmeg, cinnamon, and cloves wafted in the air of Long Island.

It was a graceful, gradual change of season from summer to fall and a chance to reflect and renew, a reminder that things can change—that life itself can change, from a moment to a series of moments, like a pebble hitting the water radiating a wave of rings, each influenced by the last's momentum.

When would that pebble arrive for Elliott's life? And what would the ripples be?

In her office, Elliott finished up her notes for the day. As she reached for her belongings to place in her newly gifted tote bag with compartments, from Dr. Heller, which wasn't that much better, her phone lit up. It was Orson. It was unlike him to call out of the blue.

After she answered, she put him on speakerphone as she neatened her desk, placing pens and notepads inside the drawer.

"I have some questions regarding the Balloon Day process," he said. "Normally I would ask Dr. Heller about this, but she is away this week, as I'm sure you know—plus, I figured I'd get a second opinion. You said you have your own Balloon Days, correct?"

He sounded concerned, bordering anxious—another unusual behavior for Orson. Similar to how Howard sounded when he said his Balloon Day had perplexed him after his first experience.

"Yes, I have my own Balloon Days." Elliott finished tidying her desk and swiveled in her chair to see the sun dipping below Manhattan, painting the horizon in burning red.

"Has anything unexpected ever happened?" he said. "Not from your conscious control?"

"Yes, but Dr. Heller said it is normal. That it's our unconscious mind showing us what we're trying to suppress. So don't avoid it. It's best to go along with it. That's how you take back control." Elliott still questioned it, wondering why her mind would be a bully. But it also made perfect sense.

Many of Elliott's patients up until now had been simpler cases assigned by Dr. Heller. Not many patients reported issues, just fears, as they were advised to purposely place themselves in situations that triggered anxiety, starting from the gentlest scenario working their way up in order to expose themselves to the situations in a safely controlled environment.

One patient had a fear of flying, and first tested out sitting on a parked plane with the cabin door open, working their way up to flying in the air, to then being the actual pilot themselves.

"Huh," Orson said. "That's what she told me too."

"Are you sure you are okay? I know you're dealing with a much more complex use of the Balloon Days." Elliott's cell buzzed with a text from Asher letting her know when he'd pick her up for the Halloween party. "Maybe try another one, or take a break from them for now?"

As soon as she said the words, she regretted it. Dr. Heller would be disappointed in her; Elliott's job was to advocate for Balloon Days, no matter what.

"The Balloon Days are extremely helpful for my grieving process," he answered. "No need to stop."

Relieved by his response, Elliott replied to Asher, then plugged her headphones into her cell phone. "I completely trust your judgment, but you are always welcome to tell me or, of course, Dr. Heller. The best suggestion I can think of is to ask for a new Day Room. Have a fresh start."

"Good idea. Thanks for your time, Elliott. Have a good night." He hung up.

Her mouth twisted to the side of her face. Elliott had to be careful to not suggest too much, to not turn into his therapist. But she also did not want to cut off communication completely in case Orson had anything "unexpected" happen again, especially since she was the one to have suggested he come to the Center in the first place. She'd hate herself if something bad happened to him, especially for Ryder's sake.

After she collected her things, Elliott made her way home to dress for the party.

It was finally the night of Dave's annual Halloween bash—a week before Halloween—and Elliott's relationship deadline. Dressed up and antsy, she peeked out her front window waiting for Asher.

She hurried to the bathroom to double check if her dark makeup had smudged or if she needed more of it. Her eye color and long lashes were highlighted by thick black eyeshadow swept across and around each eye, extending to each temple, her lips a deep burgundy.

Her irises appeared brighter with the surrounding makeup; green like granny smith apples, with darker rays fanning out from each pupil. Her hair, swept in an updo, normally swung just below her shoulders. Its color—newly dyed red-violet—was as vibrant as the autumn leaves before they crumbled like chips beneath her feet.

A car door slammed shut. Elliott made way to the foyer, and through the bay window, she could see Asher approaching the front door. Before he could knock, she swung it open.

Asher gave her a quick peck, then pulled away to check her out. "You look great, babe." She wore a black tutu with white tights underneath, the ballerina from Black Swan, while Asher wore a plain white t-shirt and a red cap.

"What are you supposed to be?" she said.

"You can't tell? I'm an off-duty baseball player," he said, as if it was the most obvious thing in the world. "Let's get going." He leaned halfway out the door. "We have lots to celebrate—Halloween and the deadline being removed. I realized it would be in my best interest to stay. Love you, babe."

"Your best interest?" Elliott started tugging at her eyebrow. Although she felt relieved, she didn't feel as happy as she thought she would. "What is that supposed to mean?"

"It means I can see your progress already. And, you know, working for your dad and everything."

"Maybe it should be my turn to give you one now," Elliott joked with a blank smile.

"You wouldn't do that. It's in your best interest, too." He smirked.

She squeezed her eyebrow.

"Don't squeeze, Ellie. Nothing is wrong. I'm messing with you. I love you."

She pinched it one more time, before returning her arm to her side. *Was it in her best interest?*

It did make things a lot more convenient. To start dating all over again seemed exhausting, and dealing with Dad's disapproval gave her a headache just thinking about it. Asher wasn't that bad outside of his stupid moments; on paper, anyone would agree he was a smart choice. This was another one of those stupid moments. Those stupid, aggravating, confusing moments.

Thirty minutes later, they arrived at Dave's, an impressive house with a grand living room that clearly could fit over a hundred people. Most rooms were lit by purple and orange lights strung throughout the place and packed with costumed guests, many of those she recognized from the gym, dancing and chatting away, talking over one another.

Mostly all who was there appeared drunk already. A guy dressed as Batman stumbled into another dressed as some shirtless wrestler with a replica of a championship belt. Thankfully, they stayed out of character and laughed it off.

Some costumes were more creative—a guy with four types of spectacles calling himself "foresight," while others were more revealing—the typical skimpy version of any career of your choosing.

Was Evan at a Halloween party, too? If Nicole was there, was she wearing something revealing or creatively stunning? A pit grew in her stomach; it was nonsensical to care about, so why did she think about it in the first place? She had to stay focused, had to figure out if Asher was the one worth her attention. Without his ridiculous deadline, she had more time to assess the relationship.

Entering the kitchen that rivaled Dad's, many were pouring mixed drinks into red plastic cups, or cracking open cans of Bud Light. Guys filled the refrigerator with more thirty packs of beer.

A girl dressed as an angel, ironically with spilling cleavage, passed by and Asher practically lasered a hole through her ass as he watched her walk. Before Elliott could slap his arm and shoot him a glare as fierce as his stare had been, Dave interrupted.

"Great costumes, you two. Hope you're having fun."

"Thanks," Elliott said, silently disagreeing about Asher's costume also being great.

"Amazing party, man," Asher chimed in. "Lives up to the hype. Where's your bathroom?"

Asher received the directions and left. After about ten minutes of enduring small talk with Dave, Elliott began to feel antsy again. Where the hell was Asher? He should have been back by now.

She grabbed another drink hoping to mitigate her restlessness. She prayed the buzz would arrive sooner rather than later. She wasn't the best in large group settings; she much preferred one on one. It quieted her brain's tendency to overanalyze both her own behavior and that of others.

Elliott left the kitchen with her red cup of vodka and Sprite, and re-entered the loud living room, with only the orange and purple strung lights to guide her. She stopped. Asher stood near the sofa, chatting up a girl in a skimpy Chucky costume. Why did they have to make a half-naked costume for everything? It limited women's costume choices and lacked creativity.

Elliott continued walking toward them, pissed off at Asher for abandoning her. She could make out the girl's face behind the drawn-on freckles and cheap bright red—more like copper—wig. It was Clara. Could this night get any worse?

"Hey, Clara. Great to see you, Happy Halloween," Elliott lied loudly over the blaring techno music.

Clara giggled. "Aw, hey there. I was just telling Asher how, like, amazingly clever his costume is. So, so adorable." She touched his arm. "Shows off his hard work at the gym, too, right?"

Who does she think she is, touching my boyfriend in front of my face?

Elliott wrapped her arm around Asher's waist. "He always looks good."

"True," Clara said, bouncing on the balls of her feet. "How fun is this party? I was worried you guys wouldn't make it."

"What do you mean?" Elliott said. Her grip on Asher's waist loosened.

"Oh, like, a few weeks ago, Asher was saying you guys might—"

Asher loudly cleared his throat and yelled, "That was going to be a surprise, Clara." He looked at Elliott. "I considered taking you to Salem instead."

"Right," Clara said with a raised eyebrow. "I am going to go dance. Want to join me?" She winked at Asher.

"Sure," Asher shouted. "Only if Elliott will, though."

Surprised, Elliott downed the rest of the vodka, then nodded. She placed her empty cup on the nearest end table. Clara grabbed both Asher's and Elliott's hands and led them to where the other guests were dancing.

As they pushed through the crowd, Asher yelled to Elliott, "I'm sorry. She has no clue what she says sometimes."

"Honestly, I don't care," Elliott yelled back, surprised she meant it. The alcohol was helping loosen her up. Although it was obvious Asher had told Clara they were fighting, Elliott was the one here with Asher, not her.

As soon as they reached the dance floor, Clara swung her hips near Asher's, and waved her hands around to the beat. Asher's eyes roved up and down Clara's figure as he began to dance too. Part of Elliott wanted to punch Clara. A bigger part of her wanted to win the proper way.

Elliott pulled Asher close, let the rhythmic music drown her thoughts, and moved her body against his. Asher's eyes shifted and fixed on Elliott. He put his arms around her.

Clara sang the lyrics at Asher; when that failed to gain his attention, she slowly twirled, her flat butt in the stupid overalls dress, now facing them. Desperate and cringey.

Dave broke through the crowd, forcing Clara out of the way. He was handing out red Jell-O shots, as if he knew Elliott needed to keep her cool to beat this Clara boyfriend-stealing bitch. Elliott grabbed one and let the cold Jell-O slide down her throat.

"I love this side of you," Asher yelled.

Placing his hand on Elliott's lower back, he pulled her closer and grazed his lips against her neck, sending a shiver down her spine.

"You want to get out of here?" she asked him.

He quickly nodded. Elliott had won.

Bye, Clara.

They dashed out and hurried to his car, the night cold, her eyes faintly blurry from the shots and mixed drinks. She scrambled into the passenger seat as he climbed into the driver's.

"You're okay to drive, right?" she said.

"Ellie, c'mon. Not everyone is a lightweight like you. Plus, I pocketed this for when we get back." He pulled a bottle of tequila out from his leather jacket and handed it to her.

Elliott smirked and shoved it in her bag. She checked her makeup as Asher drove. Lipstick must have been stolen by her red cup, as most of it was faded. She grabbed a tissue out of the glove compartment, removing the rest.

"Keep the black on your eyes," Asher said.

They rushed into her house, escaping the cold. He darted off to the kitchen to pour shots for each of them, then took a couple of swigs directly from the bottle. Two and a half shots later for her, and four more for him, the tequila was buzzing through her blood, tingly and warm. They waltzed upstairs to her bedroom.

As soon as they reached the room, Captain scurried underneath her bed. Asher unbuttoned his pants. "Wait. Do you have a condom?" Elliott said. He rustled with his jeans as they reached his ankles, then kicked them aside. Then, pulled his shirt over his head, tossed it on the floor too. "Asher, do you?"

Before she could say another word, he pushed her onto the bed, pressed against her, his lips on her mouth, biting hers and pulling with his teeth, so forcefully her bottom lip cracked. Part of it was sexy, that he wanted her that badly, but it was also painful, despite being drunk. The taste of copper hit her tongue.

It was dark, the moonlit night eerily quiet, and everything happened so quickly she couldn't keep track. Her tutu and tights were thrown somewhere on the floor. His boxers and her underwear long gone. His hands roaming around her chest, around her waist. Lifting her up, flipping over with her, repositioning her on top with ease.

"We should r-r-really get a... a condom," she heard herself slur.

"Yeah, I did, shhhh." He pulled her head down toward his and kissed her hard again.

The absorbed tequila now numbed all thought and she surrendered, unaware of anything but the euphoric pleasure firing sparks out of every nerve.

When it was over, her head spun while she was splayed on the bed. She traced a sliver of moonlight across her stomach.

Asher stood up, slightly visible in the night sky glow, mumbling some garbled nonsense. "Oh, whoops, looks like I, u-u-uh—I actually forgot. The condom. Do-y-you-have-any-pretzels?"

Elliott giggled. "H-hey, wait... what?"

"Pretzels? Mm?"

"No," she said and laughed again. "Didge you say something about a condor, I mean, the, condom?" Breaking through her inebriated trance, she suddenly remembered how she hadn't grabbed it. "Did you?"

"Oh yeah, forgot. To put one on. Oh, well, oh wellie-oh, Ellio. You're, aren't you like on the pill or something?" He belched. "Right?"

She shot up, head whirling, as he climbed back into the bed. "No... I told you I had to temporarily stop. How could you have forgotten?"

"Well... Well, you... you should've noticed." Asher nudged her. "Move over," he whined.

She crawled out from the other side of her bed, throwing on whatever pajamas were at the top of her drawer.

"What should we do?" she said.

Silence.

"Hello-o-o? Ash?" She shook his foot. "Asher. What should we do?"

Nothing. Ridiculous. How could he fall asleep, nothing else said? He was acting so irresponsible. She—she couldn't recognize herself right now. How could she have been so careless?

Maybe she wanted him to change so badly that she was changing herself.

Elliott washed the dark, heavy makeup off her face in the bathroom, the black filling the sink as it wandered down the drain. She applied

Vaseline on her cracked bottom lip. She returned to her room, turned the ceiling fan on, and climbed back into bed.

Laying herself down next to her idiot of a boyfriend, she stared at the ceiling fan buzzing its familiar hum. A noise that usually comforted her as she fell asleep. But right now, it was acutely loud and noticeable. Sleep was nowhere in sight.

Two hours went by and she still hadn't fallen asleep nor was fully sober enough to drive to a store for the emergency pill. Her stomach groaned. She went downstairs into the kitchen and ate the pretzels Asher had asked for to settle the oncoming nausea.

She should call a cab and get on with it. There was no way pregnancy fit her timeline for the foreseeable future—she had her mind set on thirty-two years old as the best age to have her first child. No exceptions.

Twenty minutes later, Elliott slipped into a taxi and was driven to the nearest 24-hour pharmacy. She asked the driver to wait while she went inside. Humiliated, she accepted the Plan B from the pharmacy tech, paid for it, and scrammed out of there in case she somehow crossed paths with anyone she knew at this hour.

God, what if Evan was there?

When Elliott arrived home, she ambled to the kitchen, poured herself a glass of water, and swallowed the tiny pill, while also swallowing the bitter truth as to what might occur if it somehow did not work. All there was left to do for now was sleep.

Elliott quietly opened the bedroom door and there Asher was, sleeping soundly, not a care in the world. She slipped into bed. Tossing and turning for nearly an hour and several calming mantras later, sleep remained nonexistent.

She read the clock. It was now five in the morning.

She lifted the covers and whispered the magic words to her dog: "Time for a walk." Asher remained on his stomach in a snoring slumber.

Captain popped his furry head up as Elliott scooted back out of bed. He jumped off and headed toward the bedroom door. As soon as she opened it, he trotted to the front of the house waiting for his leash.

Elliott and her Havenese wandered into the quiet neighborhood, meandering past glowing houses, green and orange, with headstones and skeletons and pumpkins spread out on their lawns. It had rained and the air was foggy, lending the homes an eerier appearance.

She wasn't sure what to make of the last eight hours or how to feel. If her night was a comic strip of emotions, it would appear like this: a frustrated Elliott; a jealous Elliott; a triumphant Elliott; a drunk Elliott; an ashamed Elliott—now a confused Elliott.

Should she be the one to feel ashamed? Sure, she drank way too much. She did not double check if Asher secured a condom. Undoubtedly, she took accountability for those things.

He lied. Inebriation aside, Elliott assumed a man could tell whether or not his penis had a condom on it. Unless Asher's brain consisted of nothing but gym exercises and ways to potentially ruin Elliott's life.

As Elliott stared at her dog sniffing the wet ground, realizing she nearly plucked an eyebrow hair out, she contemplated a life without Asher. Dad would be upset; it would cause tension between the three of them— but it's not as if she'd have to hear too much about Asher—she could avoid Dad for a while if so, without any hesitation.

She would feel lonely though. She'd have to start all over in the harsh dating world. Asher did keep her motivated to exercise, as well as to be a more positive person.

He lied tonight. He had given her a deadline. Also, he could really, really be a dick. The thoughts drained her.

Her dog tugged on the leash, snapping her back to reality. The dew on the grass became ink for Captain's paws. She watched as he stamped paw prints on the pavement before making her way back home.

A few days after having taken the emergency pill, Monday arrived, and Elliott was back to work. She did her best to distract herself from thoughts of babies.

She should highly likely be safe with having taken the pill within hours of the unprotected sex, increasing its efficacy. Julie agreed.

Asher didn't seem to care much about the whole thing, though. He had handed her money to cover the expense as if it were cash he owed Elliott for dinner.

Elliott had been avoiding Asher's requests to hang out since the night of Dave's party, mostly out of anger and more confusion about whether to break up with him. The control had returned to her hands, but she didn't know what to do with it.

Elliott's indecisiveness frustrated Julie and now it was beginning to frustrate herself.

She had to shake these feelings off. It was the day of her intake appointment with her new patient, Howard Nor.

A little less than an hour before Howard's arrival, Elliott slipped out to grab a coffee down the block. Once she turned the corner, the street was livelier and buzzing, with noises of drills being used inside buildings under construction, the bustling of people in their fall fashion—scarves and warm colorful layers—carrying shopping bags or work totes and talking to one another, store owners standing in front of their shops. All energizing her almost as much as coffee could.

The Split Bean was a small and quaint coffee house with a menu full of delicious seasonal lattes. As she scanned the new autumn drinks written on the chalkboard wall, debating between cinnamon fig and maple pecan, someone tapped her shoulder.

"Elliott?"

She turned around, pulled out of her indecisive daze.

To her delight, it was Evan. He waved, grinning.

It was Evan.

He leaned in for a hug.

"What a coincidence." she said. "We didn't have to plan after all, look at that." She let out an awkward laugh. She must sound so corny.

"A great coincidence." He stepped aside to let another customer forward, so she did the same. "I love this place. Do you usually come here?"

"Yup, the Center is right around the corner basically. There's another one further down the block I go to if the line is too long here—I think it's called Coffee and Chill, but I like this one more."

He laughed. "I think I know the one you're talking about. Purple awning?"

"That's the one. It's, like, woo-woo, right?" They both moved as they let another customer cut in front of them.

"Just give me a good coffee—I don't need all that crystal healing mumbo jumbo."

He held up his hands and wiggled his fingers, getting a laugh out of her. He was kind of corny too, but he somehow made it extremely endearing with his humble confidence.

"I noticed you staring at the new seasonal lattes they got going on. Which one were you thinking?"

They both turned to look up at the board.

"I'm torn between cinnamon fig and maple pecan," she said, looking back at him.

"I'm usually a simple black coffee guy, but how about you get the maple pecan and I'll get the cinnamon fig and we can trade if you prefer the other." He shrugged his shoulders.

"Deal," she said. It never occurred to her to get both. Why did she always think there was a right versus wrong decision? Not everything in life was an either/or situation.

"I'm not always the best at decisions either, truth be told," he confessed. "This one's on me." Evan got back in the line. She stood dumbfounded at how kind someone could be after revealing a flaw of hers, as well as his own. With him, it somehow didn't feel like a flaw anymore.

Maybe breaking up with Asher was not something to be so indecisive about; there was no easy fix in this situation like Evan had suggested with the lattes. Did she have to wait for her relationship to get as bad as it potentially could?

Thankfully, the line was not too long and Evan was back within five minutes, their drinks in to-go cups, receipt still in hand. Would he keep it, consider it special, add it to his collection?

He handed her the cinnamon fig one, then carefully folded and pocketed the receipt; she hid her grin behind her cup, inhaling the spiced holiday scent. "It's probably too hot to try right away," he said. "Do you have time to sit while they cool off?"

Time. Elliott forgot. She looked at her watch—only fifteen minutes until Howard's appointment.

"Oh, crap—I can't. I'm sorry, my new patient's first appointment is at two o'clock."

Damn it.

"Congrats on a new patient. I'm sure you want to get your stuff in order before he's there. I can walk back with you if that's cool. I'm sure the lattes will be cooler by the end of the block, and we can still test and swap if need be."

"That sounds perfect."

Elliott and Evan walked, and she told him more about the Center. The lattes were slightly cooler, but not by much, so they both took a quick sip of each, deciding to trade.

"I hope we can hang sometime soon," he said. "Next time, on purpose."

"I promise I won't be in a rush." She quickly hugged him goodbye and headed straight to her office.

As soon as she sat at her desk, Elliott pulled up Howard's electronic file. She then turned the sugar packet from the café over and over in her hand.

Five minutes later, Howard was sitting across from her. He was soft-spoken and quiet unless prompted, yet he spoke with depth whenever he did. She learned he had a similar love for piano and had played extremely well, but he had stopped playing after his mother died when he was a teenager.

Elliott asked if that might be a goal of his to pursue, to play again one day, but he looked uncomfortable, so she swiftly filed the thought away in one of her mind's drawers for a later time. To let talent like that vanish and waste away was a disservice to both him and the world. Piano might be an avenue to enliven him again—and one of his strengths to pull on.

Elliott was also impressed with Howard's intellect; he had dropped out of high school due to his mother's traumatic death, yet he was well-versed in musicians, artists, philosophers, history, and people from all the books he read.

He told Elliott he considered himself an observer who absorbed the world around him, whether he was any part of it or not. It was sad and sweet, pulling at her heart.

"Tell me about your Balloon Days," Elliott said.

"They seem to be giving me confidence. I'm not sure I had any to begin with."

Looking at her, he maintained eye contact longer than before, letting her see his gentle, somber eyes. Eyes that held a lot of life behind them, their color a rare grayish blue, radiating behind both pupils, each a mini solar eclipse. She wondered if her own eyes ever looked that sad, or if they ever would. It seemed the more life happened, the more there was to mourn.

"Can you elaborate on how you're working on building confidence in them?" Elliott said. She jotted down the words "HN reports BD helping self-esteem" on her notepad.

"Okay." He folded his hands in his lap. "I create a life that I'd want in real life. In the Balloon Days, I get to have an established career, and a partner who loves me and appreciates me. A home. All of the things that make someone normal. It's starting to make it feel possible for a failure like me to obtain." He looked behind Elliott, out the window. "They are impossibly real. When my first one ended, I felt confused and dejected but found myself looking forward to having more."

"What caused that confusion and sadness?" she said.

Howard returned his gaze to Elliott. "Sometimes my brother or my ex-girlfriend pops in here and there, or other things that remind me that I'm a disappointment out in the real world."

Between Orson and now Howard, it confirmed Elliott wasn't messing up her own Balloon Days and Dr. Heller was right about the unconscious poking through—as it should be, that's the whole point. She trusted Dr. Heller as much as she trusted Julie, neither of whom had ever given a reason for Elliott not to trust them.

"Then," he said, "I knock down those reminders, kind of like whack-a-mole."

"That's an accurate way to describe them." Elliott let out a quick laugh. "I'm sure the control to be able to do so helps your self-esteem as well."

"That makes sense." Howard leaned back in the chair.

Elliott leaned back in hers as well. "Do you ever find these 'whack-a-moles' helpful?"

"Mostly they are strange and upsetting. I don't want to be reminded of what I'm trying to escape." Elliott didn't blame him. She felt the same way sometimes.

If Dr. Heller was completely accurate, it should be apparent to one. Or was it a stubborn block? Mom and Dad's horrific fight, and those bubbles, were displaying situations Elliott already went through. They sucked then and still sucked now.

Although she couldn't make Asher remain kind in most of her Balloon Days, he was now seemingly more kind in real life; he asked her to go on lavish dates in Manhattan and at Michelin star restaurants, like he had been when they first met. Were his gestures only because she had pulled away since Dave's party? Should she trust her intuition?

Maybe she was avoiding something and didn't know it consciously yet.

"Is it possible that your unconscious mind is trying to suggest something?" Elliott said.

"Not unless it thinks I love being reminded of things I regret or hate about myself."

"Regrets can help us," she said, placing her notepad on her desk. "If we see a theme repeating among them, we can learn what to change. Otherwise, we let the regrets pile up and defeat us."

Howard sat with her words. After what felt like a year for Elliott, but was a minute in actuality, he said, "My theme is that I'm floating through life, accepting whatever and whoever is in my path. No matter how they treat me. I'm sick of being aimless. The last real decision I made was to drop out of school and look where that got me." He looked down and then straight into her eyes again, the sadness not so sad anymore. "But I did see her yesterday—in real life. Jillian. That woman I told you about earlier."

"Tell me more about that," Elliott said. She picked up her notepad to jot down more notes: "low self-worth, frustrated with his lack of autonomy, perked up at seeing Jillian."

"She invited me to see her in Long Island. Normally I think I would have declined," he said. "I have always wanted to be like John, and still do. But I never planned on falling in love with his girlfriend. It's further proof I'm a bad person." He paused. "Then I thought, for the first time in a long time, screw it. I guess the Balloon Day gave me a glimpse of how it could truly be with her. That it's worth exploring if given the opportunity." He began to fidget, one hand scratching the other. "She told me they broke up."

There it was. His older brother. It made sense. He envied John. Idolized him even.

Now he wanted John's girlfriend (or ex-girlfriend?), and if that was possible and he had a chance to be more like John, why wouldn't he try? This sounded like another regret in the making, albeit his deliberate decision to accept Jillian's request. Elliott's head was swirling. Should she say any of this to him? She didn't want him to feel judged.

"Howard... do you believe Jillian?" Elliott cocked her head in curiosity.

He stared at the floor, briefly pausing before he answered. "I wouldn't trust it if it were coming from Kimmy. But Jillian is different. They're complete opposites."

"What happened after Jillian told you about their break-up?"

"We talked like old times. She alluded to having feelings for me. We hugged before we said goodbye, she even held my hands and agreed to see me again on Sunday," he said, his cheeks reddening.

"That must have been overwhelming—a lot of mixed emotions, I'm sure." She wrote: "secretive relationship, rapid pace, idolizing brother, and idolizing Jillian, too?"

She wished to tell him this was a terrible idea. To date, or even secretly hang out, with his brother's girlfriend, or ex-girlfriend now, who seemed to be toying with him was bad, bad, bad all around.

Dr. Heller had once told her that stating such things to patients could appear judgmental, especially if they were not telling their therapist that they wanted help getting out of the situation. Howard showed no signs of wanting out. She had no choice but to shut up and listen.

"Was it similar to your Balloon Day?" Elliott crossed her legs and adjusted the notepad on her lap.

"The Balloon Days are better. For the most part in them, it's as if my brother never existed, unless he pops up visually or in a conversation. It's as if Jillian and I had been together for a long time.

"We live together in a small cottage in Ireland. She makes me feel good about myself. Desired, too. I never feel important otherwise, not since my mother died."

Brows furrowed with sympathy, Elliott nodded. "Jillian means a lot to you. Is she that way in person, too?"

Howard looked out the window, pensive. "For the most part. Whenever John isn't around. Otherwise, the attention goes to him."

Elliott noticed the time. "We do have to pause here, I'm afraid, but thank you for sharing all you had today, Howard. Any ideas for what you would like for your next Balloon Day before we meet again?"

"More of the same is fine—feeling like I'm needed, and being a normal, functioning person." Howard rose from the chair. "Thank you, Dr. Bailey."

"You can call me Elliott."

Howard gave a polite nod and made his way out.

Would he explore things with Jillian further? Would Howard see if she was worth pursuing or not? Would he want to play out how it could go with his brother if he found out? Or would he focus more on his other "functioning like a person" goals? She took note to ask him next time, not wanting to bombard him with the thousands of questions buzzing about in her brain.

CHAPTER 19
ORSON

As Orson hurried to the blue-illuminated elevator, his phone vibrated. It was Rose. He let it go to voicemail before shutting his phone off and tucking it back into his pocket as he ascended into the clouds of the ceiling.

Determined to have a better Balloon Day than last time, he stepped into his newly assigned Elite Day Room feeling good and hopeful. B109 smelled of fresh linen, as requested for his updated customizations. Soothing instrumental music played in the background, deepening the ethereal feel of the room. He sank into the sofa and pressed the button before his preparation time was up.

Within seconds, Orson was roaming around a neighborhood. It was dark and the air was still. A small number of houses had lights on inside; it couldn't be too late in the evening. He approached a lit house, the most inviting one, walking up its winding pathway with daisies lining either side. He reached for the doorknob, but then dropped his hand back to his side.

What if it turned out horribly again? Or perhaps he was simply acting reckless, irresponsible. Was it a stupid idea to keep doing this to himself, to others? He was risking his job, his son was acting more erratic—Orson still hadn't researched child therapists for him. His life was unraveling around him. For what, really? What was wrong with him? Was he going mad?

He closed his eyes, ready to envision his Day Room and return back to his life—but within seconds the door lock clicked open, restoring his gaze before he could escape, the entrance now wide open.

Inside was the same Summer Avenue house he presently lived in—the grand foyer, with the staircase straight ahead, and the wall of decorative mirrors laid out between the den and the dining room.

He walked beyond the foyer, past the staircase, and slowly made his way into the living room; he anticipated Madison in the hospice bed. The way these had been going, Orson wouldn't be surprised if the deepest dwellings of his brain unleashed the torture.

To his relief, all was the same, albeit with his and Madison's initial arrangement soon after purchasing the home as a wedding gift to themselves. The décor was simple but lovely, tastefully reflecting their income at the time, as well as their marital bliss.

Approaching the living room fireplace, he called out for Madison in hopes she could hear him, in hopes his imagination would take over this time.

"Madison?" he called out again. "Give me a sign. Please. I beg you." He sat down on their old faux leather loveseat, head falling in his hands. Love was turning him into a fool. "Or am I wasting my time?"

Something pushed against the tip of his shoe. He lifted his head, his gaze dropping to the middle of the floor as their old bedroom mattress appeared, the one from their first apartment together, prompting the all too familiar bittersweet taste only nostalgia could bring. Silver-gray sheets with a dark gray goose-down comforter on top enticed him now as it had back then.

Once a week, they would drag it from the apartment bedroom, move the coffee table, and plop down on it to watch movies while eating ice cream together, a tradition that stopped when they bought a two-story home years later.

Madison appeared from the kitchen outfitted in a green dress. It was unexpected and pleasant, like a cardinal landing on the windowsill bringing song into the home. Holding a sundae in each hand, she eased herself—careful to not spill any hot fudge—onto the mattress. The breath he had been holding in released.

Orson lowered himself next to Madison, her warmth snug against his skin. The sundaes floated onto the television stand, like magic, as he reached for Madison's hand and intertwined her delicate fingers with his, confirming that the solid version of herself had indeed returned. His body stirred with love, a welcome electric bolt from his heart to the edge of each cell, creating goosebumps on his skin.

He stayed there for what seemed like hours, not caring what movie they were watching—Groundhog Day. Or what they were eating—more hot fudge sundaes. Orson was simply happy to be with his best friend again, with the woman he loved. In this state it was real, her death now the illusion, his grief slipping away.

Orson must have fallen asleep. A distant voice woke him. "Why do you keep forgetting? Why do you keep forgetting about me?" The voice grew louder as Orson opened his eyes. Everything was black.

As loud as a foghorn, the voice spoke again. "WHY DO YOU KEEP FORGETTING ABOUT ME?" It was Ryder's voice.

Orson blinked, the black replaced by his quiet Day Room, and he lay on the white plush floor with the exit door open. He couldn't tell if he imagined the last part or if it was real.

All he knew was he loved his time with Madison. He wanted more and he was agitated he couldn't have it. He had to come back tomorrow or, at the absolute most, in two days. Three? No way, that was too long. He could make something up to his boss and Rose and Dr. Heller—to all of them. That he's going out of town soon. He could stay at a hotel.

As soon as he turned on his phone, it buzzed again. Rose.

"Hi, Rose I was—"

"Ryder's teacher called again. Today she said that he threw a ball at Kevin Logan's head because he didn't pick him for his team, and he kicked Dylan Shepherd simply because he didn't like the shirt he was wearing."

Orson rubbed his temples, closing his eyes. "He kicked his friend? What kind of shirt would get him that upset?"

"Does that fucking matter? You need to come home. Now."

"Yep. Straight away. And don't worry, I am setting him up with a therapist. I'm trying. I was just leaving work. I apologize."

"I don't care about your apologies anymore. Jeff and I are going to see that new fertility specialist in an hour, remember? You were supposed to be here a half hour ago. But try not to worry too much, I didn't even tell your son when you were coming back because I had a feeling you might be late again. And stop acting like therapy is the end-all solution. It's only part of it. You still have to be a parent to your child. Your child, Orson."

Orson stood, unblinking, and stared at a potentially torn, complicated future, a reality worse than it presently already was. He had to put Ryder in therapy right away to prove he was doing something.

It didn't matter if anyone else would find out anymore. Maybe the therapist could also give him ways of how to go about this all better. Hopefully, child therapists did that.

"Orson?" Rose hissed.

"Yes. Yeah, you're right. Completely. I'm on my way."

Later that evening, after Orson picked up Ryder from Rose's, and things settled down, Orson tucked Ryder into bed, then sat next to him.

"Son, I heard what happened at school—that you were upset with Dylan and you kicked him. And that you threw a ball at another boy. Is this true?"

"They deserved it," Ryder said. He picked at a thread on his fleece blanket.

"Ryder, I understand you were upset. But sometimes people won't choose us to be on their teams. Did you apologize to them?"

Ryder begrudgingly nodded. "But only because Mrs. Marley made me."

"I'm glad you had," Orson said, patting Ryder's shoulder. "That's the right thing to do. Don't do anything like that again, though. Not worth getting in trouble for."

"I already told Aunt Rose I won't."

"I see." Of course, Ryder had. It didn't matter if he told Orson the same. "Can I ask you what was on the boy's shirt that upset you so much?"

"It had a dinosaur on it," Orson looked at his son's furrowed brows, his glistening eyes.

Ryder rolled over, facing away from Orson. His son had enough consequences for the day's events; it was time to lay the topic to rest. If this were a client, Orson would do the same, knowing if he pressed or lectured beyond necessity, nothing productive would come of it.

Orson kissed the back of his head goodnight and left the room. He racked his brain as to why a shirt like that would upset his son so much.

Then it hit him.

Ryder had recently outgrown a blue t-shirt with a tyrannosaurus rex printed on the front.

The one Madison had bought for him.

CHAPTER 20
HOWARD

Being in a library was peaceful and nostalgic. Howard had years' worth of memories of perusing books of various genres with Mom every Sunday evening, all of which was kept safe in a corner of his brain: books on world history, music history; reptiles, cultural rituals around the world, cooking methods, just about everything. John, never as interested in reading as he was, would wander around the library complaining how it was a waste of his time, but for Howard it was his favorite day of the week.

Everything about Sundays as a child was special. After a bacon, egg, and pancake breakfast, Pop and John would play guitar alongside Howard as he played piano, and sometimes Mom banged on homemade drums—used paint cans with construction paper and tape, or cheered as she sipped her coffee.

After dinner was library time with Mom. She showed him how to treat books, how to get the most out of them, how to search for the right ones—to open mid-way, read one paragraph, and decide if the style of the author would be captivating enough to consume the whole book.

He loved the smell of books, the sound of the pages turning, the feel of the paper on his fingertips. With books, he could live out countless lives and go on infinite adventures without ever leaving the comfort of his home. The library had become more of a home to him than anywhere else.

It had taken him months after Mom passed to return to the public library. But one Sunday evening, a favorite novel they used to read together every Christmas Eve—The Family Under the Bridge, by Natalie Savage Carlson—fell off his bookshelf and he took it as a sign.

On this particular Sunday evening, Howard not only wanted to read, but he wanted to distract himself. It had been four days since Jillian wrote and he was a bit beside himself, restless, eager. She was likely busy or dealing with her dad. It wouldn't be like her to skip seeing Howard when she had said she would, especially without any word. It would only be a matter of time before she responded to his message to reschedule.

Howard wandered into the instrument section of the local library before heading back to the apartment. On many occasions, like today, he would poke his head in the music aisle and read about piano culture or famous pianists throughout history: Myra Hess, Philip Glass, Beethoven, Vladimir Horowitz.

Pop had liked to remind Howard how fortunate he was to play or even own an upright piano, even if it was used. Pop would explain how when the instrument was first invented, it was extremely expensive, only owned by royalty and exceptionally wealthy families. What would Bartolomeo Cristofori think today, seeing his invention much more available and widespread, regardless of socioeconomic status? Would he sneer at electronic keyboards?

A sudden rumble of dropped books on the floor shook Howard awake from his mental time traveling. To his left, an old man was slowly bending down, and it looked quite difficult for him to do so based on his cautious pace to retrieve the fallen books. He had little gray hair on either side of his mostly bare head, black skin, and a white-gray beard. The button-down, tie, and sweater vest combination suggested he lived in a fancier area of Queens—opposite side of Howard.

Howard walked toward him and squatted down to help. The old man looked up, and Howard could see his etched face, full of years of life like an oak tree with many rings, and his brown eyes, as dark as molasses, seemed to brighten as he smiled, his bulbous-tipped nose in between.

"Thank you, dear boy. Good to know kind kids like you still exist. It isn't as easy for me to get up and down these days. Life gets tougher as you get older, believe you me. It's still a beautiful thing, nonetheless." They stood, and Howard handed him his books. "We can always keep learning, keep getting better, even if our bodies don't," he said, chuckling, nodding toward the shelves.

Howard agreed. Most of his life, he had read and learned, progressing cognitively. Recently, though, things had unexpectedly accelerated in the romance department.

With the right woman this time—Jillian.

Surprisingly, Kimmy nor he had reached out to the other since their latest break-up. Howard had suppressed weaker moments of missing Kimmy (the things worth missing, like her spontaneity) with thoughts of Jillian.

"I've had some hard times getting up too," Howard shared.

"Ha. It's much easier at your age to do so, though, I promise you that," the old man said. "But you have to pull yourself up or accept help from good people such as yourself." What if there was no one to accept help from in certain moments?

That's what frightened Howard the most.

Howard observed the books the old man held. An Intro to Piano for Seniors and How to Begin Learning Piano Later in Life. Who knew such books existed? He supposed it was never too late to start something new.

"What's your name, kid?"

"Howard. What's yours?" A long "shush" came from the other side of the aisle.

"Langston," he said.

Langston. It had been a while since Howard had spoken to anyone much older than he—probably not since Pop died. There was something comforting about it. "Nice to meet you," Howard said.

Another hush.

"Okay, okay, calm your horses," Langston said toward the adjacent aisle, a human shape slightly visible between cracks in the books. "Well, I guess that's our signal to go. Thank you again, Howard. It was nice talking to someone, even if for a few moments."

"I usually come every Sunday evening." The words tumbled out of Howard's mouth. He was usually antisocial, yet it seemed right and almost vital to provide Langston with this information.

"Ah, is that so? I'm a Sunday guy myself, Wednesdays as well."

Howard raised his book to signal his best "see you then" gesture, before leaving with his newly borrowed book about piano culture in the eighteenth century, and potentially with a newly acquired friend.

Howard entered the building marked "323."

Stepping into the lobby, Howard bumped into Romalda as she placed a new painting on the wall: a field of assorted flowers in bright colors against a cloudless sky, the contrast of colors lively and immersing him at once.

"Howard, how are you?" She had on her white lab coat over a crisp white blouse with a squiggly ruffle down the center, making his eyes dance as he looked.

"Not too bad." It was strange to answer that way and actually mean it. "I have three credits to use today." He was proud. He asked John to raise his pay, and surprisingly, it had worked.

"That's fabulous. I'll let you get on your way then. Let your perception be your guide." Romalda winked and quickly patted him on the shoulder.

"Can I ask you a question?" She nodded, so Howard continued. "What does that mean, to 'let your perception be your guide'?"

"Ah, great question." She winked again. "Perception is fickle but that's how we build our own unique worlds. It can make a mockery of you, or it can totally lead you into bliss." The photograph behind her looked like someone's bliss.

"Perception is your reality," she continued. "No one ever grasps that truth. But see, Dr. Heller understands that notion better than anyone else and created the possibility for you, and others like you, to have the power to jumpstart true control over your life." Romalda gave Howard a fixed smile. It reminded him of the expression she wore on the day of his intake, after she wiped up the spilled tea.

"Enjoy it, Howard. Sometimes we ruin things with too many questions. The more technical answer is a bunch of neuroscience and brainwave jargon anyway. If you're still curious, Dr. Bailey would happily go over that version with you, if she hasn't already."

Howard was not sure how to respond. She said it in a disarming way, yet it hit hard. He had always been a curious person; he was proven right to assume there was an intricate scientific system behind Balloon Days, like the maze of strings in a piano.

"Have a great Balloon Day, the best one yet." Romalda trotted away.

Howard said goodbye, then took the silver glass elevator and made his way into his white room once the slot lit up.

It was possible he did ruin things with too many questions. Maybe it wasn't unsafe to throw caution to the wind occasionally, even if Pop's advice had been to do the opposite. Being with Jillian in her new town surely proved that.

In the meantime, before he would see Jillian again, Howard could enjoy her in his fantasy, the balloon taking him away. He stared at the control in his hand, the button, the cursive letters. An alternate version of Jillian still believable and real, like a clone only for him, admittedly gave him a rush.

What couldn't he do with this Jillian?

He could maintain the verisimilitude of real life by doting on her, spoiling her with gifts and elaborate dates, talking all night long. Or he could fly her around the world on a magic carpet and make love to her over the backdrop of the city lights—no, too creepy. Flying in the sky with her was enough. The infinite possibilities delighted him.

Howard looked at the button and pressed, surrendering to the shift. The instant floating sensation he started to become awfully familiar with took over as a hazy glow clouded his eyes, clearing up like dissipating fog as he thought of being in the Irish hillside again.

The smell of chocolate chip cookies in the oven heightened Howard's senses, sending a savory-sweet tingle to his brain. He hurried into the kitchen. The sun shone through the window.

"Good morning," Jillian said, beaming.

Ah—that winsome smile. It opened his heart, the renewing warmth of it healing the necrotic tissue of his past.

A smile that made Howard's inner Lord Byron return.

"You've been napping for so long, it was cute." Jillian looked at the golden-brown chocolate chip cookie in her hand. "And I was craving cookies. Not the healthiest, I know." She took a bite and swallowed. "Want one?"

"They smell incredible. Can I actually eat one, and taste it?" Howard picked one up. The edges were browned, and the middle gave when he pressed it. Perfectly gooey.

"Well, it isn't too many calories if you have one or two." Of course, Jillian couldn't understand what he meant. His perception created such an authentic clone, such a real person, so you should be able to eat.

"I could use a few pounds." He took a bite, and it was sumptuous; every grain was sugary, the chocolate chips melting, thick on his tongue. His body plumped up. He added some attractive abs to go with it.

When in Rome.

Well, Ireland in this case.

Or to be more accurate—when in a Balloon Day.

"What should we do?" Howard said. He could test out telling John about them. Play it out. Gain some courage for the real thing.

Maybe for the next one.

Jillian tugged on the bottom of his unwrinkled and hole-free blue shirt. "Want to venture out to lavender fields? Take me to France?" she said. To her it was a joke, but to Howard it was possible.

Closing his eyes, images of lavender fields from the books he read on France earlier this year conjured in his mind. When he opened his eyes, their surroundings now looked as it had in the photographs: rows upon rows of shooting rods; bright, lush, bruise-purple flower buds with lime green stems. Forest-covered hills lined the horizon, complemented by the setting sun, a perfect vibrant sphere of orange that cast a peach glow weaving through the purples and greens.

Howard followed Jillian in her yellow sundress through open paths between rows of lavender. The sun's heat beamed down on the back of his neck, the breeze keeping it a tolerable warmth instead of scorching bare skin. She took his hand and gently pulled.

The lavender plants became a breathtaking blur as they ran by. The earthy, crisp florals carried through the air, like butterflies in search of nectar, flitting in his nose with each labored breath.

Jillian slowed down and turned toward Howard. She stretched her arms outward, absorbing the sun's rays, like a child catching snow. "To me, this is living. John once told me that sitting out on a front porch, looking out at the distance, would be existing, not living." She placed her arms back to her sides. "That life was only truly grabbed by the more ambitious."

Heat hit the corners of Howard's eyes. John had told Howard this notion during one of their yearly conversations when John "checked in" with him, to see if Howard was pursuing any "real goals."

Howard made things up like how he was looking into getting his GED and going to community college, or scouting jobs to apply to, but inside, he figured why bother. Howard would never be as successful as his brother. He'd most likely never gain his approval.

He wished John were an ex, or better yet—a person who Jillian had never met or would ever meet. But what was Howard's real life, anyway? Could this not be his real life, the other his alternate, fake one?

Or maybe that was playing it too safely, as he had done for a majority of his adult life. Playing it safe had made him stagnant.

Jillian still held his hand, waiting patiently. "I'm sorry," he told her. "Was stuck in my head." Which was weird to say, because wasn't he stuck in his head already?

A honeybee hovered over petals nearby. The petals immediately turned iron-gray, dried up, and blew away in the wind. He didn't want to talk about John anymore.

Jillian grabbed his hand, her eyes suddenly wide. "Stay with me here. It's better here. Please." She was right, it was. Reality came with too many messes, too many rules, too many potholes in the road.

The sky turned gray and a strong breeze made it hard to breathe. In the distance, a dark cloud formed, low and large, shifting into a funnel-like shape. A tornado headed their way.

"Are you going to save me?" Jillian called out.

As the tornado neared—Howard's body locked up. The twister swept them up and both vanished.

CHAPTER 21
ORSON

The unique, fresh scent of pear and vanilla, on the verge of a cloying sweetness but still pleasant, lingered in Orson's nostrils as he placed the shampoo bottle back on the shelf. It was nearly empty, but it was Madison's and he was incapable of throwing it out. The more he threw away the more she faded. Her possessions were dying along with her, it seemed, and he wanted her ghost around the house a little longer.

He had already given away most of Madison's coats and dresses to her cousins. Several necklaces to Madison's mother, his mother, and Rose. Parts of her, in parts of him, were taken, like waves washing away words with every pull of sand.

Favorite movies, like Scrooged, and books by Raymond Chandler remained stacked atop the television entertainment unit made of cappuccino-colored wood. They picked it out together, their initials engraved in one of the cabinets, with the words "We will forever find joy together" written beneath.

Looking at himself in the mirror, his thick hair was overdue for a cut, the front pieces lingering by his pupils; dark circles under his eyes stole bits of his handsomeness. He splashed cold water on his face then drifted back to his bed, littered with photographs.

Orson continued to make a separate pile of the ones he wanted to study further. Perhaps if he looked at each one, recalled the memories and wrote them down, then he could accurately retrieve them for his upcoming Balloon Days.

He held up a photograph he captured of Madison in Europe, at a Latvian restaurant. Young and messy and proud, with a sweaty-faced grin. Madison stubbornly needed to find this restaurant, and because they were traveling on a shoe-string budget, to save up enough for their wedding, they walked from their hostel, the start of their trek the city center; it was cold, and the sun had started to set.

The path became wet grass, dark tunnels, long roads, pavement again. Finally, they'd reached the restaurant, to be told it was closing within thirty minutes. Madison should have seen her face—the amount of sweat on it, its shade of strawberry red, matching her hair. She was thrilled they made it there with enough time to eat, even if they couldn't sit for very long.

Why was everyone else able to live on? Why did she have to be frozen, moribund? Her spirit now confined to photographs and stories? He lay down, his body still with upset, trying not to glance at Madison's vacant spot beside him. Orson squeezed his eyes shut and prayed that sleep would ease his suffering.

What must have been hours later, he groggily opened his eyes, body rocking back and forth, feeling a push at his side, as if someone were failing to roll a carpet.

"Are. You. Kidding. Me? Orson? Again? Wake the hell up." Orson's sister was repeatedly shoving him, each time harder than the last. He jolted up, wiping drool and crust from his mouth.

"What? What time is it? I'm awake." Photographs fell off his chest and scattered as he got out of bed, realizing he was still in yesterday's clothes.

"It's 9:30 a.m. The school just called me and asked why Ryder wasn't there. They told me they called you a bunch of times, but you didn't pick up. I raced over here as fast as I could. Damn it." She sat on the bed. "You scared the hell out of me."

"Shit." Orson tripped over his black work shoe as he rushed to the walk-in closet, grabbing a new outfit. He snagged the first button-down he touched—maroon—and gray pants, black belt and walked back out. "I can't imagine how you must have felt. I completely messed up, Rose. I'm sorry."

"Your son said he tried to wake you—my god. He was crying. Alone. In the living room, with his backpack spilled out on the floor. Tell me, Orson, what in the ever-loving fuck is wrong with you?" Rose threw her hand at her temple and shook her head as she stood up, walked toward the door. "I understand you're trying to heal and work and who knows what else, but it cannot happen like this. Not anymore."

"I must have dozed off."

Shit, shit, shit.

Orson laid his clothes on the bed before taking steps toward her. "But, yes, I am healing, I promise. I'm almost fully there. A few more weeks, I know it. I will fix everything and be putting Ryder first." He gestured to the photographs. "I have this plan that—"

Rose held her hand up.

"Ryder should be first, always. You've been saying this for months now. You're getting worse. You seem less depressed, I'll say that, but you've gone from depressed to—I don't know what. You're not here, you're like a ghost.

"You have to still get up to take Ryder to school, feed him, take care of him—Christ, the bare minimum—and then, then you can go back to sleep again, or cry in the bathroom at work, or take the occasional day off for yourself. I would understand that, and I would be there for you even through my own grieving. Remember? I loved your wife too." She started biting her nails, her tell-tale sign that she was trying not to break down. "It killed me to see her dwindle down to nothing."

"You're right. You're absolutely right. We all lost her. But this therapy is letting me see her again. Her healthy, normal self. Please understand." Orson went over and picked up a couple of the photographs, bringing them to her. "It is helping. Because I can see her and know that, you know, know that she is... well, it's helping because I can relive memories with her and truly be there. Look at this photo, we were so happy." He waved a photograph of Madison and Orson standing in the entrance of Bamburgh Castle, in Northumberland. "When she was alive, I took it all for granted. Every moment not spent with her was a moment wasted. I get a chance to redo that."

He looked over at his slippers, Madison's still at their side. The more time kept passing, the harder it seemed to get, the more forced he was to let go of more and more—another holiday he can't take her picture, another gift to give that he couldn't include her name, another experience or milestone for Ryder she was not at his side. The number of memories without Madison would eventually amount to more than the ones with her.

"But I will take care of Ryder," he said. "I will be more involved."

Rose pushed his hand away, and the photograph fell to the floor.

"Hey," Orson snapped. He retrieved the picture, the memory, off the floor. "What the hell?"

"Honestly, I don't care if you see her in this therapy or not. Because she isn't alive, Orson. She, your wife, is dead, in an urn, and nothing will ever change that." She shrugged and shook her head. "So no, I don't get it. You are so disconnected from what is actually still here in your life." Rose's voice quivered. "We all have to move on, Orson. And it's time you stopped whatever voodoo bullshit you have going on and do it too." A tear raced down her high cheekbones, taking some of her black eyeliner with it.

All of her words buzzed around in his head. "No, we don't, Rose." He implored. "You don't quite get it. In there, she is real. I can touch her, kiss her, smell her. Maybe you could try it too, and you'd see what I see."

"You are losing your fucking mind, Orson. I didn't want to have to tell you this, but his teacher hinted at having to call CPS soon if Ryder displays more concerning behaviors. I reassured her he is in therapy now, so it seemed to hold her off. For now. But Jeff and I have been talking, and we think it's best that we take Ryder. For a few weeks at least until you sort your shit out." Orson's mouth opened, but he was at a loss for words. His fists tightened as she continued. "We packed his bags while you were sleeping, and I let the school know how badly you both are grieving. Thankfully, they understood the situation."

Orson's eyes and limbs felt heavier by the minute. How could she throw this in his face? She dared to stand there, lecturing him, acting as a savior. She played pretend parent for too long.

His fault or not, she had no right to take Ryder away.

"What the fuck do you know about raising a child?" he said.

"Excuse me?"

"You didn't lose your spouse, and you don't even have a child yet. Who knows if you ever will? Ryder isn't your son, he's mine. I make the decisions."

Rose's eyes burned into Orson, but he didn't care. "You're disgusting, you know that," she said. "I know you're grieving and all but let me lay out the facts for you. I am the one making Ryder's meals. I'm the one taking him to and from school. I'm the one spending time with him. I'm the one making sure he finishes his homework.

"And what are you doing, Orson? From the look of things, I know more about how to raise a kid than you do. So get angry, yell, shout, pout, or do whatever it is you feel you need to do. But this is happening whether you like it or not. Ryder is coming home with me until you fix your shit."

Before Orson could ruin things further, Ryder burst through the door and into the room. "Dad? Are you okay?"

"Yes, Ryder, of course." Orson smiled the rage off his face and smoothed his day-old shirt. "I'm so, so, sorry. Dad was silly and fell asleep. I was very tired, that's all." He squatted to meet Ryder's four-foot stature, darting a glance at Rose.

"Are you sure you weren't sad? Dr. Kevin said sometimes we sleep more when we're sad." Ryder patted Orson's head. "And we forget things or feel mad. He said that's why I got in trouble at school."

"Oh." Still kneeling, he took Ryder's hand. "That's incredibly wise of Dr. Kevin." Indeed, child therapy was worth the hundred dollars per session.

"Hey, Ryder, how do you feel about having a sleepover for a few days at our place? We got a bunch of new movies to watch and plenty of popcorn. Sound good?" Rose said with a warm smile.

"Cool!" Ryder jumped, his arms above his head. His excitement hurt Orson's heart. He was losing his son, and Ryder seemed all the happier for it. As much as Orson wanted to intervene, Rose was right to take him. "Do I have to go to school today?"

"Oh, perhaps n—" Orson began.

Rose placed her hand on Ryder's shoulder. "Yes, sweetie pie, you do."

"Right," Orson said. "Your aunt is right." Of course she was.

"Aw, man." Ryder pouted.

"Alright now, say goodbye to your dad."

"I'll miss you, Dad." Orson squeezed his son tightly, his eyes closed. Ryder pulled back and looked at Orson. "You can cry, it's okay to cry. Or draw the sad things. That helps a lot."

Orson and Rose exchanged glances, but she was the first to look away.

"That's great advice, kiddo," Orson said, choking back tears. He kissed the top of Ryder's head before standing back up. "Go have fun with your aunt. I'll see you soon, pal."

Ryder, his own son, was the one telling Orson how to heal. It felt as if someone had gone inside Orson's chest and twisted his heart, wringing it out like a wet cloth. He released the built-up tears.

His son didn't need him anymore. It was official. Orson was a bad father.

Digging his fingers into his palms, Orson watched from his window as Rose drove away with his son. Things would go back to normal. They had to.

Logically, he knew that. His heart needed a little more time with Madison while he still had the chance.

CHAPTER 22
ELLIOTT

It was the end of November and a slight frost bit the air as the stars twinkled above. Elliott had continued to try mending things with Asher, but she was still not as happy as she thought she would be. For many reasons—one being the cause for this CVS shopping bag in her hand, a potential cause for ruining her assiduous attempts at a perfect, well-rounded life. Another being his non-compliance of acting consistently kind. Julie told Elliott to stop accepting crumbs of love, and to stop falling for his head games. It was all so confusing, the two sides of her brain in a constant battle. But the side begging her to leave turned louder with each passing day.

Rosy-cheeked and red-nosed, she unlocked her front door. Captain immediately attacked her legs with audible sniffing. She ruffled his furry head, and hurried to the downstairs bathroom, flinging her olive peacoat somewhere in the foyer along the way and removing each boot as she walked through the kitchen, trying not to stumble on her dog or drop the plastic bag as it crinkled and bounced against her leg.

Her last period still had yet to come. She'd had irregular periods before. But this was two weeks late now, and she was avoiding the reason why. Avoiding things might not be the healthiest response to life.

That is what she told Howard and Orson, at least; it's what the textbooks and psychology books also confirmed. It was so much easier, much more comfortable, to wrap herself up in a little bubble world and evade, unless it came to her professional life. Elliott's dichotomy between work and her personal life proved Julie's theory right, but Elliott was still determined to prove Julie wrong.

She sat on the toilet, legs restless, and tossed the plastic bag from the drug store on the stone-tiled floor. She pulled the pregnancy stick out of its packaging, threw the wrapper in her bronze wastebasket she had happily picked out with Mom before Dad and Holly ruined everything. She then made herself look at the pregnancy stick again.

It was time. It had to happen.

She put the flat, plastic tip awkwardly in between her legs, trying as best she could to make sure she saturated it while not getting any urine on her hands. She sat the stick on the counter, the liquid crawling across the test window, tinting it yellow. It was the little window that would answer why she had been randomly throwing up for the last three days.

Could she still attribute it to stress or food poisoning like Asher had said it was? Suddenly, she felt so stupid. It couldn't be positive, there was no way. This was a precaution.

One line meant not pregnant; two lines meant she was. It was a cheaper brand, but not the cheapest—she was surprised at how expensive they get. The urine was filling the last bit of white left. She remained on the toilet as she peeked at the stick.

Nothing yet.

Another minute passed, and she looked at her toenails, yawning—she could use a pedicure soon.

She looked back at the stick and a thin blue line appeared, like a shark fin splitting the surface of the sea.

One line. Okay.

In the clear.

As she watched, another line began to emerge.

Two lines—it had two lines.

Two blue lines, side by side.

She laughed, dizziness swooping in. This couldn't be right. She picked it up again, staring blankly at it. She had taken the morning-after pill hours later.

How could this have happened? She did everything right, given the circumstances. Her mouth felt dry, coarse like sandpaper.

This couldn't be possible.

This couldn't be happening to her. Everything suspended in time, slow and sudden all at once, like an unexpected push off a cliff into ice-cold water, or an accidental prick from which blood, a dark thick red, oozed out. She could barely breathe.

Before placing the stick back down on the counter, she looked once more at the two lines. Then grabbed her phone and called up Julie, still sitting on the toilet.

"Is it negative?" she said.

As soon as Elliott heard Julie's voice, she squeezed her eyes shut, feeling the heat behind her eyelids. "No." she paused. "I'm pregnant."

"Oh. Fuck. Wait. What? How? You took the morning-after pill. I don't get it. Are you sure?"

"My life is ruined."

Julie's voice grew softer. "No, it isn't. It will be okay, Elle. We'll figure this out."

She continued with reassuring words, but Elliott could hardly hear them; she barely believed them. Her panic was too loud, a blaring siren clouding her mind. How could this have happened?

No, no, no.

This can't have happened. Not to her. She was a straight-A student. She performed impeccably at her job. She carefully plotted out her life. She was not ready yet for this part—she wanted to be the best, readiest-she-could-be mother when the time came. Even if she were ready, she wasn't sure that Asher would have been the one. The mere thought of him being a dad repulsed her.

She was frozen on the toilet, paralyzed by fear, as she held the phone up to her ear. Pearl-sized tears began to splash open on her inner thighs.

"We will figure this out, Elle. No matter what, you won't be alone in this. Just take a deep breath, that's all you can do in this moment. Do nothing but breathe, okay?"

Elliott inhaled as hard as she could, lips trembling, and exhaled slowly from her mouth. "Okay." She sniffled, swallowing back the urge to vomit. "I can handle—"

She couldn't handle it and threw up on the floor.

"It's okay. You can and you will. You are so much stronger than you realize." Elliott had never felt weaker, or more ashamed, in her life.

Elliott said goodbye and hung up the phone, placing it on the sink. She stood up, pulled up her underwear, picked up the pregnancy stick, and chucked it in the wastebasket.

After she cleaned up the vomit without trying to vomit again, she picked up her jeans on the way back up the stairs and to her bedroom and dropped them near the laundry bin, then sank in her bed, curling her legs up toward her head like the fetus now growing in her womb, snot and tears dampening the pillow.

She slipped into a dreamless sleep.

The next morning, Elliott had trudged to her living room couch, a box of tissues nearby, waiting for Mom. Many crumpled, used ones littered the floor, little imperfect spheres of anguish.

About thirty minutes or so later, there was a quick knock at her front door as it opened. Mom rushed toward Elliott on the couch dragging a chill in with her.

"What is it, Elle? Are you sick?" She put her hand on Elliott's lap. Mom could always soothe her.

"No, Mom. I'm pregnant."

"Oh. You scared me, Jesus," she said, her hand over the left side of her chest. "I thought you were dying."

Mom's change in mannerisms was slight, but Elliott recognized when she was uncertain and afraid. She sat quite rigidly, and her hand swept away her chin length auburn hair to the side before it landed back with her other hand wedged between her legs. She had the urge to comfort Mom, but Elliott's energy was too drained from crying.

"Now tell me, sweetheart, what happened?" She placed her hand on Elliott's knee.

Mom sat quietly and listened as Elliott explained she had not told Asher yet, that she was devastated and confused, completely frightened about what to do.

How they had been drunk, but she thought Asher would have put a condom on, how she didn't realize he hadn't until it was too late, how she took the morning-after pill the same night. If only she hadn't kept drinking, if only she hadn't lost control.

"I'm so sorry, sweetie," Mom said. "I'm trying to wrap my head around it all. What happens next? What now?"

"I know Asher won't want to keep it. I made him discuss it, months ago, what we would do if this ever happened." She had agreed with him, but it was easy then—it was a decision based on a hypothetical situation, one she never thought would happen.

Mom stared at her hands in her lap. After another overlong pause, she looked up at Elliott. "I can see how hypotheticals are easy to give an answer to. If someone told me their daughter got pregnant and couldn't keep it, I would judge them. Honestly. Now, here we are. This is reality now for my daughter." Mom rubbed her neck as she continued. "And I see how this isn't easy." Captain let out a yawn on the other end of the gray sofa. He hopped off onto the floor, stretched, jumped back on, then licked Elliott's arm before burrowing into the nearby blanket.

Elliott broke the silence. "Are you disappointed with me?"

"Oh, honey, what? No. Never," Mom said, reaching for Elliott's hand, her round eyes glistening. Elliott cupped it with her own. "If you decide to not keep the baby, maybe we should look at this as another way of preventing pregnancy, like a form of birth control. You had insisted he wear a condom, had taken the emergency pill for a reason—you already didn't want to become pregnant."

Mom was reassuring herself more than she was reassuring Elliott. Because, really, was it truly considered preventative anymore? Elliott remained clueless as to what she would consider it, aside from failure. "Either way, know I will absolutely do everything I can to support you in whatever you decide."

Dad flashed in Elliott's mind. Would he support her? Would he kick her out? Maybe he wouldn't understand, but throw money at her.

"I don't want anyone else to know aside from you and Julie for now. Especially not Dad. Unless you think I should tell him."

Another long pause before Mom spoke. She let out a quick sigh, shaking her head. "You know your father. He isn't helpful in these situations, never was. But it's ultimately your choice. You have to remember the control you do have."

Quiet tears trailed down Elliott's cheek onto the cushion as she lay back down; Mom smoothed her hair back, and Elliott could hear Mom was crying too.

Elliott wished it would all go away, be a nightmare to wake up from, a movie to turn off, a book to throw out.

After some time passed, Mom reminded her she loved her no matter what. "Please call me if you need anything at all." She kissed her on the forehead, then left.

Even more twisted up inside, every part of Elliott was screaming. She slid from the couch to the floor. As she rocked back and forth, deafening cries broke through, an agony she had never experienced exploding through her core.

She gripped her elbows in a painful hug. She was urging, pleading, begging for this paining choice to go away, or for someone to make it for her. Sitting there, with her head down, eventually the tears ran out; soon all she could hear was the occasional car driving by.

An hour later, Elliott washed her face with cold water, threw on a pair of jeans and a sweater, grabbed her coat and bag, then rode the train to the Center.

She needed a Balloon Day.

Usually, Elliott had a Balloon Day session after seeing her patients, to save money and time. Today she didn't care about the commute. The ride felt quiet—everything bland and muted—except for when the doors would open and close at each stop, letting passengers on and off.

Once at the Center, Elliott journeyed to her Day Room. Laying herself down on the fleece hammock, control in hand, she pressed the button and quickly immersed in the same fantasy-filled landscape as she conjured up in her second Balloon Day.

She hopped down from the tower and roved barefoot in the fields of bright, blended flowers—lilies, lilacs, peonies, and sunflowers—short and tall, wide and narrow, brilliant confetti of colors. She ran alongside winding creeks, as sparkling blue waterfalls popped up, beckoning her to stand underneath and wash away the heart-hurt.

Elliott slowed down and let the sun fall lower in the sky, creating a pink and orange horizon. Musical notes birthed from the center of each flower, sailing toward the sky, somber harmonies in the air.

Below the tallest blossoms and blades of grass, Elliott lay, the sunset blanketing everything in a pink shimmer. She rested her hands on her belly.

In a whisper as soft as fleece, she said, "I wonder what you'd be like if I have you. I wonder how you'd laugh and what your favorite color would be."

She closed her eyes and her belly swelled. It grew just a bit.

"I'm so sorry. I wish I was stronger for you." Her mouth trembled. "I wish I was ready to give you a great life. A life full of fun trips and cute traditions, lots and lots of books and playing and drawing. I'd tell you stories before tucking you in, kiss your forehead goodnight, touch your cheek while I stay with you, watch you as you sleep. I'd make sure you always felt so safe, so loved. So special."

Flowers around her began to shrivel, and crumble, one by one, into ash. She tried to stop it with her mind, but like her emotions, the discomfort couldn't be fixed or controlled. Like Mom said, she had to focus on what she could control. But she didn't like either choice she would have to make.

As Elliott's world broke down around her, she continued. "I wonder if you'd be short like us. If you'd get my eyes or his, if you would be kind and funny and smart." She gulped the air and released a slow breath as a light rain began to fall.

"God, this is all my fault. I was so stupid and careless. I wish I could take you somewhere. Protect you somehow." She wiped tears and raindrops off her cheek. "I want to fly us to the moon and have everyone leave us alone. I want to stop time, stop the choice, until I become the best mommy for you.

"Maybe we could still meet somehow, some day, if I couldn't have you now. Would you be there if I can't have you now?" The rain continued to pour, and a bolt of lightning flashed in the distance. "Would you wait for me? On the other side?"

The feelings within her were nameless. How could she ever forgive herself for the worst misstep of her life? She wanted to stay here, away from her soul-crushing decision.

The last of the setting sun highlighted her clasped hands upon her stomach. A starless sky took its place, the clouds foggy and gray and close enough to touch.

She closed her eyes, and when she opened them again, all was gone. But something nearby still moved. The white feathers of her Day Room. She must have fallen off the hammock. There she lay on the thick, white carpet, curled up on her side, protecting her stomach, a pool of tears against her cheek.

Her life had fallen apart within the matter of a day.

CHAPTER 23
HOWARD

Thirty-two days had passed since Howard met Jillian in person. Even worse, it had been twenty-eight days since they last spoke. Their daily streak not only damaged, but up and vanished altogether.

Sitting on his bed, Howard checked his phone. The screen he lingered on throughout each day was readily available; he scanned his last few messages to Jillian, progressing from how she was doing to if they could meet up again soon, to if she was alive and alright.

He left several apologies after that, but everything remained unanswered. Just as it transpired in June. But it had been different then— Jillian hadn't expressed any outright affection toward him, or approval at his omission of liking her—it had been clearly obvious to not translate their bonding as anything more than platonic at that point.

Had he misjudged the signals yet again? Was he that out of tune with reality? It didn't add up. He took a long swig of whiskey, then watched the rest of the contents slosh around in the bottle as he tilted it back and forth.

Over the course of such a disappointing month, he tried to keep as busy as he could by venturing to the library to see his new and wise friend, Langston. They spent a few Sunday evenings, as well as Wednesday afternoons, meeting at the library, followed by chats at the nearby coffee shop to avoid the relentless shushers.

During a recent conversation, Howard admitted to Langston that he played piano until he reached sixteen years old.

"Why stop?" Langston said. Howard responded with, "I was a stupid teenager who got caught up in stupid things." That seemed to suffice.

Minutes later, Langston then asked if Howard could stop by his house this Friday to teach him about the piano, or even show him some simple scales to play, if he still remembered and was willing.

Did Howard remember? It was possible he didn't, and that realization would crush him. It was also possible his skill would return flawlessly, and that would crush him too. He agreed to come over, but regarding playing the piano himself, he said he couldn't. The idea alone tensed every cell in his being.

Friday came and, with trepidation, Howard trekked to Langston's. The hour and a half walk was uncomfortable, not only mentally but physically—the days grew more and more frigid each day. Today's weather brought a light snowfall, but the snow didn't stick to the ground.

Few snowflakes rested on his coat sleeves as he turned onto Langston's block, the top of his beanie slightly wet and toes numb in his poorly insulated sneakers. Even two layers of socks weren't helping. In hindsight, using up the few dollars to take the subway would have been a better option.

Langston's neighborhood was a charming kind of ritzy, a quieter part of Queens. Shipshape greenery lined the avenues, each tree an array of near-bare yellows, oranges, and reds with the sun filtering through the branches.

The homes were beautiful, cottage-like townhouses, nestled side-by-side with stunning bay windows to peek through. A couple sat cuddled in the living room of number seventy-five. At least he now knew what that felt like, to live with your loved one, in glossy comfort, thanks to the Center. It was achingly pleasant.

"Hiya, Howard. Come in, come in. Get you out of this cold. I made a fresh pot of coffee," Langston said, holding the door open as Howard wiped the muddled slush off the bottom of his shoes. Patting Howard's back, he said, "Feel free to take your shoes off altogether, boy. I pulled a pair of wool socks out for ya on the sofa right there. Remember to always tend to yourself first, or you will never be able to attend to another. Not properly, anyhow." Langston chuckled. "Now, where'd I put my glass of water?" He peered around the living room, spotting it on one of the end tables.

Flames snapped and sputtered in the fireplace at the back of the living room, filling the room with a hickory-fragrant blend of pine and birch and ash, as Howard placed each foot in woolly comfort. He pocketed his two pairs of dust-stained-at-the-bottom socks.

Attentive and cheerful, Langston had the personality Howard imagined Santa Claus's would have—when he was a child, that is. There, Howard was, like an elf learning how to assemble toys, except the toys and lessons regarded life.

Langston's home was clean and timeless. It carried the warmth and ease of a log cabin yet was luxurious and filled with expensive-looking antique furniture. Upon the fireplace was a photograph of a younger Langston and a woman, side by side, holding hands and smiling.

"Ah-ha. I see you are admiring my beloved, Laura. Yes, we were quite the pair. L and L."

Howard picked it up to look more closely at a younger Langston with crew-cut hair, smiling next to a beautiful woman with corkscrew curls, joy-filled eyes, and black skin that shone like onyx, the sun setting behind them. "What happened?"

"She passed long ago, close to ten years now. I was sixty-six, and she was only sixty. A rare cancer spread to her brain. We had planned on doing so much more together.

"Now, here I am, with years' worth of our savings, lots of time, and shit-all to do with it, pardon my French. I moved here two years ago and bought myself some nice things. It didn't satisfy me. To tell you the truth, I regret not having children, and grandchildren, to spend it on. Thanks to you, Howard, I feel like there is kindness again in life. Hope in moving forward. That meeting decent people and building new skills are still possible for an old man like me."

Langston walked over and reached for the frame, sighing as he held it in his hand. It was strange to hear Howard was one to make a difference in another's life. He hoped Langston wasn't being kind for kind's sake.

Langston continued, still holding the frame. "I loved her more than anything and will always love her. What a woman. You have anyone in your life, Howard?" he said, placing the photograph back down on the mantel.

"No. Not really. I am in love though. But it's complicated." Langston didn't need to know how severe the complications were. "Not sure if she will ever love me back, or if she even likes me anymore, for that matter. I don't think I'm good enough for her."

"One of the worst kinds of complications, eh? Some say better than never having loved at all, as exquisite as the pain may be. Be careful to not let it consume you." He stoked the fire. "Before I built my wealth, I lived in poverty. My parents did what they could, but the apartment was rundown. The bathroom mirror had a sizable crack running from one corner to the other, diagonally. Not terrible enough to distort everything, but enough to get in the way of seeing your true self.

"After a while, it gets to you. After a longer while, you start to accept it. What I'm saying is, Howard, if you look in a broken mirror for long enough, you'll begin to believe the reflection. Sometimes people can be that broken mirror, but we don't realize it until it's too late and the damage is done."

Howard's reflection broke long ago. Jillian brought him joy; she had been the closest thing to it in a long time. "Are you suggesting I give up?"

Langston took a deep breath, an audible sigh in reverse. "Is she worth fighting for? Or is she a broken mirror?"

Howard immediately thought of John, and everything John represented. If he could have one part of that, someone who John didn't take too seriously anyway, then he could amount to more than a broom in the closet, only brought around when needed.

"Yes. It is—she is."

"Then there it is. I trust you. Step outside of your comfort zone and fight for what brings you happiness. No one is gonna drop it in your lap, Howard. Now come. Let's have coffee."

After filling their stomachs with hot coffee and muffins in the dark-hued kitchen and giving Howard even more wisdom to ponder over, such as "it's important to 'be', and not just 'do'" (the opposite of what John advises), Langston led Howard to the room where his piano was.

Howard stopped in the doorway, the sight of the baby grand overwhelming.

Black as night, yet gleaming, as if the moon shared its glow, the piano was pristine and polished, recently born and recently purchased, and the ivory keys pearly, like the inside of the Center. Mom and Pop would have adored it—and be floored at the sight of it, at the exorbitant expense, knowing they could never have purchased something similar.

If they could see Howard now, how disappointed would they be? At fourteen years old, he had declared that he would become a rich and famous pianist one day and buy them each brand new everything. Pop said it would be impractical, but he appreciated the thought. Mom appreciated it and believed he would be a success. Maybe she would be proud knowing he had still made a supportive friend, at least.

"You okay, boy?" Langston said. "It is a beauty, that's for sure. I guess enough to make any pianist tear up."

Howard took a step back, his feet soft in the wool socks against the hardwood floor. "Just a lot of memories returning. Anyway, thanks. But I'm not a piano player anymore."

"Howard." Langston neared the piano. "Yes, you are. That sort of thing, that talent, it doesn't leave you. I can tell your hands were meant to dance on the keys. You sure you don't want to check it out? It's all yours." He gestured toward the equally exquisite leather bench.

Howard's fingers slightly tensed and then wiggled. His heartbeat bumped inside his chest, like someone had turned up the bass of a stereo. He checked the clock on the wall. It was almost two—how had it become two already?

He had to get back to John's to run his errands by three. He could leave now, or maybe try out a scale or two before heading out. The subway, plus some walking, would only be about a half hour, forty minutes at most.

It was an honest excuse to not play for any longer than that. He plodded toward the piano seat and lowered himself, the plush leather cushion barely sinking beneath his weight.

Howard eyed the smooth white and black keys; he had not seen keys without cobwebs and dust for the last seventeen years. The piano was a ghost, an old friend from the past.

It was a thousand memories at once—memories of soaring notes, classic symphony after symphony. His own feeling-filled, impressive melodies; Mom and Pop cheering, his family content and complete.

"I'm sorry, I can't," he said, standing up to face Langston. "Not today. I have to go to my brother's."

Langston smiled gently, his voice low. "You can, my boy. You're not ready yet. But I understand. I will continue practicing simple scales from the books until you are ready to show off."

Howard rode the poorly ventilated, crowded subway, which smelled as putrid as his apartment building's elevator, and tried to avoid a mysterious liquid pooling near his feet. He safely evaded the threatening substance and arrived in Astoria, then set for the two-block walk to John's.

Saving money for the Center was priority, but he was too upset to return just yet. If he spoke of Jillian aloud to Elliott, the likely expression on her face would confirm Jillian's silence was not a good sign. He didn't need to spend money to guess that.

Although he preferred to stay in his Balloon Days forever, it was obviously unfeasible, and draining all his funds. Maybe his only other hope was to make it a reality out here, to finally take a leap of faith, like Langston said.

To fight.

Returning to this man-made moment, he again texted Jillian a message: "Can we talk?"

Scrolling through each previously unanswered text, he was suddenly in gym class again, feeling stupid and alone and vulnerable as every kid around him was chosen, one by one, by randomly selected captains.

Come to think of it, he never was a chosen captain. It was always the football kids like Keith Malone, Tommy Gendrin, and Dan Lournes—and Howard wasn't known for his athleticism, so maybe it was not so random after all.

Ambling into John's apartment, Howard turned his phone off and on again, in hopes that it was faulty. Perhaps it needed a reset. Alas, still nothing. He cracked open a beer from John's fridge.

After a couple of hours of reading and getting John's mail and tidying up, sometime between five and six o'clock, the door opened as Howard finished wiping the kitchen counters.

Still no messages. Maybe it was for the best. Although John wasn't the best boyfriend, Howard sometimes felt sorry for him. Even more, he felt guilty for talking to Jillian behind John's back.

When John trudged in, threw his coat and hat on the couch, sifted through the mail, leaving the torn-open envelopes on the table, and stated an underwhelming greeting, Howard's guilt once again dissipated.

John plopped onto the couch and untied his fancy work shoes. Brown Oxfords—the ones John had made Howard order online for him months ago. Howard studied the shoe rack, his latest sneakers on the bottom tier—a pair of black and white Vans John had graciously explained he was about to throw out before thinking of Howard. The soles were still intact at least, though gray from dirt, and the material part was quite lived in.

"Can you make dinner tonight?" John said as he headed toward his bedroom. "I think I'm going to take a nap. They might need me back in the office later."

"Okay."

Howard walked into the stainless-steel sparkling kitchen, grabbed a hanging pot, then filled it with tap water. He set it on the burner and turned on the gas, igniting the flame, half-wishing he was back at Langston's sitting by the fire.

"Oh, guess who came by last night?" John yelled out to Howard from his bedroom. He sounded smug.

"I don't know, John. Another secretary?" Howard feigned interest in his "conquests"—John's despicable terminology for the different women he slept with. It was the one thing Howard had never understood. If even one woman could love Howard, particularly Jillian, that would mean more to him than a thousand fawning girls ever could.

"Nah. Jillian."

Howard stood still, his heart suddenly heavier in his chest, like it had dropped into his stomach and out his rear. He held onto the counter for support, knowing that regardless of any acknowledgment or response, his brother would continue.

As if on cue, John entered the kitchen. Howard wished the water boiled this instant. He visualized dumping it all over John's head, melting him and whatever his next words would be.

"Yeah, so she called me up, crying and desperate. Said she wished we never split up, asked if she could come over and talk. Ha. I said she could, and I told her I was upset too and I hadn't been with anyone since.

You know I didn't want to have to deal with that, plus it isn't any of her business. Then, she came over, so, you know," John said with a smirk.

Howard's hands clenched, his head whirring.

"It was good. Probably better than it has been in a while. She has a great ass for—" he said, gesturing the position by putting his arms out as if he was pulling something toward his groin.

Howard wanted to escape; he wanted the air to go away so he could suffocate and be gone already. John was stupid, ridiculous, selfish. Tears seared the back of each of his eyes, the urge to punch John overwhelming him. John didn't deserve Jillian. Howard did. She wasn't the broken mirror. It was John who punched the glass.

Jillian seemed to have felt the same way as Howard. She had said it, she implied it. Howard was not, could not, be making that up—the hug, the closeness, her wanting to see him again. This had to be a lie. There had to be another reason, a more humane one, for why she had been absent for over a month.

The bubbles rose to the top of the water, gurgling with fury. He lowered the heat and poured the macaroni into the pot, spilling a few on the stovetop.

"What is your problem?" John said. Even without looking, Howard could sense John's eyes were fixed, boring into him.

"I need to go get more sauce, I realized, for the pasta... I'll be back," Howard mumbled, his voice noticeably quavering, as he rushed past John and grabbed his coat from the front hall closet, dashed out the door into the night.

Scrambling to the Hudson River a few blocks away, he snapped grass like picks of glass beneath his feet. He sat on the nearest bench. He took out his phone and dialed Jillian. To Howard's surprise, she answered, but remained silent.

"Jillian?" Trapped tears thickened his voice like a slug in his throat as he shivered. "Are you there?"

"I'm here." Howard was now the silent one, so she went on. "I'm guessing John told you we got back together," she began. "He wrote me a long apology. I felt horrible. I know I shouldn't have met up with him, it was so stupid. But when I was with him, I thought maybe it could work, and how maybe I had left too quickly. That we could give it a reset, you know?"

"John said you reached out to him."

"I'm sorry if I led you on."

His hand shook against the phone. Yet, she sounded unfazed. "Led me on? You are going to reduce it to that? I understand I'm not the best candidate for a boyfriend. But then at least, please, don't go back to him." Howard wanted to throw the phone. Why couldn't she be more like the Jillian in his Balloon Days? "That day alone with you meant a lot to me." It had given Howard hope.

"I guess I'm not ready to give up on him. I know he wasn't the best and he is definitely far from perfect. But that day with you was special to me too, I swear."

Howard waited for a bundled-up jogger to pass by before he spoke again, his anger taking over. "If I have to see you around him again, I don't know how much I can take. Hearing him bring you up, and in the vile way he does. You can't only come to me when you're upset with him. It's not right. I can't do it. Any of it. It will break me. This is breaking me."

He let it out. "I love you. I have for a long time." Howard's breath slowed down, so low he could barely hear it. "It sounds selfish. But I wish I met you first. Before you met John."

Quiet.

The air was still and dark.

"Jillian?" His voice broke through the silence.

"Oh—yeah, wow, um." Her voice was barely audible. Howard lifted his beanie and pressed the phone harder against his ear. She went on, her voice louder now. "This is all my fault. I shouldn't have asked you to come see me. I screwed everything up. You're so, so sweet. I didn't mean to hurt you."

"Do you feel nothing for me?" Against Howard's ear drums, his heartbeat thudded, and despite the cold, his forehead had begun to sweat.

More nothingness. More hesitant breaths.

Then, she finally said, "I do like you. You are so sweet. You make me feel more special than I think anyone ever has. But it's like there's you, and then there's my life with him. I think because I was with John first that I owe him—"

"You don't owe him anything." She was acting delusional.

"I'm sorry, but you have to understand." Her voice lowered. "Please know I never meant to hurt you."

"Sure." Howard removed his beanie, the air immediately cooling off his head. If he couldn't be happy, at least the people he loved could be. Maybe that was his lot in life. "I'm sorry too."

"Do you think we can still be friends?"

Howard winced. "I don't think we should talk anymore."

"At all?" she said.

"It's for the best," he lied.

"That will be hard, but I understand." Jillian paused. "I do have another question."

Howard stayed silent.

"Can you please not tell John we met up? No matter what. I just don't want to deal with it, I want to move forward, okay?"

If Howard had hair, this would be when he would rip it out. Instead, he sighed heavy and slumped, his rear at the edge of the chilled bench. "I wouldn't do that to you. The last thing I want to see is you hurting." As for himself, he wished to be gone completely. Thoughts of how life was before the real possibility of being with Jillian was not a life he wanted to return to.

"Thank you—for always being so kind, even when I don't deserve it," Jillian said. "I will try not to be there when you are. Until you are ready. I should go now. I'm sorry. Goodbye, Howard." Howard would never be ready.

The pain was too much. He should have told her John's a lying cheater. But something held him back.

John was sitting on the couch, remote control in hand, when Howard returned. "What the hell, man? I did have a jar of sauce. And thanks for taking forever. I had to do everything."

The sauce. Thank God John was too self-absorbed to notice the lack of a bag in Howard's hand.

In the bathroom, Howard stared at himself in the uncracked mirror. If he had the nice clothes, the expensive, shiny shoes, the modern everything, he would be considered more attractive, more acceptable.

He knew that. Maybe more weight on his frame would help as well. But staring back at him was reality. Yes, his facial structure was symmetrical, and he had features that worked well together.

He could grow a great beard and he was always told how beautiful his eye color was by many, so he must be somewhat acceptable. Why couldn't she love him back? Was having a successful career that important to her? Or was it truly her guilt keeping her away, like she said?

Or maybe Howard simply wasn't lovable.

CHAPTER 24
ORSON

Orson prepared to go into the office to speak with Jack, outfitting himself in his favorite, most esteemed suit, one he bought himself after his deserved promotion and hefty raise: navy-blue wool, Zegna Couture, complete with a burgundy Hermès tie and brown leather Armani shoes and belt.

The outfit in which Madison had advised, "Whenever you wear this suit, remember all it took to get here."

He used to think it was about enduring grueling years of school, the long hours each case required, calls in the middle of the night from his insensible boss. Now, as he stood in the mirror, he saw what she taught him all those years, the hidden lessons he missed when she was still alive.

It was important to stay humble. It was important to stay connected to what mattered. To remember and appreciate where he came from.

Orson arrived at the firm. It was in the North Shore of Long Island, not too far from home. Behind the expansive reception area was the firm's name mounted on the wall: Gabriel & Co. in sizeable gold letters.

Jack's office was modern with its shiny black desk, black floors, and a silver bar cart, a vast difference from Orson's preferred, traditional look for an office. Thankfully, Madison knew how to blend modern and traditional well at home.

"Look who it is," Jack said, slapping Orson's shoulder.

Jack was in his late fifties, of average height, his hair tobacco brown like Orson's except striated with gray and slicked over with a side part. Crow's feet around his eyes appeared whenever he smiled, and he mostly stayed clean-shaven.

"I'm back in action." Orson gave a quick nod. "How are things?"

"Great, my man. That question is more for you though. How ya doin'?"

"Things are going much better." It was not a complete lie.

"Fantastic to hear. Pulled out your finest, I see." He motioned for Orson to take a seat. "Drink?"

"I'm good for now, thanks." Orson sat down on the leather chair across from Jack's.

Jack poured himself a glass of gin, took a sip, then sat down across Orson, his imposing desk in between them. "We understand that you must be going through a lot. If you weren't so damned good at what you do, I'd say take all the time you need. But it's hard to get these clients to switch to someone else here, and once they've been with you, they're locked in, ya damn bastard. You're like a goddamned money magnet," Jack said, chuckling.

"I appreciate the praise. It certainly has been a trying time, to say the least." Orson looked at his watch. Time was extra precious today; he missed Madison, and he couldn't miss his Balloon Day appointment. He needed to use his time without Ryder well to prove to Rose he healed.

"Well then," Jack said. "Let's get down to it. Senior partner. Still interested? Eventually, you might become the top dog around here. I'm only getting older." The idea of leading a firm of his own had been a long-term goal of Orson's. He didn't feel nearly as excited about the prospect as he used to.

"Is it possible to have more time to think about it?" Orson leaned forward in his seat, realizing the error of his ways. He knew he sounded weak, and he needed to fix that. "I'm certainly interested, I just want to make sure it's all done right." He checked his watch again.

Jack stared at him for a long moment, chewing Orson's words. "I get it. That's smart." He took another sip of gin.

"Thanks for understanding," Orson replied. "I won't need much longer for the decision, but I am ready to get back to working cases. I'm ready to take on the Robert's case and close that one out for good. Should be getting a nice payday from that malpractice suit."

"Good to hear, Orson. Your expertise as a senior partner is worth having more patience for, so long as there's no bullshitting me. Ha. As for you returning to your cases, they're all yours." Jack tipped his drink toward him.

"I appreciate that." Orson snuck a look at the clock on the wall.

"You have somewhere you need to be?" Jack said.

Apparently, Orson was not as slick as he thought. It was unlike him to not keep a good poker face. His poise was one of his most treasured traits as a lawyer, one of the many reasons Jack wanted him on his team—a skill he boasted about when introducing Orson at business dinners.

"I have to visit Ryder's school about a permission slip he needs, and then I got a lead on a new, lucrative case. Gonna wine and dine 'em, then reel 'em in." The lie came out, manipulating Jack as easily as he manipulated plaintiffs into spilling the truth. What a relief that not all of his skills had atrophied.

"Of course, Orson." Jack swirled the ice in his gin, clacking it against the glass. He raised his eyebrows.

That's it, he's onto me.

Orson needed to leave before he provoked any more suspicion. He stood and collected his briefcase.

"We'll chit-chat again soon," Jack said. "Let me know if the case is worth taking on before you charm 'em too much." He rose from behind his desk. "Good to have you back full time, truly. Tell the boy I said hello."

"Will do."

After a pit stop to Shamone's Deli for a gold-wrapped grilled chicken, pesto, and fresh mozzarella panini, Orson checked in with three of his clients, Darnell, Viraj, and Mark, on his way to the Center. Once parked he said his goodbye to the most significant client of all, Darnell—he is content and won't be smearing Orson's reputation after all.

Maybe he couldn't do anything to save Madison before, no matter the top physicians or medical treatments he had found and paid for—but now he could save her memory, and in doing so, he could save her.

Somehow, some way, he was bringing her back.

Sitting in his Day Room, he pressed the glowing button on the control. Within seconds, the sofa beneath him vanished, a hand slipped into his, and Madison appeared at his side.

She pointed straight ahead and gasped. Peering from the basket of a hot air balloon tethered to the ground, they were suspended about five hundred feet above Paris; the Eiffel Tower appeared small in the distance, but no less graceful and grand.

Here they were again, in Parc de Citreon, floating high in the Ballon de Paris Generali.

She smacked his cheek with a kiss, then lifted his hand into the air and the hot air balloon vanished. Immediately, his mind took over, his perception led, and they glided over the city. Finally, he had control.

He took a breath of fresh, cool air, expanding his lungs with a chill as nourishing as water on a hot day. The scent of fresh baguettes hit Orson's nose. Below, Parisians drank glasses of red wine, smoked cigarettes, and ate pain au chocolat outside cafes, waving up at the two of them. The wind grazed his cheek. Madison's hair trailed behind her, a flowing cascade of strawberry blonde.

They stopped, slowly falling downward, like a leaf abandoning its branch, but as their feet touched the ground, the landscape around them shifted. They were now perched on a bench on Mont Saleve overlooking Geneva. Rooftops of houses were red sprinkles from afar; trees were heads of broccoli Ryder pushed to the side of his plate.

The city surrounded Lake Geneva, a rink of sparkling sapphire blue. The Jet d'Eau, a shooting geyser of a fountain, could still be seen from over four thousand feet high. Clouds hovered above the city and shadows of mountains lined the horizon.

Madison and he traveled as much as they could before Ryder entered their lives. It wasn't until earlier last year, before Madison was diagnosed, that Ryder was old enough for grander adventures. With his new passport in hand, they mapped out a two-week trip to Europe. But Ryder's passport remained blank.

Orson turned his body to look at Madison and take her hand in his.

"I miss you," he said. "More than you could ever know."

Madison lowered his hands and squeezed them back. "I miss you too, Orson, gosh, do I miss you."

"I'm no good without you, Madison. I'm messing up. Ryder's going to hate me soon, if he doesn't already. Rose resents me. I'm on my last thread at work. I need you back, I need your help. I don't know what to do."

"I'm sorry that you need to do all this alone now," she said. "I'm glad you found a way to visit me." Orson slid off the bench, feeling the soft earth beneath his knees.

"I would visit you forever if you wanted. Everyone keeps telling me to grieve, to move on." He shook his head, over and over, tears beginning to wet his eyes. "The truth is I don't know how to miss you and move on, because I don't want to miss you. I don't want to move on."

Madison brushed his hair back as the last of the setting sun slipped away.

"I think about you all the time," he said. "All the time. I won't cancel your magazine subscriptions or remove your name off our shared accounts. I order your favorite foods and drinks when I'm out. I spray your perfume on your pillow to pretend you're still there. But then I reach over and you're not there, and I'm lonely. I'm terribly lonely." Madison dropped to her knees with him, her head falling on his chest as he wrapped his arms around her.

Orson stared at the stars, releasing what he had not been able to admit to anyone, or to himself. "Every night I think if one of us had to die, I wish it had been me. You didn't deserve this. You deserved a full life with Ryder, to see him grow up, graduate, have children of his own. Being with him brings me comfort but breaks my heart—seeing you in him, knowing you aren't by my side, that I'm just a father now, his only parent, while kids around him have their own mothers they can run to at the end of the day. I don't know how to handle it, any of this, even my own thoughts."

He pressed his lips against her forehead. "I tried to save you. I couldn't. I didn't. I tried, I tried so hard, but it wasn't enough. I'm sorry. I should have never left your side that day. I should have never taken Jack's call." Orson gasped for air. "I failed you."

Sobs came in waves, stealing his breath. "Now I'm failing our son."

Madison gently pulled away, looking up at him. "Oh, Orson. Neither of us deserve what happened. Don't ever think it should have been you. The cancer—my death—none of it is your fault. None of it. Our love was beautiful. You gave me everything I needed, everything I didn't know I wanted. As for Ryder, you will do fine. He loves you. Thank God he has you. Stop trying to be something you're not. I could always tell that's when you parented the best."

Orson wiped his nose with his sleeve, then made the glistening snot disappear. Why couldn't he make Madison's death disappear too, and have her back in real life? "God, I wish I saw it all sooner. I wish it didn't take until you became sick and left, until now, to stop caring as much about money and things that don't matter. I wish I could make it all up to you. All of the years I was missing out on you," he said. "On Ryder. On us."

Madison had filled his life with her laughter, her touches, her words, her light. Yet he spent so many years taking her love for granted. When she got pregnant, he told her, as well as himself, that things would be different.

But it was a promise short-lived.

Orson had buried himself in late nights, in work again, determined to create the best life for his family. He missed out on helping Ryder with his homework and playing video games together before bedtime. Conversations at dinner time were interrupted by work calls or rushed along to get back to work. Some nights, he didn't make it back for dinner, at all.

How could he have put a monetary value on happiness? Happiness was her; happiness was Ryder; it was his sister, mother, and father. Happiness was letting yourself be fully thrown into life with the ones you love, in not only the special moments but the ordinary ones too.

He looked out at the city. The stars continued to gleam and light up the lake. "Maybe I deserve to be miserable."

"No," she said, pulling his face back toward hers. "Don't do that to yourself. Be there for Ryder now. You have time. Maybe there is a way to have us both."

They were suddenly pulled, spit back out, now in their house the way it was arranged in the present day, sitting on the living room couch.

Madison started twitching, like a television garbled by static. "Maybe... there's a way to... get me back... in your... life."

"Madison? What do you mean? Are you okay?"

"Hold me." Her hands transformed in his, the skin shriveling, then disintegrating, leaving only her bones, the wedding band dropping to the floor. "Orson, I'm scared."

"Hold on, Madison. Hold on to me. Hold on."

Orson tried to grab onto her, wrap her in his arms, but she and the room vanished as quickly as the hot air balloon had.

CHAPTER 25
ELLIOTT

How could Elliott know where to start with a decision so world-tilting, so heart-wrenching? Step one was to tell Asher. Throwing the comforter off, she placed her feet on the powder blue rug, stretching her arms upward. It was already five o'clock. She removed her plaid pajama top and tossed it on the bed.

She slid a sports bra on, opened her closet, and grabbed an oversized green sweater and threw it over her head. She dug for a pair of jeans from the pile left in the laundry basket for five days now (she couldn't exactly remember if the clothes were clean or dirty), gave up, and went with black leggings instead.

Staring at herself in her floor-length mirror, eyes bloodshot and swollen, she whipped on some mascara then concealed the dark circles. She had hidden in her bed for most of the weekend, shedding tear after tear until she'd eventually fall asleep again.

The tears were almost constant lately. She'd never cried so much in one single period of her life. She became acquainted with all types—so many shapes and sizes and durations: the quick, watery ones that were easily swept away. The quiet ones, surprising her as they wet her cheeks. The hot, stinging ones forcing themselves out from the inner corners of her eyes. The heavy, heaving, gut-punching sobs; the howling, body-curling wails.

Three quick knocks echoed up the staircase, and she went downstairs to let Asher inside. She was petrified. She had to tell him.

Asher mumbled what sounded like a hello and gave his lazy one-armed hug. It was dull and lifeless. How had she only begun to accept he would never change? Aside from the bedroom, he didn't let loose unless it was to spend a lot on dinners or gifts for her, and maybe during those few minutes he flew the kite that day in the park, and of course, when he was drunk. But after that careless disaster last time, she never wanted to be drunk with him again.

Having dated for close to two years now, she learned more and more about how mechanical he was. His precise routine: herbal tea with biscuits for breakfast, a protein shake, the gym for two hours, a shower, his moisturizers, then either work or coming to see her—it was so irritating, so monotonous.

Once, he'd left his shower basket out on her sink with a makeup concealer stick next to his fancy Oribe shampoo. He drowned in insecurities and his weird, borderline creepy, routine was to control them. Maybe she was part of that routine too. Something to control. If only she broke up with him before the party, none of this would have happened.

"So, what's new?" he said. He sat down on the couch, his toned biceps peeking out from underneath his plain white t-shirt. Would she see these same arms cradling her baby in eight months if she kept the pregnancy? More importantly, would she want to? He shifted in his seat to take his phone out from the pocket of his wrinkle-free jeans, custom-tailored to skim the tops of his black loafers. He checked the time. "You hungry, babe? Want to go get a bite to eat?"

"Asher, I need to tell you something," she said. Captain jumped up on the couch next to her and curled himself into a furry golden ball.

"Okay..." Asher's eyes squinted.

"I'm pregnant," she blurted out. Surprisingly, she felt relieved. Maybe the avoidance had made her more uncomfortable than the difficult decision itself. She had seen the same thing in patients—anticipation keeping them in agony, like kids putting up a prolonged fight before getting a shot that lasts ten seconds.

When she thought of the actual decision again, her stomach clenched.

"Oh. That sucks. But really?" Asher's voice was high and quite shrill.

"That 'sucks'?" Elliott stared at him.

"You said you took the emergency pill." He bounced his leg. "Or were you lying? Maybe you wanted this. I've read girls do that."

"I did take it—but I'm sorry, what are you even saying? Why would I have wanted this? And for the record, you played a part in this too. You told me you were wearing a condom."

"But you took the pill. You must have screwed something up."

"This was your fault," she said. "I didn't screw anything up."

"Alright, well, it's a simple fix. Get an abortion. I'll pay for my half," he said, reaching for his wallet.

Elliott stared at the rug, its delicate mix of grays and blues beginning to blur together. How could he be so casual about all of it? How could he be so damn indifferent? She was alone in her scurry, her fear. Her voice turned into a whisper as she held back tears. "I don't know anymore."

"What? Speak louder."

"I didn't know, Asher." The tears began to drop, tumbling toward her chin. "I didn't know how I would feel when I said that at the time. It was easy to say because it wasn't happening then—it wasn't anything I would imagine I'd feel now." She put her hand on her abdomen. "It's nothing I could describe."

Not to him. He would never understand. He would never understand the closeness—the fusion of another life within her, the warmth diffusing throughout her body, the love and connection she already felt; her instinct to protect her baby, especially from him, was insurmountable.

"I'm sorry. But if you don't do it then—you lied," he said pointedly, his tone suddenly low and cold. "You would be a liar. We already discussed this." He scoffed and picked a honey-blonde dog hair off his jeans.

Elliott wiped her tears with her hands. "I am not a liar. You're the liar. You told me you put a condom on that night."

. "Yeah, and then after I told you I forgot." He stood up from the couch and hovered over her. "God, Elliott, you can't be serious. We can't have a baby." He laughed again, yet this time it seemed full of nerves. "We can't. I can't do it. I do not want to be a father right now. Not now, if ever. I wouldn't be good at it..." He trailed off, staring at the rug.

Maybe he did have emotions after all. He looked scared, and part of her sympathized with him. A small part.

"Like I said," he went on as he looked at her again. "I'll pay for half of it. I can look up places, take you to the doctor, I can book it, all that jazz." He walked away to take out his phone again.

"Stop," she bellowed. "Stop. It." Stomping her foot, she suddenly felt so small, so afraid, so childlike. Captain jumped off the light gray sofa and fled toward the bedroom. "You don't understand. It is so easy for you to say, but you have no idea what it's been like for me," she said, her voice rising. "How can you not care at all?"

"It's a bug," he said, his voice rising. "Nothing else."

Those words. She cringed. Hand on stomach, she realized she was completely alone in this. Julie had been right—he wasn't going to respond how she wanted him to. Asher was emotionally vacant. He wouldn't offer the support she needed. Not now. Not ever. She felt lightheaded. It became difficult to see, difficult to breathe, the air coming in rapidly, too quickly to hold onto, in and out, and in and out, and in again, her chest heavy, her stomach tight, her throat closing. How could someone be so cruel, so manipulative? How could she have wasted so much time on him? The room spun.

Asher did nothing but stare at her as she panicked. "Your fucking anxiety shit is driving me insane."

Elliott's world steadied and with her words she breathed out her disgust. "You're heartless."

"That's a lie," he said.

"You called it a bug."

"Jesus. I meant it hasn't grown yet. Nothing I say or do is right. Not to you." He shook his head. "This is who I am. This is how I talk. If you don't like it, break up with me."

"I don't like it." Elliott took a moment to look at Asher, the man she thought she loved, before she continued. "I don't like you. I hate what we've become. I hate what you fucking did to me. You've made my life miserable, no matter what I did to make our relationship work. I might even hate you. We're done, Asher. Get out of my house." She demanded. "Now."

"You're actually breaking up with me?"

"I wish I had done this sooner."

"Look, I was only joking. You're clearly emotional right now, but that's no need to—"

"I said get the fuck out." Without thinking, Elliott shoved him. *Shit.*

"Yeah, and I'm the bad guy," Asher mumbled as he regained his balance.

Everything unraveled so quickly. This wasn't the composed break-up she envisioned.

"I'm sorry." Elliott's hands shook with regret. She took a step toward him, but Asher backed away. "I didn't mean it."

"You are fucking batshit," he spat. "It'd be my pleasure to leave."

As Asher walked toward the door, she quickly followed him, stepping in between him and the door to try again. "Wait, Asher, I'm sorry. I didn't mean it. You know it's not like me to behave that way."

Asher stood there firmly, lips pursed and eyes looking down at the floor. "Maybe it is like you. Now, I'm serious. Move." His arms and fists tightened.

"No. Stop, come on. Let's talk about it. It was stupid, I got angry. I got carried away. Please." Lips, trembling, she tried to hold his hands, but he ripped his away.

"I don't care. You wanted me gone, I'm gone." She attempted to hug him, and he immediately turned away. "Fine. I'll find another way out." He left the foyer, hurried through the kitchen toward the living room, where the sliding doors leading out to the yard were.

Elliott hastened her pace trying to catch up.

"Elliott. Don't make me have to go past you." He whirled around and headed back toward the front door. She grabbed his arm. "Get off. You're going to make me want to hurt you."

She stepped in front of him. How could he threaten such a thing? "You wouldn't do that."

Asher's eyes were icy, unblinking. He looked at her as if she was vermin. He clamped Elliott's arms and shook her, his grip full of alarming intensity.

"I wouldn't? I don't care about you. Or that stupid baby."

"I'm sorry," she yelled. "Let go of me."

He forcibly moved her out of the way, the push knocking her back against the wall.

When she looked up, the front door opened and he was gone.

She rebalanced herself and rushed out onto the front porch, coatless, barefoot, feeling the frosted stone beneath the soles of her feet.

Crossing her arms for warmth, she called out his name, but he didn't turn around. He continued to walk down the pathway from the house, onto the sidewalk, into his Jeep.

"Asher. Are you kidding me? Please. Don't let it end like this." A girl walked her dog across the street and Elliott's dignity shrank to the size of a pea. "Please come back," she said, lowering her voice.

The sounds of his car door opening and shutting, echoed against the silence of the night. The engine rumbled and within seconds he sped off.

Across the street, her neighbor continued walking her dog, pretending not to notice as Elliott stood there lonely, abandoned, teeth clattering, likely bruised. And pregnant.

A thin layer of fresh snow twinkled like sugar in the moonlight. Elliott's leftover briny tears stung her cheeks whenever the wind whipped. She didn't want to do this alone, but she didn't want to do it with Asher either.

She could not believe it.

She disappointed herself with such shameful behavior. She didn't want to lose control, especially in front of Asher. She was furious with him, with all of it. She should have gone about it differently, but he should have been understanding—he should have shown even an ounce of compassion.

She went back inside and, with the last of her frenetic energy, slammed the door shut, causing a thunderous roar. The fact Asher didn't stop to apologize, didn't look at her as he walked away, crippled her. How could she have ever dated someone with such hate in his heart?

Part of her thought maybe he would come back and apologize for what he said and forgive her, and give their break-up a proper, sufficient ending. But he had not. Instead, he had driven off.

Elliott stormed into her bedroom and found herself dumping her box of collected sugar packets onto her bed. She grabbed the ones she kept from dates with Asher and chucked them at the wall. One broke and spilled on the floor. She began to sob.

Falling to her knees, tears continued to burst through like water from a crack in the dam. A wail produced from deep within, painful and raw and heavy. Elliott searched for hope, for answers, but nothing came.

CHAPTER 26
HOWARD

Howard didn't want another Balloon Day, not yet at least. But he did need therapy, desperately. The last few days had been a whirlwind since hearing about John and Jillian's reunion.

He still couldn't make sense of it. Why did John want her back, and who was the one who initiated it? It would have been awful if she had said she was interested in someone else entirely, but at least it would have been more understandable than going back to fucking John.

"Howard, tell me what's going on. You seem distraught."

Elliott looked tired today too, the dark circles under her eyes prominent. Maybe therapists had their own life issues. He hoped she was alright, but here she was, so he continued, although he was still not used to a relationship being so one-sided. It was strange to have all the attention.

"Jillian's back with John." He couldn't stop his leg from shaking. "I found out from him."

They sat in the corner of her office, away from her desk; she must have recently rearranged her room—still smaller than Dr. Heller's corner, but he quite liked the coziness it added. The room itself smelled like cinnamon spice from the lit candle on the windowsill, one of the kinds that crackled while it burned.

Elliott leaned forward, resting her hands on her knees. "Oh, gosh, Howard. That must have hurt you. Especially after how things were going with her before."

She could have been judging him right now, she could have told him this is what he gets for falling in love with his brother's girlfriend. But she didn't. It wasn't her job to say "I told you so."

"I left John's and I called her to ask her why. I asked her why she would do that, and why she wouldn't, at the very least, tell me she had considered going back to him." Words were racing and plummeting out of his mouth and he didn't care; someone was finally listening to his pain, being there for him only, like Mom had when she was still alive.

"She said she felt bad when John called her up, saying he was upset. That he missed her. But John had told me she was the one who reached out to him." His fingers curled into fists. "The only truth I know is that they are back together, and I had to hear it from him. Not in a simple way, either. He had to slip in there how they slept together. Also, I raised my voice slightly at Jillian at one point. I'm not proud of that." His gaze dropped to the floor. "But I was spiraling."

When Howard looked up, Elliott held a look of care and sorrow, each green eye a forest floor of emotions. In that moment, he could see she knew heartbreak too.

"It makes perfect sense why you reacted that way. I am proud of you for releasing that emotion, not numbing it with alcohol," she said. "What are you going to do now?"

Everything about what she had said stumped him. He never thought in-depth about his emotions. He hadn't even read anything about what made an emotion... an emotion. Alcohol numbed them? It made sense. Perhaps one could be intelligent while being an emotional moron. He didn't want to tell Elliott how he had indeed drowned the emotions out later that night.

In terms of what he would do, well, he never had thought about what he would do or could do aside from wallow and dwell and continue onward with his monotonous life.

"What are my options?" he said.

"Well," she said, her eyes squinting in thought. "You could take the safe route—keep your head down, act outwardly like nothing ever happened, with that deep pain trapped inside. Or you could make a change." She rested against her chair again.

Howard shifted in his seat, suddenly, quite aware of her gaze—each eye, a spotlight on him.

"A small one, though. Baby steps. What would be some possible risks for you to take?"

The last time he took a risk was going out to see Jillian in Long Island.

"I don't know. I was always taught to play it safe. Now that I think about it, my father himself was not much of a change-maker either."

"You are not your father. You can make change happen. And remember, I'm not suggesting you take a giant risk here, like confronting John. What about something that meets safety and growth in the middle?"

He looked at his hands, reminding him he had not returned to Langston's since his last visit, had not met him at the library, and hadn't returned his last few calls either. There was a pang of guilt but he pushed it aside.

"I could ask Jillian to meet me and talk again, but this time in person," he said.

"What would be your goal?" She took a sip of water then placed the glass back on the white marble end table.

"To get some type of answer." He moved the pillow from behind his back and placed it on his lap. "To see the truth in her face. To know I did all I could. Maybe I could convince her to end things with him. Not to be with me, but for her own good. It kills me knowing a great person like her is with a cheater."

"I do wonder if she is as amazing as you believe. But I think that discussion requires more time."

Howard disagreed. Everything he knew about Jillian was wonderful, aside from her flip-flopping and naivety. "Maybe," he settled with.

"Completely up to you. You can let me know. But back to the main point—what would you be risking?"

The pillow was soft and comforting on his lap, its color a pleasing shade of forget-me-not blue. It had a braided edge that Howard liked the feel of against his fingertips. "She stays with John no matter what I say. Or he somehow finds out, but that seems unlikely. She made me promise to not tell him about our coffee... meeting." It was clearer now. It was not a date.

"That's your homework then," she said. "See if Jillian will meet with you for closure."

Within days of Elliott's encouragement, Howard sat in the backseat of Jillian's car, the nighttime snow frosting the windows. The weather was gloomy yet convenient for hiding. His risk was in motion.

Although the winter chill stilled the air, Jillian had turned the engine off to save gas, with Howard's blanket being one of their options for warmth. She parked not too far from his apartment. The chosen street abandoned, dark, save for the streetlights hung like suspended marigold orbs shining down on the sidewalk every ten feet or so.

He sat at an angle, feeling the curve of the door digging into his back. Jillian leaned on the opposite door, under the shabby fleece blanket. A visual reminder that she was out of his reach.

"I'm glad you suggested we talk in person. It's nice seeing you," Jillian said.

Howard looked at the chocolate strands of her hair, her face glowing a bluish white from the moonlight.

"Do you honestly think John is a good boyfriend?"

She let out a hesitant laugh. "I think so, but you keep talking like you know something I don't. Spill it, already. Did he say something dumb?"

"No, it's not that." It was now or never. "He cheated on you. Multiple times. He still does."

Jillian sat in silence, staring at the floor of the car. Faint, fragile exhales escaped her mouth. Now that it was said, Howard wasn't sure what to do next. He didn't plan for that part.

Or how she would look. Like someone told her that her parents died. He wanted to eat his words back up, swallowing them whole, to see the hurt lift from her eyes. There was no going back now.

Still staring off into nothingness, she said, "When?"

"After you've had nasty fights and don't speak for a few days. He doesn't bother hiding the evidence, it's almost like he wants me to see the women walking out half-naked in the morning, as if he's trying to prove something to me." Howard's voice was as small as he felt. "I'm sorry."

"When was the last time?" She pulled at the bottom strands of her hair.

"Before you left for Paris. After you fought about him not spending enough time with you."

"Oh God," she said. "I can't believe this. Now the condoms under the bed make sense."

"You found used condoms, too?" Howard said, astonished. How could she still not have realized?

"No, I meant a box. You've found used ones?"

"Yeah, they weren't exactly hidden," Howard said. "I'm assuming you two don't use them."

She remained quiet, but it gave him the answer, proving John correct.

"What excuse did he come up with for the ones you found then?" Howard said.

"That the box was old. From before we dated. God, saying this out loud—I feel so stupid," Jillian said, shaking her head. "I think somewhere deep down I knew all along, but it's one of those things you don't want to see. Like lies that you want to believe so badly are truths, so you try so hard to believe. I wanted to believe, at least. Obviously, the version of John I wanted him to be was all in my head." She stared off again into the distance with tears in her eyes. Howard knew the feeling.

"Why, Jillian? Why not give up and move on for good?"

For a moment, she said nothing. She looked at her hands, at that damn ring, holding her birthstone, a sparkling ruby. The ring that Howard picked out for John to gift her for their one-year anniversary. "Because I love him."

Silence again. Howard had the sudden urge to leave. She specifically said love, not loved. What had Howard done? It's as if he planted a bomb but the control was in the hands of some Howard-hating entity that could blast it at any moment without warning. His life was a never-ending series of explosions. It was officially his fault this time. If only this was a Balloon Day, he would squeeze his eyes shut and make it all go away.

Questions attacked him like a swarm of bees. What if she tells John she knows he cheated? Would she tell him that Howard was the one to let her know? If not, John would put two and two together. Howard doubted John told his friends of his affairs, but then again, maybe he bragged about it to them, too. Jillian broke the quiet and the bees fell to the ground.

"But as much as I love him, I admit, I've been thinking about what you said, about if I had met you sooner. Before John. And I think that maybe I wish that had happened too." She scooted closer to him. Howard's heart was beginning to pound against his brain. Jillian's words surprised him.

The word risk returned in his mind. So far, somehow, things had taken a turn for the better.

Risk. Risk. Risk.

It repeated in his mind like a ticking clock.

"Howard, are you okay? You're being extra quiet. Howard?"

"Yeah?"

"Can I hold your hand?"

He looked at her palm faced up, waiting. Then at her sweet-sad smile. John would not find out about any of this.

She wouldn't tell him. Howard knew that.

Maybe he didn't need closure. What did that mean anyway? Why did he think it would help? Endings, suck, separations suck, losses suck. No matter what. Whether this was an ending or a beginning, he couldn't tell yet. Either way, it should be memorable, and if it was an ending, it should be a sweet one, a romantic one, if there had to be an ending at all.

Without another thought or question or worry to ruin it, or to let the moment slip away by being too safe, too nice, too submissive to life—he placed his hand on her own. Jillian looked down, mouth slightly open, eyebrows higher, then back up at him. She interlocked her fingers with his, filling the spaces between each digit while filling the voids of his heart, his starvation of human connection, for her connection, finally fed.

Adrenaline hit him and the heat in his groin quickly spread throughout his legs, his stomach, his chest. It was unlike fear, it was unlike whiskey, unlike anything Kimmy had ever made him feel; it was something quite exquisite.

"How much time do we have together?" she said.

"However long you'd like me to stay." She was indeed a mirror, perfectly uncracked as Howard had said, and he loved every bit of his reflection.

Jillian had the same look on her face she had when last with him, right before he left on the train. Now there was no mistaking it. Howard lifted her chin, and slowly, meeting her halfway, pressed his lips against hers.

Warm and soft and full, her lips began to part. She placed her hand on the side of his head, their tongues entwining delicately. The world vanished and he was a floating body floating away with her. It was magic. It was fireworks. It was winning the gold medal.

Jillian gently lifted her leg over his waist and straddled him. Arms around his neck. He grabbed her thighs and then her waist, pulling her closer. He could smell the sweet peach as he leaned forward to kiss her again, but she stopped him.

"Wait," she said. She slid next to him. Her voice breathy. "Is anyone outside?"

"Even if anyone is out there, they can't see in. All the windows are fogged up."

"Is this a bad idea?" She bit her lip, slowly flipping her hair from one side to the other; loose strands fell upon her face, returning the rush, the fire, in his pulse.

It was a bad idea for several reasons. He didn't give two shits about those. He didn't care if she and John were still together, or if they were together last night, or not together at this point.

He didn't care if she and he were from separate worlds. Or if he was being irrevocably selfish. All he cared about was her and that she was here in this moment, alone, with him.

His hand, as if it had a mind of its own, cradled her cheek, drawing her closer.

"I think it's the best idea we've had in a long while," he said. He grazed his thumb over the divots of her mouth, her bottom lip pouting open. He kissed her harder this time, for all the times he could not, for all the love he had stored up, for all the years he was cast aside and left alone and undesired, by Kimmy, by everyone. Lips crushing together, he grew hungrier. He wanted more.

So did Jillian. She quickly unbuttoned her pants. Howard followed and unbuttoned his, awkwardly pulling them off. Her underwear was a deep crimson, a stark contrast to the gray of his. Her bare legs caused him to shudder.

Their exhalations were translucent puffs of white air, but he removed her sweater anyway and draped his blanket around her shoulders. He lowered her down on the seat, removed her underwear, grazing her outer thighs as he slid them down. He kissed her hips. The dip and curve of her side. The swell of her chest. Everywhere.

Jillian's breathing grew heavier and he listened to each response, each shudder. He kept track of every expression of pleasure. Digging her nails into his shoulders, more moans escaped, each intensifying to an orgasmic crescendo.

Howard removed his boxers and shook them off his leg. She pulled him close, kissed his lips, his chin, his neck. Howard shivered, but not from the winter air.

Their bodies synchronized to an imperturbable rhythm of their own design.

Relishing her scent, her taste, her skin, her desire—it freed his pain. Her open mouth, her eyes gazing up at him, her legs wrapped around his waist.

Howard broke his heart and placed her deep inside.

Soon after, she fell asleep in his arms. He made a mental note to document this night in his journal. He wanted to lock it perfectly in his memory, keeping it as pure as the night sky, every star in its rightful place.

After Jillian woke up, they prepared to part.

"I think we can make this work," she said, buttoning up her pants. "I think I'm falling for you, Howard."

"Are you serious?" He said.

Jillian opened the car door, and Howard followed her outside.

"Yes, I'm serious." She grabbed his hand.

Was he dreaming? Maybe he was in a Balloon Day and was too drunk to remember having gone to the Center.

"But we have to play it smart," she said, staring at the deserted street. "This has to be thought out properly." She spoke as if Howard wasn't there, then returned her gaze to him. "I'll call you tomorrow, I promise." She kissed him goodbye.

The back of her car gradually shrunk to a smudge of white on the street. He tugged at his shirt collar, a gust of fruit-filled air hitting his nose.

As Howard reached his apartment building, the familiar assault of piss and mold hit him in the elevator, snapping him back to reality: Jillian returning home, returning to being John's girlfriend, and most likely not keeping her promise to call, let alone devise a plan to be with Howard.

If only he had finished high school. If only he had a career. If only he had labels and structure and purpose like other humans, then maybe, somehow, he could have met her first and she would indefinitely be his, and he wouldn't feel so pathetic for stealing his brother's girlfriend, for wanting to steal his whole life.

He took out the bottle of cheap whiskey from underneath his bed and swallowed a shot. He stared at the half empty bottle. He took a risk tonight. Maybe when you took a risk, none of that other stuff mattered anymore. Jillian could be his—she just was.

Mom would be proud.

CHAPTER 27
ELLIOTT

On Elliott's way to the Center, she passed by a boutique with dresses on infant-sized mannequins. The sparkly, adorable onesies lured her inside. She picked one up and brought it to the register, not completely sure why she felt compelled to buy it. She didn't even know if she was carrying a girl.

"Aww, how adorable. Who's it for?" the cashier said, wrapping the onesie in tissue paper.

"Oh. Um, me. I'm pregnant." It was uncomfortable to say it out loud to a stranger, someone who had zero clue about what this pregnancy represented for Elliott. It felt, somehow phony, with Elliott still not yet knowing what she was going to do about it. She grabbed her wallet from her new white Prada leather tote bag, courtesy of Dad and Holly, although she never cared much for flaunting brand names the way they had.

"Oh, that's so great. Congratulations." The clerk handed her the small shopping bag and gave her the receipt—had Evan saved any more receipts lately?

Evan. His name made her sad. Elliott hadn't heard from him, hadn't bumped into him again at the café. But she knew why.

Julie had told Elliott it was best to focus on what was more important right now, and begrudgingly, Elliott had agreed, so Julie let Evan know to give it some time before pursuing. Unsurprisingly, and respectively, Evan had clearly understood and complied.

She hoped he wasn't scared off or gone for good, as selfish as that was. Plus, she still had yet to completely decide on whether to keep the pregnancy—and ever since she broke up with Asher, he hadn't responded to any of Elliott's requests to revisit the options. It was clear where he stood.

"Thanks." Elliott smiled politely. She placed her wallet back inside her bag. She noticed the clerk was still watching her.

"Might I be so daring as to recommend the practical but very stylish diaper bags we have in the back?" she suggested.

"Sure. Great. Thank you. I'll have to come back when I have more time."

Elliott's heart heavy in her chest, she left the store, stood on the sidewalk, and looked at her phone. She considered calling in sick, but she reminded herself of what Dr. Heller had said about healing: "Pain is a necessary part of the process, signaling that true transformation is taking place."

Kind of like giving birth.

As Elliott went to press the pink elevator button, a voice called from behind.

"Elliott," Romalda said, catching up, not her usual everything-is-exciting-shiny self. Her hair slightly frizzy. Her feet in flats—not that it's a bad thing to be so laid back. Elliott envied that kind of attitude toward life.

"I'm afraid I have some bad news," she said. "There has been an issue with another patient. Similar to your neighbor's. But don't tell Dr. Heller I told you that. She wants to speak with you before you started any of your work today. She's free now if you can head up. I think she wants to know if Orson told you anything else."

"Why shouldn't I tell her you told me? What's wrong?"

"I probably shouldn't have said it like that. But you know how Dr. Heller can be. She doesn't like it if her patients say anything outside of her office to anyone else. And it wasn't my fault, her patient kept going on and on and on and on and—"

"It's okay. I get it. Don't worry. I won't say anything."

Romalda's shoulders loosened. "Oh gosh, thanks, Elliott. You're the best."

With slight trepidation, Elliott reached the twelfth floor, Dr. Heller's frameless glass door already open. She walked along the white ceramic tiles of the waiting area and approached the open door.

Peeking into the suite, she said, "Hi, Dr. Heller. Okay to come in?"

"Of course, of course. Sit." The soft carpet gave beneath her white flats as she stepped in; the doors closed behind her.

Dr. Heller sat at her desk covered with various papers. Elliott took the chair across from her.

"Thank you for meeting with me this morning. I'll be brief. It has come to my attention one of my patients, Jillian Mark, didn't have the best Balloon Day experience. She said they leave her feeling more and more confused each time, and that her current boyfriend seems to remain 'cruel' no matter how hard she tries to change that.

"Also, she states that the boyfriend keeps morphing into his younger brother, or he transforms into her father screaming at her—even with all the progress we made for her to establish boundaries against both. The problem appears similar to that of your neighbor's, Orson, and his lack of control. How is he doing, by the way? Does he tell you anything?"

Holy shit. Jillian Mark.

It was likely Howard had no clue; he hadn't mentioned it to Elliott at least. Jillian was a lot more messed up than Elliott thought. She used Balloon Days for bettering things with John, yet kept Howard in her back pocket, even though deep down she knew Howard was the better choice of the two. If anyone could understand difficult decisions—it was Elliott.

Dr. Heller pushed for Jillian to set better boundaries. Clearly, she didn't tell her how to do that effectively.

"Did he?" Dr. Heller said, bringing Elliott back to earth.

"Orson seems well. I mean, he hasn't mentioned anything about his Balloon Days to me, at least, other than he is happy I recommended he come here," Elliott lied. "I made sure he knew anything else related to it, to go straight to you, since he's your patient."

"That's excellent to hear," Dr. Heller said. "We must do our best to not lose any patients. With that said, I will share what I have learned on how brainwave activity shifts during Jillian's sessions. There's a way we can make it better for them. A quick fix, even." She turned her laptop to face Elliott. A brainwave report filled the screen.

"Oh?" Elliott said.

"I think you will like this one, being the kind soul that you are." She paused and squinted her eyes, her head leaning toward Elliott.

"We understand emotional memories, especially when dealing with bereavement, metabolically fire up the limbic system. This creates an intensity throughout the different levels of conscious and unconscious processes. It also involves other critical areas of the brain—as seen here." She clicked around the laptop and then pointed to an image of the brain, first at the front, then the middle.

"We know from both research and personal experience, right, that it's difficult to eat, to sleep, to enjoy anything we once had for a while after a loved one passes, or leaves us in any way, or when we are in a toxic relationship.

"The brain goes into a depressed neural state and slow-wave delta activity is clearly visible. What motivates us is therefore dampened, but the emotional centers for memory, scent, touch, taste, et cetera are lit up, electrically firing at some of the highest frequencies we can possibly reach."

Dr. Heller shuffled through different reports—fMRI images of bright, white-gray outlines of brains, with red "hot" spots and blue "cool" ones, sliced in half to see the inside; and graphs of EEGs with oscillating waves, some long and slow, like ocean waves, others fast and jagged, like ribbons in a zig-zag pattern.

Elliott sat in thought, scanning the pages that Dr. Heller handed her. "It seems the brain is conflicting with itself," Elliott said. "Over-firing emotionally and under-firing in the logical and neutral areas."

Dr. Heller nodded in approval. "Precisely. As such, I have created a way for us to quickly reroute their brainwaves whenever we see the over-firing become too intense. We simply return them to a positive experience and voila! They are happy again and will want to return, no questions asked."

Elliott should have researched more about Balloon Days on her own when it came to grief, before she told Orson—although, it was not only grief cases, like Dr. Heller said, and as Elliott had personally learned within her own Balloon Days.

If Dr. Heller was quick to hide things from her patients, was she likely hiding things from staff too? Clearly it was possible. Romalda's nerves proved that—and the fact that Elliott couldn't know how much a Balloon Day credit was. Come to think of it, she never saw the inside of an Elite Day Room either. Was it bigger and better? Why were there elite ones anyway? It didn't seem fair. Howard deserved the same treatment, regardless of money.

But Dr. Heller is wonderful. She created all of this to help people. She's a neuropsychologist, bound by the Hippocratic Oath.

"Maybe there should be a different requirement for certain cases?" Elliott said, crossing her legs as slight nausea hit, reminding her of reality.

"No," Dr. Heller asserted. She gave her smile, a smile Elliott realized was distracting, a blanket over her curtness. "Elliott. Remember, we are still helping them by making it a more pleasant experience. Some pain is necessary to heal, of course, but too much pain and they won't return. From the business end, we do make most of our income through these Balloon Day sessions. It would be a shame to have to cut the staff's pay, right? Or have our patients leave us worse off than they came?"

"Yes, but—"

"Then we are on the same page. Now, tell me about your newest patient, Howard Nor. Last you told me was he had visited the woman he's in love with."

Elliott had been so brain-scattered; she hadn't spoken to Howard since his last session. Did he take the risk they'd spoken about? Add it to the list of worries: pregnancy, Asher, Howard, now Orson and Dr. Heller too. Fires seemed to burn all around her, and she didn't know which to put out first.

"Oh, um, yes. I have not heard from him for about a week or two now since our last session together."

And your patient Jillian is ruining his life.

"He hasn't wanted more Balloon Days recently, only talk therapy. We have been goal setting, and he is actually taking more risks—"

"You must encourage Balloon Day processing. That's what our main service is." Dr. Heller drew her hair up, and a few honey tendrils framed her face perfectly. Elliott was beginning to wonder if she was part robot. "I know it sounds hard to believe, but if you give too much hope in these sessions, he will feel less inclined to work things out in a world he can craft all on his own. You are removing his ability to have full control.

"Hope itself can be a risk for someone as depressed as Howard is. What if his risks cause further damage? What if the outcomes cause him to feel worse and he doesn't want to see you, or come here again? Our goal, as

---

with any patient, is to encourage them to find their own way out of their patterns, right?"

"Right," Elliott said, her cheeks hurting with heat. "I was recently reading more on that actually. How the paths we all embark on eventually become loops—and it isn't until we decide to pause, see it clearly, and consciously step off the path that we can create breakthroughs and the changes we seek."

Elliott considered a rose in the nearby vase on Dr. Heller's desk. The flowers were so gorgeous, so lively, it was a shame they eventually withered and dried up. It was in nature, in all of us, that change was ever present no matter what we did to prevent it, no matter how hard we tried to avoid.

"Beautifully said." Dr. Heller beamed with pride. "You are talking like your old self. There are indirect ways of telling Howard that. I think he is one who needs a gentle approach, which I know you seem to provide naturally. Overall, I think you are doing wonderfully, Elliott. Just remember to be a strong advocate for the Balloon Days."

Elliott reached her office and called Howard. After a few rings, it went to voicemail. "Hi Howard, I hope all is well. I wanted to know if you would like to schedule another Balloon Day. Please call me back when you can. Thanks."

Hand on her stomach, and thankful the queasiness had subsided, she waited. After about a minute of silence staring at the lifeless phone, she grabbed the onesie out of her tote and headed to her Day Room.

Her Balloon Day would take place in her second trimester. The baby would be bigger now; Elliott would be able to see her belly's growth. She likely won't get the chance to know the sex of the baby, but she felt in her heart it was a girl, with bright big eyes to look up at her, a little voice calling her mommy.

When she reached her Day Room, she stared at the teensy pink onesie in her hand. Emptiness, longing, anger, guilt—all swept through her, making her dizzy.

She hit the button and it all lifted. Like pressing a reset button, her emotional and mental canvas now clean. She began to assemble her world.

There truly were benefits of Balloon Days, but she had to wonder if Dr. Heller was pulling the strings. If Dr. Heller left it alone, or only rerouted in exceptionally intense scenarios of brainwave spiking, Elliott's concerns would be lifted, the fire of suspicion put out.

Walking through an archway, a flowing red dress accommodated her growing abdomen. It was a warm, cozy day, a gentle breeze swept through her hair. Bouncing along a breathtaking grand avenue, weeping cherry trees and storefronts bloomed around her.

The sun beamed. She clacked in black heels along the pavement, trotting by window displays filled with gorgeous pastries, mannequins in polished outfits, and twinkling diamond necklaces and rings. The scent in the air was a unique and delightful combination of champagne and macaroons.

Elliott strolled into a café, humming along with the melody in the air. The café had golden walls, golden tables, delicate, round chairs. The seats of the chairs white, the arms and legs the same sparkling gold as the tables. Tea-light candles within bubbles floated in the air above.

Elliott chose the middle table. As she considered having an herbal tea as well as a flowery-looking pastry once seen in France, the waitress was placing a white layered cake with an orchid as crimson as Elliott's hair, resting on top, and a clear mug of tea, in front of her. The tea's tiny purple lavender buds, white jasmine and rose, suspended at the surface of hot water. Both tea and pastry were intricate and aromatic.

A faraway blend of piano, guitar and accordion produced a lilting tune, whimsical and heartfelt, growing louder. The romantic sounds vibrated within her. Quarter notes, whole notes, rests strung along in the air, moving along bodies of those in the cafe, as if they themselves were the measures.

Eighth notes swirled along the arm of a brunette drinking coffee at the table adjacent to Elliott. Treble clefs danced along the bridge of a man's aquiline nose, who was buying chocolates at the register, and half notes twirled around Elliott's waist and hips. Could her baby feel and hear the music too?

Elliott sipped the warm tea, continuing to feel at ease with the world. She listened to passersby merrily chatting outside, tapping on the sidewalk with heels and fancy work shoes.

As she looked above, the café's roof disappeared. The sky, a Mediterranean Sea blue, held a whirlpool of clouds in hues of whites, pinks, and yellows. Sunrays stretched and shone brightly without stinging her eyes.

Elliott returned her gaze to the table. Asher was now sitting next to her. He reached for her hands. Musical notes swept in, figure-skating around their intertwined fingers.

Asher kissed her cheek. "I love you both, I love you both, I love you both so much," he sang.

"I'm so happy," Elliott said. "I know we didn't expect this, but it feels right. You will be such an amazing father."

"I know you will be a perfect mother. You already are." He ran his fingers through Elliott's hair.

Elliott poked his handsome, turned-up nose, then traced the lines of his face. A blue shirt complemented his steely gray eyes, a look that took her breath away.

This was everything she wanted. But an empty feeling pushed through poking reality through a hole in her imagination. Because playing house in her Balloon Days was that: a fantasy. As one of the Center's psychologists, she knew that. Trying it out as a patient, however, proved to be an obscure experience.

"I'm only joking, you idiot," Asher pronounced. "I want nothing to do with this. You dumped me for a reason—you know how it will wind up if you keep that pregnancy. You'll ruin everything"—his voice grew louder —"my life. Your life. The baby's life. Get rid of that thing now. It's a pathetic bug. Nothing special. Get rid of it now," he hissed, "get rid of this mistake. Get rid of it—" Elliott raised her hand, muting him.

She was afraid of going it all alone, no matter her final decision—but there was the disquieting truth of Asher. It was there all along. Her unconscious mind, and every part of her brain, for that matter, showed her over and over the reality of him. Why had she doubted herself? Part of Elliott had doubted the break-up too. Her insecurities had blinded her.

If she couldn't have seen that with her level of intellect and psychological understanding, how could Dr. Heller, or any of the psychologists at the Center, expect the patients to recognize the messages from within?

Talk therapy provided critical feedback. Without it, the patients floated in the middle of the ocean without a compass. Pushing more

Balloon Days on them without proper guidance would keep them in treatment longer, but for the wrong reasons.

And just like that, Asher evaporated, like a wilted leaf that drops without warning. What would it have all been like with another guy, someone like Evan? Would she want him to quickly disappear, or would he be the type she'd truly want to stay at her side, be the father of her baby, even if outside her self-made timeline? If she does carry the pregnancy to full term, who knows if anyone would want to date her at all. She'd be damaged goods, with heavy baggage to boot. Why would anyone bother?

Elliott wandered outside to the boulevard, hands sweeping along the cherry blossoms above her. In the middle of the open avenue, an orchestra, enclosed in a clear glass cube, played beguiling melodies. The angelic notes streamed out of the harps and cellos, with each stroke of string.

A large, bright-pink balloon appeared and roamed toward Elliott. She grabbed the string of the balloon, quickly ascending, everything below her shrinking as she floated toward the clouds.

"Goodbye." She waved. The bottom of her red dress rippled from the wind.

As she rose, the boulevard became smaller, shifting each time she blinked, like looking through a stereoscope—with each click the image moved further and further away into a vibrant mash of colors.

Reaching the clouds, she decided it was time to let go—but her hand would not follow as badly as she wished it would. Her legs floundered beneath her, as if trying to stay afloat in deep water. Everything turned hazy and black. Her hands wrapped around her belly.

All vanished with a pop. Elliott woke up keeled over on the white carpet, clutching the baby onesie now rumpled in her hands.

Later that evening, Elliott headed up the marble stairs of her home, Captain trailing behind her. Before Elliott showered her dog with attention, she lifted the onesie out of her bag and tucked it safely underneath her other shirts in the drawer. She eased into bed, staring at nothing but her thoughts. The ceiling fan squeaked above.

She had to decide soon—to step off the path or continue to loop around.

CHAPTER 28
HOWARD

Sitting on John's couch, Howard felt like a fool. It had been five nights since Jillian and he made love in her car, four days since her promise to call. He sent multiple texts, tried calling countless times. He was desperate to ensure her silence didn't mean that she returned to John, or worse, told him that she cheated. John appeared oblivious, a good sign she kept her promise. At least that particular one.

Maybe her silence this time could mean she was preparing to end things with John, like she had said, then ask to see Howard and leap into his arms with the good news.

Although a voice somewhere in his mind whispered that everything about this was decidedly shameful and idiotic. How could he have thought taking a chance laden with danger would work out well for someone like him?

Pop was right. Life was not salvageable. It was too late.

Howard pulled his coat out of John's front hall closet, preparing to head back home. But John stopped him, startling him, and he dropped his coat.

"You're so jumpy lately."

"I'm not." He picked his coat up.

"Anyway, I know I said you could leave soon but I was wondering if you'd be able to stay and work on that client's spreadsheet, I promised it to him by tonight," John said. "I gotta go out to dinner with Jillian."

Howard tightened his grip on his jacket, then hung it back on the hanger. "Things going well with her, then?"

"Thanks, bro. You're the best." John patted his back, jolting some life back into Howard like a defibrillator before his shoulders slumped again.

His whole body was slumping at this point. It was amazing how he was still standing at all.

After John left, Howard, barely present, typed up a financial plan for one of John's clients, finished nearly all twelve beers he could find in the fridge. Eyes blurry and body drenched in alcohol, he passed out on the couch for a quick nap to sleep it off.

Hours must have gone by as there was a sudden clicking of the locks being undone at the door, a jangling of keys, voices whispering, and Howard's thumping heart. Of course, she came back with him.

Light poured in from the hallway, the black of his eyelids now tinted yellow, reminding Howard of the unsettling fact that although his eyes were closed, his actual pupils were still seeing.

Either John or Jillian knocked into what must have been the coffee table.

"Ouch," Jillian whispered. "Shoot. Sorry."

"It's okay, he's probably drunk. He won't wake up." John's voice was barely a whisper. "Come on."

"Ah, okay."

After the sounds of John's heavy footsteps and Jillian's tiptoes ceased, John's bedroom door closed. Howard immediately shot off the couch and scrambled, grabbing his coat and sneakers from the closet. The door opened again as he shoved each foot into a shoe.

He could barely see Jillian with his inebriated eyes, but he knew her outline well. "Howard," she said. She glanced back at John's bedroom door ajar. John mumbled something to Jillian. "I am going to the bathroom quick." She then spoke to Howard. "I'm sorry if we woke you." She stepped toward him and lowered her voice. "I didn't know you'd be here."

Sorry? That's it? How could she?

She had to have known Howard would have been there unless John didn't mention it. Regardless, she was still with John and didn't have the decency to say anything at all to Howard.

Was she as awful as John? Or worse, Kimmy? Cheating and no remorse, she wiped herself clean of him as if removing a stain. Elliott was right to question Jillian's true colors.

Before she could say another word, Howard left the apartment.

Miserable and furious and freezing, he walked and walked as fast as he possibly could. He could barely think straight, let alone see. He had no idea what time it was. He traveled this way so often his feet knew the way.

The next morning, around eleven, Howard walked to the convenience store, slush underneath his feet. Liquor bottles clanked in his bag as he returned to his building.

An uncomfortable elevator ride later (the stench of urine was stronger today), he unlocked the front door, shivering off the residual wintry morning air. He had purchased five bottles of whiskey. He didn't care to see if they were on sale. Whiskey was safe—it had always been there for him, the sting in his throat a familiar friend. He had learned from his father that drinking was the way to go, despite it taking years of damage to finally end his life. Elliott was right. It numbed emotions.

Thank God for that.

As soon as Howard placed the shopping bag down on the floor of the kitchen, a voice called out. "Howard. Come in here. Now."

It was John. Howard's stomach seized as he squinted at his open bedroom door, the morning light pouring into the hallway. The last time John had arrived unannounced—let alone visited the apartment at all—was two years ago, when he briefly checked in on Howard because he hadn't heard from him in days. Howard had been busy deadening the pain with whiskey after one of Kimmy's countless disappearances. John had seen him last night; he knew Howard was safe.

He pulled a bottle of whiskey out of the bag and downed as much he could, about a quarter of it before continuing onward. His body felt like it had detached from his brain, floating by on its own, passing by dusty cardboard boxes of randomly collected objects: old photographs and home videos of he and his brother playing video games, trick-or-treating during childhood Halloweens, or opening gifts on Christmas mornings. WWE wrestling figures and DC comics he had yet to chuck; and old piano books full of sheet music, like Debussy's Clair de Lune and Schumann's Scenes from Childhood.

Howard's legs dragged like slugs in sludge. What was happening? What was he walking into? Did John somehow find out about his and Jillian's night together? Why else would John be here?

It would be highly unlikely Jillian confessed last night, shared their sacred time with John, even if she had been intoxicated. Howard racked his brain for evidence John could have picked up on, but nothing came to mind. John had seemed clueless, in his own little world. And no possible way a friend of John's, happening to be on this side of Queens, witnessed them in the car that night; unless they had known it was her car, saw Howard getting in or out. Did Howard's shirt smell like Jillian's peach perfume?

He approached his bedroom: the door was half open and ominous, uninviting like an old, abandoned house. He held his breath as he tapped the door, lightly, revealing his brother reading a small spiral notebook.

Of course. Howard's sad, stupid journal. That's how.

John looked up at Howard.

"You have something to tell me?" John, with his fancy work clothes, with his bouncy blond hair Howard envied, chucked the notebook on the ground, smacking the floor near Howard's foot. Howard squinted down at his journal. There it lay, open and vulnerable, stained by John's prying hands.

"I..." Howard frantically searched for anything in the sea of words flooding his mind, the whiskey starting to hit. John glowered at Howard, practically slicing him in half.

"Jillian dumped me this morning, right before I had to leave for work, but wouldn't give me the real reason until I kept asking. I could tell she was hiding something, the way she kept talking last night, saying she hoped she hadn't woken you up, how she didn't know you'd be there, how she didn't want to have sex with me even after you left.

"At first, I didn't believe her when she said it, when she said that she slept with you." Jillian had told John after all. Howard's heart sank so low he could see it on the floor. "I didn't believe it because I didn't believe you would do that to me. To be honest, I wasn't too surprised she cheated. She said she had found a condom underneath my bed the other day, and I figured she would level the playing field. She's spiteful like that. But with you?" There was venom in John's words, and they pierced right through Howard.

Jillian slept with Howard out of vengeance. He existed as her pawn.

Unexpectedly, the sad look in John's eyes hurt more.

Howard stepped further into the bedroom. "I'm sorry," he said. "I didn't want..." Howard's voice became stuck in his throat, cracking along its wobbliness as he forced more words out, but he had none.

"I'm ashamed to have to say you're my brother," John said. "You're pathetic. You always have been." His words hit Howard like acid, burning any shred of dignity he had left. "I work hard. I took you under my wing. I gave you money, some responsibility. I paid for you to stay in the family apartment for years before you could pay the rent on your own. I give you some semblance of a life, and this is how you repay me? You fuck my girlfriend? I would never do that to you."

Howard picked up his journal and peered at John. "I'm sorry." Howard's voice trembled. His eyes burned with tears, but he did his best to keep from releasing them.

John cackled, making Howard's insides turn. "That's all you have to say?"

Icy rain began to tap on the window.

"I didn't mean to fall in love with her. I didn't want to." Howard's speech slurred in spite of his attempt to compose himself. "But you didn't treat her well, you hardly paid attention to her in a real way. After you'd yell and kick her out of your apartment, for such stupid things—like who cares if she preferred you watched a movie instead of taking a nap? She had nowhere to turn, and I wanted to be a shoulder to lean on. To top it off, you cheated all the time—how is that love?" Howard's regret was immediate; he said too much.

"It's my relationship, making it none of your goddamn business," John yelled. "What do you know about love, anyway? Kimmy was a train wreck, then you go after my girlfriend like some pitiful leech. You're a disgrace. How about you admit what you did?" John's finger stabbed at the air, pointing toward Howard's journal. "Say what you wrote. That you fucked her. You betrayed me. Don't act like you're some saint."

The way John threw that word around made Howard cringe. To Howard, he and Jillian had made love; he never would have used her, or any woman for that matter.

"I love her."

"So what? She was in a relationship. With your own brother. Now at least be man enough to admit what you did."

Howard lowered himself on his bed. He was so miserable it was hard to distinguish what emotions he experienced lately, and truthfully, he did not care, he wished he had bought ten more bottles of whiskey and downed them all by now.

"I messed up," Howard mumbled, staring at a crack in the wall. "I shouldn't have gone to see her, I shouldn't have believed her when—"

"Say it." John stopped pacing and inched closer. "Say, you fucked her. Admit it."

"Please." Howard looked at his brother. "I can't."

He had failed John. He had failed to be a normal brother, had failed to be a functioning adult, had failed himself. No wonder Howard was so lost. He kept trying to be someone else, he kept forgetting he was important and worthy of a good life. Now he knew what Mom was trying to tell him in his Balloon Day. What she had told him his entire life before she died.

Howard's understanding of it came too late.

"You're a coward." John's eyes squinted, his eyebrows creating a v above his nose, and for a moment Howard swore tears were forming. "What the hell is wrong with you? Seriously, are you actually retarded or something? Mom would be ashamed of you."

Howard's heart launched an ache that grasped his throat.

"I'm a lost cause. You're right."

"Maybe. Maybe I didn't do enough to help you after Mom and Pop died. Maybe I enabled it by giving you everything and not letting you find a way on your own," John said. "But not anymore."

John pushed past Howard and a few seconds later, the apartment door slammed.

The tears lining up in his throat were suffocating, ready to burst forth like a spider egg preparing to hatch. Howard grabbed the bag with the bottles of cheap whiskey, turned back, and shut the bedroom door behind him. He opened one, downing as much as he could.

He deserved all of it. John was exceptionally horrible with women—but they were his relationships to deal with like he said, not for Howard to swoop in and steal while lying to himself that he was saving the day, that he was doing a good thing.

John was right about Mom. She would be ashamed. Howard couldn't save her when she was alive, and now he shamed her in her death.

Days after John and Howard's fight, Howard woke up sometime around noon, peeling his lips apart like a sticker off John's shirt when they were little. The sun was bright through the window, making his eyes sting and head hurt even more.

He went to close the blinds and block the paining sunlight, but instead, he observed the sidewalk far below. The sidewalk reminded him of the one he peered at while sick, having stayed home from school when he was fifteen. Waiting for Mom to come back from the store with his medicine. The day she was murdered.

Howard used to love looking out his childhood window. He'd look forward to five o'clock every weekday, the time when he would watch Mom walking back from work. She'd wave from below as soon as she was close enough to spot him. Sometimes she'd carry books or new piano music, a special bundle in her arms for him. Howard never would have guessed that her wave on the day he was sick would be the last wave of hers he'd ever receive.

He left the window blinds as they were, letting the sunshine win. He gave up on the idea of more sleep.

After a glass of water and ibuprofen, he left for the Center. He needed to escape, so he had made an appointment, even if Balloon Days was just a false pause button. In real life there was no such thing. "Going" was life's factory setting. If there was a real pause or reset button, Howard would have pressed it. There wasn't a self-destruct button either, but he'd pressed that imaginary one plenty.

What did John mean by enabling him? Howard would likely have to find a new job.

Would John ever speak to him again?

His thoughts, like his life, rotated on a wheel he could not step off, no matter how hard he tried.

CHAPTER 29
ELLIOTT

"Have you decided then?" Julie said. She took a sip of water as the waitress brought their meals.

"I think so, but also, not really." Elliott rubbed her aching shoulder. Everything was achy in some way lately—her breasts were swollen and sore, her lower back cramped at times, her stomach queasy, her neck and shoulders tense. "Still going back and forth. I go from being dead certain to leave every tie to Asher behind me. But then I question my life again, and life in general. I keep wondering, how will I feel at thirty years old? Forty? Fifty?

"Will I always regret this decision? I wanted to have a baby by thirty-two, you know? I wanted to be married by thirty. Here I am, twenty-eight years old and I don't have someone I want to marry but I thought I had, and then wonder if maybe I could somehow still make it work with Asher, and I could have the child I wanted but what if he is telling the truth, that he won't be there for the baby and me?

"What if I do go through with an abortion but I never get the chance to have a baby again? What if something happens to me where I'll never be able to get pregnant again? I mean, what if I do have one in the future, and I feel guilty and undeserving?"

"Alright. Slow down. Take a breath," Julie breathed in deeply for Elliott to follow. "I cannot imagine what you're going through, and I see how absolutely torn you are. It breaks my heart. I wish I could make this all go away for you. But we have no idea what will happen that far off in the future. All I know is you are an amazing person and will be an amazing mother—when you're ready. And if you are not ready now, that is completely understandable."

Elliott looked at her plate as thoughts of that night tumbled around in her head. Stupid Clara, all the drinking, the pushing Elliott into having sex without making sure he secured a condom, his careless attitude about it all...

She slammed her fists on the table, causing the silverware to jingle. "I should have made sure he put that fucking condom on. I should have dumped him long before that night. I should have dumped him when he treated the state of our relationship like an assignment. I fell for it all like an idiot. I don't know who I am anymore."

"Elliott." Julie put her fork down. "Don't punish yourself for the past. Look at me," she said, causing Elliott to actually notice her for the first time since sitting down.

Julie looked so comforting and beautiful in her pumpkin orange sweater complemented by the skin that kept its summer glow. The sight of her brought stability amongst the unknown, the security of a familiar face—marked with love and concern and years of friendship.

Elliott locked into her gaze.

"This. Is. Not. Your. Fault. Mistakes happen, and I hate calling it that, but none of us are perfect. And life-changing situations happen even when we don't want them to. Especially when we don't want them to. It is only human to want to be competent and in control all the time, but it's also human to not be. Focus on one thing at a time."

Elliott frowned.

She pulled at some of the silver and gold garland on the wall by their booth. She was human, she had to accept it, even if she desired infallibility. "I keep hearing my dad's voice in my head. How could I have been so stupid?"

"Who cares what your dad would think? He's far from perfect. This isn't about him, anyway. You don't ever have to tell him. This is about you, Elliott. Only you." A busboy came over and filled their waters. Julie said thanks and waited until he left before she spoke again. "Forget your dad. Forget Asher."

"I don't know what's right for me. I don't want to make a mistake I will regret forever. Part of me is hoping if I did have the baby, Asher would change his mind and be there for me, and my child would have her father. And part of me is wanting to end it with him and get the abortion so that my baby would not have to suffer without a father and having entered this world as an accident. But then I wonder if I stayed with him even if I didn't have the baby, would it eventually get better and then we could still have a baby down the road, and then I wouldn't regret it as much."

Julie gave her a look of disappointment, her ice-blue eyes softening into compassion.

"I know. I must sound so ridiculous."

"No," Julie said. "You're not being ridiculous. Or stupid, as you like to think. You're actually being highly rational to not make an impulsive decision. To keep the baby or not, regardless of him, or anyone else's opinion, is the major decision right now. Make that choice first based on what you know is best for you and your situation. Trust your gut."

Elliott held back tears. "Julie?" she said.

"Yeah?"

"I'm scared."

"I know. It would be strange if you weren't." She smiled tenderly at Elliott, and Elliott smiled back.

"Off topic, but how is it going over there with corrupt Dr. Heller?" Julie said.

Elliott almost choked on her water. "No, don't say that. Yes, I have my concerns, but I wouldn't say she's corrupt. Do you really think so?"

"From what you tell me, I'd trust your gut on that one too. But again, one major decision at a time."

The next day, Elliott followed Julie's advice. The first major decision had to be made. And it wasn't a decision for Elliott to take her time with.

Red and green flannel pajamas on, she sat on her cozy living room floor, back against the soft gray couch, creating a list of how either choice would change her life. Applying the logical side of her brain was a challenge; this decision was freighted with such a mess of emotion.

Starting with keeping the pregnancy, she wrote down her thoughts: scared, anxious. What if Asher kept his word this time and left? Would he support her at all, or the baby, in any way—financially, emotionally, physically?

Clearly not emotionally. Would he help her raise their child, pop in occasionally, or be completely absent altogether? She wanted to cry just at the thought of him abandoning them.

No—no crying. Logic.

Would she resent him? Resent the child? Resent herself? Having a child held many people back in life. Young parents said it derailed all their plans. Would she have to give up seeing the same amounts of patients, or quit being a psychologist altogether? Money would also be an issue.

Endless expenses and the thought of relying on Dad more made her cringe. It's possible he would disown her too, kick her out of the house, not wanting any of the neighbors knowing his daughter got knocked up like some brood mare before marriage. Oh, and her body would change, go through a transformation she wasn't yet prepared for. She liked her body how it was.

Abortion.

Writing the word, underlining it, at the top of a fresh page, how quickly her eyes sizzled with tears—why were they always so hot, so stinging, right before they drenched her face?

She had to suck it up, deep breaths, one at a time. She tried again. Abortion; the word alone depleting, draining. It comes with negative societal connotations she had to ignore, shirk the influence of—it's not about those.

The procedure itself would be expensive. But Asher said he would pay for half; he was unwavering about that little nugget of knowledge. Boyfriend of the Year material. An abortion could depress her. She would have to learn to accept it—and any feelings that came after. Emptiness. Numbness. Scared it would be the wrong decision. There were also the effects of anesthesia, effects of the procedure, risks involved.

Would she turn into a shell of a person? Would she be a failure, a coward?

Or was it stronger to see that the best decision, and the right decision, are not always the same thing? Morally, an abortion would not feel right. But was it best for all involved?

Elliott did want to grow more as a person. She envisioned herself being the best mother she could be, by the time she tried for a baby. Be as ready as she could be. Be excited, be certain, be settled.

She felt far from that. It wasn't fair. It wasn't fair to bring a life into this world with unfit parents, without happiness, no matter how wrong, no matter what people said, no matter what society said.

The voices of her friends and family, reminding her they would support her either way, filled her head. Asher's concrete, "I won't be there when the baby is born, it's a bug," flashed brightly.

She was so tired, so worn, so alone and defeated. No one was going to tell her what to do. She couldn't force or pray the choice away either. She had to choose what was best even if she thought it wasn't right.

She searched the internet and found a women's clinic describing itself as a private practice environment. She dialed the number and a few moments later a receptionist answered.

"Hello, Women's Care, how may I help you?"

Elliott's body sat on her floor, yet her mind, her soul, her essence, was detached, somewhere else entirely. The living room grew colder despite the warm décor and fireplace aglow. Snow fell outside. It clouded up the window, some of the snowflakes imprinting little, unique webs on the glass.

"Hello? Hello? Anyone there?"

"Oh, hi, yes. Sorry. I need to schedule a" —she squinted at their website open on her laptop— "voluntary termination."

Her voice faraway, she provided her personal information and confirmed a date with the receptionist. She sounded like someone else. She wished she was.

"How about December 29th, 9:00 am?"

"That works fine. Thanks." Her vision grew hazy. Her head spacey and body lifeless, like a wobbly doll.

Was this right? She wanted to escape but there was nowhere to go. She wished there were a third option, like keeping her fertilized egg in the womb without growing until she was ready. Taking back control apparently can feel horrible.

"And someone supportive is best," the woman said. "Don't forget to not eat for six hours beforehand."

"Oh. Sure. Okay," Elliott said. She missed half of what the receptionist told her.

"Great. If you have any questions or need to reschedule or cancel, give us a call. Take care."

Elliott hung up and stared at the floor, motionless and quiet, as the clock unapologetically ticked the hours goodbye.

CHAPTER 30
ORSON

Ryder stood in the living room bundled up in his puffy red jacket and snow pants, shoving each foot into his waterproof boots. Orson, already in his snow gear from head to toe, covered Ryder's head with earmuffs, then a gray knitted hat over them and his strawberry hair for extra warmth.

Madison had knitted hats for the two of them last winter. With Orson on vacation this week, Rose agreed it was best to give Orson a "trial run" to see if he truly had shaped up. He was ready to prove it.

"Dad," Ryder whined. "That's too many things on my head. It itches." Orson tugged on the braided strings dangling on either side of the knitted hat as Ryder tried to pull it off.

"Oh, shush, silly. You'll be appreciating it when your nose is running and the snow hits your face." He tapped Ryder's small nose; it was perfectly symmetrical like Orson's. Ryder wrinkled it and turned his head away.

School was closed for the holidays. It was days before Christmas and the suburbs were filled with merriment, holiday parties, traffic, and stores full of frantic last-minute shoppers.

There were plenty of Balsam Firs for Orson and Ryder to choose from last week. It rested beautifully in their foyer in front of the bay window, with a silver and gold theme, arranged as best as they could the way Madison had done.

"Can we get the sled now?" Ryder said.

"Sure, son. I'll meet you out front. Why don't you start building a snowman while I fetch it?"

"Okay." Ryder dashed out the door. Orson could see him hastily gathering snow from the living room window. Orson's phone buzzed in his pocket, stealing his attention—it was Jack.

He hit the ignore button and walked into the attached garage, collected the sled fit for two off the shelf, and joined Ryder outside.

As Orson walked to the front yard, flattening snowflakes, a crunchy-squeaky sound with each step, there was someone on the other side of Ryder's snow mound. It looked like he or she was leaning over, gathering more snow. He neared the mound but no one else was indeed there.

"Ryder, was someone with you just now? Did someone help you gather this snow?"

"Huh? No. I did this all by myself, Dad," he said, standing tall with pride.

"Of course, you did, because you're my astounding, wily son." Orson lifted Ryder up into the air, made a whooshing noise, and plopped him into the soft, snowy landing. Ryder burst into a fit of giggles, asking what the word "wily" meant.

The town surrendered in the snowfall, and all was quiet save for Ryder's occasional laughs and pats on the mound. The snowflakes collected on him and Orson like sprinkled sugar from the sky. Only those with all-wheel drives dared to leave their homes. The rest waited for plows.

"Did you know that when I miss Mom, I write about my memories with her? Dr. Kevin says it helps us remember and keep the people we love alive."

"I am learning a lot from you and Dr. Kevin, especially when you let me join your last session. That sounds like a lovely way for you to keep your mother alive. I do something similar in my therapy." Orson understood completely what it was like to keep Madison's memory alive.

"Cool," Ryder said.

After Ryder was content with his snowman, they hopped in the car, sled in trunk, headed to their favorite park.

"The one with all the hills," Ryder pressed.

"Yes, son. The one with all the hills."

"Yay." Ryder was not old enough to sit in the front seat, so Orson played DJ, playing every single requested song. He hit the back button for Ryder's favorite Disney song for the sixth time in a row. Ryder belted out the lyrics each time.

Two hours later, the snow glowing in the purple night sky, Orson pulled in the wide driveway, which was pointless now, until Ryder learned to drive, he supposed. He turned off the ignition and—a silhouette of someone was visible through the kitchen window, below the raised white shades.

"What the—?" he said under his breath.

"Come on, Dad," Ryder whined. "I want hot chocolate."

Orson quickly shook his head, hoping to erase or make clearer what he witnessed. He squinted but the silhouette was gone.

"Uh, sure, son. Wait." He turned in his seat to face Ryder. "Did you say please?"

"Puh-leeeas-uh," Ryder said, baring the gap of newly lost baby teeth. Orson noted how as a child, this look was endearing, but as an adult, it was bizarre and considered unattractive.

"Alright, alright, I'm going. Give me a second, please."

After Orson and Ryder settled inside, hanging their wet gear over the glass shower stalls, they met in the kitchen and poured packets of cocoa powder with mini marshmallows into their mugs. The teapot hissed and then whistled.

Orson poured boiling water into his mug and then into Ryder's favorite. The black ceramic, like magic, came to life with an image of the famous Disney castle wrapped around the exterior.

Ryder stood near the counter, mouth open, watching the miraculous shift as Orson stirred the hot chocolate in each. Orson grabbed their mugs to carry into the living room, but as he turned, it was now his mouth that dropped, and he shattered both mugs on the porcelain tiles.

"Dad. My cup," Ryder cried. "Nooo. My cup."

His shoulders sank, and he dramatically flung his head forward, burying his face into his hands. The Disney castle was now a ceramic black and white puzzle, the hot chocolate a river of brown liquid and white goo winding through its pieces.

"I-I-I thought I saw your... never mind. I am so sorry, bud. I will clean this up and buy you a new one as soon as I'm done."

"But what about the hot chocolate?" Ryder said. Orson reassured him he would make a fresh mug as soon as he finished cleaning the mess. Ryder groaned, but when he was told he could play video games he made a beeline for the living room.

"Pajamas first," Orson called.

Orson swept, mopped, and wiped until he was sure there were no ceramic slivers left behind. The recent image of Madison was stamped in his mind: she stood there, arms open, her hair a strawberry-blonde pile atop her head, reaching to relieve Orson of the mugs.

Was he hallucinating? Was he losing his mind? He hadn't been to a Balloon Day in over a week. The last one was so lovely and positive. He had been afraid of returning and something treacherous happening again.

Ryder cheerfully yelped, dressed in his Grinch pajamas, at the sight of his Goofy mug full of steaming hot chocolate. Orson played A Christmas Story on the living room television, the area recently adorned with fake snow and tinsel. He informed Ryder he would be back soon.

Sitting at his office desk, the room essentially a smaller version of the one at the firm and furnished with cherry wood, Orson stared at the hourglass on his bookshelf. He racked his brain for who would understand best—Dr. Heller always seemed to brush his concerns off, but lately, he wasn't buying it. Not yet at least. He thought of Elliott as he lit the holiday candle on his desk. Although she worked there, he was hopeful she would be honest with him.

Elliott picked up after the second ring. "Orson, hi. How's it going?"

"I have another question about Balloon Days. I'd appreciate your honest insight." Orson breathed in the scent of cinnamon pluming from the lit three-wick, cherry-red candle.

"What's going on?"

"This might sound funny, but the reason I am calling is because, well, I think I'm seeing Madison. In real life. The way I would see her in the Balloon Days. But in real life." Orson rubbed his temple. Did he sound nuts?

"What? Do you mean in your imagination and it is very vivid?" she said. "Or in your dreams?"

Elliott's questions poked at Orson's unease. This quandary never occurred for other patients. "I meant in my dreams, but a highly vivid version of some sort," he lied, attempting to assuage her concerns and pacify his own.

"Well, grieving is personal for everyone. I mean, your imagination is stronger right now—those areas of your brain are lit up because of you exploring the grief during the Balloon Days. So, maybe the vividness of her image is because of that?" What she said was logical—perhaps it was his imagination playing tricks on him.

"I'm guessing then, this hasn't happened to you—things you've done in your Balloon Days, happening outside of them? You know, like you said, in dreams?" He peered out the window. The snow had stopped.

"No, it hasn't, I'm sorry. There are situations I might be able to get through with little anxiety now when I experience them again in reality, but nothing fantasy-like.

"But that doesn't mean anything is necessarily wrong with what you're going through. If you want, we can talk more in the morning, in person. You and Ryder can come over for breakfast?"

"Yes, breakfast sounds wonderful. Ryder would love that. Would I be able to invite Rose too? She hasn't seen him much this week. She could watch him while we chat."

"Absolutely."

"I'll see you in the morning then." Orson got off the phone, blew out the candle, then returned to find Ryder curled up on the couch, fast asleep. Orson scooped him up and carried him upstairs.

Ryder used to weigh merely nothing, and now here he is, a full grown seven-year-old boy heavy in Orson's arms. As sweet and hopeful and strong as ever, despite all he's endured in his little life.

He was better than Orson, teaching him more than anyone else could about grief. Children are funny that way—somehow, they are more resilient and adaptable than adults; they have so much to teach. Fewer defenses built up, fewer experiences to have turned them jaded.

Ryder still needed Orson's protection, his guidance, his attention. Not in the way Orson had previously thought.

Momentarily fussing as he reached his bed, Ryder rubbed his eyes and rolled over. Ever since Ryder and his therapist worked on better ways to self-soothe, he was no longer sucking his thumb to fall sleep. Orson tucked him in warm, car-covered blankets. He kissed his forehead. Ryder's chest gently rose and fell, his face soft and angelic, his worries turned to dreams.

Tiptoeing into the master bedroom, Orson checked his phone after peering out the window to find the snow was falling again, a gentle downward drift.

Jack had written: Hey. Tried to call. Did the new case work out? Thnx – J

Orson had forgotten to follow up with his lie. He had to make something up; he had to stall for more time.

He replied: No—but I received several calls today for new inquiries. Two consultations set for tomorrow and a third the following day. Meeting them at a coffee shop. Will update you soon when I return to the office on Friday. Thanks.

Within a few seconds, Jack replied: Sounds good. See u soon.

Why did he say three new inquiries? The lie was abysmal. He was not used to deceiving others so frequently. Given his unnecessarily elaborate response, he knew he was feeling remorse—it was a way he caught others in court. Elaborate lies always had cracks, it was a foundation built on sand. Would Jack be onto him?

He certainly would if it were the other way around. Orson could always say the imaginary clients canceled or could not afford his services, cover the tracks. Jack should believe that—it was a common scenario. He would undoubtedly approve of Orson staying rigid with his fees.

He put his phone back in his pocket and thought of Ryder, and how wonderful it was having spent more time with him. How could he have missed out on so much of this, for years now?

Guilt sloshed around like acid in Orson's gut. He did not care as much about lying to Jack anymore—it felt markedly worse to neglect Ryder and continuously lie to Rose.

"Things are finally changing," Orson said to himself.

"Yes, they are, my love," a voice whispered behind him and he froze.

It was not Ryder's voice. It was a woman's voice, and it sounded like Madison's. Orson drew in air and closed his eyes. A hand delicately touched him, her fingertips like a graceful ice skater tracing patterns on his back.

Orson didn't know what to think or feel. He was afraid, he was excited, he was confused. He swallowed and turned around, opening his eyes. There she was—a glowing beauty in the moonlight. She put her finger to her mouth, signaling him to stay quiet, before wiping a tear off his cheek.

She slipped her hand into his, then looked out the window. He stared at her profile, her straight-edged nose, its round end dipping delicately, her high cheekbones, her beautiful rosy ginger hair. Could he keep her forever?

The Madison in his Balloon Day had said there was a way. Is this what she meant? Or was he hallucinating?

CHAPTER 31
HOWARD

Howard stood in a room of endless white. Red rose petals fell from nowhere like snow.

"Howard." A hand touched his shoulder and turned him around.

It was Mom.

He hugged her tightly. He hugged her for all the missed hugs. For all the hugs he could never have when he needed them most. For all the hugs that had never been or could ever be replaced by anyone else. As they embraced, Howard shrunk in height, becoming his fifteen-year-old self again. The scent of French lavender hit him. It was comforting and filled his lungs with home.

Howard knew he had less than ten minutes now, as he could only afford one credit for today's Balloon Day. He had to do what he could. Now was the time to save Mom.

He had to prove to himself he was still useful.

A tug pulled Howard from behind, as if someone had thrown a lasso around his waist. Mom looked startled. He pulled away from her, lifting into the air. As Howard traveled upward, the whiteness was replaced by the block outside his childhood apartment building. Whatever the force was, it had thrust him into his bedroom. Mom stood below on the sidewalk, waving, her reddish-brown hair spilling out beneath her winter hat.

Snowflakes fell around her, and the shadow of a hooded man, dressed in all black, speed-walked his way toward Mom from behind her. As Howard went to jump and rescue his mother, he couldn't.

Howard froze. Just as he had then.

His feet were glued to the floor, and his legs were useless. He attempted to lift them again. They bowed and snapped back like a rubber band as he continued to try.

Howard was struck with panic and desperation. He was stuck. The man yanked at Mom's purse. She let him take it without a fight. When he grabbed at the pharmacy bag of medicine for Howard, her grip tightened.

Howard banged on the window and watched helplessly as the man pulled a knife from the inside of his jacket. Mom shrieked.

"Drop the medicine, Mom. Please," Howard shouted out the window. "I already feel better. Please." He pounded on the wall over and over, his knuckles bloodied, like he had done when he was fifteen. "Don't hurt my mom," he yelled. "Let her go."

Mom had not dropped the plastic bag. He did hurt her. He stabbed the side of her waist. She screamed, yelling for help. As she realized help wouldn't come quickly enough, she looked up and yelled to Howard. "Close your eyes, Howard."

The cruel man knifed her chest. Her stomach. Her heart.

An outpour of bright red rose petals fell from her stab wounds and her mouth. The murderous thief fled down the street clutching Mom's belongings. The petals reached the pavement and melted the snow into a pool of blood.

Mom looked at Howard, and her angelic voice filled his head as if she were in the room. "It wasn't your fault. You were so young. You can't save me from what happened. No one could have. But you can save your—"

Suddenly the scene wiped away as if someone erased a chalkboard, and Howard was on a tropical beach. Children laughed and ran around, and Mom and John lay on beach towels as if nothing prior had occurred. Balloons of all colors were released into the sky.

Before Howard could figure out what the hell was happening, he returned to his Day Room in complete disarray. The shift from such a horrible memory he had tried to control to a la-la-land "everything is great" atmosphere he couldn't control at all was jarring.

He couldn't save Mom in his Balloon Day. He was as useless as he was when he was fifteen.

Useless. Pathetic. Worthless.

Confused and saddened, Howard tried to see Elliott on his way out, but Romalda told him she would be away for the rest of the week. There was no offer to see Dr. Heller, but he didn't make it seem urgent, so maybe, it was his fault.

Howard was going to have to take care of himself from now on anyway. He didn't deserve care from any others at this point.

Safely back at home, the sun had sunk into the horizon as Howard stared at his most recent text message. It stared back, challenging him, and he was losing.

The text was from Jillian: Meet me at ten o'clock tonight. Where I picked you up last time. Please.

John already hated Howard. He had nothing else planned. Did it matter if he saw Jillian one last time? What else was there to lose?

He finally typed K and hit send.

Nine-thirty came around. He didn't mean to get drunk, but alas, there he was. He put on a pair of jeans, a white t-shirt, an old navy-blue sweater with a dark green stripe across the chest, his new wool socks from Langston.

Howard grabbed his jacket and a thicker, knitted beanie from the closet and slipped out. He passed by restaurants and bars. The doors occasionally opened and closed, letting music and laughter momentarily pour out into the streets. Smokers on the sidewalk huddled together outside venues.

Some slurred their words.

A drunk girl with glossy eyes and wiry blue hair stumbled out of Beery's, a hole-in-the-wall bar, with its slanted sign on the front door—a bar he used to frequent with John. The shivering blue-haired girl poked Howard's arm.

"Hey, got a light?" she slurred.

"I'm sorry. I don't." If she wanted liquor, he could help her with that. With the amount Howard drank lately, she likely got drunker with her poking him alone.

"Aw, really? Bummer, man."

How disappointing he was, even to a random stranger.

Hands in his pockets, Howard walked a bit further. Then there it was—the white Nissan Altima parked and waiting.

He was nervous but suddenly exhilarated; what if this would be the night for getting what he wanted? To finally prove himself wrong, that good things could happen to him. This could be what he yearned for. Prove therapy worked and the risk-taking worth it. Maybe Jillian would deeply apologize, tell him she loved him, and they would have a secretive relationship until John approved.

John. No. He didn't deserve that. He had to remember Jillian was the one who created this mess. Or at least the reveal of it.

He walked to the passenger door and tapped on the window. The door locks clicked. He opened the door and slid inside.

Jillian drove them to a nearby park in mostly silence aside from small pleasantries. The only other noise was the Christmas music playing low on the radio.

S-i-i-ilent night, h-o-o-oly night, all is calm, all is bright...

Once parked, they found a vacant bench facing the water, the lyrics lingering in his mind: sl-e-e-ep in heavenly peace, sl-e-e-ep in heavenly peace...

Christmas lights—red, green, blue, white, pink—lit up the area from the houses behind them. The crystal lights and pine garlands wrapped around nearby streetlamps made him forget everything for a few moments.

His beloved holiday was around the corner; it carried precious memories from childhood. Christmas was cinnamon sticks and cloves and cider. It was shreds of wrapping paper on the floor, red and green lights snaked around a tree—it was pine-scented air. Christmas was trailing in snow that dampened the carpet and Pop who stayed sober until dinner time. It was Mom smiling as each opened their small piles of gifts.

This year Howard spent most of his own money on what now seemed trivial, unless this was his miraculous turning point in life, like in the movies when everything suddenly changes because of love.

The sting of John punctured through the fantasy. Would any amount of liquor make Howard forget? Depending on what Jillian said, this Christmas could be as forlorn and pitiable as the first Christmas after Mom died. Possibly, worse.

"So," she began, swinging her legs underneath the bench. "I'm sure John told you that I broke up with him. I felt so guilty. I had to. I couldn't stand hurting the two of you any longer. Especially you." She placed her gloved hand on his, relieving him like the first gasp of air after being held under water.

"Did you sleep with me out of vengeance? Like he said?"

She held her head down, and when she lifted it again, her cheeks shone with tears in the moonlight.

Suddenly, he sensed it.

He was being held under water again and the build-up of suffocation tightened his throat and pained his lungs. It was the unbearable tension of having no control or knowing when air would come again to rescue him. He stood, took a moment to steady himself, then weaved toward the river overlook, wishing he could jump in and suffocate for real.

What was this feeling? The want to lash out and break her the way she was breaking him, to make her realize what she was doing—this was not some stupid movie and he was not a disposable character, or part of some melodramatic, sappy plot she was auditioning for; he was real and he was hurting.

Yet he begged and pleaded for every part of her to love every part of him. Instead, she tore him open—the knife was deep in his chest, his ribcage willingly wide and open, bleeding out.

Why did he act like she was a deity, something so precious to save—and why did he act like he had any potential to save anyone? He couldn't save himself.

He turned to look at her; she was already walking over. She locked her eyes on his, and he did not shift away. He had to hear her say it. He had to see her as she did.

"Howard." The gap between them thinned. "I do care about you." He could feel her jacket brush against his.

She fixed her hazel eyes on him. The eyes Howard loved had ruined him.

"Please don't be mad," she whispered.

He was more than mad. He was shattered.

"I am not an angry person." His hands trembled in his pockets. "I don't want to feel this way. I don't want to hate you. All I have ever done is ask you why. I tried to understand why you kept coming back. But too often I have only my mind to work with, because you are there and then you're not there." He swallowed, his throat dry and lodged with pain. "I have you, then I don't, then I do. But it was all fake, wasn't it? You used me to hurt my brother."

Langston had almost been right—Jillian was a mirror. She wasn't broken. She was like the trick mirrors at carnivals. An illusion. And after some time, he had believed its reflection.

"That's not true," she said, touching his hand.

He pulled away from her touch. "You should go."

She shivered. Her cheeks red from the cold, her eyes glossy from tears. "Please, let me explain," she said. "I swear I didn't use you. When I'm with you, I do care for you. It's the truth. You make me smile. You're there for me. You're everything I could ask for. But as soon as I leave you, it can't be. We don't fit, you know? It's like a phantom thing. I know that doesn't sound right. That sounds awful, actually... I am so, so sorry. I feel horrible. Nothing I'm saying is coming out right. All I know is I didn't mean for it to happen this way."

One by one, everything was fading. A phantom thing. Like she said. Like him.

"I want you to know... I do love you," she said. "I'm just not capable of loving you the way you deserve. I don't know what the fuck is wrong with me."

There they were. The words Howard wanted to hear for so long. But instead of giving him happiness, they fell into the empty well that Howard's heart had become.

"You need to figure things out." Howard resisted the urge to hold her as she leaned her head against his chest. "And not use people in the process."

Christmas lights rattled from a whipping breeze. Jillian's shoulders shook up and down with each wave of tears. Who knows anymore where her feelings truly stemmed from? Was she crying for Howard, or for John? He felt numb inside.

He was drained of tears. He was empty not only of food, but of any drop of joy the world could offer him. He wanted to transform into a sere leaf to be shriveled up and stepped on.

She peeled away from his chest. Howard felt the chill where her tears soaked through his shirt. He kissed her one last time. It was a tender kiss, soft and gentle.

A kiss reminiscent of a scene in a book he recently read, when two lovers knew they were about to die.

.

CHAPTER 32
ELLIOTT

The winter sun burned brightly and melted most of the snow off Elliott's Mercedes by early morning, in time for her to have run out for eggs and maple syrup before breakfast with the Thatches. The smell of French toast and bacon still lingered in the air; used dishes and forks filled her sink as food stuffed their bellies. Christmas tunes continued to play, the current one being, "There's No Place Like Home for the Holidays."

Ryder pointed out Elliott's window to the front yard of his house, showing her the blob his snowman had become.

Elliott raised her eyebrows and gasped. "Oh no, I wonder why," she said. Ryder's mouth widened, an amused look on his face. "I guess he wanted to take a nap," Elliott said in a deep voice. She then raised her pitch to that of a mouse. "Oh no, he's losing weight."

Ryder roared with laughter. Elliott came up with more silly reasons for why Ryder's snowman melted, cracking him up, while Orson and Rose washed the dishes—they had insisted.

Ryder smashed himself into Rose's hip as she entered the foyer, wrapping his arms around her, Elliott's Christmas tree as their backdrop. Rose squatted down to meet his height. "Ready to head over to your house while Dad and Elliott talk about boring grown-up stuff?"

"We can finish my giant Lego village," Ryder said, holding his hands far apart to display how giant his Lego village actually was.

After Rose and Ryder left, Elliott led Orson into her kitchen and sat on one of the stools surrounding the kitchen island. Orson followed but remained standing. On a casual morning, Orson still wore his black suit pants and gray button-down.

For an older man, he was handsome, but not her type. His hair was ever darker than Asher's, whereas Evan's was a lighter brown; she didn't care much for always looking so put together outside of the Center, but Asher had made her feel uncomfortable, commenting on her lack of effort when she wore a sweatshirt and jeans, like today. Just like Dad, come to think of it.

"So, did you see Madison again?" Elliott said. "In your dreams?"

"Yes, actually. Except, it wasn't in a dream this time."

"What do you mean?" Elliott sipped the remainder of her orange juice.

"I think I'm having hallucinations. Is that possible?" He pressed his hands together in a prayer position. "Is that a side effect?"

Elliott stared at the leftover pulp at the bottom of her glass. She had to carefully choose her words.

"Elliott? Is what I'm experiencing normal?"

She looked at him. "In the time I've worked there, Dr. Heller hasn't mentioned the possibility of hallucinations—but that doesn't mean it's not normal. How realistic are they? Do they last for long?"

Orson slid on a stool opposite of Elliott. "Very realistic. I can hold her hand." He reached his hand on the island's surface to the left of him. It looked as if he was holding something, but nothing was there to be held.

Was he becoming delusional? Was this all her fault? Could she fix it? Worse still, was something wrong with Balloon Days? Every patient would suffer from long-term effects.

"Orson, is she here? Can you see her now?"

"Yes." Orson held a slight frown on his face. "But the odd thing is, I don't know if I want to fix it."

"I'm going to grab a water. Want some water?" Elliott offered.

"Sure."

Both stainless steel doors of the refrigerator were covered in quotes about growth and grasping life, postcards and magnets of Croatia, Italy, New Zealand, and other various countries she wanted to travel to—reminders that she could continue to move on, to "live the life" she would not get to if she had a baby. To "make it count" like her mother had advised.

She shifted chicken broth, almond milk, heavy cream, and a half-full jar of sauce out of the way, as she sifted through her thoughts of what to do for Orson. She grabbed him a bottled water from the group of them in the back, then closed the door.

When she turned around, Orson was patting the air and muttering to himself. When he realized Elliott was nearing, he quickly reached out to take the water.

"I think we need to fix this," she said. "This can go very badly. And I know I shouldn't say what I'm about to say, like at all, but can you promise to not mention this to Dr. Heller? Please?"

"Promise. Go on."

"I think Dr. Heller is not telling any of us the truth, or the whole truth anyway. Who knows what long-term effects of her 'proprietary blend of oils' has on our brains? Clearly, you're already experiencing one. All Dr. Heller seems to care about is money. I think if you told her, she would manipulate you into staying. She'd tell you it's normal. But Orson, I don't believe it is."

"I know a thing or two about manipulative people. My boss is a similar way. Hell, most lawyers are..." Orson took a sip of water. "What do you suggest then?"

Elliott peered out the window. She could see the side of Orson's house, icicles dripping off the roof. Was it wrong speaking how she was about Dr. Heller? But her gut reassured her that saving the people she cared about from harm was more important than all the money in the world. It was more important than the Center.

"That you let me perform a brain map on you. To see what your current brainwave activity is without the influence of the chemicals and regulate it where abnormalities appear. I think your brainwaves got stuck somewhere they shouldn't. Something went wrong in your last Balloon Day."

"I see." He tugged at his collar briefly. "I have to admit, having Madison at my side right now, seeing her in person, even if no one else can, gives me great joy and comfort. I don't know if I can deal with her death again. It would be repeating the worst moment of my life."

"I understand. Really. I do. But did you ever truly grieve? I know you saw her in the Balloon Days, but it is different when you still return to real life. They do feel so real. That's why they're alluring, addicting even.

"And they do help me in ways too. But I think the Balloon Days system needs tweaking. I think Dr. Heller can make the induced states safer, gentler, so each patient is in more control. Meanwhile, she's giving them less. She recently started altering the Day Room oils if she sees a Balloon Day going haywire. Her new oil blend instantly reroutes the brainwaves to make it a more positive experience, so the patient keeps returning.

"She banks on your obsession. On your grief remaining intense. I know grief is forever, but you aren't truly healing or learning to live with it in a healthy way. It isn't authentic joy and comfort that you're experiencing. It's avoidance, and relief from real life. In that respect, you never truly lost Madison. So, in a way, this death would be the real one."

Orson nodded. "I have to accept grief lasts forever. It's not often people say that, so thank you. The whole notion of 'it gets easier' is a temporary thought to blanket the pain. A lie, really." He gazed at his silver wedding band. "It gets harder. I miss her more every day. I long for more time to make up for what I took for granted." He looked back at Elliott. "But I think you're right... I know you are right. I see Ryder learning to live with the grief. I see him experience happiness again. I must do the same for him."

"We will always want more time with the ones we love," she said with deep sincerity. "I know this is going to be painful. But you're right. You owe it to Ryder. And your life here, now. Madison will always be with you, just in a different way. Your relationship will never end if you don't let it."

"Thank you. You will make a great mother one day." His words stung. "You are wiser than I ever was at your age." He looked to his left, where the hallucination of his wife likely was, then looked back at Elliott. "If you were me and lost a loved one, would you have done it all the same way?"

Elliott paused to decide what answer would best help Orson. But the truth was, if possible, she'd have tried it too. The honest answer meant the right answer. "Yes."

"Right. Thanks for making me feel less alone. And less insane." They both laughed. "Alright then. What do we have to do?"

"I'll have to take you to the Center after hours," Elliott said. "How does two nights from today sound? This way you can enjoy Christmas with your family."

"Sounds like a plan."

Christmas day arrived, and Elliott unhappily stepped through the threshold of Dad's house. A "house" that was more akin to a manor. The property was large enough to fit the in-ground pool in the back, a grassy area with a net set up for badminton, a patio with furniture, an immaculate flower garden, with plenty of room left over. All this luxury for Dad and Holly. And the sparse occasions when Elliott could stomach staying in the guest room for holidays.

Now here she was again for Christmas dinner. With not only some of Dad's side of the family, but Holly's pretentious side too. She much preferred the Christmas brunch earlier with Mom and her much kinder side of the family—Elliott's fun, open-minded grandparents Sue and Arnold, Aunt Melanie and Uncle Joe, and her cousins Amelia and Scott, both around Elliott's age. That was nice, calm. Why did she bother to come here?

"Where's Asher?"

Of course, that was Dad's first question.

"He's not coming," Elliott said, handing over her winter coat and gray, sparkly scarf. She was surprised yet relieved to hear that Asher hadn't told Dad about the volatile breakup, including Elliott's shove.

Holly kissed the air beside her cheek, creating an annoying smacking sound by Elliott's ear. "Aw, why not?" she said.

"Yeah. What'd you do?" Dad said.

"I didn't do anything." *He's the one who got me pregnant and ruined my life.* "He's with his family. Remember?" Elliott could see a bit of her reflection in the ornate accent mirror on the wall opposite the front door.

Lately, she hadn't cared much about her appearance. Hair in a bun, a few rogue strands here and there, with raspberry lipstick complementing her emerald green A-line dress and a slapdash swipe of mascara for each eye.

"That's no reason to not join us. I'll have to have a word with him. He should be here." Just like Dad to make sure everyone is proper, doing everything according to his rules of how the world should work.

Should, should, should.

If only he knew Asher's nasty side, then he would "should" Elliott to death about her picking the wrong guy and tell her to dump him immediately.

Maybe Dad would still blame her for Asher's heinous behaviors, the way he had always done with Elliott and Mom for his own rash decisions—the affair astonishingly included. "I have to talk to him about his business performance anyway. He's seemed distracted lately. Are you sure you're not pestering him?"

"Just drop it. Jesus, Dad. It's fine." Elliott pulled her cheeks down, already drained. She wasn't ready to deal with their break-up opinions that would follow if she confessed the real reason for Asher's absence.

"Stop that, dear," Holly chimed in. "You'll give yourself wrinkles." She merrily offered her unsolicited suggestions as always. But her helpfulness was as fake as the rest of her body.

Elliott removed her heels before facing Holly. "Or maybe I should start a suggestion box for you both to submit your advice for me to review for hours on end."

To Elliott's surprise, her rebuttal felt great. Like relieving an impossible itch—and it was then she realized as a little girl, what she was trying to pull out was not her eyelashes. It was her voice.

"Elliott," Dad bellowed. "What has gotten into you today? It's Christmas. Apologize to Holly now."

Elliott walked into the dining room and sat at the table, Holly and Dad following. Holly stood there, her bronzed nose up in the air.

"No." Elliott gave a phony smile, and Holly's mouth dropped.

What got into her today was she simply did not care anymore about what he, or anyone unsupportive, thought of her anymore. She was hormonal, possibly depressed, and there were more important things to care about now over their stupid, obnoxious comments.

"I have the best beauty tips—you should accept and appreciate my advice." She laughed. "But you always did have a rebellious streak, didn't you?" Holly always thought she knew more about Elliott than Elliott herself.

As more of the family arrived, including Grandma, who was somehow worse than Dad (and maybe Holly too), the table became filled with bread baskets and platters of lasagna, chicken parmesan, prime rib, mashed potatoes, sage and rosemary gravy, dark leaf salad, spears of roasted asparagus, honey-glazed carrots, and plenty of overly priced bottles of Bordeaux poured into every glass. Elliott would have loved to have already downed her first glass before any of the food came out, but even knowing the termination was tomorrow she still felt wrong for drinking.

"Holly, have you been to Bora Bora lately?" Jackie, Holly's younger, blonder sister said. Her diamond bracelets dangled as she filled her plate with asparagus. "Nate and I went last week to relax. Last month we were in Marseille and walked everywhere. Beautiful sunsets against the Mediterranean, but I felt the variety of restaurants lacking."

"Actually, Warren and I are flying out tomorrow morning to The Hilltop Villa in Fiji. We enjoy the private islands. We did Bora Bora years ago. It was more like boring-boring," Holly cracked up while she loaded her plate with salad, carefully avoiding the goat cheese crumbles and candied pecans.

"Good for you." Jackie gave Holly the middle finger.

"Be respectable, ladies. We are with company," Holly's mother, June said with eyes as big and round as an owl's, her voice full of arrogance and luxury. "However, your pettiness is disgraceful in any setting."

Jackie and Holly quieted. The only sounds heard were forks and knives clinking on plates, Dad's obnoxious chewing.

Nate attempted to break the tension. "This food is delicious, Holly," he said. Nate and Jackie married two years ago. He also came from money but held a more down-to-earth feel. Believe it or not, that was possible. "Especially the prime rib. Did you and Warren cook it?"

Elliott couldn't help but laugh as she pictured Holly cooking. They catered everything or hired chefs. "Yeah, right. They don't boil pasta for themselves," Elliott said. "Holly did attempt a charcuterie board once, though. But she put brie as the only cheese option, so..."

Holly cleared her throat and hit her fork against her plate as she put it down. "We prefer hiring Chef Toussaint for such special occasions over slaving in the kitchen for hours. Allows more time for important matters, like business and setting up the décor. Something you could learn, Elliott. I hear your house is a mess."

"You're all boring me," Grandma Bailey declared. "Elliott, tell us about your career at the Center with the renowned Dr. Heller. I've bragged about it to everyone. So proud, though we did hope you were to become a medical doctor instead," Grandma said. "Never too late." She winked.

"I'm glad I still meet at least some of your expectations." Dad shot Elliott a glance, warning shots off the bow demanding she change course. She attempted a pleasant tone. "It's going fine."

Elliott loaded her plate with more lasagna. She could feel Holly's judgment like an annoying fly she couldn't swat away.

"How is Asher? You better be engaged by the end of the year," Grandma said, snickering. "I want some grandchildren before I'm knocking on death's door."

Elliott closed her eyes, doing her best to keep her composure.

"Give her a break, Gwendolyn," Grandpa said.

The only kind one is another outsider, one with no blood relation to this hedonistic coven. She had no idea how Grandpa put up with her, but his soul did seem further sucked out of him with each visit.

"My goodness. Answer, Elliott. You are being so rude again," Holly said before turning to Grandma. "She's been rude all evening, Mrs. Bailey. I don't know what's gotten into her."

"Why isn't he here, anyway?" Grandma pressed. "You must have upset him. Or is he as rude as you? I hope you don't turn out to be single and lonely, or worse, a divorcée like your mother."

Elliott stood up so quickly the knowingly expensive chair flew back, slamming on the hardwood floor. "Do NOT speak about my mother. Ever. She is better than all of you combined, all your money, all your stupid trips and your dumb materialistic bullshit. None of that matters, because none of you are kind-hearted like she is. I'm sick to death of all of you.

"You are all so... so arrogant. And so is Asher, it's no wonder you like him. He's not here because I fucking dumped him." They all stared at her, mouths opened. "Except you, Grandpa, and you, Nate—you two are actually great, sorry. I'm leaving. The rest of you, enjoy your phony, vapid bullshit-filled dinner."

Everyone remained silent as Elliott stormed into the grand foyer, collecting her coat and scarf and shoes.

"Elliott Grace Bailey." Dad stomped behind her, arms swinging at his sides, like pendulums with fists. "You stop right there, young lady. This is unacceptable—this is not how I raised you." His face was pinched with fury.

"Yes, you are absolutely correct. You tried to raise a perfect little princess, right?" She picked up her clutch off the table, next to the ornate lamp. "You tried to hold me to some lofty ideal that doesn't exist. I'm sorry I'll never be good enough to reach your high standards, Dad."

"Oh, Ellie, come on, you know that's not true. Come into the parlor with me and sit down. I may not be the best father at times, but I can still tell when something is troubling you. And you aren't exactly hiding it tonight."

Elliott followed him into the room, resigned and wishing to leave, but something made her stay. He turned on one of the lamps, then sat down on the leather recliner as she took a spot on the matching sofa. "Look, I know I can be hard on you, but that's because you are better than the rest and I know your full potential," he said. "But sweetie, no matter what happens, you'll always be my perfect daughter."

"It's hard to believe that. I make mistakes. I make huge mistakes in fact." She tried her hardest to keep her tears back. "I'm pregnant," she said. Before he could answer, she added, "But I am getting an abortion."

Dad put his hand to his head as he leaned back in the chair. "I guess that explains it. First, your display at the dinner table. Then lying about Asher. Why didn't you say you broke up with him from the start? And now—you're pregnant. I'm a Grandpa." He stood and began to pace. "But I guess I won't be one soon enough."

"Is everything okay?" Holly peeked in.

"Not now, Holly," Dad said. "This is private. Go entertain our guests."

Holly's mouth dropped, giving Elliott momentary joy. She turned on her Christian Louboutin heels and left the room, and Dad resumed his pacing.

He stopped and looked at Elliott. "Help me understand," he said.

"I didn't want to say anything to you because the breakup was horrible. I wanted to avoid the topic entirely, not only with you, but everyone..." Elliott said. She was too ashamed to tell Julie how bad it had become.

"What the hell happened?" Dad said, and in the dim light she could see the worry in his eyes. "What are you not telling me?"

She took a deep breath. "When I told him I wanted to end it, Asher was angry, scary even," Elliott said. She squeezed the edge of the sofa, the cool leather against her skin. "He told me I was crazy for considering keeping the baby. That I would be a liar if I did. But he is the liar."

The words poured out and she couldn't stop them. "I couldn't take it anymore, the things he was saying were just so awful and I shoved him, I couldn't help it, I know that's not like me but the hormones, you know, and the way he was acting, it was all too much for me and then he tried to leave, but I didn't want him to because I felt ashamed and wanted to make it right again, but that was a mistake, and he shook me, then pushed me against the wall right before he left, and I couldn't believe how—"

"He did what to my daughter?" His dark blue eyes were a storm in the sea. "I am going to kill that piece of shit." He whipped out his phone. "I can get Gary and Roger to take care of it." He scrolled through what must be his extensive contacts list, apparently equipped with hitmen.

"No way, you can't do that," Elliott said, standing up.

"They could beat him to a bloody pulp, leave him in the middle of nowhere, teach him a lesson or two. If he makes it out alive. And to think I let him work for me, that petulant so-nova-bitch."

"Dad, seriously, stop." She put a hand on his arm. "Put the phone away. That will make things worse—for everyone. Fire him, sure, but leave it at that. God forbid you and your friends go to prison."

He paused again and looked at her, then at his phone. "I'll take that risk."

"Please, Dad. Please."

When he looked back at her, the storm in his eyes had begun to calm down, and his voice softened with it. "Oh, honey. This is all my fault. I pushed him on you. I encouraged this." Dad pocketed his phone. His shoulders slumped and he looked defeated. "I failed you as a father."

To hear Dad admit failure overwhelmed Elliott, yet relieved her at the same time.

"It isn't your fault," she said. "But it is nice to hear you admit flaws for once."

"Of course, I have flaws. I'm sorry for it all." The creases on his forehead showed his age and his despair, and she knew what he meant by "it all"—the affair, the abandonment, the constant criticism. "I don't know what else to say, what else to do aside from wanting to kill that little shit. My head is reeling."

"I don't know either." It was the truth. "I just need your support. Just say that."

"What exactly am I supporting here? Your outbursts? Your lies? I don't know where to begin with the pregnancy." He rubbed his throat.

"It doesn't matter. Trust me for once. Support me. That's it. Just me. Be there for me." Elliott started to cry, and to her surprise, Dad embraced her which made her cry more. "And stop pressuring me to be perfect."

"You're right. I'm sorry," he said, his voice gentle. "I can do that."

They sat in silence, and he held her in the warm-lit room until she left.

CHAPTER 33
ORSON

Around nine o'clock in the evening, Orson drove with Elliott to the Center. He parked his car in the nearby garage. Full of dread, they headed to the building's entrance. Elliott hesitated before putting the key in and unlocking the door to the main lobby.

"Hide your face from the cameras, keep your head low," she whispered as soon as they stepped in.

Orson felt like a criminal. It stirred a nerve-racking thrill within him. He had always been the one to defend those for their wrongdoings; now here he was on the other side. The lack of control was liberating. He should let go more. He could certainly get used to this feeling.

They took the red elevator to the eleventh floor but then Elliott hit the button for the tenth floor, too.

"What is that for?" Orson said.

"I want to see if the Elite Day Rooms are larger."

"I had no idea that was even a concern."

"Believe it or not, Dr. Heller assigned me to a normal Day Room," Elliott said. "I remember she told me not to worry about it because the average client doesn't use those rooms, and it would be more beneficial for me to be in the same type of room as them. But with how much she's already hidden, there must be a better reason for her not permitting me to see an Elite Day Room."

"I agree," Orson said. "Smells like bullshit to me."

The elevator reached the tenth floor, its melody chiming upon their arrival. They stepped out into the gleaming pre-room. Orson pulled out his Day Room card, then scanned it.

"Well?" Orson said. "Is it larger?"

Elliott took a moment to observe the room, and he could tell by her expression the news wasn't good. "No. Nothing different aside from the etched words 'Elite Day Room' on the sliding door. Everything else is positioned the same."

The white feathers swayed quietly in the snowy glow like kelp on the ocean floor, something that used to bring him peace. His hands turned into fists and he could feel his nails digging into his palms.

"One other difference is the ceiling is of the day sky instead of the night sky," she added.

He was a downright fool.

"I should sue," Orson concluded. "She clearly overcharged me, took advantage. And anyone else who used one of her bullshit Elite Rooms. I can't believe I didn't pick up on that."

"She took advantage of your grief. That's what she was counting on," Elliott said, shaking her head. "Disgusting."

They walked through the pre-room and returned to the elevator; its illuminated light was as red as the anger inside Orson.

"Now that I think about it, she sounds more like a salesman than a psychologist," Orson said as he pressed the button for eleven.

"God, Orson, this is all my fault," Elliott said, staring at the elevator floor.

"No. You couldn't have known. I made my own decisions, ultimately."

Elliott gave a small smile, appearing momentarily relieved.

"And look," Orson continued. "You know now and as soon as you had a hunch, you helped me. That's something."

"I appreciate you saying that, it's kind of you."

"I'm learning more and more how to see the brighter side of things," Orson said. "But don't tell my colleagues that. Not very lawyer-like to be upbeat and happy about the finer things in life."

Orson chuckled, as did Elliott. As the elevator doors opened, reality hit him. They walked down the hallway in silence.

Once inside the brain-mapping suite, Elliott positioned a red plastic cap with holes throughout the material on Orson's head. She then secured the tiny electrode sensors with a gel that felt cool on his scalp with each application.

"All nineteen wires are in place," she said. "They connect to the electroencephalogram device, and it will give me a read out of your overall brainwave activity. You'll then be able to view the results on the screen." She dimmed the lighting in the room to a warm golden glow.

"Will I feel anything?"

"Not a thing. It's a gentle re-routing process. Now do your best to not move or speak so it can get the most accurate reading possible."

Computer on, they waited for the scan to complete in complete silence.

Twenty minutes later, Elliott reported his brainwaves in the limbic, visual, auditory, and somatic areas were a mess: spiking and active where they shouldn't be, while dull and short in others. As she had predicted.

"Okay, I am going to reroute your brainwaves now. Again, you won't feel any physical pain. But you won't be able to see Madison anymore." She lowered her voice. "Would you like to say goodbye? I can leave the room."

A tear slid out of Orson's eye, soft and warm against his cheek. "No. Stay. I don't trust I won't rip this thing off my head and run out the door if you don't."

He closed his eyes and took a deep breath as more tears quietly rolled down his cheeks.

Moments later, he opened his eyes again, and Madison manifested before him in a flowing white dress, her arms outstretched toward him. He clasped his hands around hers. Like his tears, her hands were soft and warm.

"Hi," Orson whispered.

"Hi," Madison whispered back.

"I love you, Madison."

"I love you too, sweetheart," Madison said. "Don't forget, we will always find joy together."

Orson repeated the words, their words, back to her. "I wish you didn't have to go. I wish the cancer and you dying had all been a horrible dream," he said.

She pressed her lips against his, gentle yet fierce with love, as if all the love in the world transferred into his heart.

"I'm always with you," Madison said. "Even when you don't see me. Remembering is what keeps me alive. Our stories. Sharing our memories and our favorite things."

She was right. It was enough, because it had to be enough.

Nothing more could be done to preserve a lost life.

"You promise?" Orson said.

"Of course, Orson"—she placed a hand upon her chest—"I promise."

Elliott was right. True grief would begin. He would have to accept that more than ever now.

Orson closed his eyes, releasing more tears. Madison kissed him once more.

"One day my love, we will meet again," she whispered in his ear. "Take care of yourself and take care of our little boy. I'll be watching over the two of you."

"Hold my hand, one last time," Orson whispered. He closed his eyes again as Madison's fingers interlaced with his own.

"We'll be okay," Madison said, squeezing his hand. "We have to be. It's time now."

Orson nodded; his eyes remained closed. "Elliott? I'm ready."

He wasn't truly ready but as Madison's hand disappeared, he knew he'd never be.

CHAPTER 34
ELLIOTT

It was December 29th and Elliott was sorry.

So sorry.

And scared, and ashamed.

But she needed to be strong. For herself. For the growing cells inside of her. She refused to give a baby a scattered life and a difficult upbringing with a distant father. She knew firsthand how awful that would be.

Elliott had reached out to Asher a few times since the breakup, hoping he would respond and forgive her. It wasn't until she asked him if he could drive her to the clinic, so he could help her pay for the procedure, that he finally responded. She could have chosen Jillian or Mom to take her, but the thought had upset her.

If she brought either of them, somehow, she wouldn't have been strong enough to go through with it. Dad flew off to spoil Holly in Fiji, although she wasn't sure he'd be the best to take her anyway. Asher reminded her of the main reason why the choice was best, why it had to be done.

The obnoxious honking of Asher's Jeep ricocheted off the wall, causing a stir inside her.

The appointment was finally here.

The chill and brightness of the early morning snow woke her bloodshot, swollen eyes. Elliott had barely slept. She tentatively lowered herself into Asher's car. As soon as she sat down, he handed her a gift.

"What's this?" she said, turning the box over to look at the back. All sides were blank; nothing but stretched-out black.

"A belated Christmas gift, duh. Why are you surprised? Didn't you get me one too?" Asher said. "I figured this meant we were getting back together."

"No, I did not get you a Christmas gift, and me asking you to accompany me did not at all mean that—"

"Whatever, I'm sure you'll change your mind. You came to your senses to get the abortion."

"My God, Asher." Snow began to cover the windshield.

"What? Are you going to shove me again?" He laughed.

"I said I'm sorry multiple times." Elliott turned to look at him. "You hurt me too, and I've yet to hear an apology."

"It was in self-defense."

Just as Elliott went to further refute his incorrect conclusions, Asher cut her off. "Just open it," he said, excitedly clapping his hands.

Elliott gave up. She found a loose corner and realized it was a flap that, when opened, revealed a thick plastic covering with what looked like a fake rose inside. It reminded her of the boxes her childhood dolls came in.

"It's a forever rose," he said with pride.

"What the fuck is a forever rose?" she said, holding the box up.

"It's soaked in some chemicals so that it can't wilt. It can never die. My mom told me about it. Isn't it great? Here, let me take it out for you." He took the box from her hand.

Chemicals. A sort of everlasting embalming fluid for flowers. The rose had become robbed of change, shut away from life.

Essentially, it was lifeless.

He handed her the rose, with its long pine-green stem, then tossed the box in the backseat. Elliott rotated it and poked at the petals. They were soft and silky, fully budded, and blood red.

"We cannot have the baby, but you can have this rose forever," Asher said, with glee in his tone. "Get it?"

Elliott stared vacantly at the perfect rose, with its perfect stem, and perfect leaves, and perfect petals, from her perfect-looking ex-boyfriend.

She snapped it in half.

She lowered the window and threw it on the frosted ground.

"What the fu—"

"Drive."

After a half hour they arrived at the women's clinic, now sitting side by side in the waiting room. A sense of nothingness filled her head, her thoughts hard to hold onto. She wished to be anywhere else.

The car ride to the clinic had been strange. After Asher loudly complained about Elliott's destruction of his "very kind, very thoughtful gift," and how she was extremely ungrateful, he seemed fine, as if he were driving them to the mall or a diner for breakfast.

He transitioned into his weak argument for why they should get back together: they could now start fresh after the abortion; they looked good together. Her dad would rehire him at the gym. And Elliott owed Asher a redo for having shoved him.

The waiting area was cold and crowded with other pregnant women; some were alone, some accompanied. A girl with long curly brown hair, who looked slightly younger than Elliott, twiddled her thumbs as she stared down at them, transfixed, as if they held all the answers about life.

The girl's pacing fingers reminded Elliott of the up and down motion of one's feet when riding a bicycle. The idea of speeding away on one tempted her; she envisioned a bicycle awaiting her outside in the parking lot. She doubted Asher would notice if she dashed out now and escaped. He buried himself in NFL stats on his phone.

The brunette's thumbs stopped, and as Elliott looked upward, the girl regarded her too but then quickly looked away.

Their brief eye contact said it all: I'm alone, and I'm scared.

Who was the father? Why wasn't he there with this girl now? It's possible he immediately dumped her, and she too, like Elliott, didn't want to raise a child without the dad.

That notion was simply a farce. Undoubtedly, this girl could raise her without him. Elliott wanted to rush over there and tell her if it's because the dad is gone, she should leave while she still can. That she was fierce enough to do it all on her own. But the girl was called next, and in she went.

Asher typed out a text and nudged her shoulder. The words on the screen made her want to punch him.

Ur lucky. Lots of lonely grls here. But not u. I'm here for u babe.

Every cell of her being screamed, and she wished he could be blown away by the force onto another planet, like a sonic boom of hatred.

Instead, Elliott went back to staring at the floor as Asher watched muted videos on his phone of weightlifting competitions. Was Asher robotic, sociopathic, or incredibly talented at escapism?

It was easy for him to stay detached, while Elliott had become attached in every sense of the word. She had sought out voices of reason, hoping someone else could make the decision for her. She had secretly wished for a miscarriage.

All remained quiet except the news channel on a small television bolted into the top corner of the room repeating the same stories at the top of each hour that passed by. Occasionally, a nurse would open the door and call in the next patient. The staff bustled around charts behind the receptionist area.

The torture of it all was crawling around in her like a parasitic worm.

After nearly three hours of waiting, a nurse appeared at the door. "Elliott?" She scanned the waiting room.

It took Elliott a moment to connect the name to herself. Part of her had liked the long wait and wished for more time. Part of her wanted to get up and leave the building entirely, hoping the imaginary bike would be real and waiting.

Her legs barely responded to her brain's demand to rise. She forced herself to follow the nurse inside. Asher wasn't allowed to accompany her.

Elliott had to get a sonogram before moving into the next waiting area. In a small consultation room, the technician spread the cold gel on Elliott's lower abdomen. She also stupidly left the screen slightly facing Elliott, enough for her to see.

Don't look—this image was for women who were keeping their babies, the women who get to see that image and yelp excitedly, who get to take a print-out to show everyone they could before hanging it on the fridge.

She couldn't help it. She looked. Her heart fell silent.

A nurse came in and led her into a smaller waiting area for the patients only, and as much as she hated Asher, she kind of wished he were allowed here so she wasn't so alone. There were other women sitting in hospital gowns; an old television played children's shows on a table nearby.

Barbed wire wrapped itself around Elliott's heart, squeezing with each child's giggle on the screen—the girl to her right, freckled and fragile, made a comment about it being awful, while an older woman with long, pointed nails cursed and turned the television off entirely.

Soon, she was called into another room that was poorly lit with a cluttered desk, to meet with the counselor on site. As soon as Elliott sat down, she shed tears.

"It's okay. You want to do this," the counselor said with complete assurance, handing Elliott the bill. "While Joe and Mary are providing karate classes, nice clothes, good food for their kid, you'll be rubbing two pennies together to give yours a PB&J. You're doing the right thing." She paused and Elliott handed her Asher's credit card, along with four hundred dollars in cash, a small part of her generous holiday bonus from Dr. Heller, to pay for her half.

Elliott followed another nurse back into the small waiting area to change out of her clothes and into a hospital gown, in the bathroom off to the side of the room. She had never been so ashamed and lost.

The nurse walked her to the procedure room.

Elliott was taken aback at the sight of the medical room. It was cold, both in presentation and temperature. The metal procedure table looked like a death cot with black leather stirrups. She lay down, her thin gown a poor barrier to the chill against her spine.

The anesthesiologist, who barely introduced himself and mumbled his name, attempted to insert her IV. Fumbling and huffing, impatient with the veins in both of her arms, he then switched to her hand. Still dubious. As the needle pierced her skin, and he fished around again, wiggling it in search of a vein, Elliott yelled.

"Stop," she yelled again.

He pulled the needle out and looked alarmed.

"I can try another vein, or a smaller needle," he said, reaching for her other hand.

"Don't touch me." Elliott pulled her hands away.

Another doctor walked in.

"Hey now, I'm Dr. Stagers, your obstetrician for today's procedure. Everything is alright," he reassured. "Just relax."

She curled her legs up toward her chest. "No. Stop everything. I don't want to do this. I don't need another doctor to try. I need to leave." Elliott clambered off the examination table. "Now—right now. I've changed my mind."

Asher dropped Elliott off at home, where Mom and Julie were waiting. He drove away as fast as he could without so much as a "goodbye" after Elliott denied his myriad requests to get back together with him.

"You didn't do it? Really? Oh my God, Elle," Julie said through smiles.

Mom put her hand on Elliott's shoulder. "Elliott—what does this mean—are you keeping it, honey?"

"Yes," Elliott said. She was relieved. Yet, she was still crying.

She could tell they were relieved, too, that they wanted to celebrate—but she remained outside the realm of excitement, unable to feel the same way. Because everything was going to change—everything.

"What did Asher say?" Julie said.

"I—I didn't tell him."

"Oh dear," Mom said as Julie's eyebrows raised and mouth dropped, in an "oh shit" kind of way.

"Are you going to?" Julie said.

"I don't know, I have to figure things out. All I want to do is go to sleep right now."

After a few more minutes of Mom and Julie consoling her the best they could, reminding her they will support her the entire way, Elliott laid in her bed in nothingness. There were no sounds, no colors, no smells, or tastes. Everything was static and lifeless, quiet and deafening all at once.

Mom had once said that life was full of pushes. Pushes that caused people to make tough choices, choices we have to eventually face no matter how hard we try to avoid them.

It required acceptance and compassion whenever those choices felt wrong, even if they ultimately worked out. At the time, Elliott had tucked it away, unsure of what Mom's rambling meant.

Elliott understood these things now.

CHAPTER 35
HOWARD

Howard sat in his living room writing nonsense in his journal, his handwriting visibly shaky, words not nearly as eloquent as he'd prefer, but he continued onward anyway while downing almost an entire bottle of whiskey with no plans to stop.

Thoughts were strange when highly intoxicated. He was evaluating everything and nothing at the same time. An unreachable life Howard always desired. A vast emptiness. Howard's existence was a state of perpetual misery—things were given to be ripped from his hands, no matter how tightly he squeezed.

A wonderful mother. A talented father, regardless of his flaws. Music. Unconditional love. Friends. With all of that gone, not to mention Jillian and John's disappearance, it only solidified the fact that there was no hope. He was a non-being incapable of experiencing love.

Simple as that.

He sat by the window staring at the rain as it melted some of the snow away, drop by drop, creating a sprawl of gray freckles on a winter landscape. Even the rain was something to envy. It restored life. It washed away a bad day when he needed it most. When it was paired with a gray sky, it matched Howard's mood while he read, making him feel less alone in his sorrow. Sunshine always seemed to deride him anyway.

Howard chucked his journal in the wastebasket by the door. It was a book to never be read. He hated it. He hated the details of his lonesome life. Loneliness ate away at his heart.

He flipped his phone open and scrolled through his contacts. There had to be one last hope out there, one last person worth living for—or believed that Howard was worth living for, rather.

It didn't take long until he landed on the "K" section of his contact list and found her.

Two results awaited him if he called Kimmy: she'd be glad to hear from him, or she'd laugh and hang up. Howard expected the latter, but he didn't mind either outcome at this point. He had already sunk deep under the sea of life.

He clicked her name and pressed the call button.

Ring, ring.

Perhaps she wouldn't answer at all. That wouldn't be that bad either. He wasn't sure what time it was, but it had been dark out for a while now.

Ring, ri—

"Hel-lo?" She actually answered. She sounded annoyed. Maybe she thought he was a solicitor.

"Hey, it's me... Howard." He walked into the living room and sat on the squeaky, burnt-orange corduroy couch.

"Yeah, I know," she said. "But why are you calling me?"

Why was he calling her? This was stupid.

"I don't know." He pictured his words on a scale, wobbly and out of sync.

When he expected vitriol and annoyance, Kimmy's voice softened. "Is everything okay? You sound drunk."

"Any chance I can see you?"

"You know what? That's not a bad idea. I would like that, fuzzy head," she said, whipping out the old nickname already. Although it seemed phony, it felt nice too. "I feel bad about how we ended things."

"We did not end things. You did."

"Whatever. I'll be there in ten. I'm in the neighborhood."

He didn't tell her where or when, but Kimmy was like that. She made her own plans. He always admired that about her and succumbed to the familiar thrill of not knowing what's going to happen next with her.

Fifteen minutes later, there was a knock at the door. Howard took one more swig of whiskey and walked over to open it.

Kimmy hadn't changed much. Her eyes were lined with black, her cheeks glowing with a slightly overdone plum blush. The only thing that was different was her hair color—well, two colors—and her haircut.

One side of her hair was dark purple, the other side bubble-gum pink. She had thick bangs, and her hair fell an inch below her chin. Ashen skin gave her a spectral appearance.

An alluring illusion, always.

"Wow, don't clean up for me," she said as she barged her way into the living room. She dropped her coat on the couch.

Howard hadn't taken care of the apartment in weeks. Even in the candlelight, visible crumbs collected on the coffee table alongside used napkins; empty bags of Lay's potato chips stuck out from underneath the couch. His worn hoodies covered the upright piano in the corner. But as he looked around, embarrassment never came. To him, this was normal.

"So, you are drunk," she said, picking up the bottle of whiskey off the table. "And I see you can't be bothered with a glass no less."

She laughed, licking her lips. "But don't fret, I'm back at it too, fuzzy head. Those therapists can go circle jerk to their ignorant advice. A life without drugs and drinking is incredibly dull." She grabbed the whiskey and downed about two shots worth.

She then kneeled on the floor near the coffee table and pulled out a familiar film canister, the one she kept her drugs in. She popped it open.

"As much as I love the romance vibes from the candles, I can barely see. Put the lights on for a second."

There was a clumsy silence before Howard answered. "I can't."

"What do you mean?"

"I couldn't afford the electric bill this month." He had spent all his money at the Center. With John having fired him recently, he hadn't had time to replenish the lost funds.

"Um. Kind of sad, but whatever." Kimmy's lack of surprise, or concern, reminded him he's the type where poverty suited his existence. "X?" she said, offering the canister.

"No, thank you."

Regret tugged at his sleeve. He shouldn't have called Kimmy. What was the point of all this? He felt sleazy and ashamed, like a hypocrite. He drank more than the average person, but the pills and cocaine and judgment caused him discomfort, and he'd never get used to it. He'd never get used to Kimmy.

"You're no fun, choir boy," she said. She crushed an ecstasy pill on the table with the bottle of whiskey, then retrieved a mini straw from her pocket and snorted it in one well-practiced movement. "What about coke?"

"No."

"Cigarette? Goes well with whiskey, especially your cheap-ass kind," she said as she picked up the Evan Williams.

"No. I didn't invite you over for your arsenal of drugs."

"Oh. I see." She sauntered over and traced a finger along his chest, sending a spark from her touch to his groin. He backed away from her hand, but she stepped forward again, leaving little space between them. "Playing hard to get, love?" She used the same finger to pull at the waistband of his jeans, sending another spark through him like a shooting star.

"No," he said. "I guess I thought we'd talk." He couldn't tell if his head was cloudy from the alcohol or anxiety, but his heart pounded suggesting it was a little of both.

She laughed. "Talk? Sure, we can talk. After you get naked with me."

Before Howard could answer, she removed her sweater and then moved on to pulling off her black skirt and tights. She had lost weight again; he could see her rib cage and the peaks of her hip bones. Slowly, she moved toward him and took his hand.

"I don't know if this is such a good idea." He wished he was doing this with Jillian right now, not her. But that will never happen again. Kimmy is the best Howard will ever get. Kimmy is what he deserves. "Can we please talk first?"

"Always the Boy Scout." She dropped his hand. "This is what we do, fuck and make up. Now take your pants off. C'mon." She kissed his neck as her hands explored his waistband again, unbuttoning and unzipping his jeans. The electric bolt didn't occur this time. If anything, it struck outward to protect him, and he wished she would stop. "Dance with my body," she whispered, "like old times."

"We should change that. Get back together in a healthier way," he said, turning his head as she went to kiss his mouth.

She stepped back and snapped. "Oh, come on. You know you want me." She began to sway, caressing her pallid skin. "Can you not handle me anymore? Have you gone soft?"

"I didn't say that, I said—"

Her hands fell to her side. "Forget it. You're pathetic, you know that? I'm going back to my boyfriend's house. He's boring too, but at least he'll put out."

"You have a boyfriend? What the hell is wrong with you?" Howard said as she began putting her clothes back on. Why should he be surprised that she'd have a new boyfriend and be willing to cheat on him? At least he now knew she'd do this to anyone; it wasn't just Howard—he wasn't special enough to be the "only one" of anything.

She laughed wildly. "What's wrong with me? Ha!" She didn't stop. "Look at you. You're a sad, balding loser who lets people walk all over him. You called me but you don't know what you want. You never did. You never make choices for yourself; you never do anything. You sit and let the world go by. You're a fly on the wall. You're nothing."

She shimmied into her tights. "And your head isn't fuzzy in a cute way. I said things like that because it's what I thought a girlfriend should say to make her boyfriend feel better about himself. But nothing works with you. You will always hate yourself, as you should, because you are a sad sack of human waste that will amount to nothing. And to think I was going to pity-fuck you."

Howard stared at one of the stains on the beige carpet. He couldn't look her in the eye. As brutal as she was, he knew what she said was the truth.

Kimmy grabbed her coat from the closet, then opened the front door and paused.

"I'll forget you," she shouted, before slamming the door.

After Kimmy left, Howard put a bottle of whiskey into a plastic bag with an umbrella and a blanket. He foggily thought back to Jillian enshrouded in his blanket that night in her car. He looked at his phone— another missed call from Langston and one from the Center. A tinge of guilt gnawed at his stomach along with the awareness of it being empty. He had not had an appetite for days. He barely lived while he was alive.

Howard's eyes shifted toward a photograph of Mom on the wall. "I'm sorry, Mom." The dusty wall clock beside it told him it was nearly midnight.

He left the apartment. Walked. And walked. Nothing to see but cement, crumpled wrappers, old cups near trash bins, occasional cigarette butts sticking up in a zig-zagged pattern or completely flattened on the sidewalk.

The first time he finally tilted his head up, he was already at the park by the river. He stumbled toward a bench and spilled whiskey, leaving a patch of amber in the slush. It was the bench where he and Jillian had sat over a week ago.

He steadied himself onto the seat, reached for the umbrella, but took the blanket out instead. He wrapped himself in it, then threw his hood over his beanie-covered head. His heart ached, cracking like glass—the cuts of pain widespread like wandering streams carving lines deeper and deeper within.

The devastation of living without love, or family, or society or belonging somewhere or to someone, to be tethered in a pure, lasting way wrapped around his throat. Howard grasped for rescue, for warmth, for any sign of welcoming.

His entire being screamed for affection and acceptance. Things that come normally to most people. Things they would never have to think about. To live in a world where you searched for love, but no one searched for you.

Howard looked up at the curved moon as he tilted his head back, guzzling the whiskey with shaky hands—its burn hardly registering. Even the moon looked wan and dismal tonight. It was barely visible behind fog-like clouds stretched across it like gray cotton.

He touched his cheek. He was unknowingly weeping, the tears rolling themselves out. He had come to understand why Pop acted the way he did after Mom died. Maybe he drank himself to death on purpose.

A languid snowfall returned, snowflakes swaying in the moonlight as his vision blurred in and out.

His breathing was labored and sluggish, his body suddenly heavy. Howard shifted downward on the bench. The near-empty bottle of whiskey almost slid from his hand, the glass of it twinkling from the Christmas lights still strung on houses behind him.

"Sle-e-ep in heavenly peace..." he slur-sang to no one.

Images flashed in his head like a happy montage. Mom and Pop cheered him on as he played piano. Jillian snug in his arms. John proud of him for starting therapy with Elliott, and Langston doing his best to guide Howard. Images of what life took away. Images of what he no longer deserved.

As Howard's eyelids lowered, he dropped the bottle, its remaining golden liquid slowly spreading throughout the snow.

CHAPTER 36
ELLIOTT

Elliott sat on her couch with her laptop, researching attachment theory and its application in the private practice setting, trying to distract herself from her breast tenderness and swelling that was growing increasingly painful each day.

She tapped her finger on her laptop, gawking at the words on the screen.

Tap. Tap. Tap. Tap. Tap. Her phone rang. It was Asher. Again.

Elliott silenced it. Again.

She wasn't ready to tell him she kept the pregnancy yet. She wasn't sure if she'd ever tell him. She had been ignoring his calls and text messages for days, the relentless attempts about getting back together. He had transformed into a delusional stalker.

The doorbell rang, and her legs jerked underneath the computer, disturbing her sleeping dog. She closed the laptop and got up. Slowly stepping out of the living room, Elliott edged toward the door, Captain trailing behind her.

Knock, knock, knock.

"Elliott? Hello? Are you alive?" Asher yelled from behind the door. "Hello?"

Knock, knock, knock.

Well then. It would have to be now.

Knock-knock-knock-knock

She opened the door. "Oh my God, seriously," she said. "When will you give up?"

"Hello to you too," he said, pushing his way past her. Winter's chill emanated off his body. He took a seat on the living room couch and tossed his coat on the cushion next to him. "You've been ignoring me for days."

"Okay?"

Asher shook his head. "Seriously, that's it? 'Okay?'" he mocked, sounding like a high-pitched buffoon. "What's going on with you?"

Elliott stood by the entrance to the living room, leaning against the wall, arms crossed.

"Well? An apology would be nice," he said.

"I have nothing to apologize for." Elliott uncrossed her arms and stood up straight.

"Are you about to start a fight? I thought the time apart was great—gave me space from all your negative vibes." He put his hands behind his head and leaned back on the couch. "Thought you were thinking things over too about how to be better when you finally came back to me."

"What the fuck are you talking about?" Through the window behind him, she could see the sun setting. As beautiful as the layers of orange and fuchsia along the horizon were, she couldn't enjoy it; not with Asher's stupid face staring at her.

"Just apologize"—he eyeballed the fireplace—"and put our photos back on the mantel. Stop playing games. Let's move on, like you said."

"I did not come back to you," Elliott fired. "You misinterpreted."

"Yes, you literally did." He pulled out his phone from his pocket. "Let me read your last text in case you forgot: 'Hi Asher, I know you are still mad at me and that's why you're not answering. But I am truly, truly sorry. I hope you can forgive me and move past it. I was also hoping you would accompany me to the clinic. I have decided to get the abortion and put all of this behind us.'"

"I know what I said. But it had nothing to do with getting back together."

"Jesus Christ." Asher's voice began to rise, and he scooted toward the edge of the couch. Not only anger. Slight nervousness. "You've been acting weirder ever since you got that bug inside you. It's gone now, let's move on—together. Stop this bullshit act already."

"I'm done." She stepped further into the room. "With all of this. I'm done with you. I'm done with your lame ass skin-care routine. Your manipulation. Your narcissistic ignorance. You seriously need help. You're the one who needs to go to therapy. I'm sick of all of it, and I'm sick of you." Asher's true ugliness was under a magnifying glass, and she would never again turn away from seeing it. Her idea of him—the reality of him—had been worlds apart. "You repulse me. And guess what else?" She placed her hand on her lower abdomen. "That bug—your child—is still inside me."

"You're joking, right?" His cackle was unnerving. He shot up off the couch and moved so close to her she could feel his breath.

Her fists tightened. "No, Asher. I'm not. Let me tell you what else. I do not love you anymore. It's done. We're done." She couldn't stop her tears from forming. She was frustrated, exhausted, hormonal, and more than anything else in the world she wanted him to go away.

"Oh, stop. Look at you. All you do is cry. We can't talk about anything without you crying," he said with a sneer.

"At least I can feel."

"Come on, you don't want to break up. You'll be over this tomorrow morning, like always. I know you're screwing with me. You're not actually pregnant."

Elliott rushed out of the living room, ran up the stairs, and into her bedroom.

"Where the fuck are you going?" Asher called out.

Elliott reached her room and rummaged through her dresser. She pushed aside sweaters and cardigans until she reached the bottom. There it was: the adorable pink onesie. She hugged it, smiling. She would now be able to use it for her baby.

"Hello?" Asher yelled again. Elliott's smile quickly faded.

She made her way back to Asher in the living room, onesie in hand.

"What is that?" he said as she waved it in his face.

"I'm not screwing with you. I'm still pregnant. Oh, and I found out she's a girl. So, this is for my future daughter. Get over it and get the fuck out."

"You're not joking, are you?" Asher paced around the room, then stopped and walked up to her. "What the fuck is wrong with you?" He grabbed her shoulders and shook her. "Why would you do that? Why would you keep it?"

Elliott pushed away from his grip this time. "You didn't listen to me. You didn't see me, you didn't care. I wanted to keep it. But I thought I shouldn't, and truthfully, I thought that only because of you. But I don't need to explain myself to you anymore. Now get out or I will call the police."

"Fucking shit," Asher yelled, punching the palm of his hand. "You won't see a goddamn dime out of me. I'm not helping. You wanna play mommy, go right-a-fuckin-head. I won't stick around. You're psychotic."

Pacing back and forth, he was mumbling under his breath. "Fuck."

Swiftly, he turned toward the wall and punched it, forming a crater of drywall around his hands. Thick, glossy blood seeped through his fingers.

"Leave." Elliott's voice was firm and steady. "Don't worry about sticking around. I'll be better without you." She placed a hand on her stomach. "We will be better without you."

Asher's face reddened as veins bulged in his forehead. "You're a nightmare," he said, clutching his injured hand. "And to think I could've cheated on you. Do you know how many times I turned Clara down?"

"Give up already. Give up." Elliott walked toward the foyer, and he followed, rushing past her. "I honestly feel bad for you," she continued. "You're the one losing everything. You might not see it now. I know you won't admit it if you already do. But you will."

Asher glared at her, his eyes ablaze. "You'll be begging me to come back. You need me."

Elliott laughed. She laughed loudly. Because she realized, Asher was not important anymore.

"What is so funny?" His eyes scanned her face.

"You're nothing to lose. And absolutely nothing to need."

He stared at her, dumbfounded, like a wounded child. Finally, after a few seconds too long, he stormed out. The front door slammed.

Elliott slid down to the floor, breathing heavily. Her heart was beating rather fast from the adrenaline rush, but she hadn't had one urge to pull at anything on her face, despite how unhinged Asher had become.

She never recognized just how rigid of a person he was, until she became more tolerable of the messiness in her own life. Life proved to be restless. Flexibility was crucial for living in such a constant stream of questions and answers. Being preoccupied with the unknown ruined the peacefulness of living in the known—of living in the here and now.

As Elliott paced her breathing, allowing it to slow down, she scanned her body for any signs of heartbreak. Her emotions were quieter than they had been in a long time. Although she was single again, and pregnant, she was not afraid.

Above all else, she felt hopeful—free.

"Everything is okay," Elliott whispered to her baby.

She had finally stepped off the loop.

Elliott jerked awake to the sound of her alarm. The room filled with early morning sunlight. Smiling, she stretched her arms upward and squinted at the clock on her wall: 7:30AM. As she rolled over to retrieve her phone off the nightstand, a missed call from Dr. Heller flashed on the screen. It was highly unusual for her to be calling this early. Elliott shot out of bed as if she had already downed ten cups of coffee.

She called her back.

"I'm deeply sorry but I have terrible news," Dr. Heller said, her voice gentle. "It's about your patient... Howard Nor."

Elliott's head began to spin; she stopped listening, her hand reaching back for the bed as she lowered herself onto the mattress. What was Dr. Heller saying? Elliott had to latch back onto Dr. Heller's words, but she was frozen.

"Elliott? Elliott, are you there?"

"Oh—I. Yes. What happened, is Howard okay?"

"I said he is in the hospital. St. Mary's. It appears he attempted to take his life last night through alcohol poisoning. It would be appropriate if you would visit and represent the Center for us."

Is she really making this about the appearance of the business?

What a joke. Dr. Heller's empathy was a shell hiding greed at the core.

"I cannot believe this." Elliott ran through their last few sessions together in her head. "There were no obvious clues last time we spoke."

"These things happen in our field. It's an unfortunate reality," Dr. Heller said plainly. "We work with ill people and sometimes treatment, no matter how hard we try, does not equate to steady progress. He was terribly depressed."

"I should have checked in again. Tried harder." Elliott was his therapist. Howard had trusted Elliott, and she failed. Her relationship with Asher had made her become so consumed, that she followed Dr. Heller's orders without question. Elliott should have trusted her gut that talk therapy alone was best for now. "I want to see him, make sure he's all right."

"It will be okay. We will fix this. You are still in your first year of working with patients. This could happen with our thousandth patient, to the utmost, experienced professionals, although it hasn't happened to me now that I think about it.

"But I'll have Romalda reach out and make sure he sets up appointments with you for his return. Please discuss better use of the Balloon Days because I believe it will help. I'll allow it to be free of charge for his next one."

Elliott stepped near her window and peered at the morning sky. She refused to push Balloon Day sessions on someone who attempted to permanently escape his life.

Dr. Heller continued. "We will follow the ethical protocol as well—encourage him to join a group for alcoholism and a day group for further community-based support. The hospital should be able to set up those resources for him."

Elliott's personal issues had finally collided into her professional life, and in one of the most serious ways possible. Breaking up with Asher should have been taken care of long ago.

Chasing perfection caused nothing but chaos.

CHAPTER 37
HOWARD

Howard lay in a foreign bed, blurry-eyed, the world around him a smear of white and gray. His eyes burned from the light. He could hear a cacophony of sounds: machines beeping, metal clanking, wheels thudding and rolling by, the buzzing of distant chatter.

Each eyelid was stuck together with goop and opening them was proving to be like pulling gum off the bottom of a shoe. An IV stuck out of his forearm.

What the hell was going on?

Suddenly, a touch on his shoulder brought him back. "Hi," a woman said in a low, soft voice. "Are you feeling alright?"

It was Elliott, his therapist.

"Oh." Howard's voice cracked. His throat was as dry as dirt in a drought. He tried to sit up, but nails hammered into all sides of his head.

"It's okay, rest. Drink some water."

"Where am I?"

"You're at Saint Mary's." She passed him a glass of water.

"The hospital?"

"Yes... you were found in a park near your home in the middle of the night, around three o'clock this morning. The nurses said you suffered from severe alcohol poisoning." She briefly held her head low. "But you're better now, and that's what matters."

Howard sipped the ice water, its restorative tingle traveling down his throat into his stomach.

Elliott took the glass from him and placed it back on the table. "The doctor said your blood alcohol level was close to point three percent.

Thank God you're alive. He said the nurses had pumped your stomach on the way over in time."

"Who found me?"

"Oh, um—I believe they said your brother had."

Everything was suddenly overwhelming. John found him?

Howard dropped his gaze to the IV in his arm, then up toward the saline bag hung on the pole. Little pearls of liquid dripped and swam through the thin tube. Had he tried taking his life? Truth was he didn't know. He couldn't remember. If he had, he wished no one had found him.

He couldn't even do that right.

"I appreciate your help," Howard said.

Elliott nodded, and gave his shoulder a brief, gentle touch.

"I'll send John in. He's eager to see you but wanted me to talk with you first. He said he figured you'd prefer that." It was odd for John to act so thoughtfully. "I'll see you soon, Howard."

Howard said his farewell, thanked her again, then prepped himself for his next visitor. To have his brother find him that way... Howard was ashamed. And afraid. John still must be angry with him.

Moments later, John walked in. As he came nearer, his features became clearer. Blonde hair. Strong jaw. Fancy clothes. A brother to be proud of.

John lowered himself in the seat next to Howard. He shook his head, looking down at the floor. "God. I haven't felt so terrified since we lost Mom. Then, you know, Pop. You should have come over. Or called me. Or your therapist. If I knew. If I knew how badly you were hurting, if I knew you were... I would have..."

John's mouth quivered. "I couldn't sleep last night again. I finally got up, said screw it, and headed to your apartment around two in the morning. My excuses sucked more and more of why I shouldn't talk it out with you. Reminded me of Pop's lame excuses."

Howard let out a small laugh. "Like the one where he canceled playing guitar at that café because he suddenly had to disinfect the bathroom?"

"Oh my god, that one might have been my favorite." They both laughed. "But it wasn't fair for me to take everything away from you. To take myself away from you. We're the only family we have."

Howard teared up, worsening his headache. "How did you find me?"

"I checked your room. I found your journal in the bin and read it. I saw the empty bottles in your kitchen, your bathroom, your bedroom. Figured you went out to get more, but when I didn't see you at the store or the bar, I started piecing it all together. It wasn't long before I found you at the park. I figured you might be there. I know you like to think there. But I didn't expect to find you like that. We lost Mom and Pop, Howard. I can't lose you too."

Howard's mind was whirling.

"I'm going to grab a coffee from downstairs," John said. "You want anything? The muffins looked good. The nurse said she was bringing you food up soon, but I'm sure it'll suck."

"Muffin sounds good."

As John walked away, Howard called out to him.

He turned around. "Yeah?"

"Thank you," Howard said.

Evaluations, rehab pamphlets, an intensive outpatient program, and a newly prescribed antidepressant later, the hospital had allowed Howard to finally return home. They made sure he had at least three appointments lined up with Elliott—she had been in contact with the hospital and helped arrange everything.

John asked Howard to move into his apartment as Howard recovered and stood on his own two feet; he offered to pay for his medication and treatment, too. Howard promised he would meet John halfway.

All of the help—it was nice.

He was trusting it. He was trusting himself. How could he have almost let this all go?

He should have reached out to John. He should have apologized more. He should have groveled for forgiveness; he should have begged. John had every right to be as angry as he had been, and he was beyond grateful John forgave him. Howard was all too eager to start a better relationship between the two of them.

John made sure there was no alcohol in either apartment, and also made sure Howard re-blocked Kimmy's number for good. Both blocked Jillian's number.

His brother was there all along and Howard was the one to never ask for anything, the one who pretended all was okay, the one to believe he would disappoint his older brother if he continually needed help. He had already been ashamed relying on him financially. He learned from Elliott he could be both independent and need support. It didn't have to be one or the other.

Howard put his coat and beanie on and headed to the Center for a session with Elliott. Once he was inside her office, he cried. He cried for what felt like hours. He wept for all of it. His hands shook from emotion and withdrawal.

"We were all so worried," Elliott said. "I can't imagine what you must have felt. Do you remember anything from that night?"

Howard told her how the risk he chose sacrificed too much, but he was greedy. How he lost Jillian, how she used him to get back at John. How he didn't know what was true anymore. How horribly wrong his last Balloon Day session had gone. How he had lost John. How he had nothing left to live for—that his presence was confirmed by Kimmy, by all, that he was worthless, useless, a nuisance. So, he drank the pain away.

"The substance abuse counselor told me the depression blinded me to all that was good. That it drives people to cling to anything that could relieve it, like I had done with alcohol, the Balloon Days... and love. Even if it wasn't healthy. Both Kimmy and Jillian were relationships riding on hope. A hope that they would want me back, and a hope their love would make me become a better person."

"Yes," Elliott said. The midday sunlight made her white outfit look even crisper. "Untreated depression, especially paired with unprocessed grief, can certainly lead to that. With that knowledge, we can keep looking at how to move forward."

Howard grazed the perfectly braided edges of the pillow in his lap. "It's hard to move forward when all I feel is regret."

"I understand. We all act in ways that are problematic at a point in time because up until then, we only had that level of wisdom, only that level of skill to manage hardships.

"I mean, in hindsight, it's so easy to bring up the should-haves. But if we use each experience as an opportunity to grow, we get wiser as we get older. So, let's see how we can move forward from here with all of what you do know now."

Elliott picked up her pen and notepad. "First—did you cut off all communication with Jillian?"

"I blocked her," Howard said. "Along with Kimmy, in case they tried to reach out, or in case I became tempted to. I do love Jillian. But like she said, it was a phantom thing. And striving for someone who does not let you materialize into her world in a real way, even if she said she cared about me—that is enough to drive anyone mad, I think.

"I thought she saved me when she came into my life, but now I know she saved me more by leaving. I painted this perfect image of her and how it should be and when she messed it up, every single time, I still tried to go over the mess and fill in the image again with only the good. But that's not fair. To me or to her."

Truthfully, some days were better than others as of late. In the moments Howard remembered Jillian—it broke his heart.

"Well said." Elliott nodded and lightly clapped her hands together, causing Howard to let out a laugh. "It's important to see the reality of people. I believe you saved yourself, though, Howard. Just like you had when you kept reading and learning after dropping out of high school. You also embraced the opportunity to work for your brother. You already have many strengths you tend to discount."

"It's hard for me to see that," Howard said, although Elliott had a point.

Elliott leaned forward toward Howard. "I do believe—once you are ready—us processing the trauma of your mother's death will be a significant piece toward your growth. It directly impacted your self-worth, there's no question about that."

"I don't doubt it," he admitted. "But I don't think I'll be ready any time soon."

"That's totally fine. I think right now our main goal together is to focus on you alone. Let's find ways to have you feel materialized in your own world. Fill in your own image, so to speak, so that you transform into your genuine, fulfilled self."

She smiled at him, sweetly. In that moment, he was beyond grateful for being less financially fortunate—he might not have ever met Elliott, he might have been assigned as Dr. Heller's patient instead. Money could buy things, and temporary happiness. It could never buy meaningful, genuine connections with people.

That came from the heart.

"Whatever it is, choose what feels meaningful for you. Something that is all your own."

He repeated her last words in his head. Something that is all your own. He teared up again, but it did not feel like sadness. Something within him was released, unlocking the chains of his mind.

Howard was seeing more clearly now all those who were there for him, unconditionally. And the ways he could truly save himself.

As beautiful and euphoric as the Balloon Days could be, they were an illusion. It was time he built his life in the real world.

"I would like that," he said. "And I want to add in another part if I could?"

"Of course."

"I want whatever I choose to also honor my mom's memory."

"Then I think we both know what that means."

CHAPTER 38
ORSON

Waiting for Jack to return to his desk, Orson played a game on his phone.

"You sure you don't want any, Orson?" Jack said, carrying a demitasse cup of espresso. "It's from Italy."

"I'm quite alright, thanks. I had some coffee before I got here. But it does smell delightful." Orson pocketed his phone.

"Suit yourself, cowboy," Jack said. "Me? I can't get enough of this shit." He sat down across from Orson and pulled out a manila folder. "So, my man, while you've been dilly-dallying with consultations—which, I still don't understand how those last few could have considered us if they aren't ready to pay the big bucks—despicable."

He scoffed and shook his head. "Who the hell do they think we are? Anyway, I'm gonna play it straight with you. We decided we'd like to offer you senior partner but not until next year. We want to make sure you get fully back on your A game."

"Jack," Orson said.

"The decision's been made. Sorry, son. Now, as for what we'd need to see, I—"

"Jack. I need to say something." Orson's heart rate escalated.

"What is it?" He put the folder down and gulped half the espresso, placing the cup back on its saucer.

"Thank you, Jack."

"I'm sorry?"

"I don't want to become a senior partner. Not now. And probably not ever. I'm fine where I'm at. To be honest, ever since Madison died, I've realized how absent I've been from my son's life. I was certainly absent

297

from Madison's life these past few years and that will be a regret I carry with me for the rest of my life. I won't make that mistake again for my son." Jack remained quiet. "I would like to stay at the firm, and I'll manage the cases I've already been assigned. But if that doesn't work, I'll pack my things, no hard feelings. I hope you can understand." As he finished speaking, his muscles and mind loosened, letting go of all burden, like releasing a balloon into the sky.

"Okay, then." Jack leaned forward on the desk and clasped his hands together. "I never knew too many lawyers who talked themselves out of work, but there's a first time for everything. Were you not so damned good at what you do, I would have told you to hit the bricks. I understand. And to be honest, it sounds like you have more wisdom in that beautiful brain of yours than me.

"My wife filed for divorce. Got the papers yesterday. Can you believe she hired those hacks over at Gunter & Gunter? Anyway, she was sick of me not being around enough, but to tell you the God's honest truth, this job is where my priorities are. If I ain't arguing, I ain't living, simple as that." He leaned back again, arms up behind his head. "If you ever change your mind, let me know. I do have other candidates in mind, but you're the top star around here in my book, Orson. But I can't force you into anything. It isn't for everyone."

"I appreciate that. And I'm sorry about your wife."

"Eh, it was a long time coming. Well then, if I'm still blessed with your presence at this firm, that saves me a mighty headache. Tell your kid I say hey."

It was a bright and colorful Saturday morning when Orson walked into his kitchen. His son sat at the table stuffing pancakes into his mouth. New Year's Eve was a day away, but new beginnings had already begun. Letting go of the chase to be with Madison again, ironically, made him feel closer to her, carrying her onward with his every step.

"I can't wait to go to the Iffer Tower," Ryder said, licking syrup off the back of his fork.

"Eiffel Tower, son. I look forward to it too. And showing you all of your mother's other favorite spots in Paris."

"Awesome. All the ways to keep her alive like you said, right?" Ryder spoke his next words under his breath. "Eif-fel Tower." He grabbed the maple syrup, turned it upside down over his already saturated pancakes, and squeezed.

Orson sat down, chuckling. "Exactly. We can miss her and carry her with us wherever we go. That's enough syrup, bud. You're sweet enough. Your Aunt Rose and Uncle Jeff should be over soon. We can tell them the great news about our trip to France together."

Ryder nodded happily, dunking a sausage in the collected pool of syrup on his plate, the sticky substance pulling upward like gooey, melted cheese.

"While you work on pronouncing the Eiffel Tower correctly, I'll keep working on those Harry Potter spells. I know I've said it before, but you impress me with your skills. I look forward to reading the next book with you," Orson said, pointing his fork at Ryder as if it were a wand.

Ryder beamed. "Woo-hoo."

He pumped his arms in the air, then pointed to his feet at his favorite Harry Potter socks, the ones with the gold and red stripes. Orson joined in the celebration, pointing to the identical pair on his own feet.

Orson had left the front door open for Rose and Jeff, and soon their footsteps and the shuffle of coats being hung in the foyer announced their presence. He was eager to share the good news—not only of his travels— but of his firm decision to help them pay for their infertility treatments like he had once promised.

What was the point of having bountiful amounts of savings and investments? What was he saving for? He couldn't think of a better way to spend his money than on his family, and the potential of bringing a new life into it.

"Oh my god." Rose squinted. "Wait. Is this because you are getting a huge settlement from the lawsuit?"

"Rose. This is truly from the heart. Settlement or not. I'm donating all of that money anyway."

Although settled on his decision to sue Dr. Heller, the choice was difficult. At the end of it all, he had been able to see his wife in the Balloon

Days—something he'd never otherwise be able to do, to say a proper goodbye to her.

Because of Balloon Days, Orson now understood the true meaning of embracing life was to see—to really see—and absorb all of life's beauty with every sense of his being in every moment with the ones he loved. That lesson was priceless.

There was simply no questioning of how to use the money received. To donate every last cent to foundations for breast cancer, as well as fund a new organization created by Elliott, providing free bereavement therapy for children losing loved ones to cancer.

"Really?" Rose said, tears filling her blue eyes.

"Absolutely. The check is already written." He handed it to her, and she and Jeff stared at it, the relief and joy in their faces swelling Orson's heart.

"We actually have good news, too," Jeff said, a big grin on his rosy plump-cheeked face.

"That's right, Orson." Rose left the kitchen, then returned with a gift. "Open it."

Orson pulled the red and green tissue paper out of the gift bag, revealing a blue t-shirt. He lifted it out. Rose took the bag from him and placed it on the kitchen table.

"The treatments have worked," Rose said. Jeff placed his hand on Rose's shoulder.

"Number one uncle?" Orson looked at the words on the front of his new t-shirt and then at Rose. "Does this mean what I think it means?"

Rose beamed. "I'm pregnant! We are finally having a baby." Rose hugged Orson, and he wrapped his arms around his sister. "Finally."

"Congratulations to the both of you. This is incredible news." Rose and Jeff deserved this for too long now. "The best news we've had in a long time. Mother and father must be ecstatic." Orson turned to his son. "Ryder, you'll have a new baby cousin to play with."

"Hooray," Ryder cheered, catching on. "Can we go outside now?"

Orson, Rose, and Jeff laughed. "Yes, son," Orson said. It was one of those enlivened winter days with pale sunshine and brisk, fresh air. "Now, get your—" Before he could say another word, Ryder dashed into the closet and back, rushing past Orson, coat in hand, racing into the kitchen and out the back door. Orson nodded. "Coat."

Orson stopped at the glass doors leading to the yard while Rose and Jeff ventured onward, joining Ryder. Rose pushed Ryder on the swing set, the sunlight streaming through his strawberry hair.

CHAPTER 39
HOWARD

I t's about time, kid. Ya nearly scared me to death," Langston said to Howard, his hand on his chest. If Pop was still alive, he would be around the same age as Langston.

"I'm sorry. Life got dark for a while." Howard stood near the crackling fire in Langston's living room; the warmth relieved him of ·winter's chill. Langston sat on the couch with plaid pillows on either side of him, listening.

"I see. I'm truly sorry to hear that."

Howard took a seat on the recliner. "I needed to figure out how to stop staring at the broken mirror."

"I see," Langston repeated. "Talk to me."

"That's a story to shelf for another time. Piano is the focus for today. I owe you that."

"Well, I'm always here if you want to talk. As for the piano, I'm ready, but only when you are—I could tell something caused a stir within you last time."

Howard glanced down the hallway toward the room where Langston's piano resided, shiny and calling. "It's time for me to be ready."

"Sometimes the things we resist the most are what creates the biggest breakthroughs." Langston stood.

Howard followed him to the piano. He took a breath in, prepared to speak, prepared to share parts of his story with someone who cared—the type of risks Elliott helped him to see were the right ones to take.

"My father taught me how to play. He and my mom cheered me on, especially my mom. She was my number one fan. She brought me music books home, encouraged me when I wanted to quit. She bragged about me to everyone she knew.

"We couldn't afford a great piano, let alone lessons for me to take, and I never played in any recitals. I played for my family on holidays. But I mostly played for her." The heat of tears lurked behind his eyes, but this time, they were tears of gratitude rather than of pain.

"Thank you for sharing that. Your parents sound wonderful. I am so sorry for your tremendous losses. You playing will mean more to the both of us, then."

Howard stared at the piano. It was as gorgeous as he remembered—the kind Mom and he would look at in books or catalogues, dreaming about the day they could save enough money to buy him one.

The smooth ivory, the shimmering black. It was as intimidating as it was beautiful, a full moon on a stormy night. Elegant and grand and expensive. The sound it must create, the melodies, the notes—must sing and swirl and stir movement within, enough to close the cracks of his broken heart.

This was Howard's moment. It was now or never. He had nothing to lose anymore. He had seen the worst of life, the worst of himself. He already could have lost it all in the most permanent of ways and was beyond grateful he had not. This was the risk, he now knew, that would set him free on a path of his own.

He sat down, the glimmering keys waiting. He placed his fingertips on them, pressing down gently enough to feel the weight of the keys without emitting a note.

"Go Howard," Langston said, his voice a gentle cheer.

Howard closed his eyes. There was Mom. Her reassuring smile. Her proudly holding a new book of piano music from the library, the first one to borrow, Pop playing guitar at his side. A young John clapping along.

It's a wonderful thing how the brain can retrieve something from so deep inside its walls. With his eyes still closed, Howard's hands began sweeping across the keys to a waltz all their own. He and the piano, in harmony, their relationship restored. A melody began to bloom, growing faster with fervor, his fingers flying from note to note, a symphony from within, gliding, gliding, gliding from one measure to the next of a song unseen but visible in his mind, a melody pouring out his pain like a bursting pipe, filling him with love and light and agony all at the same time. What a heavy ballad he had trapped inside, one he had drowned and deafened for years. He was sober and he was alive. Silent tears fell down his cheeks, a decrescendo accompanied by relief.

When he stopped, Howard opened his eyes. Langston looked awestruck.

"Howard—you must accept payment for my lessons, I don't care what you say anymore on that matter. I insist. I bet a café would hire you to play, you could tutor children. Oh, the possibilities. Hell, you should be booking yourself at Carnegie. That was," —he started clapping— "marvelous. Simply marvelous. Your parents would be more than proud."

A warmth spread throughout Howard's body like honey, trickling from his chest and oozing outward to the tips of his fingers and toes.

Was this hope? Or something else?

Acceptance. Belonging. Love.

But he knew, above all else, that he was healing, the year to come brand new.

CHAPTER 40
ELLIOTT

"I'm totally quitting my job," Julie said in between sips of her mocha latte. She and Elliott had met at one of their favorite Long Island coffee shops, Grains de Café.

"Finally made the decision then?" Elliott said, smelling the coffee in the air. She looked forward to being able to drink it again. For now, she enjoyed the thick hot chocolate, especially because hers had a delightful scoop of peanut butter melted within.

"Yup. I was right," Julie said. "Maria is a complete mess. She kept submitting insurance claims improperly, using incorrect psychotherapy codes, and refuses to hire a proper biller. Then she told us she'd be withholding our checks until she was reimbursed—which could be months from now."

"That's so messed up," Elliott said.

"Yeah, no thank you. The decision to leave made itself," Julie said, dunking a chocolate cookie in her latte, the steamy foamed milk dripping from it as she quickly brought it to her mouth. "How is yours going?" She said with a half-filled mouth. "Is Dr. Heller still acting like a Balloon Day-pushing maniac?"

"She is. I don't get it. Maybe something isn't going well at home and she's burying herself in work. Otherwise, I have this other theory that she is actually a robot powered by greed. All she wants to do is become famous to keep making money, no matter who it will hurt. Her corruption would make for a good documentary, now that I think about it."

"Well, as plausible as a greedy robot is, whatever her reasons are, it isn't worth harming any more patients. I think you should tell her to fuck off and quit too," Julie said. "We can become quitting buddies, maybe start our own practice together—a properly planned one."

"What about my patients?" Elliott said. "I can't bail on them."

"I'm sure they'd follow you and continue with the good old traditional therapy." Julie then glanced around and lowered her voice. "The Eeyore guy definitely would."

Elliott appreciated Julie's attempt at keeping Howard's name confidential, although continuing to nickname him Eeyore reduced his growth. He was more of an Eeyore mixed with Owl type of guy now: sweet-souled and humble, full of wisdom.

"It sounds like Balloon Days are basically an addiction for most of your patients anyway."

She was right, the patients who appreciated talk therapy more than Balloon Days would transition with her—especially Howard, given their rapport. The idea of Elliott's own solo practice had terrified her. The amount of detail and responsibility was overwhelming—she'd have to create her own schedule, take care of the billing, the insurance calls, pay rent, all on top of seeing her patients. To have a partner, and an intelligent one like Julie, lifted some of the angst.

She remembered the reason why she couldn't have coffee.

"I don't know. To tackle all of that with a newborn seems impossible. I'd bring the practice down, bring you down."

"No. We could gather a team. We have enough in our savings to hire some people. We'd be okay," Julie said, smiling. Her confidence was contagious.

Elliott smirked back. "Do you think we'd kill each other?" she said. "They say never to mix friendship with business."

"Whoever 'they' are, never met us. We will be a power team," Julie reassured. "I already have some well-respected colleagues quitting too and I know they're interested. Don't worry about needing time off for little Juliette on the way. We will be a very parent-friendly practice. Plus, Lily said she'd be happy to watch her, so if things continue to work out with her and I, you have a free babysitter, too."

Julie's thoughtful planning reminded Elliott of her own take-charge attitude. She perked up in her seat.

"Well, I guess that settles it then," Elliott said. "Time to tell Dr. Heller to 'fuck off'."

A train ride later, Elliott made her way up to Dr. Heller's suite with slight shakiness in her hands, but strength in her mind and heart. As the doors opened to floor twelve's waiting area, Elliott was taken aback to see Romalda crying in the corner, blowing her nose into a tissue.

"Romalda, sweetie. Are you okay?"

"No. Um. Oh gosh. I didn't realize you would be here so soon. Don't mind me." She tucked the tissue into the pocket of her lab coat.

"What happened?"

Again, Romalda burst into tears. Elliott picked up one of the nearby tissue boxes and handed it to her.

Romalda lowered her voice and shared. "I accidentally told Dr. Heller's patient Jillian—oh gosh, I shouldn't have said her name, there I go again."

"Don't worry about it," Elliott said. "My lips are sealed. Go on."

"I told the patient that there was a new mechanism in place to make the Balloon Days better when they weren't going positively. Obviously, that didn't go over well, and the patient demanded her money back, telling Dr. Heller that it robbed her of her having full control and understanding."

"Jillian deserved to know the truth." Even if she did break Howard's heart. "You did nothing wrong. You did what anyone would. You're not a robot."

"It sure feels like"—Romalda sniffled—"she wants me to be. But I can't do it. I can't be perfect all the time. How can I both keep the surfaces clean, while staying out of sight of the patients? They come and go all day." She blew her nose into another tissue. "She's also more on edge than ever—she ranted about some pending lawsuit. I'm trying to not take it personally, but it's difficult. She's scary when she's disappointed."

Elliott lowered her voice further. "I'm quitting for those exact reasons. She wants everything and everyone to be perfect here. But perfection is a barrier to who we truly are. No one should deny that."

Romalda's mouth dropped in shock. She wiped her eyes, then tucked another crumpled tissue into her pocket. "You are so brave. I wish I could quit, too."

"You can be brave too. You don't have to quit right away. But you do deserve better." Elliott placed a hand on her arm. "I trust you'll know what to do when the time comes. It will suddenly all click into place. Just don't think too much. Overthinking hides how we truly feel deep down in our gut."

Romalda wrapped her arms around Elliott, giving her a big hug. "You're right. You're such a great therapist. Good luck with wherever you go next in life, and please stay in touch."

"I will," Elliott said.

Stepping through the sliding doors of Dr. Heller's office, Dr. Heller immediately rose from her desk and carefully shifted to her chair in the left corner. Elliott joined, her heart barreling out of her chest.

I am in control.

"I was happy to hear you wanted to meet this evening. I was about to ask you myself." Dr. Heller paused to sip her tea. "Orson left. But I am not surprised. It was incredibly interesting seeing you and him on the cameras the other day. I also see Howard has terminated his time here as well. Both of whom, coincidentally, and quite clearly, happen to be linked with you."

She placed her mug on the ottoman. "Any inkling as to why your patients are leaving so suddenly? Clearly our discussions have been grossly misunderstood."

Elliott bit her tongue as the fire spread within her, Dr. Heller hailing the barrels of fuel. "Orson was your client. Wouldn't he have told you his reasons?"

Dr. Heller looked taken aback. "We did great work together and he felt he was better, despite my persistent concerns. That's all. But I have a feeling that there is more to it neither of you are telling me. He should have stayed. Howard should have stayed as well."

"The Balloon Days were doing them more harm than good." Elliott's throat tensed up.

Dr. Heller stiffened. "You are being insubordinate and have no idea what you are talking about."

"Believe me, I do."

"Quite frankly, Elliott, you are the one doing harm to your patients by not pushing them to continue. Furthermore, you revealed to Orson the lack of size difference in an Elite Room, which simply is not true.

"There are many additional perks you do not know about, but perhaps that is my failing. I could promote you and inform you better, but only if you keep in line and do what you can to promote Balloon Days. Otherwise, you force me to consider your termination."

Elliott rose from her seat, the sofa area meant to be a safe space. But it proved phony, all manipulation of the highest magnitude. The Center was merely Dr. Heller's puppet show and everything within her puppets. She pulled the strings, controlling them behind neurological terms, beautifully tinted windows and doors, expensive tea and compliments and heavenly décor.

And for what? To what end? Regardless of whatever the answer was, Elliott wouldn't let herself or the ones she cared about be deceived any longer.

If working at the Center taught her anything, it was this: The lure of another's power made one forget their own.

"You don't have to be forced to do anything, Doctor. I quit."

Dr. Heller's mouth twitched. For the first time ever, she looked defeated. "You've made a monstrous decision." She stood, her white gown falling neatly into place. "Before you leave and realize this, I'll bestow upon you the only sound piece of advice I've learned: be fierce and selfish with your success, because at the end of it all, no one cares about you. Once you realize this simple truth about making money, you'll be begging me for your position back."

Elliott smirked. "With all due respect, Dr. Heller, you are delusional and corrupt. Your advice is worthless."

Elliott rode the pink exit elevator down to E 75th for the last time.

The new year was twelve hours away, and Elliott could barely feel her toes as she unlocked the front door to her home. She placed a bag with a bottle of sparkling apple cider, newly purchased for herself for Julie's party, down on the hardwood floor of the foyer. She disturbed a few fallen pine needles.

The Christmas tree had shed, but Elliott did not want to throw it out yet, so as per Dad's warning, she had made sure to not turn on the Christmas lights anymore lest she start a fire and "burn the whole damn place down."

Elliott hurried to her bedroom and found Captain laying next to the clothes she had laid out for Julie's party. She scratched behind his ears, and he flopped to his side, displaying his fleshy pig-pink belly.

Mom walked in.

"Hi, honey. Hope you don't mind I'm a bit early."

"No, you're right on time. Thanks again for coming to take him for the night."

"You know I love my Captain. Billy wants to meet him—I figure after four months, he is worthy of Captain." She winked. Elliott liked Billy, too. He was good for Mom. "Plus, I have lots of treats ready to go for when the ball drops," Mom said.

Elliott leaned against her dresser. "I told Dad, by the way. About keeping the pregnancy."

"Go on," Mom said with keen interest.

"He said he was excited to spoil his future granddaughter. He also told me to ask 'that lawyer' Orson about hunting Asher down for child support. I said I'll think about it. I'm not sure how I'd feel with him back in my life—in any way. I still have to figure out when and how to tell my future daughter that her father didn't stick around."

"Asher is somethin' else. I thank the Good Lord that you dumped that monster. You'll be an even better mother without him." Mom sat down on the bed and Captain relocated to her lap. She was right; Elliott would be a much more attentive, happy parent—she already was. "As for your father, maybe he can change for you, after all. And, Holly?"

"He said she's eager to buy lots of gifts for the baby. I don't care what she thinks though."

"Of course not," Mom said, "and you shouldn't. That bimbo's worth less than two nickels rubbed together."

"You know what's funny?" Elliott said.

"What's that?"

"Ever since I stood up to Asher and Dr. Heller, I've had less anxiety. I haven't been picking or pulling at things." Elliott looked at the new bed sheets she bought herself, hole free. "I mean, once or twice, here and there, I'm tempted to—more out of habit than anything."

"I'm so proud of you, sweetheart. You know, anxiety isn't necessarily bad, despite it feeling dreadful. It is a sign you're going against your intuition. Living to please others in expense of yourself isn't a life at all. I'm glad you've learned that lesson sooner than I had." Mom gave Elliott a kiss on the cheek. "Now go get ready for the party and have fun. Go do the young things you young people do—but be safe."

Elliott laughed. "Love you, Mom." Elliott turned to look at Captain. "Okay, okay. If I get sucked into your cuteness, I won't leave," she said, giving him one last pet before Mom took him and left.

After putting on dark jeans, flats, and a sparkly top she soon wouldn't fit into, Elliott straightened her hair, put on mascara and eyeshadow—a smoky look—and shimmied her way out of the house.

Julie's apartment bulged with friends. She had the lights dimmed and white Christmas lights around the place, giving it a warm touch. Decorations strung and dangled. A banner with Happy New Year hung in gold and silver letters. Between music and everyone's conversations, it would be another night of projecting her soft-spoken voice.

"Hey," Julie yelled. She kissed her cheek and took Elliott's black overcoat. "You look amazing."

"So do you," Elliott said. Julie curtsied in her sequined skirt and black top. "I love what you did here." Elliott looked around the room. As she did, it was like the sea parted. Evan was there, too. He was looking at Elliott.

"Evan actually helped me out," she said and smirked. As he walked over, Julie whispered, "Happy New Year," and blended into the crowd.

"Hello there," Evan said loudly, leaning in for a peck on the cheek. But it was more than that: it was a lightning bolt to her nerves, yet one that was gentle and soft and sweet, its imprint lingering warmly on her skin. He spoke to her ear, so she could hear him better.

"I'm so glad you made it. Julie mentioned things have been tough for you lately." He pulled away, hand remaining on her elbow. "If you ever want to talk, I'm here."

"I appreciate you. I mean, I appreciate that." Hopefully he couldn't hear her flustered stammer too well over the noise.

It would be so great to have him to talk to other than her mom or Julie, for a change. And that is what a healthy partner would do.

"Same goes for you," she added.

"Actually, I was wondering if you wanted to step outside and chat for a bit, away from all of the noise."

"Oh. Sure," Elliott said. Confused, but curious, with a dash of butterflies, she bundled up and followed him outside into the courtyard.

"I don't know how to begin," he said, his breath visible in the air. "But please don't be upset with Julie—she told me you're pregnant."

Jesus, Julie. Elliott stayed silent, unsure how to respond.

"I'm happy for you," he said. "And I want you to know I'm here for you. Asher is a piece of shit." He shook his head. "And I won't pressure you for a date or anything like that. Not until you're ready. Well, now I'm sounding stupid and assuming you'd ever want to, so maybe you should completely ignore me."

Elliott processed his words. His wonderful and extremely unexpected words. "No, no, you're not stupid at all. I still can't believe she told you, and I cannot believe she did not tell me she had. It isn't like you wouldn't find out eventually, I'm not going to be able to hide it much longer. I'm still going to yell at her," Elliott said and they both laughed. She made a mental note to do so tomorrow.

"Deservedly so," he said.

"I also would have never guessed it wouldn't bother you."

"You're human. And you're an awesome one. I'm excited to meet a cool, tinier version of you one day. If you'd let me, that is." His yellow, blue eyes glowed with sincerity.

"I would."

"I look forward to it."

"Me too," Elliott said.

Evan's gaze landed near her mouth.

Melinda stumbled out of Julie's apartment with an unlit cigarette in her hand and a lighter in the other. She was too drunk to notice them but would soon enough.

Elliott shivered.

"You look cold," Evan said. "Let's get you back inside."

As wonderful as the prospect of having Evan in her life was, Elliott didn't pressure herself any longer for the perfect scenario, or perfect timeline, a totally unrealistic bullshit notion anyway. Meeting life where it's at proved more enjoyable than forcing it to be what you wanted.

For the rest of the night, Elliott and Evan found a corner inside Julie's apartment and talked loudly over the crowd about which Twilight Zone episode was the most thought provoking, the glory of instrumental music, and how relieved she was to have finally left Asher, relieved to have left the Center.

Everything had changed for the best within a matter of days. The ripple effect had finally presented itself. Elliott was the pebble.

It was then Elliott noticed Nicole and Melinda through the sea of friends. Tasteful and tasteless, as expected. Her stomach did a quick somersault. Could baby Juliette feel it? It was time for the countdown.

Nicole conveniently squirmed next to Evan. Elliott glanced at her, then Julie who snuck up behind Nicole with Lily at her side, shook her head, cupping her mouth, but Elliott couldn't understand the muted words. Julie waved it away and instead cheered her drink with the air.

Around the room, glasses of champagne were ready to sip. All faces were veiled in moon-blue, staring at the Times Square Ball on the television set.

Ten ...what if Nicole pulled Evan in for a kiss?

Nine ...would he kiss her back?

Eight ...if he did, I shouldn't care.

Seven ...

Six ...but I do care.

Five ...Nicole and Evan just looked at each other.

Four ... he does care about the whole pregnancy thing.

Three ...

Two ...Evan's hand is brushing against mine.

One ...he's looking at me.

Within one swooping moment, her life became confetti, horns, fireworks, kisses.

AUTHOR'S BIOGRAPHY

Kristi Strong was born and raised in Long Island. She considers herself to be the human version of her dog—the exceptionally weird and affectionate Rat Terrier named Sophia. Kristi loves to wander the planet as much as she loves being nestled in the same spot of her couch most evenings, curled up with a good book.

Kristi's writing draws upon her professional experience as a trauma-informed mental health therapist. Highlighting the human condition and the power of resilience—whether it be through fiction or non-fiction—is Kristi's calling and passion. She has the honor of witnessing all facets of what it means to be human, and she wrote her first novel Balloon Days to remind readers that they are worthy and capable of change.

Keep in touch with Kristi Strong via:
Website: https://kd-rose.com/
Instagram: @Kristi2paper
Twitter: https://twitter.com/kristi2paper
Tiktok: @krististrong.author

CPSIA information can be obtained
at www.ICGtesting.com
Printed in the USA
LVHW082320160523
747145LV00026B/1369